Willful Impropriety

Also available

Truth & Dare: 20 Tales of Heartbreak and Happiness
Edited by Liz Miles

Corsets & Clockwork: 13 Steampunk Romances
Edited by Trisha Telep

Brave New Love: 15 Dystopian Tales of Desire
Edited by Paula Guran

Willful Impropriety

13 Tales of Society, Scandal, and Romance

Edited by Ekaterina Sedia

RP|TEENS
PHILADELPHIA • LONDON

Constable & Robinson Ltd
55–56 Russell Square
London WC1B 4HP
www.constablerobinson.com

First published in the UK by Robinson,
an imprint of Constable & Robinson Ltd, 2012

This is a work of fiction. Names, characters, places and incidents are
either the product of the author's imagination or are used fictitiously,
and any resemblance to actual persons, living or dead,
or to actual events or locales is entirely coincidental.

A copy of the British Library Cataloguing in Publication
Data is available from the British Library

UK ISBN: 978-1-78033-348-9 (paperback)
UK ISBN: 978-1-78033-349-6 (ebook)

1 3 5 7 9 10 8 6 4 2

First published in the United States in 2012 by Running Press Book Publishers,
A Member of the Perseus Books Group

Books published by Running Press are available at special discounts for bulk
purchases in the United States by corporations, institutions, and other organizations.
For more information, please contact the Special Markets Department at the Perseus
Books Group, 2300 Chestnut Street, Suite 200, Philadelphia, PA 19103, or call
(800) 810-4145, ext. 5000, or e-mail special.markets@perseusbooks.com.

US ISBN: 978-0-7624-4430-4
US Library of Congress Control Number: 2012932639

9 8 7 6 5 4 3 2 1
Digit on the right indicates the number of this printing

Published by Running Press Teens
An Imprint of Running Press Book Publishers
A Member of the Perseus Books Group
2300 Chestnut Street
Philadelphia, PA 19103-4371

Visit us on the web!
www.runningpress.com

Printed and bound in the U.S.A.

Contents

Foreword

Scott Westerfeld

For the people living through it, the era of Queen Victoria's rule in Britain was one of constant revolution. Steam power and Marx's *Capital* gave rise to a new, more antagonistic, relationship between workers and bosses. The discoveries of germ theory and anesthetics brought medicine into its modern form. Networks of gas lines erased night across London, and telegraphs and railways shrunk distances around the globe. Even the novel was transformed, by a notion called "realism", which posited that a story could carry a reader into another person's life across barriers of gender, geography, and social station.

Given this maelstrom of change, it's odd that today we view the Victorian era as a tableau of stuffed shirts, fancy frocks, and good manners. Or perhaps it's this juxtaposition between decorum and chaos that makes the period so compelling. We imagine of the lord of the manor sipping tea while reading in his morning *Times* that slavery has been abolished, or that Mr. Darwin has forever altered the horizons of religion and natural philosophy. These contrasts make for good drama. After all, the most theatrical place to deploy a flame-thrower is a tea party.

Teenage readers, of course, have a stake in flame-throwing. They're too young to have been co-opted into the social order, but are old enough to test its limits. They relish discovering how arbitrary social mores can be, and how identity is imposed both from without and within. At the same time, teenagers are exploring how their own bodies work, and all the biological realities that underlie the abundant customs surrounding race, gender, and even clothing.

It's into this rich stew that this anthology takes us. Many of its young protagonists live inside the systems of Victorian privilege. But as ladies of class, their fortunes aren't secure without a proper husband in their future. Other stories are about young people whose race, sexuality, or simple poverty leaves them outside of the circles of power, and whose improprieties endanger them every day.

In the Victorian era, behavioral codes were at once stronger and more fragile than they are today, with all the dangers of the magic spells you'll find within these pages. The wrong word, the wrong hemline, even the wrong flower in a bouquet could result not only in humiliation, but in social banishment and–for the working classes–deadly economic isolation.

So the stakes are high, here in these tales of ancient manners and traditions at war with young bodies and wills. These are stories about revolutions, after all, some as small as a proper dance turn, some as large as the solar system's movements. But all of them are driven by the human heart, that most potent engine of rebellion.

Scott Westerfeld

Introduction

Ekaterina Sedia

Adult writers and editors enjoy arguing about what makes a book suitable for a young-adult audience. While there are probably as many answers as there are writers (and editors), we can still agree on a few things. Most notably, books for a young-adult audience are by no means restricted in their tropes, but thematically they are more likely to deal with coming of age, identity, and rebellion than books for adults. After all, what other age category is so often defined by defiance?

Recently we saw a great rise in both Victorian and young-adult categories of fiction, and to me these two go hand in hand. If being a teenager is about disobedience, the notion of Victoriana (at least the way it is perceived by a modern reader) is often centered around propriety and convention, rigid social structures, and impermeable class, race, and gender barriers. Yet, where there is convention, there is also defiance, and the opposite side of this Victorian coin is the realization that as long as there are barriers and conventions, there will be those who will rise up against them–suffrage, human rights, notions of equality all find their beginnings in that rigid age.

So it seems to me that the Victorian age is a perfect medium to tell these stories of defying convention, of individuals chafing against the constraints of what was considered to be the unchangeable order of things. Against the expectation that one should know one's proper place, determined by one's race, class, and gender, against the notion of marriage and binary gender constructs, against the expectations of strictly heterosexual attraction. These struggles are universal and recognizable, but they take place in the world in which the stakes are very high.

In these pages, you will find stories of young people who manage to wilfully violate the rules. You will also find stories based in reality as well as fantasy. (After all, Victoriana has become a fertile medium for fantastic stories–just look at the latest big-screen iteration of Sherlock Holmes!) But whether the stories are realistic or fantastical, the conflicts are always recognizable, and the tropes will touch a familiar nerve. Be it cross-dressing or dancing or improper use of magic, I hope that the readers will recognize themselves in the protagonists.

In collecting these stories, I was hoping to put together a collection that spoke to modern readers about the eternal themes: love and trespass, betrayal and loyalty, and above all the defiance in the face of disapproving society, and the sacrifices people will make to be true to themselves and to those they love. Because even though the times have changed, there are still restrictions, and there are many improprieties we are willing to commit for love–be it love for ourselves or for others.

New Jersey/Mexico, December 2011

At Will

LEANNA RENEE HIEBER

With a name like Portia Nightingale, the girl was destined to become an actress.

That, and she was born in a dressing room.

That, and she was abandoned to be raised by a roving theater troupe.

That, and she had a terrible time telling the truth.

Considering these factors, it's safe to say that from the earliest age, Miss Nightingale's sense of reality was entirely subjective. One might say warped.

But she knew every single word Shakespeare had written, even the "problematic" plays, and that was a priceless skill in a profession that was respected only a fraction more than prostitution. In this elegant, gilded age of Her Majesty, Queen Victoria's inimitable, empirical reign, skilled adaptability meant survival.

The day she met Mr. Smith in some northern province, however, her methods of survival would broach new and intriguing territory. He quickly became the most interesting thing that had ever happened to her in her eighteen years of life.

The production was *The Tempest.* The town was drab, dull, unresponsive, and her Ariel was praised with lukewarm applause. She knew it was her very best, and that Will Shakespeare would be proud. She didn't need an ovation to prove it. A tiny candle of confidence flickered deep in her bosom, kept alive by a more minuscule bellows of pride.

Dusting the white powder out of her brown-blond curls kept reasonably short for maximum adaptability between roles, Portia padded barefoot backstage to her "dressing room" (a few set flats angled to create a simulation of privacy). She began to wipe the pale greasepaint off her face that had made her into an androgynous, colorless spirit, revealing fair skin, a few freckles and youthful color brushing high cheekbones.

She had a "classic" beauty, "one those Pre-Raphaelites would covet," a theater manager once told her before trying to seduce her. She resisted. She was fired. Thus, she hesitated plying her trade in the London circle. Directors, producers, and patrons expected too much of an actress, in every way. In the provinces, a girl could get by without all the sexual politics, and Portia played whatever roles the rest of the small touring company didn't want, which was the only reason why they kept her around and reasonably well fed. She was unbuttoning her vest to access and unravel the binding that kept her small breasts flat against her torso, when she noticed an intruder standing at the corner of her dressing-room flats. Whirling to look him dead in the eye, Portia snapped to attention, her posture tall and defiant against attack or interrogation.

He was tall and angled. A mop of unruly dark locks poked out from beneath a weather-worn, wide-brimmed hat, his burgundy coat was long and a striped cravat was undone but looped loosely about his neck. Portia honestly couldn't tell if he was attractive, but he was compelling, young, and vibrant and yet full of gravity. Ageless, somehow. His expression enigmatic, his stare parceled her out piece by piece like Olivia's personal inventory to Viola in *Twelfth Night*: *Item, two lips, indifferent red, item, two gray eyes, with lids to them* . . . His dissecting stare continued as he spoke.

"Don't undo your paint," the man said, holding out a long-fingered hand. "Don't undress. Please. In fact, tell me nothing about you. If you are male or female, I cannot tell, and I do not want to know. You've an incredible timbre to your voice–it's just that perfect, median range, do you know that?"

She cocked her head at him. "I've been told my voice is useful. Malleable. Keeps me working. Any part, whatever needs playing, doesn't matter to me. Why?"

"Just tell me your last name. Please."

Portia blinked, baffled. "Nightingale."

The man laughed and bounced on his feet. "Perfect. Nightingale you shall be! Tell me, do you have any interest in breaking out upon the London stage?"

Portia folded her arms. "I was just thinking I'd rather avoid the politics."

"What if we *created* the politics?"

"What if you told me who you are and what you want?"

"I'm not asking who *you* are, am I?"

"You asked for a name. What's yours? Coming backstage uninvited is a piss-poor way to introduce yourself."

"Mr. Smith. Just Smith. Will you come with me? You could be anyone. Anything. Just as you say, whatever needs playing. I could make you anything. You are utterly brilliant on the boards. Come with me."

Portia blushed beneath her greasepaint despite the unexpected boldness of this conversation. "I don't know you. It would hardly be wise to follow a stranger to London."

"You've a family?"

"No."

"No one to miss you, then. Come on."

Portia set her jaw. She hadn't expected pity, but she did expect the man to talk a bit of sense. "Tell me your full name, your aims, and why I should entertain your company a moment longer."

"My aim is to make you a London sensation. Something and someone they've never seen. I am a manager and director and I've great plans, I just needed the right actor. I have found, now, in you, the right actor for *every* role. And I've no name other than Mr. Smith, so don't go around asking about it. You'll not find a thing save for the various Covent Garden theaters where I built my roving reputation. Together we will build something far greater–"

"What do you mean, you don't have a name other than Mr. Smith?"

"I mean exactly that. Now. Give me Viola's speech, if you will. 'Build me a willow cabin–'"

"Shouldn't you have auditioned me *before* absconding to London with me?" She scoffed, unsettled and intrigued. How did he know she'd just been thinking about *Twelfth Night?*

"Who said anything about absconding?" Smith scoffed. "I shall take you as my willing companion. And my star. With no obligations other than rehearsing, performing brilliantly on the stage, and maintaining your mystery. Now, 'Build me a willow cabin–'"

Portia shook her head and began the speech she could recite in her sleep and backward.

How could someone not have a name? Or not wish it to be known?

What scandal did he hide?

How could she trust a man who didn't have a name?

A name was everything. It told the world who you were.

Considering her tenuous world was made up solely of characters, greasepaint and foreshortened walls, a birth name was something to grab hold of. Something personal and real. She found his refusal to tell her his name profoundly upsetting. But possibly freeing. She finished the speech.

Smith clapped. "Very good. Now, give me some of Sebastian–"

"But I–"

"But you *do* know it. You're a talent that knows every word, don't deny me, I can tell."

How could this man grasp anything, truly, about her? Smith seemed to know her, though. His bright brown eyes, more gold than brown really, pierced her to the core. It was as if he'd anticipated how she'd respond, as if he'd written the script of these moments himself. Had he spoken with her castmates, who might have told him that, yes, she could step in to play any role (and had, often) at any time? She couldn't imagine any one of her crew that would say kind words about her. While they were civil, none of them was kind, and all of them were jealous. Smith's expression was more kind than any look she'd received in a long time.

Her protests at Sebastian clearly would mark her as a female. Surely he *had* to see the truth of her–but it seemed Smith refused any clues. Considering she did know every word the Bard composed–and that was her only useful trait to offer the world–Portia felt a deep, compelling urge to impress this strange man.

And she was quite sure, as she performed the lines of Viola's male twin, Sebastian: "I am yet so near the manners of my mother, that upon the least occasion more mine eyes will tell tales of me . . ." that Portia's eyes *did* tell tales of her. She was sure her eyes spoke of a hunger she didn't know she had, an emptiness she didn't know she needed filled until this stranger had appeared, dangling a curious carrot of adventure before her.

"Brilliant!" Smith applauded. "No one would question you as Sebastian. Or Viola. Or any of the young persons of the great canon! I'll set you up at the Royal, playing Sebastian in *Twelfth Night* for one week, and then the following week, at the Lyceum, playing Viola. I'm not going to have you be some poor patron saint of one house and one company. True freedom means gracing every London stage, never overstaying your welcome, and never answering questions. It will add to your mystery. I promise you. I only take risks I believe in. And I believe in you."

He was so passionate and yet so matter-of-fact that Portia found herself struck dumb, unable to argue, unable to refute him. Unable to say no to this *mad* proposition. Her awestruck silence was apparently enough for him. A contract.

"Good, then!" Smith bounced forward, handing her an envelope. "We'll begin rehearsing tomorrow. Ten A.M. The Royal. Don't say goodbye, don't tell anyone where you're going or what you're doing. If you have second thoughts about disappearing, then this conversation and this idea dies and ends here, and you hand me back that envelope with notes and train tickets. Are you willing to discard your old self and life for a grand new experiment?"

Her mind spun. She thought of the many petty goings-on of her days on the road. She thought of how little anyone truly cared for her, how much she longed to lose herself in London and be rid of the countryside forever. She'd always loved London but she'd been so scared the city, and the people in it, would eat her alive. But with Smith, this odd, indomitable Smith as her benefactor, and a new life with a malleable identity as only she could create it . . . Why not?

"All right then."

"Good!" Smith shook Portia's hand. "Very good! Now. You arrive male, Nightingale, and you see to it that no one thinks otherwise. You have no first name, no pet name. I'm Mr. Smith, you're Mr. Nightingale. The following week, for the reversal, Miss Nightingale, we'll need to arrange chaperones and all that nonsense," he muttered.

How odd.

No one, even Smith, would know who she was beneath the changing trappings.

In a way, it was every actor's dream to wholly invent, reinvent, and invent again, on the grandest of stages, one's very life.

Fascinating.

That night, she packed her meager bag of things, said nothing, and slipped out at first light without so much as a second glance behind her as the distant whistle of the train approached the tiny station.

Smith must have gone on ahead to London, for Portia was alone on her morning train ride. But that was all right, in a fine suitcoat, waistcoat, and top hat (stolen from the dressing room with a few pence left behind for poor Heidi, who would throw a fit to discover her finest contemporary male pieces missing) she needed no chaperone. While she'd seen the world through a male lens via Shakespeare's text, all the sixteenth-century words of fools, nobles, and gentlemen could hardly have prepared her for the freedoms of being a contemporary male in Queen Victoria's England. She was *free* . . .

Of course, freedoms had their limits, even in the *terribly* modern 1890s.

Mr. Wilde was about to be brought into court on charges of "gross indecency" with young men. Some things, even for men, were off limits. If men in her company were of *that* persuasion, they were utterly discreet. But from what she knew of Mr. Wilde, that simply wasn't his style. A flamboyant, generous, genius soul, an innovative, modern, luminescent candle against the constant rehashing of the Bard, his trial and shame would prove a loss for the theatrical community. And a warning shot across the bow for any who dared veer from a "moral and upstanding lifestyle."

The train into London gave her food for thought of the myriad possibilities for her life. She watched how people watched her, and felt reinvented down to the very bones. Small towns grew larger and larger until the hulking, sprawling behemoth of London, great sooty London with its dragon-bellows factories and its hellfire of industry and innovation, rose before her like a great Tower of Babel, its denizens thronging its labyrinthine streets. Everyone and everything she gazed upon became a course of study, and she took note of all attributes and quirks, anything that would be useful in imitation and foolery. She had to blend in with London, she had to be one with its multifaceted spirit.

As per instructions and a key left in the envelope, Portia arrived in London and hailed a hansom cab to take "Mr. Nightingale" to "his" new home, a small Covent Garden flat, the address of which would change every other week around the environs. Smith did not give her long to settle in before it was time for rehearsal.

Portia tried not to gape as she set foot inside the theater, all golden and velvet and sparkling gaslit sconces that were about to be wholly replaced with the new electric light . . . She realized how used to unadorned, provincial places she'd become. This was a palace. A palace of her new birth. Reborn a star who no one could get too close to, for she would burn *so* bright . . .

Smith presented Mr. Nightingale to the company with quite an introduction.

"I told you I would go out hunting and fetch you the most promising buck of our generation!" Smith cried, standing upon a chair in a box seat. "Nightingale here will surprise you, and the world. You just wait. We'll make history, friends."

Her new company looked at her appreciatively, both the boys and the girls, and she got the distinct impression she was being flirted with by both sexes. Since she had arrived as Mr. Nightingale, she was sure to give the women more attention from the first. This wasn't difficult, as she'd always tended to seek more female company–men got the wrong ideas and assumed actresses were quick to lie flat on their back at the least advance.

The rehearsal process was smooth. Any English actor worth their salt could offer up Shakespeare in their sleep, and Smith was just inventive enough in his staging and interpretation to be interesting. He worked with them from a theatrical box reserved for wealthy patrons, pacing the velvet-lined stall and occasionally exclaiming random truths and new interpretations. His carefree, quirky nature infused all of them with a youthful sense of play.

And the audiences *loved* them. They *particularly* loved Mr. Nightingale. The papers were full of praise.

> Mr. Nightingale's performance as Sebastian was refreshingly genuine and particularly moving. A compelling young face one finds it hard to look away from. Here we have a young man of the stage Mr. Henry Irving himself would kill to have in his company.
>
> —*The London Times*

Mr. Henry Irving. No faint praise. Portia had thought about seeking out the most successful actor of the age in hopes of working at the Lyceum. But Irving was quite the man for a special effect at the cost of his castmates. Sparks literally flew from his sword-fighting scenes, and she just didn't know if she had it in her to be on the receiving end of the electrical charge as she stood on a metal plate. Acting for a passable wage was one thing—allowing England's foremost actor to sizzle you with an electric shock was another. Still, having one's name associated with Irving's in a review was money in the bank.

And the next week, at the next theater, the press was similarly glowing.

> Miss Nightingale's Viola lit the stage with luminous charm and beauty. Easy on the eyes and ears, we find ourselves her new devotees. Considering last week's production featured a Mr. Nightingale, perhaps, dare we hope, that there is a new theatrical dynasty that has emerged?
>
> —*The Evening Standard*

It was the week *after* that they realized the two performances were the same person. The question then rippled through London—who was Nightingale?

Growing up backstage hadn't prepared Portia for the limits

and contradictions of the world offstage, and Smith hadn't prepared her for the scandal. But he did at least try to cover both their behinds.

Smith published a brief letter to the editor of the *Standard.*

> I understand there is some confusion as to my two Nightingales. The Nightingales are twins, one boy and one girl. I've a certificate to prove it, lest anyone court libel or say that the law should come down upon my company. But even if there were only one Nightingale, what law could stop him? Her? The fact that a Nightingale is a damn fine actor is the only law of my land.
>
> –Mr. Smith, theater manager, director, visionary

The fact that the Nightingales were never seen together meant the public didn't believe in any such certificate. They preferred to embrace the scandal. Soon schooled in the fickle, forked tongue of the press, what to Portia and Smith was playing a bit of a game, it seemed that to London they had struck a deeper chord.

> It's a positively shameful scandal, this confusion of identity. It is sacrilege, *unnatural* that someone should be paraded about, no matter how talented they are, as fluid between two sexes. I realize the theater is perverted, but this spits in the very face of our refined, civilized culture. This stunt of Mr. Smith's company makes fun of what it is to be British, that is, entirely self-possessed and proud men and women of the Empire who present themselves as God intended.
>
> –*The Pall Mall Gazette*

Scandal, of course, was phenomenal for business.

The dinners and the intrigues soon followed.

If she thought the theaters were grand, they were nothing compared to the homes in which she was entertained. She tried not to make her awe evident, but she was still young and her wealthy benefactors seemed to find her wonder an additional charm.

Countless patrons and endless flirtations, from men and women, were laid at Portia's feet like bouquets, each trying to draw her out. Each sure that they had her pegged.

"Ah, but look at how he carries himself–a woman could never hold that sort of bearing and piercing stare. Why, look at how he doesn't even blush or bat an eyelash as he gazes upon me," flirted countesses and merchants' daughters in husky voices dripping with need, daring Portia to look them straight in the eye and mouthing behind their fans an invitation for a secret rendezvous. Portia did not take them up on it. But she did return their stares. Hard.

"Ah, but see the artful cheek, her delicate ringlets, the demure tilt of her head–why, the fairer sex, the *gentler* sex, it is positively written all about her!" cried aristocrats and Members of Parliament who stood too close and "accidentally" brushed their hands across her to search out her most obvious feminine parts, murmuring indecently in passing that she could reveal herself to them, that they'd never tell . . . She knew enough of the average man not to trust them as a species. The many layers and starched fabrics she put on, large and lavish dresses she'd never have dreamed of being able to wear were they not a part of Smith's costuming for her life, made it impossible for anyone to come away with a physical impression.

But it seemed that the mystery made her all the more appealing to each, and men and women, boys and girls fought over her as if she were a prize, sometimes forgetting she was a human being in the room with them. Not a toy. Not a theory. A person.

As the weeks went on, she wondered if she'd transcended humanity and become an idea instead–one of Shakespeare's pants roles like Rosalind's or Viola's disguises come ludicrously to life and trapped in a cycle of a madman's making, wondering who would write "The End."

No one ever touched her true contours. Only she did, when she bathed. She was the only one who knew her most private, and now most sought-after, secret. Well, and God. She supposed "He" knew. She could not have predicted how shatteringly lonely this life soon became.

Clearly, thought Portia, detaching herself from among lush dinner arguments over her body parts, those who waged war over her identity as if it was something that touched on their own pride, hadn't been around enough actors. She knew men who could pass as very convincing young women. It was, after all, the theatrical tradition in Shakespeare's day, when women weren't allowed on stage. But the former was something a man did in utmost secrecy, and the latter had been an accepted custom of previous centuries. What *she* was doing–what Smith was doing to her–was unprecedented.

From Romeo to Juliet, from Lysander to Helena, from Ophelia to Hamlet–oh, yes, they tempted the favor of the theater gods even with the melancholy prince himself–Portia began to feel that she was as much one sex as the other. Each of her two sets of behaviors came organically from within her, and she lost herself in the trappings of the clothing she stepped into, her body's mask.

Never had it been so glaringly proven to her that people

believed only what they wanted to believe. She heard them arguing after every show as she retreated into the shadows, their ardent suppositions about her hanging in the air like moths to the footlights.

Smith was ever present during the company fetes, a mischievous, delighted soul who needled on each side until opponents were nearly frothing at the mouth in indignation for their "cause" of proof of her gender–he was a mad scientist adding his powders to an impassioned brew. All that ever seemed to incite Smith in turn was a good analysis of a well-made play. He clearly enjoyed sitting back and watching the distinct yet utterly titillating unease his Nightingale's unconfirmed presence had on everyone. And to Portia, Smith remained an enigma. She wondered if he'd ever loved, had family, or other professions–she knew nothing about him other than his unfaltering belief in her.

Which was the only anchor she had in a life of secrecy.

Portia had been instructed to always dress at her apartments–mysterious lodgings that changed constantly and that no one but Smith knew the location of. She hadn't seen the sense of this at first, but it wasn't long before castmates were bribed exorbitantly to spy upon her changing rooms, and certain patrons felt they had the right to charge backstage and see if they could intercept Portia to see for themselves.

She started to fear for her safety. But Smith was ever on guard, which calmed her. Still, she wondered how long before paying audiences, press aside, were fed up with her too.

That question was answered when an angry mob burst into their rehearsal of *Lear*, on stage at the Savoy. She was Edmund at the moment, the bastard. Next week she would take up Cordelia. Edmund's glory in the base and unnatural was an uncanny herald to the evening.

The leader of the protesting mob, a stout, scowling man in a bowler and fastidiously trimmed mustache, called for an end to their nonsense, that it was a bad influence on London.

"It will corrupt our sons and daughters, this charade of yours," he said, huffing like a walrus. "The youth will think they can play games with what makes the world turn–men and women in their proper place. We here have an injunction–"

Smith appeared from his usual place in rehearsal, popping out from the shadows in one of the front boxes–he liked to be above things, and he leaned down to examine the mob of ten buttoned-up men and sour-looking women, his loose cravat hanging low over the gilded railing.

"Oh, *you.* You of the *striving* classes. You've the most to lose and the most to gain, which means you are *always* tense. You want your world ordered and methodical, full of rules so that you may advance properly when you understand the formula. My Nightingale is every freedom you feel threatened by."

"You, Smith, just who do you think you are?"

He shrugged, grabbing onto the rail and shaking it. "Just a madman in a box! You give me too much credit! It's the *idea* that has caught hold! The *idea* that has London on fire. The idea that life is nothing but costuming and choices! It can be rewritten as we choose! It is our right! That all the world is indeed, one big, bloody stage!"

At this, the mustachioed leader produced his legal document and began to recite his indictment on numerous moral grounds. In response, Smith pulled out a revolver from the breast pocket of his long coat. Everyone, including the stunned company on the stage, screamed.

The crowd dispersed with harrumphs and threats. Smith

trailed them with the barrel of the pistol until they were out of the stalls and into the street.

He clicked the gun and a kerchief spat out. Smith giggled. His company stared up at him, wondering just what he'd gotten them all into, and none so much as Portia. "It isn't *real*, of course." He waved the gun. "I abhor violence," he said, horrified that anyone should think otherwise.

"You know, Mr. Smith," came a commanding voice from the back of the house, stepping from the shadows into the blazing gaslight. He was tall, auburn-haired, hazel-eyed and devilishly good-looking, and he strolled down the red velvet center aisle in the finest of new suit fashions from Paris. "The small-minded have to put people in boxes in order to understand them. They do not like it when you defy their constraints."

"I *am* in a box," called Smith, challenging the newcomer with a grin. "Do you understand me?"

"Not in the least, Mr. Smith," the man replied.

Smith laughed. "Good, then. I like you. Who are you?"

"My name is Lord Rothschild, and I've just sponsored your company indefinitely. I think you, and particularly Mr. or Miss Nightingale–*whoever* this songbird may be–are the finest actors that have ever lived, and damn anyone who tries to ruin your sacred and daring mystery. Don't worry about the injunction. I'll have my lawyers dismiss it before you can say 'To be, or not to be . . .'"

The company applauded.

That night, they were feted at Rothschild's grand London apartments, and Portia fell swiftly for her host, feeling her body waken, tingle and ache in ways that were utterly foreign to her. This, she knew, was a profound development. Her physical body complicated her mystery. And her mystery was her survival. The loneliness reared an ugly, desperate head. But she maintained her exterior cool, even if her insides roiled with heat.

She was dressed as a male that evening, and she and Rothschild, who was six years her senior, struck up an immediate rapport. It was the sort of kinship that felt fated, as if they had always been bosom friends and it just took their meeting to confirm what they'd always been waiting for–a certain missing piece.

Rothschild was jovial and generous, possessed of a razor-sharp wit and a keen eye for everything artistic and philosophical. By the end of the night, the rest of the company having tired of the two of them finishing one another's sentences, Rothschild had invited "The Nightingale" to be a regular at his club–an exclusive club–as his guest. Portia opened her mouth to protest.

"Nay, I *insist* upon it," Rothschild declared. "But you'll have to be male. No women are, of course, allowed in gentlemen's clubs," he said, his hazel eyes sparkling.

"But Lord Rothschild," Portia countered, squaring her shoulders in the way men tended to, "you've said that I am 'everything of humanity in one soul.' Every facet. Unlimited identity. You say it thrills you. But if I am to only remain Mr. Nightingale in your presence, where are my other facets–"

"Oh, only at the club," Rothschild smirked. "I fully intend to take *Miss* Nightingale to the opera. It will be the talk of the town."

He spoke knowing she'd not deny him. Portia wondered if her blush betrayed her right then and there, the knees of their fine black suit pants nearly touching.

They'd almost forgotten Smith was in the room. But he didn't seem to mind, he just grinned. The puppeteer appeared to enjoy retreating into the role of quiet audience, director and voyeur.

In the next weeks, as the papers took up new ammunition

with Rothschild's complicity in Nightingale's ambiguity–first at the club as friends, and then at the opera possibly in courtship–soon it was forgotten that The Nightingale was a superb actor, and the pressure became personal. Vicious.

> Today's theatrical breed continues to prove its unnatural tendencies. From Wilde's upcoming trial to the likes of Lord Rothschild, now a patron of mad Mr. Smith's shifting, restless company, cavorting about with a creature who refuses to tell the world what it is, the thespian life drops its curtain to reveal a perverted bacchanal. Perhaps Smith and Nightingale think they remain charming, alluring and at the height of parlor conversation. Instead, this reporter wagers the carnival attraction has lost its appeal. The curious masses have no wish to see Miss Nightingale's take on one of Shakespeare's female pants roles, only to take on the very pants the next day as the lead hero in some sort of mockery of the sexes. Has Darwin not sufficiently undermined the order of things? One cannot elude destiny forever, Nightingale. You'll be outed soon enough, and this whole tedious charade will fade into the obscurity in which it ought to have remained.
>
> –*The Times*

It was a threat.

Rothschild remained unruffled, much like Smith, laughing that society's psyche should be so insecure. So needing validation of its rigid, righteous mores that its populace flouted in hushed secret. So needing to keep up its untenable hypocrisy.

Rothschild never asked about her sex. Portia respected and abhorred this equally. He stood too close and brushed up against her like all the rest of the men did. But with him it was natural, and she hoped it wasn't her imagination that sparks flew when they inadvertently touched. Because he did not pressure her to give up the secret, it only made her want him more.

She would never know if the pressure of newspapers and biting editorials pushed her over this line, or merely her body's own need to be recognized at last, that she did indeed out herself. But only to him. Perhaps she wanted it to be on her own terms, not anyone else's.

They'd spoken like bosom friends all evening at the club, her in a suitcoat and fine silk cravat, posturing as stiff and elegant as any proud young man might, reveling in her handsome companion who glowed in the gaslight. He'd placed a hand upon her shoulder, firmly–a commanding hand, a suggestive hand.

He offered up his London apartments, as the hour was quite late . . .

But she had another idea. There in his apartments would be servants, and servants would talk . . . She needed someplace vacant for what she had planned.

"Come to the theater, Rothie. I've something I need to show you."

She had a stage-door key and a private dressing room that only herself and Smith had access to, a room even Rothschild as benefactor didn't know about. She led her darling Rothie backstage, giddy as she approached the precipice of danger. She bid him sit upon a chaise in the small room that lit up brightly the moment she turned on all the new electric lights. The bulbs buzzed, garish, revealing.

She passed him a brandy and took a double. The draught was as strong as her desire. They hadn't said a word for maybe the last hour, only stared at one another, Rothie curious, his lips partly open.

He was so beautiful, sitting across the clothing-strewn room, his perfect, seamless look and presentation such a contrast to the mess of the space backstage. The ten feet between them felt like an impassable gulf when all she wanted was to throw herself at him.

"What do you have in store for me, my little bird? A new poem?"

They'd taken to reciting poetry to one another. All the latest works, the suggestive ones. The pump had been primed for this moment, she knew it. Did he?

"No. I cannot hide anymore," she said finally, whipping her cravat open, exposing her throat. "See me as I truly am. Please," she whispered. "I can't go on–*we* can't go on like this . . ." Her heart thudded in her ears as she began to undress.

"No," Rothschild protested quietly, "don't, you–"

"I *have* to, Rothie. How can you know everything about me and nothing about me all at the same time?" she snapped, tearing open her vest, waistcoat, undershirt, tossing them aside. And then came the silk-paneled modified corset that fastened up to her throat to keep her small breasts flat against her body, something she'd had made in secret as it was more secure than winding cloth or bandages about her bosom. Turning away, she loosened the strings and popped the hooks and eyes. Her breasts strained and ached to be released, to be free and acknowledged. As much as clothing had given her certain freedoms, so was it her prison, too.

She turned back around to face him. Naked. Trembling.

She stared, first down at herself, her waiflike, young woman's body, and then up at Rothschild, who had lost his ruddy color suddenly, as if seeing a ghost.

She wanted to be proud of that body but she was scared. It was foreign. It was a secret.

"I love you," Portia murmured. "I've loved you this whole time, and I can't stand it."

Tears filled Rothschild's hazel eyes. He approached. Portia trembled.

She'd be touched. At last. Finally, someone was *seeing* her. *Truly* her. He reached out a wide hand which entirely cupped the side of her face. Oh, was he going to kiss her. . . . She nearly swooned into him, her bare body against his fully clothed one made her so deliciously vulnerable . . .

"Oh, you beautiful creature," he said quietly. Sadly.

Why was he sad?

His hands did not travel down her body as she craved. He did not cup her in a passionate kiss. He did not lay her back upon the divan and take advantage of her, as she'd imagined so many nights alone in her rooms. Instead, his tears splashed down upon her cheeks as he placed his wide, luscious lips upon her forehead.

"You beautiful creature," he repeated.

Creature?

"Beloved friend," he continued, still in that gentle, sad tone. *Beloved* was a welcome word. *Friend* was not. Lover, yes. She needed a lover, and wanted to hear *that* word. Portia blinked up at him, not bothering to wipe his tears from her face. "I love you as well," he murmured. "But not in *that* way. I . . . if you were . . . I truly thought . . ."

The realization was like a knife into her vulnerable, exposed flesh.

"You thought I was a boy . . ." Portia choked. She thought, since he knew her so well, he had to *truly* know . . .

People believed what they wanted to.

Tears were in her eyes in turn. Her cheeks burned with red-hot shame. She snatched at the adapted corset that kept up her male appearance, the layered boning that enslaved her, that had tricked him . . . that had let them both down. She furiously began trying to dress herself again, haphazardly, the wrong layers first.

Rothschild grabbed her hands, kissing them, dragging her close and she fell against him, feeling like a ruined fool but unable to resist his insistent embrace.

"I am so sorry . . ." he murmured. Portia wept against him, for everything she was not. For everything she did not have. For everything she could not be. For Rothschild's sake, she wished to God she had been born male. She wished society would have permitted their love. She wished Mr. Wilde was not about to go to trial. She wept harder.

"Now we know our deepest secrets, we two," Rothschild murmured, still keeping her folded, all long limbs tucked like a paper crane against him as he bent to lift a silk dressing gown, a simple, sexless gown that bore no particular mark of masculinity or femininity, and slipped it onto her shaking body. She could not look at him. But he forced her gaze to his. He was never kinder, never more loving. Yet not in *that* way.

"And we must keep our secrets, take them to the grave, must we not? Does your very existence not require that your secret be kept?"

Portia nearly blurted out that she'd have given it all up to be Rothschild's lover. But she held her tongue. No use making a further fool of herself . . .

"And must you not keep mine?" He pressed. "The law is hardly on my side. And while I likely could have kissed you and enjoyed it, while it certainly would be easier if I could just lie with you, be with you, I can never lie *to* you. I love you too much for that."

"But not enough–"

"It isn't about enough, my Nightingale."

"My *name* is *Portia.*"

"It isn't about enough, dear Portia."

"Then what is it about?"

"Who I am."

Portia wasn't sure she understood, because she wasn't quite sure who she was, at the end of the day. Other than a woman. But that wasn't enough . . .

Rothschild tied the silk ribbon of her robe around her waist and stepped back. The absence of his heat was eviscerating. The robe made her less chilled, but she'd not stopped shaking, her cheeks nearly the same scarlet as the gown.

"Come," Rothschild rallied with the gusto that had brought him into her room, the sacred, sanctified space, now tainted . . . "Shall we to the club–"

"No, Rothie." She stared at the hem of her gown. "No."

Silence. Rothschild's tread retreated. They knew their secrets. They were strangers once more.

The dressing-room door quietly opened and shut. Portia sank onto a pool of red silk. She was there for a very long time. She remembered one of the box cleaners saying that a woman had killed herself from a broken heart in a laudanum-induced haze in that very dressing room ten years before.

While she admitted that suicide was attractive at that desperate moment, killing herself over a man was not the sort of woman she wanted to be. She was young–the world prized a pretty girl of eighteen. Yet she sat broken, her womanhood rejected in a cold theater by a man who meant her no harm. She sat hollow and empty–an idea. But ideas didn't die. They couldn't.

Eventually, at some point, Portia collected herself from the pool of silk. She bound her breasts, donned her waistcoat, tied her cravat. Smoothed her short, sensible locks with a pinch of pomade. This week she was a male youth, and she needed to remain so. The only way to lie was to be consistent. Her sanity depended on lies and consistency.

Just as she moved to the door, Smith burst in, startling her.

"There you are, Nightingale. Was out looking for you everywhere. We mustn't keep the Vicomte waiting! He's a late-night creature, but really, don't be rude!"

"Sorry," Portia mumbled.

She'd forgotten about the company soirée with a French aristocrat. Rothie had made everything else unimportant. The last thing on earth she wanted to do was to be charming to a patron. A sudden rage filled her, and her nostrils flared.

"No. I'm not sorry, Smith. I'm not going. I'm quitting. I cannot do this anymore."

"Of course you can. What's gotten into you?" The matter-of-fact way he asked her, and the frank, uncanny way in which he always stared at her made Smith the one person she could not lie to.

"I just had my heart broken, if you must know."

"Oh. Terribly sorry. By whom?"

"No business of yours whom," she hissed. He likely knew very well who, but was being kind and playing ignorant.

"Can I make it better?" he asked. Portia clenched her fists and nearly punched the wall.

"No, damn you, Smith, you're not God, you're not a *doctor*, you can't *always* make things better!"

"Yes I can," he stated with the maddening, unwavering confidence that at once drove her mad and that she coveted passionately.

He stared at her, up and down, and his doing so made her glance in the mirror. And there she was–the perfect picture of a young, handsome man of Her Majesty's gilded age.

"You are my greatest creation," Smith declared, smiling proudly.

Portia bristled. No one should think themselves God. Other than, perhaps, God. Even then she thought the divine Creator was more humble than He was made out to be. He. Or *She*. Portia knew, better than anyone, how the world's idea of someone's true self was entirely fabricated. Mortals confined God into a gender for their own purposes. God, she imagined, could change at will, *Deus* making its own *Ex Machina* to suit its purposes, ones mortals could hardly guess.

So could she, of course. Change at will. But she–unlike Smith–didn't think herself God. Smith qualified his statement as he took in the look on Portia's face. She saw herself in the mirror, furious and beautiful.

"I have given you all the tools you need in this limited, polarizing age. Think of it, Nightingale–you can go out into the world as whomever you choose, however you choose. The world only knows what you want them to see. I have helped you be utterly free."

She allowed his words to sink in.

It was true, tonight had not changed that fact.

And suddenly, unexpectedly, Smith moved forward and kissed her.

It was a tender kiss, soft and sure yet confident. Passionate. Deep.

Oh. She'd wanted a kiss.

She'd so longed for Rothie to be her first kiss, yet this was better. She loved a surprise, and this was most certainly unexpected. It could just be a ploy to get her to stay. It could just be another experiment. She didn't care, and returned the kiss eagerly.

Smith broke away, flushed, looking rather pleased with himself, as usual. And suddenly that confidence she'd coveted seemed somehow attainable. Because she had been part of making that confidence. They were an incredible, inseparable team. And then he solidified that sentiment.

"And no matter *who* you are, or *how* you choose to be known, I will love you either way. You are wholly beautiful, and I love the *all* that you inhabit, the all of you that has no limitations. Our grand experiment has opened two cages. Our flesh is one truth, but our minds and hearts might be another. We are ingenious, fluid beings. We can change at will. Be whomever you will, only promise you'll remain with me. I'd rather not imagine my world without you."

She stared at him, appreciating his words, letting them fill voids and hollow places, letting them assuage her loneliness.

"Yes. I will," she agreed. Another kiss.

She thought about demanding his name, and telling him hers. A further intimacy. She thought of again baring her naked flesh once more this night, to test him.

And then she thought better of it. She kept on kissing him instead.

His name was whatever she wanted it to be. And she would reveal herself whenever she chose to. Maybe yet tonight. Maybe next year. She was an ingenious, free creation of unlimited potential, and all the borders of the world could not vanquish such endless possibility.

The Unladylike Education of Agatha Tremain

Stephanie Burgis

At the age of sixteen, Agatha Tremain let down her skirts, pinned up her hair, and set herself to running her father's household. Her first step was to forge her father's signature and dismiss her hated governess. Miss Blenheim left with her perfectly straight nose held high in the air, trailing bitter premonitions of disaster like wriggling serpents in her wake.

Agatha's second step was to teach herself magic, using the books in her father's library as her guides.

The first time Agatha entered the library to find an introductory text, her father looked up at her with vague approval from his customary seat by the fireplace. When Sir Jasper's eyes focused on the book she took from the shelves, though, his normally mild face darkened into anger.

"Do take great care with that work, my dear. There are no fewer than five different points of contention in his arguments, and three outright fallacies. I should hate to see you taken in by such folly."

"I'll take care, Papa," Agatha promised. She came down off the wooden stepladder, brushing dust from her fingers. "I shan't believe anything without proper evidence."

"I'm very glad of it. But, I say . . ." Sir Jasper blinked. "I don't mean to be rude, but are you permitted to be in here at all? I thought that creature Blaggish–Blagmire–"

"Miss Blenheim?" Agatha waited for his nod. "I sent her packing this morning. I'm old enough to look after myself now."

"What a relief. I never could abide that woman." He began to subside back into his chair, but an expression of sudden surprise halted him mid-movement. "Good Lord, I am hungry. Have I missed luncheon, by any chance?"

"You've been in here for two days, Papa." Agatha sighed. "I've ordered a hot supper for you. The servants should bring it shortly."

"Oh, good. I was afraid I might have to leave."

Her father settled happily back into his book. Agatha pulled up a second armchair beside him. Carelessly crushing her skirts beneath her, she set her booted feet upon the footstool in front of the fire and began to read with a feeling of vast contentment.

The Tremain land was set fifteen miles out of town and nearly three miles from their closest neighbors. As a young girl, left to the sole care of Miss Blenheim and her malevolent admirer, the butler Horwick, Agatha had frequently regretted the distance. Keen-eyed adults might have been salvation to her then.

As she grew into her own, however, free of Miss Blenheim and able at last to cow Horwick into a sullen form of near submission, she realized that isolation had its benefits. With no irritating supervision, or near neighbors to gossip, Agatha was free to forget all the oppressive rules of dress and proper maidenly demeanor. After all, what were such fripperies to her?

As Miss Blenheim had explained hundreds of times over the years, Agatha's unfortunate nose, unnaturally red hair, and general lack of grace meant she would certainly never be capable of winning any man's heart. Only her dowry could ever appeal to a potential husband . . . and Agatha refused to ever marry any man who took her on such terms.

She understood only too well what it was to live with one who scorned everything about her; she would never repeat the experience.

With no prying eyes upon the spacious lawns of Tremain House, Agatha was free to practice her spells in perfect ease, ignoring the irrational social law that deemed the practice of magic unladylike. The only people ever to be alarmed by her experiments were a few of the weaker-spirited maidservants, and by the time that they finally fled the house, Agatha was nearly seventeen. She had learned by then to summon and control her own helping spirits, who filled their places to a nicety.

Moreover, the sight of the dark spirits moving about the house, eerily silent and obedient, miraculously transformed Horwick's complaints from snarls of contempt to mere unintelligible muttering underneath his breath, which suited Agatha far better.

By the time Agatha turned eighteen, she had become so accustomed to her freedom that she no longer feared to lose it. So when an imperious knock sounded on the front door of Tremain House one morning, it never even occurred to her that it might be the sound of approaching doom.

In fact, engrossed in one of her more challenging experiments in her own private study, Agatha barely noticed the sounds of bustling arrival in the rest of the house. It was only when Horwick appeared, looming in her doorway, that she even recalled hearing the knock.

"Well, Horwick?" As she spoke, Agatha kept her commanding gaze fixed upon the inch-high imp who slouched on the desk before her.

This was her first attempt at multiple transformations, and by far the most complex set of spells she had ever attempted to master. The imp, who was a startling bright blue and currently engaged in making horrible faces, had begun its life as a common field mouse. If Agatha spoke every word of the spell correctly, it would next become a housecat and remain one, too, a sensible and useful addition to the household. As Agatha hadn't yet recited the second (and intimidatingly intricate) spell, though, the imp was still enjoying its first, highly dangerous transformation. She couldn't afford to take her eyes off it for an instant.

"What is it?" she asked impatiently.

"A caller for you, Miss Agatha," Horwick intoned. "A *lady* caller," he added dolefully.

"Well, tell her I can't attend on her, for Heaven's sake." Agatha narrowed her eyes at the imp. It had far too mischievous a look on its blue face, almost as if it knew something she did not. Of course she did not believe that for a moment, but it made her uneasy nonetheless.

Agatha realized, with a sudden flash of irritation, that Horwick had not moved from his pose of ominous warning. "Tell whoever it is to go away," she said. "I don't have time to wait on some gossipy neighbor who wants to nose about the house. Get rid of her!"

"Now, my darling girl, you cannot possibly mean that." A rich, velvety female voice spoke from the doorway, rippling with amusement. As Agatha half turned, caught by surprise, a woman wrapped in floor-length furs swept past Horwick into the study.

"Dearest Agatha. Don't you remember me? You were only a little tiny girl when I saw you last. I'm your aunt Clarisse, finally back from Vienna. Now, take off that silly gaping look from your face, my love, before it freezes there!"

Chuckling, she patted Agatha's face, which was stiff with shock. "My goodness, I can see you have been in need of a proper woman's influence, haven't you, my poor child? Oh, I've worried so much about you! You wouldn't believe how many sleepless nights I've spent agonizing over the injustice of your situation, a beautiful young girl like you trapped out here with my absurd brother for years on end with no London season or eligible suitors in sight."

"I don't–"

"No, of course you needn't worry any longer, dear. I'm here now, and I shall take marvelous care of everything. I've come to live with you and your father and take all the burdens from your shoulders. Now, doesn't that sound perfectly wonderful?"

Slim, scented arms closed around Agatha. Soft fur pressed into her face and covered her eyes. The imp leaped off the desk with a yip of glee and darted toward freedom and mischievous adventure. It would undoubtedly cause nightmarish catastrophes all throughout the household, and even more of the maidservants would resign their posts.

Agatha couldn't bring herself to worry about any of that, though. She was too overwhelmed by the far greater and more terrifying disaster that had closed her in a loving auntly embrace.

• • •

"My dearest Jasper." Clarisse swept into the library ten minutes later, still draped in furs despite the heat. Agatha trailed behind her, speechless with horror. "Aren't you utterly delighted to see me?"

"Ah . . ." Sir Jasper blinked over his book. "I say, Clarisse. Is that you?"

"Of course it is, you absurd creature. Didn't you read my letters? I told you I would arrive today."

"Letters?" Agatha croaked.

As a matter of course, she read every letter that arrived for her father. It was a question of necessity rather than interference, as his post piled up on every available surface otherwise, ignored for years as their estate accounts languished. She had learned to pass on only those notes to which he was likely to pay attention—fat packets of argumentation from scholars in Germany and the Netherlands, written in spidery scrawls with every line crossed twice as they fiercely debated the most abstract theories of magic.

Estate management and personal gossip were both equally tedious to Sir Jasper, and Agatha had learned long ago that it was best to simply forge his signature on any checks, business letters, or notes of polite regret that had to be posted on his behalf.

"Oh, I sent piles of letters." Aunt Clarisse smiled ruefully. "How could I help myself, missing home and family as I did all these long years?"

Agatha said, "They never arrived."

"Those dreadful continental mail carriers!" Clarisse shook her head sadly. "But never mind that. I'm here now, at last. And of course, our first order of business must be your social debut."

"My *what*?" said Agatha.

"But what else, my dear? Jasper, I am ashamed of you." Her furs rippled as she made a moue of disapproval at him. "It's one thing to bury yourself down here for years on end, but to bury your young and"–she glanced Agatha up and down, managing to look both skeptical and kindly at the same time–"not *entirely* unattractive young daughter along with you? There is that nose, of course–and that dreadful hair–but a multitude of sins can be concealed by her dowry. Still, how in Heaven's name is she to find a husband and home of her own out here in the wilds?"

"This is my home," said Agatha.

"Nonsense," Clarisse said. "Every young girl dreams of an establishment of her own and a husband to give her status in Society. I shall launch you upon London immediately. We must thank our blessings that the season is not yet over. Jasper, all that I require from you is your checkbook–but if you don't immediately surrender it to me, I promise I shall nag you unmercifully for weeks until you give in."

"I beg your pardon," said Agatha, "but this is absurd. I don't wish to be launched into Society. I have no interest in going to dances or to London, and I certainly do not desire a husband. All I want is to stay here and study–just like you, Papa."

"Just like my brother?" Clarisse let out a tinkling laugh. "My dear, haven't you yet learned? You are a young lady now, not a child to be so wilful. Your duty to the family is to marry, just as your grandmother, great-aunt, and I all did before you–and I can tell you that *studying* is hardly required for that vocation. Gentlemen are none of them so very difficult to understand."

"Papa!" Agatha said. "Pray tell my aunt that I do not need to be launched upon London!"

"Jasper," said Clarisse, "do you really wish me to settle myself here in your hermit hole for the next full month, talking nonstop until you finally agree with me? You know it is my right to chaperone your daughter into matrimony. It was promised to me by our own parents, all those years ago."

Clearly, the weapons had been drawn. Agatha pulled out her own most ruthless stratagem. "If I leave, Papa, who will take care of all the practicalities? Who will listen to the housekeeper's complaints and deal with the estate manager? You will have no time to devote to your own studies."

"Well . . ." Sir Jasper looked pained. "It is true that I shouldn't like–"

"We will only be in London for a matter of weeks," Clarisse said. "A few months at the absolute most. That is the longest it could possibly take me to find our dear Agatha a fiancé. I am certain you can allow the practicalities to pile up that long, Jasper–indeed, I am more than certain that you have done so in the past. And our dear old Horwick may see to all the rest."

"That is true," Sir Jasper said, with obvious relief. His gaze lowered stealthily toward his book.

"Papa!" Agatha said, and snatched the book from his hands. "Aunt Clarisse means to marry me off. If she succeeds, I will be gone *forever.*"

"Have no fear," said Clarisse, and smiled kindly. "I shall remain here, Jasper, to look after everything for you. It will be as if nothing had changed–except that you had done your duty to your daughter, and to me, at long last."

"Oh, well," said Sir Jasper. "That does make a difference, I suppose."

Agatha stared at him. "Papa? Haven't you heard a word I said?"

"Yes, yes, my dear," Sir Jasper said peevishly. "Indeed, I haven't been forced to listen to so much tedious debate in a very long time–not since Clarisse left the last time, I suppose." He sighed. "You do not know how difficult your aunt can make it for a man to study, Agatha. And Clarisse is right–marriage is what young ladies are meant for, particularly in our family. If only you had been born a boy, it would have been different . . . but there are promises, you know, that must be kept, whether we care for them or not."

"But–"

"You forget, my dear," said Clarisse softly, "you are entirely in your father's care until you find a husband. You must abide by his decisions–and I shall stand as your guardian in his absence." She smiled warmly. "Have no fear. We shall make the decisions that are best for all of us, even if you are too young to understand them now. You will be grateful in later years, when you have a daughter of your own."

Agatha fisted her hands and did not reply.

It might have been two years since she had finally escaped Miss Blenheim, but she had not forgotten how to fight.

• • •

It did not take long to think of a plan. That night, supper was served in the dining room for the first time in years. Agatha allowed her aunt's stream of scandalous continental gossip to pass over her unheard, while her father sat looking miserable and casting longing glances in the direction of the library.

There was no expecting Sir Jasper to stand against his sister, that much was clear . . . and unfortunately, Clarisse had the right of it: according to law as well as custom, Agatha was her father's property, little though she might relish the reminder. She might be the heiress to his estate, but at the moment, her only legal possession was her dowry. Sizable though that was, she could not even touch it–that privilege belonged to her future husband.

Should her father and Clarisse desire her to be forced onto the marriage market, Agatha had no legal or financial means of resistance.

Fortunately, she had spent the last two years developing every magical recourse available. It was time to make clear to her fashionable aunt exactly what sort of young lady she really was.

The first shock of the evening came when she slipped out of her bedroom and down the corridor to her private study, which she'd left unlocked in the confusion of her aunt's arrival.

The handle refused to budge . . . and her key, as she remembered only too clearly, sat inside upon the desk, beside a stack of unused candles and all of her notes.

"Blast," Agatha muttered.

It was the imp at work, of course, causing trouble as she'd expected. She turned with a swish of her dressing gown and strode into the next room–a guest bedroom, never used–to give the bell pull an imperious tug.

For once, Horwick did not make her wait. Indeed, he slipped through the servants' door hidden in the tapestry as swiftly as if he had been waiting nearby for the summons.

"Yes, miss?" His normally doleful tones sounded suspiciously self-satisfied. To Agatha's shock, she saw the corners of his narrow lips twitching as if he were repressing a grin, the first she'd seen on his face in years.

She had poor memories of his grins. They had generally coincided with some new witticism Miss Blenheim had made at her expense, or a particularly humiliating punishment the two of them had devised for her.

Now Agatha scowled at him and reminded herself that she was a mature eighteen years of age. She was no longer a child to cringe before her old tormentor. "I require your assistance, Horwick," she said.

"Indeed, miss." Horwick's jaw moved convulsively. Under Agatha's disbelieving stare, he even rubbed his hands together in delight. "Always happy to be of assistance in any way I can, miss."

"I am glad to hear it," she said. "If you would simply unlock my study using your copy of the key–"

"It can't be done!" Horwick caroled the words with open glee. "No, I can't do that, miss."

"Why on earth not?"

"Because I don't have that key anymore. No, miss, I don't. Your aunt, Miss Clarisse as was, had it off me this evening."

"But–"

"Every copy to be in her keeping," he said happily. "That's what she said, and that's what she did. The key from the desk and the key from my ring, and I saw her lock the door herself. 'Much better for all of us this way, eh, Horwick?' she said. Oh, that Miss Clarisse. The memories she brings back . . ."

Chortling happily to himself, he backed away and closed the hidden door behind him while Agatha stood numb with shock.

Every note, every grimoire, every carefully prepared brazier and specially ordered candle she possessed sat behind that closed office door. Without them, she was as helpless as . . .

No. Agatha set her jaw. She might not have magic at her command anymore, but she was no longer a helpless child. Miss

Blenheim and Horwick might have found a young, motherless girl an easy target, but Clarisse would not find the same.

She stalked down the corridor to her aunt's room and threw open the door without a knock.

"My goodness." Clarisse looked up, eyebrows raised, from the dressing table where she sat. A maid stood with her back to Agatha, brushing Clarisse's rippling, waist-length golden hair. Even dressed for bed, Agatha's aunt was still draped in lush furs–this time, a lavishly fur-trimmed satin dressing gown in royal blue, with skirts that spread in draping folds around her chair.

A fire blazed in the hearth, raising the temperature in the room near boiling point. Clarisse's maid stepped back, turning away discreetly as Clarisse shook her head in amused disdain.

"We really must work upon your manners, mustn't we, dear? In polite society, you know, it is customary to knock before entering a lady's bedroom. Or a man's, for that matter, although perhaps we'll wait until your wedding night to discuss such delicate questions."

"In polite society," said Agatha, with icy control, "it is customary not to steal other people's keys. *Or* their homes, for that matter. I don't know what may have brought you back now after all these years abroad, but if you think you can bundle me off like an unwelcome parcel just so that you can take my place–! Well, you do not know who you are tangling with."

"Oh, don't I?" Clarisse raised perfectly arched eyebrows. "What do you think, Blennie?"

The maid's shining dark head tilted up. She turned to meet Agatha's gaze.

Agatha's breath stopped in her throat.

The maid was smiling with open amusement. The same expression was mirrored on her aunt's face, but Agatha barely noticed it. All her attention was fixed on the maid's glittering green eyes and her perfectly straight nose.

. . . Just as she remembered them.

"Oh, you are just as my dear Blennie had described to me," Clarisse said. "I cannot begin to express how helpful it was, all those years, to have a faithful friend in my old home, keeping me apprised of everything that mattered. And of course she knew just where to come when you staged your childish little rebellion."

"*Blennie?*" Agatha mouthed. But she couldn't say the name out loud, not with Miss Blenheim grinning at her over her aunt's fur-trimmed shoulder.

Agatha knew that grin, even after two years of freedom.

"Oh, you might be surprised at how well I know you already, my darling niece," Clarisse said. "But never fear. Once we leave for London next week, you shall grow to understand me as well . . . and you may be surprised by just how much we have in common."

Agatha couldn't answer. All she could do was stagger out of the room before the strength in her legs deserted her.

The helping spirit who assisted her in lieu of a proper lady's maid never made its appearance in her room that evening, but Agatha took no note of its absence. All that her senses could encompass was the sound of her aunt and Miss Blenheim's mingled laughter, ringing in her ears all night long.

• • •

Many new visitors to London notice first the miasma in the air, a thick, dark substance pumped out from the thousands of chimneys and coal stoves that fill the capital. The unsavory pollution can stagger noses still accustomed to the more innocent countryside, especially in addition to the overwhelming and inescapable aroma of horse dung.

Other newcomers gasp first at the sheer size and variety of the crowds pressing about their carriage, from the pedestrian throng that chokes the streets to the peddlers who sell everything from eels to china, and the thin children who sweep the dung away and dart through the crowd in rags more fit for the Dark Ages than a supposed Age of Progress.

Clarisse, needless to say, ignored it all. She maintained a steady stream of chatter about the Great Exhibition that was taking place in the Crystal Palace, to show off the technological advancements of the age . . . and Agatha, with Miss Blenheim's sardonic gaze resting upon her, sat silent and icy cold on her side of the carriage, numb to the press of humanity and the sights outside.

Over the past four days, she had come to understand the full extent of her aunt's new dominion. The helping spirits Agatha had summoned so carefully over the years were all dismissed like smoke blown through the air. The grimoires she could have used to summon reinforcements were locked out of her reach, and, worst of all, when she had stepped into her father's library the day after Clarisse's arrival, Sir Jasper had reacted with an embarrassed cough.

"I say . . . should you really be here, Agatha?"

Agatha stared at him. Her armchair still sat beside his in its regular position, her footstool stood prepared before it. "Why would I not be?"

He looked pained. "Well, as a young lady . . . that is, if any of those gossips got wind . . . I mean to say . . . well, it's not quite the done thing, is it?"

Agatha folded her hands together to keep them from curving into claws. "Has my aunt Clarisse instructed you not to allow me in here anymore?"

"I wouldn't say *instructed*," said Sir Jasper. "But you know, if anyone in London did ever find out that you'd been practicing magic out here, as an unmarried female–well, if Clarisse hasn't managed to snag you a husband first, that is–oh, blast it, Agatha, you simply can't be here anymore! I cannot have Clarisse breathing down my collar for allowing it despite all the promises our parents made her. You have no notion of how she can discompose a fellow!"

"No?" Agatha asked, her spine rigidly straight. "You think not?"

But Sir Jasper had already turned back to his books . . . and Clarisse's carriage took both ladies to London four days later.

When the carriage finally drew up in front of a row of redbrick terraced houses in a relatively quiet London square, after eight full hours of travel, Agatha lunged for the door like a sailor reaching dry land after a year at sea.

"My, such undignified haste." Clarisse clucked disapprovingly and pulled her furs tighter around herself. "You may wait for a footman to hand you down, dear. And don't take too long about making your toilette–we must sally out once more as soon as possible, to visit the modistes at Cranbourne Street before the end of the day. Our first engagement is tomorrow evening, you know, and we cannot have you still looking like such a country yokel. Not when so many gentlemen are waiting to meet you there."

Agatha felt, more than saw, the curl of Miss Blenheim's upper lip and the quick flick of Miss Blenheim's gaze cataloging her features, no different now than they had been throughout her childhood.

She kept her mouth shut despite all temptation. She would not humiliate herself by protests that were clearly futile.

The next evening she entered Lady Sherington's glittering drawing room in a new gown of deep golden silk, with a domed skirt that swept two full feet in either direction of her nipped-in waist, sustained underneath by uncomfortably thick and heavy horsehair petticoats. Her hair was, of course, still unmistakably copper, but it was also carefully teased into silly ringlets and puffed over her ears before rising to a chignon behind her head.

("This is all useless anyway," Miss Blenheim had muttered, as she'd held the hot curling tongs by Agatha's face. "We can't disguise the color, can we?"

And Clarisse had sighed in regretful agreement.)

The drawing room was richly lit by candles, and a dozen mirrors flung the candlelight's reflection onto the velvets and silks of the assembled company. The reflected light flashed against the diamonds and garnets on the bare skin of the women and the ornamental dress swords strapped to the sides of the officers.

Agatha lifted her chin and glared defiantly at them all. She refused to duck her head to hide her nose or her hair. All the better to frighten off any would-be suitors and save her the trouble of refusing them.

"My dearest Clarisse!" Lady Sherington rustled toward Agatha's aunt, emeralds and rubies glinting on her outstretched fingers. "How delightful to see you home at last. And this is your dear niece? Oh, yes." She exchanged a conspiratorial glance with Clarisse, as Agatha's back stiffened. "I do see what you mean. Well, I may tell you that every gentleman on your list is here tonight, and they are most impatient to make her acquaintance." She turned a kind smile on Agatha. "You needn't worry about being a wallflower tonight, my dear."

"I wasn't worrying," Agatha said, through gritted teeth.

Lady Sherington's eyes widened. Then she and Clarisse both burst into laughter as they linked arms and steered Agatha into the room.

Two hours later, Agatha took ignominious shelter in the lady's retiring room. Thankfully, it was empty, but she could still hear the laughter and voices from the dance nearby ringing through the walls and grating against her ears. She tipped her head against the cool glass of the mirror and closed her eyes.

I am ice. I am stone. This cannot affect me.

"Oh, where has that foolish girl got to now?" Her aunt's voice sounded through the door of the retiring room, and Agatha gave a start that rapped her head against the mirror. As she straightened with a jerk, her aunt continued, "Have no fear, Captain de Lacey. She shall be only too delighted to dance with you a second time–couldn't you see how ecstatic she was to be noticed by you in the first place? Just let me . . ."

The door handle began to turn. Agatha spun around. Her gaze landed on the servants' door hidden in the wall. She lunged for the crack in the wallpaper, slipped through into darkness–

–and bumped hard into another girl already hiding there.

"Oof!" Agatha's breath was knocked out of her.

"Quick!" hissed the other girl, and pushed the door shut just in time.

"Agatha?" Clarisse's voice sounded in the retiring room. "You aren't trying to hide somewhere in here, are you? Because you know there's no use . . . ah, well." Her voice softened to wry amusement. "Probably gone to the library," she murmured.

"Not that that fool will care. All the better not to let her muck it up, anyway."

Footsteps moved away. The door opened and shut. Agatha finally breathed again.

In the unlit, windowless corridor, she couldn't make out any of the other girl's features, only a general impression of warmth, soft breathing, and a shape a little smaller than her own. Their domed skirts were so bulky, they took up all the width in the narrow corridor, and Agatha could feel her silk skirts being crushed by the enclosing walls. Thinking of Clarisse's irritation at the sight was her one consolation for the indignity of her position.

"Your mother?" the other girl asked sympathetically. From her matter-of-fact tone, it might have been a perfectly customary experience to have a casual social meeting in a darkened servants' corridor.

"My aunt." It came out as a growl from Agatha's throat. "She's determined to marry me off."

"Aren't they all? Well, apart from mine, anyway. She gave up on me ages ago."

"Why?" asked Agatha. Then she realized, too late, all that the darkness might be hiding. She winced. *Graceless as ever, Agatha.* She could almost hear the amused, scornful words spoken in her ex-governess's voice. *This* was why she was better off alone with her studies, not trying to make conversation with party guests. "I apologize," she said stiffly. "You needn't answer if–"

"Oh, I'm not deformed," the other girl said cheerfully. "Only hopelessly poor, and not beautiful enough to make up for it. Worse yet, I'm bookish, to round it all off. In fact, I'm a naturalist, like Mr. Darwin."

There was a pause as Agatha assimilated the news. An inexplicable feeling of warmth and ease was slipping through her, relaxing the muscles in her back for the first time in five days. The dark, narrow corridor felt seductively safe, the close air like a protective bubble that held the two of them separate from reality. She felt a dangerous urge to reveal all her own secrets in response to that warm, cheerfully open voice.

As she struggled with herself, the other girl spoke again, this time sounding subdued. "You probably think it's unladylike or absurd to call myself a naturalist, don't you? I shouldn't have told you, I suppose."

"No!" Startled, Agatha reached out. Her fingers found the other girl's gloved hand. "I think it's wonderful, actually."

The other girl's fingers felt warm and strong through the fabric of their gloves. The weight of their skirts seemed to push them closer together in the narrow corridor. Suddenly dizzy, Agatha said, "I practice magic. That's not ladylike either."

"Do you really?" The other girl sounded delighted. "I knew there was something about you! From the moment I saw you in that doorway . . ."

Agatha dropped her hand as if she'd been burned. "I know," she said. Her shoulders hunched as her voice turned flat. "My features and my hair color and my deportment. You needn't remind me."

"I beg your pardon?" Agatha could feel the other girl's astonished stare, even though she couldn't see it. "What are you talking about?"

Agatha gritted her teeth. "Large. Red. And awkward. That is what you meant, isn't it? Believe me, I harbor no illusions about my lack of attractions, so you really needn't–"

"That's not what I meant at all. Who was ever mad enough to call you unattractive?" Warm fingers closed around Agatha's gloved hand in the darkness. "But there is something about you, something different. I didn't know what it was until now. It's the magic, isn't it? I can feel it sparking in your skin. It's amazing."

Agatha swallowed. Her throat was dry, her pulse oddly rapid. She could feel sparks, too, suddenly racing up and down her skin, but they didn't feel like magic. They didn't feel like anything she recognized. "That's not how magic works," she said. "Magic is all about using the proper grimoires, with exactly the right words in Greek. It has nothing to do with talent, only diligence, and using the right supplies. You can't even use normal candles, they have to be specially prepared. They're very expensive . . ."

Her voice trailed to a halt. The air in the servants' corridor felt so hot, she was tingling and lightheaded. She spoke almost at random as she finished: "My aunt stole all my grimoires and supplies, so I can't do magic anymore."

The other girl laughed, a shockingly intimate sound in the darkness. "Who told you that?"

Agatha blinked. "Everyone! All my father's treatises say–"

"Well, isn't that what gentlemen always say? And no wonder. If you need to mouth exactly the same Greek phrases some man came up with three hundred years ago, you'll need money and education to get hold of the texts and make use of them, won't you? And if you've been told you can't even try it without expensive supplies . . ."

"The treatises all say it would be too dangerous," said Agatha.

"Then that keeps women and the lower orders safely in their place, doesn't it? Leaving the magic to the gentlemen who rule the Empire." The other girl snorted. "Of course they don't want anyone else sharing their power. They wouldn't let me into university either, even though I'd taught myself Latin and Greek as well as any Eton student. But do you think I'm going to let them stop me?"

"No?" Agatha said. Somehow, they were standing even closer now. She could feel the other girl's breath brush warm against her cheek. It felt like a spring breeze waking her at last from the icy chill of helplessness that had gripped her for the last five days. Every inch of her body tingled with reaction.

"Never," said the girl. "If they won't let me study at Cambridge with the gentlemen, I'll simply teach myself. That's the message of the Great Exhibition, isn't it? Times are changing, at long last. And when I start publishing treatises about my discoveries, no one will care whether or not I ever sat in a university classroom with a whole crowd of wealthy idiots."

"I believe you," Agatha said. And she did. She felt more wide awake than she had in days, and wild with curiosity. "What's your name?"

There was a long pause. Then, "Isobel," said the girl. "Isobel Cunningham. I'm Mrs. Wesley Stanhope's companion, for my sins. She's probably calling for me again by now." She sighed, her fingers relaxing their warm grip around Agatha's. "I should go. But thank you. It was lovely to meet you, whoever you are."

"Agatha Tremain," said Agatha. She moved forward when Isobel stepped back. "Wait," she said. "Can I call on you tomorrow? If I can escape my aunt–"

"Mrs. Stanhope doesn't like me to receive callers," Isobel said.

"But–"

"We'll be at the Tennants' ball tomorrow," said Isobel. "Who knows?" She moved closer, her voice lowering to a whisper.

"Maybe you'll find me in a servants' corridor again, where no one else can see us."

Her breath brushed against Agatha's mouth. Agatha felt her heart begin to race. She held perfectly still, waiting for . . . for . . .

"Goodbye, Agatha," said Isobel softly.

She opened the door and slipped swiftly into the retiring room, revealing only the back of her rich brown hair and her modest gray bombazine dress in the candlelit doorway. By the time Agatha forced herself out of her trance to push the door open again and search for more, Isobel had vanished from the room.

• • •

Agatha moved through the rest of the evening in a daze, dancing without protest with each gentleman her aunt presented to her, but making only monosyllabic, distracted answers to the conversation that sounded like buzzing insects around her ears. No matter how she craned her head over her various partners' shoulders, she couldn't catch sight of that plain gray bombazine gown anywhere in the crowd.

All she lived for, in the endless hours that remained, was the moment when she would be allowed to return to her room in the rented townhouse, to turn over every memory of that brief, electric meeting in her mind. As she and her aunt rode back in their carriage, she let Clarisse's icy stream of words wash over her, as harmless as rain against a sturdy umbrella.

The Tennants' ball would be tomorrow. She would have another new gown by then, the modiste had promised. Not that appearances mattered in a servants' corridor, of course. But still . . .

When she started down the corridor toward her bedroom, Clarisse's hand shot out as quickly as a striking snake to fasten around her arm. "Oh, no, my dear. We have important matters still to discuss."

Yanked out of her thoughts, Agatha pulled her arm free. "I'm sure tomorrow will be soon enough."

"Tomorrow," said Clarisse, "we shall announce the news of your betrothal. I will compose the notice to the newspapers tonight."

"What?" Agatha stared at her. "But I haven't–no one has even proposed to me yet."

"Goodness, what a romantic you are. I had no idea of it!" Clarisse tittered as she walked gracefully into her own bedroom, her vast skirts and petticoats rustling and her Indian shawl wrapped tightly around her shoulders. "Your fiancé arranged it with me himself, of course, just as mine did with my own parents. You have nothing to do with the decision."

"But . . ." Stopping short in the doorway, Agatha stumbled to a halt. Miss Blenheim stood at the dressing table, holding Clarisse's fur-lined dressing gown. Under her ex-governess's gleaming gaze, Agatha's instinctive urge was to freeze or, better yet, retreat to safety.

She remembered Isobel's words. *Do you think I'm going to let that stop me?*

No, Agatha told herself, and her shoulders straightened. "I believe," she said coolly, "it is customary for a gentleman to ask for a young lady's consent as well."

"Oh, well, in love matches, perhaps . . ." Clarisse waved a careless hand in dismissal.

Miss Blenheim tsk'ed compassionately. "Did you really expect someone to fall in love with *your* face, miss?"

Even as Agatha started to shrink, she remembered that warm, delighted voice. *Who was mad enough to call you unattractive?*

Of course Isobel had only seen her for a moment in the doorway–the words meant nothing, really, not when she thought logically about them. Isobel might well change her mind in the light of day. But still . . .

Agatha's chin lifted. "The law may not allow me to choose a husband without my father's consent," she said, "but you cannot force me to marry against my will. I will say 'no' all the way to the altar itself."

"Now, my darling girl." Her aunt sank down in front of the blazing fire, as Miss Blenheim wrapped the dressing gown around her solicitously. Tucking her chin into the lush fur collar, Clarisse said, "I believe it is time for you to understand the truth about the women of our family."

As Agatha saw her aunt shiver and lean into the fire, her newly wakened senses grated at her.

"It's as hot as a furnace in here," she said. "Why are you wrapping yourself up so tightly?" She frowned, thinking back. "You always do, don't you?"

Miss Blenheim's lips curled as she leaned over to stoke the fire higher. "It took you this long to notice, miss?"

"Now, Blennie. I told you she must be clever enough to put together the pieces eventually, did I not?" Clarisse gave her niece an unfriendly smile. "Well done, my dear. But I would attempt a bit more compassion, as you'll be sharing my condition yourself soon enough."

"What do you mean?"

Clarisse rolled her eyes. "Why do you think all your little magical experiments at Tremain House were so successful?"

Caught off guard, Agatha answered with involuntary honesty: "Because I had nothing and no one to distract me from my studies. They're the only thing I've ever been good at." Then she felt herself flush, as she realized the truth of it . . . and exactly who she'd said it to, as Miss Blenheim let out a soft snort of contempt.

Still, it was true, wasn't it? And it had been all she'd wanted . . . or all that she'd allowed herself to want, at least. She frowned.

She had believed all that Miss Blenheim had told her about herself. She'd sworn never to be humiliated again by trying for anything she couldn't have.

Agatha remembered again Isobel's warm voice; the soft breath whispering across her mouth.

I can have more, she thought suddenly. *I can believe what I want about myself. I don't have to settle for less.*

But her aunt regarded her with a jaundiced eye. "It is all that makes you valuable, I agree," said Clarisse. "But then, you are a Tremain female, and that means you have an affinity for magic, just as I have, and my aunt and my grandmother before me. How do you think your great-grandfather acquired Tremain House and all his fortune in the first place? That is why you have a duty to the family to marry, for the sake of your older female relatives. It is why a particular sort of gentleman will pay so well for the privilege of having you to wife, and it is why you *will* marry, dear girl, whether you like it or not, and you will marry with some speed, too. It is your turn now to step into the breach, and I have waited quite long enough for a younger Tremain female to finally pay me back what I am owed."

"For what?" Agatha gaped at her. "What have you ever done for me?"

"It is the sacrifice every female in our family has to pay," said Clarisse. "Magic ripples through our veins, you see. If you were a man, you could make use of it. As a woman, you were born to be a source of power, just as I was for far too many years to contemplate. But just think . . ." She gave Agatha a look of mock sympathy. "Your husband may make marvelous advances for the British Empire using the power he draws from you. In return, he will give me what I need with the first magic he extracts. And then . . ." She sighed, leaning closer to the fire. "I shall never be cold again."

Agatha's head spun with more than the heat of the room now. She held still, refusing to retreat. "Why can't you take for yourself what you need? Why do you need my future husband to do it?"

"Because those spells are never taught to women," said Clarisse wearily. "You've never come across them in your father's library, have you? No, Jasper may be the most useless and impractical creature ever born, but even he is not so careless as to allow any of those texts to be kept in public view on his shelves.

"But none of that matters now." Clarisse shook her head dismissively. "All you need to understand, dear, is that my magic was drained out of me over and over again across the years while my husband rose ever higher in the Austro-Hungarian court. Simply dismissing your creatures from Tremain House took nearly all that I had left." Her lips curled into a smile. "Nearly . . . but not all."

Slowly, sinuously, she rose to her feet, while Miss Blenheim smiled behind her, a smile of deep satisfaction.

"I have been waiting for this day for two long years, miss," said Miss Blenheim. "Did you really think you could dismiss me so easily? Knowing all that I do about you and your family?"

Agatha could only shake her head numbly.

"It was tremendously helpful of you to keep all your books and supplies so carefully organized in your little office," Clarisse said. "When combined with the supplies that my dear Blennie found for me in Vienna, I am more than prepared to take on this last spell. And I think we can agree, can we not, that I am the only person in this room with both magical power *and* the spells and supplies that are needed for it?"

Agatha looked from her aunt to Miss Blenheim. Her chest tightened.

She had wanted so badly to believe herself free.

"What are you planning?" she asked, through dry lips.

"That," said Clarisse, "is entirely up to you. If you are a good girl and follow your part in the plan, like every Tremain girl has before you for the past hundred years, I won't need to do a thing–and you may have your payment in return as soon as your own daughter is old enough to be sacrificed.

"If not, though . . ." She shrugged gently. "I have both the supplies and the spellbooks to make you mouth any words I wish until you are safely wed and drained. I could not care less which choice you make."

Agatha stared at her aunt's face, so similar in shape to her own father's. "And you would really do that to me, after everything that was done to you?"

Her aunt's blue eyes were as cold and hard as sapphires. "My darling niece," she said. "I would do anything, and sacrifice anyone, only to be warm again. In twenty years, I daresay you will feel exactly the same."

Bright, hard flames leaped in the fireplace, and Agatha tasted the bitterness of defeat. If only she had managed to salvage a single grimoire, a single sanctioned brazier . . .

Wait. She closed her eyes. Suddenly, with the flames shut out, she was in the darkness again. And in that darkness, she was not alone.

She heard Isobel's laugh echoing in her ears. *Who told you that?*

Agatha had always believed she could do magic only by mouthing an expert's words. But Clarisse said magic rippled in her veins . . . and unlike her aunt, great-aunt, or grandmother, she had been allowed to devote two full years, as an unmarried girl, to the uninterrupted study of her father's grimoires. She understood the very essence of the spells she had performed, better than any Tremain girl before her.

Sparks ran up and down Agatha's skin, and this time, she knew that Isobel had been right. The sparks were magic—*her* magic, sparking through her. Her own personal magic, which she had never believed in until tonight.

Her magic, which she would never allow anyone to take away from her again.

"This is an Age of Progress," she said. "Things are changing for all of us, now. We don't have to follow the old ways anymore."

She opened her eyes and looked from her aunt to Miss Blenheim. "Do you know what the last spell was that I worked on, back at Tremain House?"

Clarisse frowned. "I can't imagine that it would be relevant, dear."

Miss Blenheim sneered. "Do you think we care about any of your little games, miss?"

"No," Agatha said. "But I'll tell you anyway . . ."

She smiled as she finished: "Transformation."

She lifted her arms and magic swept out from them, changing the world around her.

• • •

The Tennants' ball was packed with ladies in sparkling diamond tiaras, ropes of pearls, and gowns that swirled across the crowded floor. Footmen bellowed out the names of each new arrival. Officers smiled down at admiring girls, and black-coated gentlemen swept their dance partners around the room.

Agatha ignored them all. Whispers rustled around her as she forced her way, unchaperoned, through the crowd, but she barely even noticed.

Her hair was pinned into a plain bun with no ringlets or waves. It was all that she could manage without the help of a maid. Her corset was undoubtedly laced too loosely for an absolutely perfect waist, and her new blue gown didn't fit as well as it had in the modiste's fitting room.

In the dark, though, none of that would matter. If only she was still in time . . .

She stepped into the ladies' retiring room and forced herself to wait for the giggling, excited crowd of other girls to finish fixing their appearances. The moment the door to the main corridor closed behind them, she pressed her hand to the crack she had glimpsed in the flowered wallpaper. More female voices were coming down the corridor. She rushed headlong into the darkness before they could arrive.

Warm, ungloved hands caught her, and pressed the hidden door shut behind her.

"You came!" Isobel said.

"You waited," said Agatha.

"I've been waiting for an hour," Isobel said, so softly that Agatha could barely hear her. "I had to take off my gloves after the first half-hour–it's so hot in here. Mrs. Stanhope probably thinks I've run away by now. I suppose it was silly to hope you would really come, but–"

"I hope you will run away from Mrs. Stanhope," Agatha said. "I mean . . ." She stopped, gathering her breath. Her corset laces might be loose, but she still felt lightheaded. She was gasping for air. She could feel Isobel only inches away; could feel their heavy skirts brushing against each other.

She had never been so frightened in her life. But she couldn't give up now.

"I'm going back to Tremain House," she said. "I hoped . . . will you come with me? Please?"

There was a pause. Agatha couldn't see Isobel's face, couldn't guess at her expression.

"When you say I should come with you," Isobel finally said, "do you mean as a companion? As I am to Mrs. Stanhope?"

Agatha swallowed hard. "If you want," she said. "That is, I could do with a friend, and a companion. I think I've spent too much time alone. But also . . ."

She closed her eyes in the darkness.

She had sworn never to humiliate herself by asking for what she couldn't have. But she had also made a vow to never hide again.

Agatha leaned forward, holding her breath.

Isobel's lips were soft and full.

Magic sparked between them.

A long time later, Agatha drew back. She was breathing quickly now, flushed with a warmth that left her unsteady. She wanted to laugh, or cry, or dance in the darkness. She forced herself to hold perfectly still instead as she waited for Isobel's reaction.

"Well," Isobel said consideringly, "in that case . . ." She laughed suddenly, and her voice was bright with joy. "Yes. Yes, yes, yes!"

"Really?" Agatha caught hold of the rough wall to support herself as her legs turned limp with relief. "You'll really come? You really want to . . ."

"Well," Isobel said teasingly, "as a committed naturalist, you know, I can't take any of my first observations on faith. So perhaps . . ." Her warm, bare fingers curled around the nape of Agatha's neck, her words whispered against Agatha's lips. "Perhaps I ought to repeat the experiment one more time, for Science's sake. And then again, and again, and again . . ."

• • •

Even Sir Jasper seemed pleased, in a vague sort of way, to learn that Agatha had brought Miss Cunningham home for good.

"Good for a young girl to have someone to talk to, isn't it?" he said. "She seems like a very decent companion for you, my dear. Very quiet. Doesn't bother a fellow in his library. Understands that it's the right place for a man to take his meals." He beamed, settling more comfortably into his armchair. "Thank goodness Clarisse gave up and took herself off, so we can all be comfortable again. Did she go back to Vienna, did you say? Or was it Paris this time?"

"Somewhere warm, I believe," said Agatha. "I'm certain she'll be happier now."

"Yes, yes," Sir Jasper said. "I'm sure you're right, my dear. But you brought back a set of animals from London, too, you say? What on earth did you do that for?"

"Only two animals, Papa," said Agatha, "and they won't bother you, I promise."

"Oh, no," Sir Jasper said, sinking back into his book with relief. "No, I am quite sure of that."

Agatha closed the library door behind her and went, with a spring in her step, to find Isobel. Her dearest friend would be walking in the woods at this time of day, as she did every morning while Agatha worked on her own magical studies; the woods of the Tremain estate were apparently bursting with interesting animal life.

Agatha had finished her studies earlier than usual, though. Something about the scent of her latest experiment had reminded her of Isobel.

A smile deepened on her face, and she lifted up her skirts to run. Magic sparked in the air around her, carrying the sound of her laughter to the woods before her.

Isobel was waiting for her there . . . and they were both distracted from their work for the rest of that morning, in the most delightful manner possible.

The two animal additions to the household, as promised, disturbed Sir Jasper not a whit. The housecat, a sleek black creature with an oddly straight feline nose, kept to the kitchens, where her bad temper made her a perfect mousecatcher and a useful addition to the household . . .

. . . and the elegant, golden-blond cocker spaniel with her coat of thick, soft fur rarely moved from her preferred spot in front of the fireplace. As Miss Tremain had given explicit orders that a fire always be lit for the dog's comfort, regardless of what heat might bake the house, she could be certain of at least one thing.

Clarisse would never be cold again.

Nussbaum's Golden Fortune

M. K. Hobson

New York City, 1889

It was a golden October day, bright and sweet as fresh apple cider, but darkness clouded Peter Oesterlische's brow as he walked along Fifth Avenue toward the Calacacara Club. He was deeply absorbed in thought–so deeply, in fact, that when his old friend Astor Nussbaum rounded the corner in a mad sprint, Oesterlische failed to notice him and was, as a result, knocked sprawling into a decorative pot of frost-wilted nasturtiums.

"*Ostrich!*" Nussbaum compounded the indignity of the unorthodox reunion by greeting Oesterlische with the nickname he'd been formally saddled with in college. He reached down to help Oesterlische to his feet.

"*Ass,*" Oesterlische rejoined, using a nickname that had been applied to Astor Nussbaum on several occasions, but never formally.

Nussbaum had the chubby cheeks and vaguely petulant mien of the Astor family, his storied forbears. He slicked sweat from his forehead and attempted to breathe at a more casual pace.

"Well! Ostrich!" Nussbaum cast a worried glance over his shoulder. "Fancy meeting you here." Another glance. "How're things?"

"Things?" Oesterlische brushed potting soil from the back of his trousers. "Why, *things* are just peachy, Nussbaum." Oesterlische caught sight of two large, rough-looking men rounding the corner. "*Things* seem a damn sight better for me than you at the moment."

Nussbaum saw the direction of his friend's gaze, saw the rough-looking men pointing at him. He turned a rather elegant shade of pearly gray. He was about to resume his flight when Oesterlische clapped a hand on his shoulder and pointed toward a brass-handled door at the top of a high stoop.

"Follow me," he said. "The Calacacara's right here."

When the young men had achieved the inviolable security of the Calacacara's carved-walnut vestibule, Oesterlische gave the doorman–a wiry old bantam with flaring gray mutton-chops–a meaningful nod. He did not have to explain why there were rough-looking men pounding up the stairs after them–the doorman just nodded back and posted himself at the threshold, thick arms crossed and bandy legs braced.

"You sure grandad can handle those bruisers?" Nussbaum cast a thumb over his shoulder as they walked through the marble foyer. "Maybe we hang around and make sure."

"Old Sullivan's more than a match for those bully pups." Oesterlische swept the air dismissively. "He was with the 137th at Gettysburg. *Warlock* division. Claims he can turn a man inside-out by snapping his fingers and speaking a word entrusted to him by an old Yankee goomer-doctor." Oesterlische lifted a conspiratorial eyebrow. "Also, he keeps a lead-shot sap in his back pocket."

They reached the coat room. Oesterlische tucked his kid gloves neatly into his black bowler and handed it over, along with a camel-hair overcoat and ebony cane with a head of chased silver. Nussbaum had nothing to leave. His threadbare appearance caused the attendants in their gartered sleeves to very pointedly refrain from shaking their heads and clucking their tongues.

"Now, there's a back door if you're in a rush," Oesterlische said. "Otherwise, why not tell me why you have a couple of Bowery b'hoys cracking their knuckles for a chance to rough you up? Over lunch, of course."

Nussbaum licked his lips and nodded quick acceptance. The gleam in his eye indicated that a free lunch was nothing less than a gift of the fates. Oesterlische, too, thanked the fates that Nussbaum had stumbled upon the scene. For listening to Nussbaum describe what was sure to be a fascinating panoply of calamity, disorder, and dismay would keep Oesterlische from spending his whole lunch brooding over his own problems–most specifically, the Wildish Disaster.

It was pickled pig's feet and chicken salad on the club menu that day–pretty uninspiring, so the young men called for a bucket of oysters and three shots of whiskey each. They lined the little glasses up in front of themselves, and stared at each other over them like a couple of pulp-novel gunslingers, eyes squinted steely-cold.

"To your health, old friend," Nussbaum said, assuming an air of congenial menace.

"To yours, old pal," Oesterlische countered, through gritted teeth.

They grimaced at each other a moment longer, hands hovering near to the shot glasses without touching. Then, by some silent accord, they exploded into action. They threw the liquor back shot by shot, slamming the glasses down as they emptied them.

Nussbaum slammed his last glass to the table a fraction of a second before Oesterlische did.

"Hah!" he crowed, jabbing a triumphant finger skyward. Then, wiping his mouth with his sleeve, Nussbaum reached into his coat and withdrew a long rolled piece of what looked to be thin leather. He swept the empty shot glasses to one side and smoothed out the scroll. It was vellum, brightly illuminated with delicate miniatures of gold-trimmed lovers in towers twined with red roses. It was covered with tightly cribbed writing and crusty brown splotches of what looked like old blood. In places it seemed to have been stabbed through with a broad, sharp knife.

"Was this what those brutes were after?" Oesterlische lowered his voice in respect for the marvelous document.

"Oh no, those were just a couple of fellows from down on Cherry Street that think I owe them some money," Nussbaum snorted, apparently having already forgotten about them. "This . . . *this* is my golden fortune!"

Oesterlische regarded his friend with fond, whiskey-soft indulgence. This was Astor Nussbaum in a nutshell. Born on the wrong side of the Astor sheets (the largely unwelcome result of a bittersweet mésalliance between John Jacob Astor's insane firstborn son and an overly sympathetic German housemaid named Grunde Nussbaum), making his way in the world should have been a simple matter of properly leveraging the Astor family's well-known aversion to scandal. But no, Astor Nussbaum was always looking for his golden fortune in the unlikeliest of places–perpetual motion machines, hot-air balloon messenger services, or crusty old pieces of goatskin.

Oesterlische was about to ask how this particular crusty old piece of goatskin might be translated into a golden fortune, but at that moment the oysters arrived, a big silver bucket of plump briny Blue Points fresh from the cool waters off Staten Island. The waiter laid down blunt silver knives and a tray of lemon wedges. Nussbaum set to work, knifing a hapless bivalve with the expertise of a back-alley assassin, slurping the salty juice then gobbling the pearly flesh with gusto. Oesterlische did not reach for an oyster for fear of losing a finger.

Nussbaum did not speak again until, having pitched two dozen oysters down his throat, he released a satisfied belch redolent of the sea. He wiped his mouth once more, this time with the napkin, as if the shellfish had exercised a civilizing influence.

"It's a magic scroll that can do amazing things," he answered Oesterlische's earlier, unspoken question as if the oysters had never interfered. "Teleportation, I think the warlocks call it." Nussbaum leaned in close, his voice taking on a conspiratorial tone. "You want a demonstration?"

Nussbaum cast a swift glance from side to side. The club's lunch room was largely deserted–most other young men, diligent types, had already betook themselves back to their offices. A superannuated attendant snoozed on a chair by the door.

Nussbaum took Oesterliche's hand and laid it palm down on the scroll with his own hand over it. Then he whispered a word in Latin.

Vado.

There was a whoosh and a blinding, eye-watering flash. The whole world deformed, bent out of shape, and then suddenly they were sitting at their table–oyster bucket, empty whiskey glasses, and all–before a massive red-brick building with arched windows. Down a sloping hill, Oesterlische could make out the tall masts of ships at dock . . . he peered up, saw a gilded grasshopper weathervane . . .

"My God!" He sputtered. "Faneuil Hall! We're . . . in Boston!"

Reverto, Nussbaum said, as it was becoming apparent that two young men sitting at a white-linen-spread table in the middle of the sidewalk before Faneuil Hall were attracting the astonished comment of pedestrians.

And just like that, they were back within the Calacacara's cozy, walnut-paneled walls. The snoozing attendant hadn't even twitched an eyebrow.

"Amazing!" Oesterlische poured himself another whiskey with a shaking hand. "Incredible!"

"I'm going to deconstruct it, figure out how to make it work on a larger scale. Why would anyone ride on dirty old railroads if I could set up magic portals all over the world? Imagine it. Walk in one, end up wherever you want. I already have a name for them. *Nussbaum Doors.*"

Oesterlische nodded, though not at the name. No one in their right mind would walk through a Nussbaum Door. Now, an *Oesterlische* Door, on the other hand. . . . No, no. It would have to be something that fired the imagination, something with punch but that wouldn't scare the women . . . "Fairy Door!" Ugh. "Merlin's Archway?" Ridiculous. Oh well, he'd find some wideawake advertising copywriter to think something up . . .

"Well?" Nussbaum's eyes were bright. "What do you think?"

Oesterlische wrinkled his nose, made a show of thinking. If he'd learned one thing in his life, it was never to reply to such a question in haste. He thought for a moment more, his mind encompassing many things–the threadbare figure of Nussbaum sitting before him, the Wildish Disaster, the unimaginable riches that could be theirs . . . *his*. He scratched his chin.

"I see problems," he said gravely. "Mantic enterprises are tricky to start up. They're often subject to strange and arcane regulations. You have to pay expensive experts to sit on your Board of Directors. You know warlocks, they don't sell their services cheap. They're like lawyers, but with fancier hats."

Nussbaum's face fell. Oesterlische stroked his chin.

"Does it only go to Boston?"

"It goes . . . various places," Nussbaum said. "I'll admit, I haven't quite figured out how to control it yet. I can only read the Latin writing, you see. The rest is in some ancient gibberish."

"I'll bet everything you need to know is written in that ancient gibberish. If only you could *decipher* it!" Oesterlische paused, examined his nails, which were polished to a gleam. "Listen, I have a friend. He's a Mantic Consultant. He's a sharp fellow, I bet you he could . . ."

"A warlock?" Nussbaum squeaked and snatched the vellum protectively to his chest. "No, sir! I'm not showing this to a warlock. He'll steal it!"

"If you want to use this scroll to make a big fortune, you'll need a small fortune to start with. Money to get the business off the ground. Seed capital. Now, I can get seed capital for you . . . *if* you trust me." Oesterlische spoke coolly, as if the very hint of distrust were a personal offense to him. It was a very practiced skill, and was how he was often able to get older men to invest much larger sums than their common sense might otherwise approve.

"I will arrange a meeting," Oesterlische said, ignoring the fact that Nussbaum was pressing his lips together like a petulant baby. "But of course we'll have to finalize *our* deal first. Secrecy must be upheld. Confidentiality, nondisclosure, all of that. You'll want to be completely protected . . ."

"*Our* deal?" Nussbaum squeaked. "What do you mean, *our* deal?"

Oesterlische leaned forward. "Astor, you're right. This *could* be bigger than the railroads. Which is precisely why going at it half cocked is so dangerous. What are you going to do when Jay Gould comes knocking at your door with a half-dozen of his Union Pacific boys, bloodthirsty and wielding knives gleaming in the moonlight?" Oesterlische leaned back. "Honestly, I'm having second thoughts about getting mixed up in it at all. We'll probably both end up dead. Now, do you want me to help you, or not?"

Nussbaum silently contemplated the image of Jay Gould and his bloodthirsty railroad boys with the gleaming knives. Finally, he sighed and extended a hand across the table.

"I'll draw up the paperwork this afternoon," Oesterlische said, mentally earmarking fifty-one percent for his own share. "The warlock is named Elden Marinus. Meet me Thursday. Four o'clock. Central Park at 57th. I'll take you around to see him."

• • •

The warlock Elden Marinus lived far uptown in a large suite of rooms in a recently completed apartment building called the Mazeppa. The Mazeppa represented the last word in esthetic dignity, with black marble hallways, block-printed wallpaper from France, and awnings of verdigrised copper. This earnestness, touching as it was, was only slightly debased by the concession to the practical–modern elevators and bountiful steam heat were present but not excessively touted, as they might be in a less high-minded establishment. The building turned one shining marble face toward Central Park, but the building's focus was undeniably inward, toward the large interior courtyard where sunflowers nodded and children and dogs were strictly forbidden to play.

Oesterlische and Nussbaum were handled by no fewer than four individuals on their way to see Marinus. The apartment's doorman bowed them respectfully through the wrought-brass entrance, a sober reception clerk guided them the three steps to the elevator as if he were a native guide leading them through hostile territory, an elevator man with gold braid on his shoulders whisked them swiftly up to the fifth floor. They were greeted at the door, relieved of their coats, and ushered into Marinus's consulting room by a young Japanese man who wore an impeccably tailored livery of crisp white linen.

The room was quite large, with tall windows that looked onto the park. It was decorated with elephantine palms in enameled Chinese pots, black lacquered furniture, and embroidered silk throws. It was masculine, meticulous, and mysterious. It not only made certain promises about Elden Marinus, they were far more interesting and ambitious promises than anyone would think to bring in all on their own. It was an astonishing effect, and for one not used to it, overwhelming.

"All a bit much, eh?" Nussbaum suggested timidly, as if afraid the draperies might contradict him.

Oesterlische, settled deep in a comfortable leather chair, said nothing. Of course it was too much. That was how Marinus made his living.

But the best was yet to come. The room, spacious as it was, suddenly became crowded when Elden Marinus entered it. A tall and fleshy man, with the build of someone who could afford to eat well, he moved with exceptional briskness. He had fierce eyes and a nobly hooked nose. He wasn't any older than Oesterlische or Nussbaum, but he was obviously far superior in all regards. He was able to wear a red velvet fez and a satin-lined smoking jacket without looking the least bit ridiculous. He had graduated with a degree in Corporate Sorcery and had since commanded higher and higher consulting fees, scrying competitive motives, summoning servile djinns who could foretell the movement of the marketplace, casting glamours on advertising campaigns of particular importance.

"Welcome, welcome!" Marinus boomed, arms wide. "How pleasant to have you come, Ostrich! It's been far too long. How have you been keeping? Well, I trust? You've met Bob Ghent, haven't you?"

Marinus gestured to the corner of the room, where a small man, whom both Nussbaum and Oesterlische had entirely failed to notice, sat on a wicker chair, the rim of his bowler clenched between nervous-seeming fingers. The turning of attention onto him was like an electric shock. He jumped to his feet.

"I was just going," he said, in a soft and cultivated voice, bowing apologetically to Oesterlische and Nussbaum. He edged toward the door, but Marinus clapped him on the shoulder and drew him forward.

"No, no! You must meet Peter Oesterlische, one of my oldest and dearest friends. Fantastic fellow, wonderful old family, doing marvelous things for himself down on the street. And this is . . ." Marinus let his voice trail off as his gimlet eyes raked Nussbaum, lingering on his shabby suit jacket as if to gauge its capacity for hiding things under.

Introductions were made all around, but they were not enough to calm the nervous Mr. Ghent–he tipped his hat over and over then hurried from the room under the tender care of the Japanese butler.

"Nervous constitution," Marinus said, annexing a divan like a large invading army. "Bad digestion. Poor fellow. Now, Ostrich. Let's get down to cases. I got your telegram. You say you have some kind of wonderful artifact to show me?"

Oesterlische nudged Nussbaum in the ribs. Reluctantly, Nussbaum drew out the vellum and handed it to Marinus.

Marinus spread it out on a low brass table, holding down the corners with a pair of chased-silver incense burners in the shape of writhing dragons. He perched a pair of gold-rimmed pince-nez on his hawkish nose and peered down at the parchment for quite a long time before speaking.

"Well, this is something *quite* different," he said. "Moorish. Second century, if I don't miss my guess. I can tell you, I've never seen one like it. Most of this writing is in ancient court Arabic that has been dead for twelve hundred years. The Latin incantation was appended much later." He looked at Nussbaum. "You've recited it?"

"That's how I made the scroll work." Nussbaum said. "I mean, I knew the scroll was magic. So I read the Latin aloud, and it transported me to different places in the wink of an eye."

"You've quite an empirical streak!" Marinus stared at Nussbaum in horror, letting his glasses dangle helplessly from his long fingers. "How did you know it wouldn't blow you up or turn you into some variety of slime mold?"

Nussbaum scratched his chin, shrugged.

"I guess I never thought about it."

"Well, all's well that ends well." Marinus shook his head as if he didn't believe it. "So. You were transported to different places. What kind of places?"

"Just . . . places," Nussbaum said. "I always arrived somewhere completely random. I couldn't control where I showed up."

"No one makes a scroll like this just to travel randomly," Marinus said. "There must be some kind of control mechanism, but to find it, the writing on the front of the scroll must be deciphered. I can pick out a few words here and there–'beloved' and 'longing.' They hardly provide me with much to go on. I'll have to take more time in my translation." He rolled up the scroll, and was tucking it away as he said, "I will need to keep this for a day or two."

"Absolutely not," Nussbaum said, reaching for the scroll. "Out of the question."

"Not a problem at all," Oesterlische interposed himself between Nussbaum and the scroll. "We can trust Marinus."

"What if he copies it?" Nussbaum hissed. He thought he'd hissed it low enough, but Marinus laughed.

"Oh, there's little chance of that, Mr. Nussbaum. To recreate a scroll like this would require a huge amount of magical energy of the type typically generated by the sacrifice of innocent human life on a most grotesque scale. While that wasn't out of the question in second-century Araby, it is in modern-day New York." He paused, looked at Oesterlische. "Your colleague's concern, however, does raise a point of importance, Ostrich. My services come with a price. I want a piece of the action."

Oesterlische lifted a cool eyebrow.

"What *action* might you be referring to?"

"Please. I can't say I have the pleasure of a long acquaintance with Mr. Nussbaum here, but I do know *you*, Ostrich. You wouldn't be involved if there wasn't the possibility of money–a lot of money."

Nussbaum knit his brow, his eyes darting nervously between Oesterlische and Marinus. "I already have one partner I didn't expect . . . I can't just keep adding them on willy-nilly!"

With a shrug, Marinus handed the rolled-up scroll back to Nussbaum.

"Then I'm afraid I can't help you." He looked at Oesterlische. "Sorry, old buddy. But I have my money needs, just as you do."

"Oh, I know all about your *money needs,*" Oesterlische said. "And we were thinking of paying you for your services. How does two hundred dollars strike you?"

Marinus barked a laugh.

"Two hundred dollars! Two hundred dollars wouldn't pay my tailor to stitch a hole in my pants. How does two hundred dollars strike me? It strikes me as a vile bargain indeed!"

Oesterlische shrugged, examined his nails. His diffidence made Marinus draw a deep, indignant breath.

"Listen, this isn't some simple business you're talking about here! I've never seen a scroll like this. And other than a very old gentleman in Cambridge who *might* be able to puzzle out the ancient Arabic–if his eyesight held out, that is–I'm the only man in New York City who can read it. Thus, I want a piece of the pie."

"And yet you won't get a penny more than two hundred dollars," Oesterlische said. "I believe the Board of Inquiry still hasn't returned its report on last year's . . . *events*, has it? I believe there might still be an opportunity for interested parties to provide further testimony?"

The color drained from Marinus's face. He fell dreadfully silent, and when he spoke next, it was through clenched teeth.

"That's low dealing, Ostrich."

"We'll be back tomorrow afternoon with the agreed-upon fee," Oesterlische said. "You'll have some findings for us by then, I trust?"

"You know, there's an old saying in my business, Ostrich." Marinus's voice filled the room, rich and heavy with menace. The power of it made the room's silver-hinged skulls, brocaded Tibetan hangings, and vases of peacock feathers rattle and tremble and sway. Marinus's fierce eyes glowed with light, and strange eldritch flames seemed to illuminate the folds of his smoking jacket. "You don't *fuck* with warlocks."

"Save it for the showgirls," Oesterlische snapped. He gestured to Nussbaum. "Come on," he said. "It's getting *thick* in here."

• • •

"I can't take you anywhere!" Oesterlische scolded, once they were back on the street. Snow drifted down from a lead-dark sky. He lifted his collar against the cold. "If you can't follow my lead, I don't know how we're going to do any business at all."

Nussbaum was still pale after the demonstration of Marinus's power. But the recrimination made color rise in his cheeks as he jammed his hands deep into his pockets.

"That scroll is all I have!" He said. "My golden fortune is back in that overdecorated apartment with that warlock! I don't know Elden Marinus, I certainly don't like leaving my scroll with him to do who knows what with it on his own time!"

"I have Marinus under control," Oesterlische said. "He will do what I say, and he will not double-cross me, or he knows what will happen."

"Yes, what was that all about, anyway? He went pale as a sheet when you referred to whatever it was you referred to."

Oesterlische looked around for passing pedestrians.

"You remember the Great Blizzard we had last year? Snows like the town had never seen, buildings buried in a hundred feet of snow, trading ships frozen in the harbor, thousands of dollars of commercial damage, et cetera?"

"Well, of course I do," Nussbaum said. "A strange series of events during that time resulted in me being locked on the top floor of an abandoned pickle factory. I nearly lost a foot!"

Oesterlische frowned at him.

"You do know how to steal one's thunder, don't you?" He pressed his lips together tightly and walked on. Nussbaum jogged to keep up.

"Aw, come on." He said. "Don't be like that. I get locked in abandoned pickle factories all the time."

"I know," Oesterlische said. "Which is why I wish you wouldn't ruin the dramatic impact of the few good stories I have to tell with your incessant pickle-factory adventures. I was leading up to quite a bombshell."

"All right, fine," Nussbaum said. "The Great Blizzard of 1888. Buildings buried in snow, commercial damage, shivering young men locked in pickle factories burning empty boxes for heat and fending off rats driven crazy with some kind of strange disease they picked up on an Indian cargo ship. Go on."

Oesterlische sighed.

"Marinus did it," he said, curtly.

"What do you mean, *did it*?"

"Caused it. Made it happen. Was the instigator of."

Nussbaum stared at him.

"No."

"He was fiddling around, summoning some kind of weather elemental. He was trying to impress a showgirl. Surprisingly, the fez doesn't always do the trick."

"I am astonished to imagine that it might not."

"Anyway, things got a bit out of hand. So I helped him hush it up, got the girl back to the cabaret . . . which was no small task, with raging weather elementals storming around."

"My goodness." Nussbaum rubbed a hand over his mouth. He turned nervous brown eyes onto Oesterlische. "And you can prove this?"

"Prove what?"

"His involvement."

"It wouldn't be hard," Oesterlische said. "The only reason no one's accused him of anything is that no one's thought to look. If someone went to the Commission and called their attention to poor Marinus, got them asking some questions, the jig would be up. But I wouldn't do that to a friend. Marinus is a good egg. Fez notwithstanding."

Nussbaum thought some more.

"And you've just gone and cheesed him off. You heard what he said. Not wise to . . . well, *annoy* a warlock. You sure we want him as an enemy?"

"Who, *Marinus*?" Oesterlische raised an eyebrow. "Marinus is all black lacquer and enamelwork and consulting fees. The dust that runs through his veins occasionally catches a glitter. His whole game is to overawe you, but you mustn't let him."

Nussbaum nodded, but didn't seem convinced. He thought for a long time.

"Peter . . ." he said softly. "Hundreds of people died in that storm. If he was responsible for it, as you claim . . ."

Oesterlische waved a hand.

"Some drunks on the Bowery died because they couldn't find enough cardboard to crawl under. Hardly Marinus's fault."

Oesterlische stopped when he saw Nussbaum's fist clenched at his side.

"Drunks. And children. And old women." Nussbaum said. But he said nothing more, and Oesterlische quickly mortared over the awkward moment by pulling out his pocket watch and scrutinizing it closely.

"Well, well. Look at the time." Oesterlische had a couple of hours before he had to get himself ready to attend the party at the Wildishes'. "What do you say I stand us to a round of drinks? I think we've earned them."

To his surprise, Nussbaum refused his offer, tipped his hat stiffly, and hurried off into the milling crowds climbing onto a streetcar headed downtown. Oesterlische watched after his retreating form for a moment, eyes narrowed.

Now, what kind of bee had gotten into his *bonnet?* Oesterlische wondered. Oh well. Never mind.

He had a party to get to.

• • •

Artemus Q. Wildish had made his money in mercantile stores and international shipping. He lived on 60th, in the newly fashionable uptown–even Oesterlische could remember when everything above 40th was nothing but mud lots and wandering goats. But now it was the playground of the wealthy, with cobblestoned roads and freshly planted trees, and huge concretions of white marble.

The specific context of his attendance at the Wildish party was as a dependable, acceptably bred spare man, one of the many eligible bachelors intended to balance out the superabundance of ineligible widows, antique grandmothers, and sharp-tongued maiden aunts. He was expected to be charming to such ladies, and take their arms when it was time to go in to dinner. Beyond that, his time was his own.

In his pocket, he had tucked a blue satin box with an enameled bonbonnière he'd purchased earlier in the week. He would look for an opportune moment to give it to Winifred Wildish. She would pay the gift hardly any notice, just as she hadn't paid much attention to the other little presents he had brought her–chocolate drops, small volumes of poetry bound in kid, fragrant satin pomanders. They were gestures merely, each one a formal token of his continued suit. She would refuse to accept it at first, then would finally succumb with a smile and a distancing word. In a day or so, she would send him a thank-you note scented with perfume, and he'd send her a teasing little reply. It was pat as a contract negotiation. And why shouldn't it be, when Winifred was old Wildish's only daughter, and stood to inherit a $30 million fortune?

The negotiations had been in danger of floundering of late. The specifics of the Wildish Disaster were not particularly exotic. Over the past fortnight, Oesterlische had lost quite a large sum of *père* Wildish's money as a result of unwise speculation in pork belly futures. But with an attractive new business opportunity to present to Artemus Q. Wildish, Oesterlische felt that he'd found a way to extricate himself from the Wildish Disaster–and indeed, radically transform it into the Oesterlische Triumph.

The hack brought him through the porte cochère and he climbed out, taking the low, broad front steps two at a time.

Masses of white roses and swags of silver bunting decorated the vast marble entry hall. Beyond, through the open doors, he could see that the ballroom was already crowded with dozens of beautifully dressed notables in silk and satin and lace. He breathed in the smell of money.

Winifred was nowhere to be seen, and after an hour of trading barbs with other spare males of similar circumstance and downing glasses of champagne liberated from passing waiters, he began to grow annoyed. He went out the side door for a private cigarette, and as he was pulling the silver case from his inside pocket, he was surprised to see Winifred bustling up the street. She was still in a simple afternoon dress and her cheeks were flushed with hurrying. She was being followed at a slight distance by two rather unseemly looking men in threadbare overcoats, their heads down and their hands jammed into their pockets. He was about to leap out into the street and tell the mashers to shove off when Winifred paused at the gate and turned back to them.

"Thank you, Mr. Lamb! Thank you, Mr. Gussy! Goodnight! Goodnight!"

The unseemly men stopped. Each one tipped his hat to her. Then they melted away into the dark street. Winifred hurried up the stairs toward the back door, jumping when she saw Oesterlische standing there.

"Mr. Oesterlische!"

"Late for your own party?" he said, as he helped her off with her overcoat and took her small purse. He looked up the street. "You know those thugs?"

"Oh, they aren't thugs! That's just Mr. Lamb and Mr. Gussy. I was down at the soup kitchen on Cherry Street handing out soup, and they walked me home. They often walk me home. They call it *watching my back.*"

Watching your bustle, more like, Oesterlische thought with disapproval. But the discussion quickly left Mr. Lamb and Mr. Gussy as Winifred broke out in a flustered dither: "Oh, I can't believe I'm so late! I've been running around all day, and everything's started and I'm not even dressed!"

"There, there. It's all right," he said. He always adopted his most soothing manner with her, because she was always so much in need of it. Volunteering at soup kitchens and distributing double-eagles to widows with eighteen children and things like that gave her whole existence the frothy consistency of whipped cream. Such activities took her to the worst kinds of neighborhoods at all hours of the day and night, which made Oesterlische worry. Charity was all well and good, but he certainly hoped, over time, she could be enticed to perform her good works at a greater distance. And without unseemly looking men in shabby overcoats walking her home.

But he didn't share these concerns with her. He carefully avoided chaffing her about anything that could possibly be a point of controversy. There'd be time enough for all that later.

"No one's missed you yet, except me." He gave her another winning smile.

She pressed his hand with hers before vanishing up the back stairs in a storm of small footsteps.

He found himself standing in the vestibule, feeling rather silly holding her coat and her gloves and her purse. He chuckled at the ridiculousness of it. He hung the coat on a nearby peg, dusting the snow from her gloves and tucking them in the pocket. He hung the purse on a different hook, and was suddenly struck by a clever inspiration.

He reached into his pocket and took out the blue satin box. With the small pencil that he carried around in his address book, he rubbed out the tedious inscription he had written and wrote "With fond regards from your coat-check boy." Yes, that was rather clever. He opened her purse and tucked the present inside.

As he did, his fingers came across a rectangle of stiff poster-board. He could not help but draw it out for a look. He stared at it for a moment. It was a round-trip train ticket to Boston, canceled two days ago . . . Tuesday.

What an odd coincidence, Oesterlische thought, remembering his own magical trip to Boston with Nussbaum. That had been on Tuesday as well.

He stared at the ticket, brow wrinkling. Why on earth would she have gone to *Boston*? Shopping? But who shopped in *Boston*? Visiting friends? But who had friends in *Boston*?

The strangeness of the coincidence firmed a resolution that had been building in Oesterlische since he'd parted from Nussbaum earlier in the day. He had already decided he was going to go pay Marinus a private follow-up visit. He wanted to make sure the warlock was keeping detailed notes, for one thing. Oesterlische didn't want to be left flat should Nussbaum's worrying persnickitude induce him to take his scroll and go home. This strange new Boston connection was worth talking over, too.

Hearing people coming toward the door, Oesterlische swiftly tucked the ticket back down in her purse, along with the blue satin box. He closed it up, left to hang there for her to find. He was already composing the teasing little reply he'd send her when she sent him her thank-you note.

• • •

Winifred came down a half-hour later, wearing a dress of gray silk tissue, draped up in the back with a spray of pink satin roses. She hadn't done much with her hair, Oesterlische noticed, but what she'd forgone in coiffure she'd made up for with jewelry–a high diamond choker, dangling earrings, and a massive hair clip. The effect was dazzling. Oesterlische watched her glitter all the way down the stairs.

It took her a while, but finally she made it through the crowd to where Oesterlische stood casually discussing Wordsworth with some superannuated pastor. After Winifred had given them both a polite greeting, Oesterlische turned his back on the little pastor, drawing Winifred to one side. He had better things to talk about than Wordsworth, now that he had a better partner.

"Thank you for helping me," she said to him, in a low voice. "You're right, nobody missed me."

"Except me," he reminded her. "How could I possibly enjoy myself without you? Like a faithful dog, sitting on the stoop, waiting for his mistress's return . . ."

"Oh, nonsense," she said. "You were out to have a smoke."

"Well, perhaps I *was* going to have a smoke while I pined miserably for you," Oesterlische said, in a somewhat hurt tone. "But it was only to soothe my longing and despair."

"Longing and despair?" Winifred's voice was soft, and she turned her eyes down in a very maidenly fashion. She even blushed. "For me?"

Oesterlische seized his opportunity. Making his voice very low and serious, he said: "Every moment I am parted from you is one I pass in agony." He let these words hang, which was a risky move given that the party around them was bustling and swirling and the resonant effect of them was likely to be lost. But they did not seem to be lost on Winifred. She blushed deeper. He calculated his chances, decided that they'd never be better than at that exact moment.

"I love you, Winifred," he said, clasping her hand. "Be my wife."

Winifred pulled her hand away, pressed it to her hot cheek.

"Oh, Peter!" She looked up at him, her eyes moist and pleading. "If only you knew how happy those words make me . . ."

she paused, looked away. "But . . . my father is so terribly angry at you. He says you've lost him a lot of money, and that he can't forgive you for it. He'll never consent, never!"

"He'll consent," Oesterlische smiled down at her. He touched a finger to the side of his nose. "I've got a new business opportunity for him. It will make him millions."

Winifred's lower lip trembled. Hope kindled in her eyes, but then, just as quickly, she stifled it.

"No," she said. "I daren't dream of the joy that could be ours. He won't give you any more money. I'd bet my life on it."

"Oh, so you want to *bet*, do you?" Oesterlische said. Silly girl, she knew he could never pass up a wager. Oesterlische lifted his chin. "Your father'll give me not a penny less than $25,000. If I win, you marry me."

"Make it $50,000," Winifred returned, with the quickness of a Bowery card sharp. Oesterlische's eyes widened. He must have looked a little unsure of such a large raise, because Winifred's face became soft and pleading again.

"You *can* get $50,000 . . . can't you?"

"Well . . ." Oesterlische lifted his chin. "Of course I can! Just watch me! It's as good as done!"

"And then I'll be yours," Winifred said, in a low, thrilling voice. "*All* yours."

Oesterlische was so taken by this dazzling concept that he hardly noticed Artemus Q. Wildish standing behind him until the older man tapped him heavily on the shoulder.

"Young man!" Artemus Q. Wildish's voice boomed in Oesterlische's ear, making him wince. "Step into my office."

• • •

"You've lost me a lot of money."

Artemus Q. Wildish's voice was stern and disapproving. It almost ruined the pleasure Oesterlische felt at being in Wildish's den. Wildish's den was a wonderful, masculine place, wallpapered in bookshelves with acres of expensively bound books. Everything smelled of leather and hound dog and brandy. There was a roaring, welcoming fire in the hearth. Oesterlische felt quite certain that if he were to own such a den, he would never leave it, even to fetch spendthrift young brokers with designs on his daughter in by the ear.

Wildish went to a humidor and withdrew a pair of fat, fragrant Cuban cigars and handed one to Oesterlische. The old man went through all the fussy motions of cigar smoking–clipping the end and piercing it, rolling it between his fingers contemplatively, sniffing it.

"You've lost me $10,000, to be precise." Wildish lit the cigar, looking at Oesterlische through the flame. "And I want to know what you intend to do about it."

"I intend to hit you up for another $100,000," Oesterlische said, letting his cigar rest between his fingers, unfiddled with. The older man's eyes widened as he waved out the match and puffed out a mouthful of smoke.

"Indeed?" he said.

"And with that $100,000, I'm going to make you $10 million. I've got a proposition for you that will make all other propositions seem like mere suggestions by comparison."

"That's what you said last time," Wildish said, drawing another mouthful of smoke.

"It's magic . . ." Oesterlische began, ". . . which I know isn't usually in your line. But this is fantastic magic. Exceptional magic. Magic that could make the railroads obsolete."

"That's hardly appealing to me." Wildish's eyes narrowed. "You should know better than anyone how much stock I hold in the railroads."

"I'd advise you to get out of it, quick," Oesterlische said. "In a year's time, those certificates will be worthless."

"Poppycock," Wildish said. But his eyes narrowed by another precise degree. "Tell me more."

Oesterlische described the scroll, and his lightning-quick trip to Boston and back. He left out all the troublesome details, like the fact that they didn't actually know how to really make the scroll work. He painted visions of fairy transport achieved in a twinkling, travelers veritably blooming with delight at the opportunity to wave money at the providers of such a wonderful service. By the time he was finished, Wildish's eyes, once suspicious slits, had widened to the size of California grapefruits, and his expensive Cuban cigar burned to ash in a brass tray, forgotten.

"How about side effects? Strange loopholes? Odd anomalies?"

"I've got Elden Marinus looking into that," Oesterlische said offhandedly.

"Marinus? Why, he's quite an up-and-comer! Charges exorbitant rates! How can you afford him?"

Oesterlische yawned extravagantly, did not answer.

"And you've got a license on this magic?" Wildish said. Despite his best efforts, eagerness was creeping into his voice. "You've got the rights?"

"The scroll is mine," Oesterlische rolled the cigar between his fingers. "But I'll need that money to get the ball rolling. A hundred thousand should do nicely."

"You're not getting a penny more than fifty," Artemis Q.

Wildish grunted, throwing open the heavy, leather-bound check register on his desk.

• • •

The party dragged on for hours after this extremely satisfying interview. Artemus Q. Wildish locked himself behind the closed doors of his den to smoke more Cuban cigars and drink whiskey and play poker with a select coterie of fat-bellied chums. Oesterlische would dearly have liked to join them, but his acceptance as an "Old Man" would have to wait until he was actually betrothed to Winifred. He would have to play the callow suitor until then, and speak with old women and priests, and pretend to thrill to the emotional appeal of poetry. It was frankly horrible, but Oesterlische was a young man of determination and purpose. Luckily, all the old women and priests got tired by midnight, and the party broke up, carriages heading home full of drooping egret feathers.

As he was fetching his coat to leave, he was surprised by Winifred, who grabbed him by his satin lapels and drew him into a private vestibule near the front door. She jerked the curtains shut behind them. He looked around, appalled at the thought that someone might have seen.

"How'd it go?" She whispered breathlessly, pressing her hands against his chest, leaning her body against his.

He lifted an eyebrow at her, surprised but not entirely undelighted by her zeal.

"Fifty thousand," he said, drawing the check half out of his pocket. "As promised."

She kissed him then, throwing her arms around his neck.

"Really, Winifred," he said, enjoying the cool press of her diamonds against his throat. "At least let me get the ring first."

She pouted up at him.

"So you *didn't* make arrangements?"

"No, not tonight," Oesterlische said. "I thought asking for $50,000 *and* a daughter might be a bit much for your father to swallow. Let me put this money to work and start showing him a return on his investment. *Then* I'll ask him for your hand."

"Oh, Peter, you're so wise!" she said. "You always handle everything so well."

"Yes I do, don't I?" Oesterlische said, glowing with warmth.

After untangling himself from Winifred's embrace, Oesterlische skipped out into the chilly darkness, reflecting that while he'd walked in with almost nothing, he was walking out with both a $50,000 check *and* a $30 million fiancée in his pocket. A smattering of snow covered the dark gaslit sidewalks. He felt like scooping it up and letting it drift down over his head in a glittery cloud.

He had her! He had Winifred Wildish! She'd promised to marry him! Of course, he still had to get her father's approval, but once Marinus had the magic figured out, it would be nothing but smooth sailing.

Thinking of Marinus, Oesterlische turned his steps downtown, toward the warlock's apartment. It was late, but warlocks in general, and Marinus in particular, were known to keep late hours. Oesterlische knew from experience that a friendly call at two in the morning would trouble Marinus far less than a business call promptly at nine.

When Oesterlische arrived at the Mazeppa, he was handled by three of the accustomed people–the doorman, the entry clerk, the elevator boy–but when he came to Marinus's door expecting to encounter the fourth, Oesterlische's heart dropped into his shoes. Marinus's door stood wide open, and Oesterlische could see wreckage within.

He stepped inside, gingerly kicking aside the flotsam of destruction as he moved. Most of the smashing had been done in Marinus's office–silk pillows had been disemboweled with knives, frondy palms had been toppled, and everywhere, papers and scrolls and vellums were scattered.

"Marinus?" Oesterlische called, but only silence answered. Hurrying out the way he came, fearing to be found standing there if the Japanese butler happened to suddenly return with the police, Oesterlische noticed something he hadn't seen coming in.

Stuck to the front door with a heavy, thick-handled knife was a piece of paper–blank, save for one stark, paint-smeared mark.

A black hand.

• • •

With the silver-headed top of his cane, Oesterlische rapped on Astor Nussbaum's door. Nussbaum came to the door bleary-eyed, blinking.

"For heaven's sake," he said. "Don't tell me the Wildish reception lasted this late! How'd it go? Did you get the investment?"

"I got the investment," Oesterlische patted his pocket. "But we've got problems. Marinus is gone. And the scroll, too. The whole place has been busted up. I found this on the front door."

Nussbaum's eyes widened as Oesterlische showed him the paper with the black handprint.

"Come in," he said.

Nussbaum lived in a small, clean apartment in a part of town that had once been fashionable, and was at least still respectable, but hardly impressive. His rooms were small but tidily kept. He lit a coal-oil lamp and banked up the stove and put some coffee on. It was terribly cold–Nussbaum kept his blanket around his shoulders, and Oesterlische kept his coat and muffler on. They sat at the small table in what the landlady had probably called a dining room.

"The Black Hand," Nussbaum said, grimly. "The men who were chasing me yesterday, before you rescued me into your club. They were Black Hand thugs. I owe them money. They must have followed us to Marinus's."

"Wonderful," Oesterlische said. "I've got Artemus Q. Wildish on the hook for fifty grand to get the ball rolling . . . and now we have no ball."

The memories of Winifred's diamonds scratching at his throat came back to Oesterlische in terrible mockery. His marriage to Winifred . . . she had as good as said she would marry him if he obtained her father's approval! But how the hell was he going to do that if he didn't have the scroll?

The two men drank coffee, thick and boiled on Nussbaum's coal hob. It was bitter but powerful, rather like the glare Nussbaum kept giving Oesterlische.

"This is all your fault, you know," Nussbaum grumbled. "You and that weather-witching warlock of yours. None of this would have happened if we'd held onto the scroll, like I wanted to."

"If you hadn't surrendered the scroll, it might have been you who was kidnapped," Oesterlische said. "As I see it, I've saved you from a terrible fate."

Nussbaum pondered this grimly as he sipped his coffee.

"How much money you got on you?" he asked.

"What? Why, about a hundred dollars in cash."

"You walk around with $100 in your pocket?" Nussbaum shook his head. "I know quite a few poor folk in this neighborhood who'd knock you down for less. It's better that I take it off you."

"That's the finest explanation for a touch I ever heard," Oesterlische said.

"I'm not putting the touch on you. This is business. I can bribe a lot of people downtown with $100. I'll poke around, see what I can find out. That'll make a start, anyway."

"What makes you think you can manage that?" Oesterlische said. "You don't seem to have too cozy an arrangement with the underworld. Last I saw, the underworld was chasing you up Fifth Avenue."

"I think I can muster the discretion required to make effective enquiries . . . I have so much at stake here, you see." He gave Oesterlische another sad look, that Oesterlische thought was most unbearably reproachful.

"I will find out how we might go about getting it back. I'll meet you after work tomorrow and let you know what I find out." Nussbaum heaved the blanket off his shoulders and reached for his heavy overcoat. "Now I'd better get out there and see if I can find people while they're still drunk."

• • •

Oesterlische didn't tumble into his bed until five a.m. He slept until noon, at which time he was unceremoniously launched upon by his mother, a hard thing for a fellow to have to endure before he'd even had his first cup of coffee.

"There's a letter for you from Miss Wildish," his mother trilled in the drawn-shade darkness of his room. Through sleep-gummed eyes, he could see her waving a pink envelope in his face. "Delivered this morning!"

No doubt it was the perfumed thank-you note he'd expected. But Oesterlische had no time to bother his mind with flowery sentiment from his almost-fiancée. He left his mother to brood over its potential contents all day–it would provide her with ample intellectual amusement, and he felt generous in giving it to her.

Oesterlische was employed at the firm of Rudnick & Culpepper–to say that he worked there, however, was to somewhat overstate the issue. Mr. Rudnick and Mr. Culpepper understood that the young men they employed as Junior Brokers–well-bred young men of taste and distinction–had to be given some leeway. Thus, when Oesterlische slid into his seat at one p.m., fully intending to stay for an hour and then make a hasty break for it, no one raised an eyebrow other than the slightly less well-bred young men in ink-stained sleeves to whom the work actually fell.

Oesterlische sat at his desk and stared at his shiny black desk phone. He thought about the situation, thought about the similar shiny black desk phone that Wildish had on *his* desk. Bringing the two desk phones together in any kind of communicative arrangement was completely out of the question. He imagined the conversation that would occur between them, then knocked such awful fantasies out of the air. He couldn't call Wildish. He couldn't tell him that he'd lost the scroll. He'd already had one failure. Fail one time and it could be dismissed as a mistake. Fail a second time, and it started to look like a habit. No, there was nothing else for it. He had to get the scroll back.

There was the sound of a commotion near the reception desk. Oesterlische saw, with a sudden rush of joy, that the commotion was in the shape of a large, loud warlock. It was

Elden Marinus. He looked quite a bit the worse for wear–there was a huge goose egg over his eye and scratches along the side of his face. When Marinus saw Oesterlische, he brushed aside the receiving clerk imperiously and came to tower over Oesterlische's desk.

"What kind of insanity have you mixed me up in?" Marinus bellowed. "Rough trade! Wharves and warehouses! I am not accustomed to being engaged by clients with one foot in the camp of thuggery!"

Oesterlische shushed him, all too aware that his powerful voice was carrying into the offices of the partners. While they understood young men of taste and distinction, they most certainly did not understand the bellowings of warlocks.

"Come on, quiet down," Oesterlische murmured. "We'll go have a drink."

"He thinks he can buy me off with a drink!" Marinus said even more loudly, looking around the office for some sane man who would sympathize with his plight. "A man whose shady dealings have led me to such a pretty pass!" And suddenly Oesterlische realized that Marinus meant for his voice to carry–it was subtle revenge for the dirty trick Oesterlische had played him before. Oesterlische stood swiftly, took Marinus's arm, gave it a jerk. He put his lips close to Marinus's ear.

"All right, you've made your point," he growled. "Now do you want a drink or not?"

Marinus turned his head, looked down at Oesterlische with a mean, silky smile.

"Why, yes." He said. "I suppose I *would* like a drink."

They hurried downstairs to a bar called Mamma Ri's, where Oesterlische called for whiskey. Marinus called for absinthe, lighting the lump of sugar atop the silver spoon with a small snap of his fingers. After downing one or two of these sorcerous concoctions, Marinus became far more pliable and easy to work with.

"Tell me you have the scroll," Oesterlische pleaded.

"I regret to say it was taken from me."

Oesterlische swore. "Are you, or are you not, a mighty warlock? How does it happen that a bunch of hooligans from the docks are able to wrest a master of eternity's great mysteries from his own hearth and home?"

"Peter, I am a *corporate* warlock," Marinus hiccuped. "I scry competitive motives and polish up magic for rollouts. I do not specialize in martial sorcery of any sort. If you wanted *that* kind of magic, you should have looked up someone like Bob Ghent."

"Who?"

"Bob Ghent. You met him. He was at my office when you came by the other day."

Oesterlische searched his memory, to no avail.

"Mousy chap, unassuming . . ." Marinus offered. "He was hiding behind a potted palm when you came in."

"Oh, *him*," Oesterlische said. "He reminded me of a bowl of cold oatmeal."

"Yes, he gets that a lot," Marinus said. "He's a salamander."

"A what now?"

"A salamander. He changes color and spits fire. All the things that a salamander does. It's his specialty. It's more useful than it sounds, I assure you."

Oesterlische pressed his fingers to the bridge of his nose, briefly attempting to ascertain how cold oatmeal, firespitting, and salamanders had entered the conversation.

Marinus must not have noticed this action, for he pressed on blithely: "He's really quite an angry little warlock underneath that cold-oatmeal exterior," he said thoughtfully. "But he keeps it all inside, under careful control, and uses it to send forth flaming jets of doom upon malefactors of all stripes. Terrible for his digestion, as you might imagine."

Marinus frowned at the bartender for being quite so far down the bar, gestured to the man impatiently. "I was going to hire him to talk to some clients who've left their bills go too long. His talents really are spectacular."

"Leaving aside Bob Ghent and his amazing fire-spewing talents," Oesterlische gently attempted to return the conversation to his own particular set of digestion-disturbing troubles, "How the hell am I going to get my scroll back?"

"I don't know, but I can tell you it's one amazing magical artifact. I didn't get as far in taking it apart as I would have liked, but there was a lot of language about love and promises and faithfulness and those separated coming close. The words 'betrothal' and 'beloved' occurred quite frequently."

"Aha!" Oesterlische lifted a finger. "Then *that* was why Boston!"

Marinus looked at him quizzically.

"Was that a sentence, or have you lost the capacity for rational speech?"

"Miss Wildish–you know her, Artemus Q. Wildish's daughter?"

"Thirty million, right?"

"Thirty million. I'm *this* close to announcing our engagement." Oesterlische pinched the air to indicate the closeness of his expected betrothal. "She was visiting Boston the day that Nussbaum took me there. Remember how Nussbaum said that he always traveled to random places? We must have traveled to Boston that day because my almost-fiancée was there!"

Marinus nodded thoughtfully.

"That would be consistent with what I was able to discover of the scroll," he said. A look of worry came over his face. "But, old friend, your mention of Miss Wildish does bring up another point. A rather disturbing point. When I was down on the wharves, or the warehouses, or whatever grimy hole they threw me in, I saw someone. Someone you know."

Cold foreboding washed over Oesterlische.

"Who?"

"Miss Wildish."

"Miss Winifred Wildish? My almost-fiancée, Miss Wildish?"

Marinus nodded soberly.

"She was speaking quite forcefully to the men who were my captors. She was screaming loudly at them, saying that they were a bunch of low cads. She asked . . . no, rather *demanded* . . . that they return the scroll immediately, and that she certainly would not allow you or her father to pay a $50,000 ransom because you were such a wise, loving, decent, hard-working man and it was shameful that they would do something like this to you. She said she betted you'd come for her, and then they'd pay for what they'd done, double quick. While she was berating them, the thug who'd been guarding me went over to watch. He was highly amused by her high-pitched antics. Given that he was thus distracted, I took the opportunity to slip out."

"And you didn't take her with you?" Oesterlische fairly screamed.

"Once again, you've confused me with someone possessed of derring-do. But I remember where they are."

"They will have moved once they found you gone," Oesterlische said.

And once they found you gone, they certainly kept their hands on another captive, he thought, looking glumly into the bottom of his glass. Visions of $30 million fortunes in the dirty grabbing arms of desperate men danced before his eyes.

This was getting serious.

Marinus snapped his fingers, contemplated the little tongue of flame he made dance there. He touched it to the sugar cube on his fresh glass of absinthe. "I tell you one thing. If those ruffians had been unfortunate enough to grab *Bob Ghent* in my place, your almost-fiancée would be as good as rescued. He would have barbecued the lot of them, and stayed for lunch after."

Oesterlische sighed. His fingers went to his coat pocket to the $50,000 check that repined there. And of course that was just the amount of the ransom they wanted, the damn dirty scoundrels. He could get the scroll back, but it would leave him with no money to get the ball rolling.

"Yep," Marinus said, sipping his absinthe. "Ol' Bob Ghent. He's just the man for this kind of show. Breathes fire, you know."

Oesterlische snapped his fingers.

"Marinus, old chum!" Oesterlische slapped the warlock on the shoulder, making him choke on his absinthe. "I believe you've given me an idea!"

• • •

Oesterlische didn't get home until much later, where he found Nussbaum waiting for him in the entryway of his family's house. His mother had apparently let young Nussbaum sit there for quite a long time.

"Well, you sure have done a peach of a job handling this," he greeted Oesterlische, a greeting which Oesterlische took rather hard, given all that he'd already been through that day. "By the way, who is Miss Wildish?"

"My almost-fiancée," Oesterlische invited Nussbaum into the parlor and poured him a shot of whiskey from a locked cabinet. "Why do you ask?"

"The Black Hand sent a ransom note to her father, and she somehow managed to intercept it, and now they've got her *and* the scroll locked up somewhere." Nussbaum shook his head. "They're going to send another ransom note tonight, if we don't go down and get her first."

"We certainly can't let them do that," Oesterlische said. "Otherwise the jig will be up and old man Wildish will know that I've lost the scroll with which I promised to make him millions of dollars."

"Then I guess we just have to go down and get her," Nussbaum said, fiercely. "And *my* scroll."

"How are we supposed to get her? We don't even know where she is!"

"I've been given directions," Nussbaum said darkly. "I met with some shady gentlemen. I told them I represented her father, and that he'd sent me down to deal with them. They told me that they'd hand her over, and the scroll too, for the $50,000 Wildish gave you. You have the cash?"

Oesterlische felt a spasm of possessiveness. "It's Wildish's cash."

"You think he wouldn't want us to spend that money to get his daughter back? And *my* scroll?"

"Can we trust them?" Oesterlische said. Nussbaum looked at him. Actually, he didn't so much look at him as *give* him a look.

"Oh yeah, *sure* we can trust them," Nussbaum said. "They're completely trustworthy. Butter wouldn't melt in their mouths.

They're the picture of respectability, the apex of integrity, the . . ."

"Shut up," Oesterlische said. Oesterlische rubbed his chin. He was still thinking long and hard when his mother bustled in, making a point of ignoring Nussbaum's existence entirely. She had Winifred's fat pink letter between her fingers, where, Oesterlische had no doubt, it had been the recipient of her close scrutiny all day.

"Peter!" she said. "The note from Miss Wildish!"

"Yes, Mother," Oesterlische said wearily, taking it from her and tucking it into his pocket.

"Such a nice young lady," his mother sighed, starry-eyed. "Her family has money, I believe."

"Yes, Mother," Oesterlische said again, taking her shoulders and steering her out of the room. As he closed the door behind her, he looked at Nussbaum.

"All right," he said. "For Winifred. And *our* scroll."

• • •

Assembling $50,000 in cash was quite a feat, especially as it was past three o'clock and all the banks were getting ready to close. Luckily, though, Oesterlische knew one of the clerks at the First National, a rosy young blonde with dimpled elbows, and she smoothed the process in exchange for a tickle under the chin and a promise to take her out to a show the next weekend. He whispered a suggestion in her ear about what they might do after the show that made her giggle and blush.

"I thought you had an almost-fiancée," Nussbaum said coolly, as they left the bank with a large suitcase full of cash.

"Oh, I admire her tremendously, and I do intend to marry her." Oesterlische said. "But really, she's just *business.*"

"You don't say," Nussbaum's eyes narrowed. "And does she know that she's just business?"

Oesterlische pressed his lips together. Of course she didn't know. Why on earth would he go around telling her something like that?

"What difference does it make?" he decided avoiding the question was the best route, given that Nussbaum seemed to be on the verge of breaking out in persnickitude once again.

"I should think it might make a lot of difference to her," Nussbaum said, persnickifying as expected. But he said nothing further.

The appointed time for the meeting was midnight, and the young men passed the cold afternoon and evening fortifying themselves with whiskey and nervous boasting about each one's pugilistic skill, and how each intended to employ it if things got rough. At eleven, they began their walk down to the appointed meeting place, a warehouse on the wharves along Fulton Street. As they walked, Oesterlische took deep gulps of cold air to clear the whiskey and bravado from his blood, but Nussbaum strode forward with confidence, like a dog looking forward to a romp in the park. Oesterlische watched him with amazement.

"I say, Nussbaum. Aren't you the least bit worried by the fact that we're walking around the wharves at midnight with $50,000 in cash? That doesn't give you the slightest turn?" He tapped his chest. "You know, right here?"

"They know we're here," Nussbaum said, after a moment's thought. He glanced at the suitcase full of cash in Oesterlische's hand. "No one's going to take the money from us. It's Black Hand money now. If anyone stole it, they'd have to answer to the Black Hand. Don't worry, everything will be fine."

Oesterlische tightened his grip on the suitcase and wished he could believe that.

The warehouse was a dark and brooding building that stood out over the East River on spindly stilts. The sign above the door read *Schumann's Condiments and Fine Comestibles* but it didn't seem that Schumann had made a very successful go of things—there was a "For Lease" sign hanging in the office window. They cracked the door open, peered into the darkness. It smelled of musty wood and old vinegar, but Oesterlische had little time to notice anything other than Winifred, lying in the middle of the warehouse's vast empty floor, bound, gagged, and struggling.

As he hurried toward her, he noticed that she was not alone. Two men in shabby overcoats stood behind her, their faces hidden by loose hoods with ragged eyeholes. Both men held revolvers, and these were pointed straight at Oesterlische and Nussbaum. The thugs, seeing Oesterlische and Nussbaum moving toward them, gestured menacingly.

"Stop right there," one of them said in a low voice. "Drop the cash, then we'll give you the girl."

"And the scroll!" Nussbaum added, coming to an abrupt halt behind Oesterlische.

Setting down the money, Oesterlische took two steps backward. One of the men rushed forward, knelt down, unbuckled the suitcase's leather straps. He ran his fingers over the greenbacks, nodded back to his thuggish compatriot. His thuggish compatriot stuffed a rolled vellum into Winifred's hands. Then he cut the ropes that bound her. As the ropes fell to the floor around her, she ran into Oesterlische's arms.

"Oh, Peter!" she breathed. But Oesterlische did not look at her. Eyes narrowed, he watched the filthy thug paw over the

$50,000 in the suitcase. He watched the man close the suitcase, buckle its leather straps. Then he nodded.

"Now, Ghent!" Oesterlische cried.

At the command, Bob Ghent seemed to materialize almost out of thin air, though really he just magically reoriented the color of his body from the dingy gray of the warehouse's tin walls along which he'd been hiding himself. The filthy thugs jerked their heads and guns up as the salamander took two steps forward. Taking a deep breath, the warlock blew a stream of brilliant golden fire on the closest one, the man kneeling over the suitcase. The sudden light of the oscular conflagration cast dancing shadows on the corrugated tin walls. The man's overcoat burst into flame.

"Watch the money!" Oesterlische screamed at Ghent, visions of $50,000 in cash going up in smoke. But the money remained undamaged as, with a scream, the man who had been pawing it toppled sideways to the ground, rolling desperately to extinguish the flames that engulfed him. Behind him, the second man lifted his gun uncertainly. Ghent took another two steps forward, breathed in and spat a thin, precise incendiary stream. It blasted the gun from the man's hand, and the man bent over, yowling, clutching his burned hand to his chest with a little whimper.

"Oh, no! Stop! Stop!" Winifred winced in terrified agony against Oesterlische's chest. Oesterlische lifted a hand, and Ghent stopped, smoke curling from between his lips. He gave Oesterlische a quizzical look.

"Yes, I suppose you'd better stop, Ghent," Oesterlische said, looking down at Winifred. "I wouldn't want Mr. Lamb or Mr. Gussy to be hurt anymore than is strictly necessary."

Winifred made a small sound, her hand going to her mouth.

"What are you talking about?" she said softly. But once again her voice held the note of a Bowery card-sharp, and Oesterlische sighed.

"Winifred, my dear," he said. "Forgive the crudity to which I am about to subject your delicate ears. But even you should know that you can't *bullshit* a *bullshitter*."

• • •

With a growl, Winifred tore herself out of Oesterlische's arms and hurried over to the man whose overcoat was still smoking. She fell to her knees beside him. She lifted him to sitting.

"Oh, his hair's all burned off!" Winifred fussed. "Astor, fetch me some water, quickly!"

Nussbaum leaped to comply. Then, as if realizing that he was impeaching himself, he stopped, looked guiltily at Oesterlische. Oesterlische rolled his eyes.

"Yes, Nussbaum, I'm well aware that you're in on this too. Go fetch the goddamn water. I'm sure you know where it's to be found, given that you were locked in this pickle factory for the entirety of the Great Blizzard. When you get back, we need to have a *talk*, the three of us."

Nussbaum went and swiftly returned with water in a grungy bucket, and Winifred used it to soothe the groaning Mr. Lamb. Oesterlische strode over, snatched the suitcase from her side, and stepped back, setting it firmly down at his side. Ghent stood behind him, arms crossed, burping smoke. Oesterlische watched as Nussbaum stood at Winifred's back, his hands resting gently on her shoulders as she wiped cinders from the burned man's face.

"So, I take it the two of you have already been introduced?" Oesterlische said frostily. Two pairs of eyes started up guiltily. Nussbaum looked at Winifred, and Winifred looked at Nussbaum.

"I met her doing good works down on the Bowery," Nussbaum said.

"Really," Oesterlische said, the word a drawl of insinuation. Hearing it, Nussbaum's eyes darted up.

"All right then, I admit it! We're in love! We're in love, and there's nothing you can do about it!" Nussbaum gazed down on Winifred with the most disgusting cow eyes Oesterlische had ever seen. "She's *wonderful*! So good and kind and decent. Money hasn't spoiled her, like it does some people. I worship the ground she walks on."

"And I love Astor," Winifred returned, standing and pressing close to Nussbaum and staring deep into his eyes. "He has been so shabbily treated, and yet he is so good and kind and decent. He is also manly and forthright and . . ."

"All *right.*" Oesterlische hoped sheer volume could put an end to the absolutely appalling display before him. He thought about taking the grungy bucket of cold water and pouring it over the both of them. "I get it. You're in love."

"How did you know?" Winifred said.

"Well, the two of you are standing right there pawing each other . . ." Oesterlische began.

"No. I mean how did you know that it was me? Or us?"

"It was a lot of little things," Oesterlische looked at Nussbaum. "The fact that you knew that I'd come from the Wildish party that night, when I'd never told you I was going . . . then later, you behaved as if you'd never even heard of Miss Wildish! And Marinus. Why kidnap him? Why wouldn't a bunch of Black Hand thugs just take the scroll and be done with it? Why bring him here, and then so conveniently let him go, unless a *witness* was needed?"

Oesterlische paused. His fingers dipped into his pocket for the little pink envelope.

"Then there's this." He opened it, his eyes swiftly scanning the contents. He nodded. "I didn't even have to *read* this to know that it would tell me exactly where to find you. Which you'd have no way of knowing, given that any kidnappers worth their salt would have moved you to a different location once Marinus slipped their grasp."

Winifred swore under her breath, a most unmaidenly combination of words streaming from her lips.

"But it was that poor fellow lying at your feet, Winifred, that put the frosting on the pastry. He was one of the fellows who walked you home that night . . . *and* one of the same fellows who were chasing Nussbaum outside of my club." Oesterlische leveled an accusing finger at Mr. Lamb, at his smoking overcoat. "I never forget a houndstooth, no matter how shabby."

There was a long silence. Nussbaum sighed.

"I knew her father would never consent to our marriage," Nussbaum said. "So I swore to better myself. And honestly, for a while there I really did think I could use the scroll to make a fortune. But we soon discovered that the scroll has no commercial value whatever. So we resolved to get some money another way, so we could live even after he disinherited us."

"You were going to try to *live* on $50,000?" Oesterlische goggled. "That has to be the most crack-brained plan I've ever heard of! Winifred, $50,000 wouldn't keep you in dresses for a week."

"I don't need dresses!" Winifred lifted her chin resolutely. "I'll wear rags and eat bones to be with Astor! Plenty of people do, Peter. But of course *you* wouldn't know that. You don't have a heart to feel with."

"Leaving my heart aside," Oesterlische said, "I know that rags are uncomfortable and bones make a most unsavory broth. You may think it's noble and attractive to cast your lot with the teeming masses, but you won't like it quite as much when you're shivering in a cold garret and picking lice out of Nussbaum's hair."

"You're wrong," Winifred said fiercely. "I'll love him and his lice forever and ever!"

"And what a bunch of convoluted nonsense." Oesterlische continued, not bothering to comment on Winifred's defense of Nussbaum's imagined lice. "Scrolls and kidnapping and all of that. And what precisely do you mean, the scroll has no commercial value whatever? What brought you to that conclusion?"

Winifred and Nussbaum exchanged guilty glances.

"We already had a warlock look at the scroll," Nussbaum admitted. "A very educated fellow at Harvard, an old chap with bad eyesight. He figured it all out for us. He said it is indeed a very powerful teleportation spell, but that it will only return a person to their true love. That's why I always ended up wherever Winifred was." He smiled down on her, she smiled back.

"So that's why *you* took that jaunt to Boston," Oesterlische said, looking at Winifred. She looked surprised. "I saw the ticket in your purse. You must have been hiding around Faneuil Hall somewhere. Because you both knew I wouldn't be impressed enough to hit old Wildish up for $50,000 if the scroll had teleported us to some soup kitchen on Mott Street."

"If we couldn't make money off the scroll directly, we had to find a way to get money some way else," Winifred said. "I knew that you'd figure something out, Peter. You have my father wrapped around your manicured pinky."

"Quite a dirty trick, all things considered," Oesterlische frowned at her. "Played both on me, and your father."

"Well, how could we make money with a limitation like that?" Winifred snapped at him. "We had to do something!"

"My dear, it's obvious that your father's business brains were not handed down to you. No way to make money on a true love scroll? A scroll that lets wives check up on their husbands while they're off on business? That allows parted lovers to reunite for passionate assignations in the blink of an eye? The possibilities are *endless*!"

"We can call it the Love Hole!" Sudden inspiration lit Nussbaum's eyes. Oesterlische winced, thinking once again about that wide-awake young copywriter he was going to have to find. He encompassed Winifred and Nussbaum in his sorrowful gaze.

"You see, why didn't you just come to me in the first place?" Oesterlische said. "We all could have avoided a lot of indigestion."

As if punctuating that remark, Ghent hiccuped, issuing quite a quantity of blue smoke.

• • •

The wedding of Winifred Wildish and Peter Oesterlische took place the next spring.

It was, unquestionably, the event of the season. The bride wore white satin trimmed with alencon lace, and carried a bouquet of waxy orange blossoms. Everyone commented on how radiantly happy she looked.

The elegant morning service, held at Grace Cathedral, was followed by a sumptuous lunch at the Wildish Mansion that featured Westphalia Ham *à glace*, *Ailes de Poulets à la Hongroise*, and canvasback ducks stuffed, rather improbably, with lobster. Oesterlische's mother cried through the whole thing, even the canvasback ducks.

Oesterlische, in a beautifully cut morning coat, comforted his weeping mother, shook hands soberly, and greatly enjoyed receiving the little bundles of money those hands pressed into his. He spoke of the regretful resignation he'd tendered at Rudnick & Culpepper, and how he was looking forward to his new position as Senior Vice President with Wildish Shipping & Mercantile & Magical Transportation. His new father-in-law hovered behind him and beamed, slapping him on the back at various appropriate intervals, heartily pleased to have such a pleasing new son-in-law.

Astor Nussbaum, who'd been hired as Oesterlische's personal secretary, served as best man. While he made every effort not to frown throughout the ceremony, his persnickitude did get the better of him once or twice. Indeed, Oesterlische had to kick him in the shins while they were watching the bride come down the aisle.

"I don't know why you're being such a pill," Oesterlische had hissed at him furiously, as everyone had oohed and aahed at Winifred's approach. "It's just the ultimate culmination of our Plan, after all."

Nussbaum had been against the Plan from the start. But Winifred had seen the advantages, and once Oesterlische had managed to get Winifred to agree, Nussbaum had no choice but to grudgingly accept.

In outlining the Plan, Oesterlische explained what they'd already figured out for themselves–if Nussbaum and Winifred got married, they'd certainly be disinherited, and there'd be bones and rags and garrets and lice and all that.

"So that's out," Oesterlische said.

But if Winifred *didn't* get married to someone eventually, Wildish was sure to leave her a rather small spinster's portion, and pass the bulk of his estate and thriving business concerns to his brother's sons.

"I know how men like your father think," Oesterlische had assured her gravely, "because I happen to think quite the same way. And then you don't have the money *or* Nussbaum, so that's double out."

But, if Winifred married Oesterlische, then everything would work out just fine. He assured them that he would press no matrimonial claims–not physical ones, at least–and that he'd promise to love and cherish the $30 million he'd gone through so much to get.

"I'll see that you both have plenty of money to go feed beggars with," Oesterlische said. "We'll set up a foundation, and I'll let Nussbaum here run it. Think of the good you can do!"

In short, if Winifred married Oesterlische, they could all enjoy the fruits of the Wildish fortune in their own particular ways. Nussbaum and Winifred could live happily ever after (and who would dare question the devotion with which Nussbaum served Mr. Oesterlische's wife, if Mr. Oesterlische himself deemed their relationship above reproach?). Oesterlische could smoke Cuban cigars, take blonde bank clerks to shows, and generally continue to live his life as he liked it.

"Here's to scrolls and salamanders!" Oesterlische said, after the trio had repaired to the Honeymoon Suite of the Fifth Avenue. He lifted a celebratory glass of champagne as Nussbaum carried Winifred over the threshold of the bedroom. "Here's to love, magic, and $30 million!"

Nussbaum slammed the door in his face, rather sharply, Oesterlische thought.

Oesterlische laughed to himself as he sipped his champagne. Then he retreated down the hall. He was going to find himself a poker game in a smoky room with the old men.

The Colonel's Daughter

BARBARA RODEN

"Miss Constance! Miss Constance! Drat the girl, where have you gone? *Miss Constance!*"

The sound of Miss Martin's voice drifted into the library, and Colonel Kingsley winced, breaking off his Crimean War reminiscences in mid-sentence. Walter Somers, his secretary, allowed himself a brief sigh. Such interruptions were all too common, as the young man knew.

"Drat the girl indeed," muttered the Colonel. "And drat that fool of a governess, for not being able to keep her in order. Four sons I've raised, and all of them put together never caused half as much bother as that slip of a girl. I had less difficulty maintaining discipline among my soldiers in Sebastopol."

"Perhaps there is another school which would take her?" asked Walter, conscious that he was on delicate ground. Miss Constance's escapades at her most recent school–which had resulted in the establishment declining to accept her for a further term–were still all too fresh.

Colonel Kingsley made a noise halfway between a groan and a sigh. "I have made enquiries, but they all appear to have no vacancies, either now or in the foreseeable future. It would appear either that a sudden mania for sending girls to boarding school has swept the nation, or that my daughter is not welcome at any of them."

"Another governess, then?" suggested Walter, knowing he was moving on to equally delicate territory. "Miss Martin seems an admirable woman, from what I have seen of her in the short time she has been here, but she does not appear to be quite the companion Miss Constance needs."

As if on cue, a knock sounded at the door of the library. Before the Colonel could answer, the door opened and Miss Martin's face appeared. Her pale complexion went an unbecoming shade of pink when she saw her employer.

"Oh, I am *so* sorry, Colonel Kingsley. I did not mean to disturb you. I was looking for Miss Constance."

"So I gathered," said the Colonel drily. "I would have thought, Miss Martin, that of all the rooms in the house in which my daughter might be, the library is the most unlikely."

"Oh, I agree, Colonel," said Miss Martin hastily, prompting Walter to suppress a smile. She might not have been in the house long, but the governess had obviously taken the measure of her charge. "I've looked everywhere else, though, and not a trace of her have I seen. She is to go out with your sister, to pay a call on the Meades, and I promised that she would be ready on time."

"Very rash of you, Miss Martin, to promise anything like that where my daughter is concerned." The Colonel sighed. "I suggest you–What in the name of heaven is *that*?"

That was a bellow of rage from the grounds outside the library, the windows of which were open to allow the late-April breeze into the room. The Colonel moved to look outside, with Walter behind him, and Miss Martin–clearly suspecting that the outcry had something to do with her charge–bringing up the rear.

A horse and rider were cantering across the lawn, with the figure of Perkins, the groom, vainly pursuing on foot. The bellow had clearly come from him, as the onlookers could tell when he paused, shaking a fist in the air.

"You come back here right now, Miss Constance! Right now, d'you hear? That horse ain't fit for you to ride; half wild, it is! What would the Colonel say if he knew?"

Judging by the shade of red the Colonel's face had gone, Walter could guess that anything he might have to say would not be fit for the ears of respectable company. The horse drew to a halt opposite the window, and the rider waved in the direction of the watchers.

"There he is now, Perkins, ask him! Hello, Father! Hello, Mr. Somers! Why, Miss Martin, *there* you are!"

"Constance! What on earth do you mean by this–Good heavens, girl, are you riding astride?"

Constance laughed, and moved the prancing horse closer to the window. Strands of light brown hair tumbled down her shoulders, and her eyes flashed with delight. She looked far older than her sixteen years as she kept the horse–clearly skittish and ready to bolt at any moment–under control.

"Yes, I *am* riding astride, and I can see why men do it. It's *so* much easier and more comfortable than riding sidesaddle. I think I shall start a movement to encourage more women to try it."

"You shall do no such thing," retorted her father. "And if you carry on in this way, there shall be no hunting for you this season, sidesaddle or in any other fashion. Do I make myself clear?"

"Yes, Father," replied Constance, in a tone which fell far short of the perfect deference the Colonel was seeking. Perkins had, by this time, caught up with her, and after a quick nod toward the window he seized the horse's bridle.

"Now back to the stables with you, Miss Constance, so I can get this horse rubbed down. You'd no business taking it, and as for riding astride–well, all I can say is that I had no idea she'd done such a thing, Colonel."

"I'm sure you didn't, Perkins." Colonel Kingsley sighed. "Please assist Miss Constance down from the horse. Miss Martin, be so kind as to retrieve my daughter and do your best to ensure that she is ready to go out with her aunt. Perhaps then we might all have a little peace, at least for a time."

The Colonel stayed at the window for some minutes after the various players had departed the scene. Walter, who had returned to his seat, waited in silence. Finally his employer turned toward him.

"What am I to do?" he asked in a plaintive tone, which would have surprised everyone who knew him as a man who had more than once stared down death. "I really am at my wits' end, Somers. My sister is a good woman, and she does her best, I know, but she has her hands full running the house. My dear wife was able to keep some measure of control over Constance, but since her death–" His voice trailed off.

"Well, sir . . ." began Walter, after a respectful moment of silence. "I have had an idea," he continued, "although I've hesitated in broaching the matter. I thought that I would see how Miss Martin worked out before mentioning it."

"Please do go ahead," said the Colonel. He sat down. "I am, at this point, willing to entertain almost any suggestion."

"It occurs to me, sir, that Miss Constance might benefit from the presence of another girl. She has grown up with four brothers, but no sister to act as a tempering influence. A governess is all very well, but someone closer to her in age would be more in the way of a companion, and might well achieve what a governess cannot."

"Or what a string of governesses cannot. Your idea has some merit, Somers, but where on earth am I to find such a companion? I can advertise for a governess, but I cannot very well put a notice in *The Times* asking for a girl to come live with us. We have no relations who would answer, and there is no one suitable in the village."

"I think I might know the place to look, Colonel, if you will put your trust in me."

Colonel Kingsley rubbed his brow, closed his eyes, and sighed. When he looked up it was with an air of profound resignation.

"Do what you will, Somers," he said resignedly. "If you can find a solution to this problem, you are a better man than I am."

• • •

Dusk was falling over London, and Walter marveled–not for the first time since his arrival in the city, three days after his conversation with the Colonel–at the contrast between the place he had left and the place where he now found himself. It was not only that the weather had taken a turn for the worse, although that was undoubtedly part of it. A chill wind snaked through the streets, doing little to dispel the thick pall of smoke that hung over the metropolis. The air was laden with the smell of food, the vendors of which thronged the pavements, and whose cries–"Chestnuts, all hot, tuppence a score!" "Potatoes, fresh-baked!" "Buy my hot spiced gingerbread!"–fought against each other to be heard by the crowds of people hurrying about their business.

The great market at Spitalfields, which Walter passed, was quiet, although a few workmen could be seen finishing their day's business of constructing the new market buildings, a few of which were already complete. His business lay in nearby Albert Street, and he made his way to the quiet building, above which hung a modest sign: Refuge Aid Society, Mile End New Road.

He had contacted his brother-in-law, Mr. Audley, the director of the society, who greeted him warmly, and led him to a small, modestly furnished office within the building. After the exchange of a few pleasantries, Mr. Audley addressed the matter at hand.

"I have, my dear fellow, given your letter a great deal of thought, a very great deal. If I understand you correctly, you are looking for a girl, aged sixteen or thereabouts, who is suitable to act as a companion to a well-born young lady. If you had asked me a week ago, I should have said there was no one here who would answer that description, either in terms of age or character. On the very day your letter arrived, however, we took in a girl who came to us of her own volition. This is somewhat unusual, as most of the girls who come here are brought by others–a concerned friend or relative, usually, who cannot look after the child but wants her taken care of so as not to fall into bad ways. I have met with her, and she strikes me as well-spoken–at least, compared with many of the poor wretches I see–and intelligent."

"Do you know anything of her history?"

Mr. Audley nodded. "She has told me some of it, but I should like you to hear it for yourself."

"You say that the girls come here–or are brought here–to avoid falling into bad ways. Is that the case with this girl?"

Audley hesitated for a moment, then said slowly, "No. She has confessed that she has already fallen into a life of crime." Seeing the look on Walter's face, Audley added with a rush, "However, I believe that the child is sincere in her desire to take a different path." There was a sound of footsteps in the hallway outside, and the director said with some relief, "Ah, that will be her now. I would like you to talk with her, then tell me what you think."

There was a knock on the door. A large, pleasant-faced woman, naturally red of cheek and cheery of countenance, entered, holding a young girl by the hand.

"Here she is, sir," she said, with a neat bob of her head to the director. "Come in, child, and don't be afraid," she said to the girl, who entered the room with some hesitation. She looked from one man to the other; then, with a belated realization that something was necessary, dipped her head toward the two men, and eyed them with curiosity.

"Please sit down, Mary," said Mr. Audley, his voice kind. When the girl had done so, he continued, "Mary, this is Mr. Somers. He is secretary to a gentleman who lives in the country, and he is very interested in your situation, for reasons that he will explain by and by. However, I want you to tell him your story, as you did to me."

Mary turned and looked at Walter, enabling him to see her properly. She was dark haired, and her skin was pale, with the pallor of one who seldom sees the sunlight, and to whom fresh air and nourishing food were but passing acquaintances. She was slim, and somewhat above the average height, so that she looked thinner still. She remained silent, however, and Walter tried to put her at her ease.

"Mary, is it? And what is your last name, Mary?"

"Daniels," she said. "Mary Daniels, I am. Sir," she added. She had a pleasant voice, somewhat coarsened by her recent circumstances, Walter suspected, but firm and clear.

"As Mr. Audley said, I am most anxious to hear your story."

Mary's gaze had not wavered from Walter's face, and he could not help but feel that the girl was making up her mind. She appeared to come to a decision, and after gathering in her breath she began to speak.

"My da was a groom at a big house in Shropshire, and my ma was a schoolmaster's daughter," she said. "When she married Da her family turned their back on her, on account of her marrying beneath her station, and she was taken on at the house as a maid. She taught me how to read, and write, and do some ciphering, and tried to bring me up genteel. Then Da got kicked in the head by a crazed horse, and were never the same man after. He took to drink, and then one day he up and left us, and we never heard tell of him again. Ma got let go then, and we had to leave. Ma had no family who would take us in, and there was no work to be had thereabouts, so we came to London, and got took on by a firm of dressmakers in the West End. It was all right for a year or so, but Ma took poorly, and died when I was fourteen. As I was a good worker I was kept on by the dressmaker, but not long after, one of the young gentlemen of the family what owned the firm tried to have his way with me, and when I complained I was turned out."

Mary had recounted her story in so matter-of-fact a tone that she might as well have been speaking of someone else. Walter, by no means ignorant of what went on in the metropolis, was still shocked at such a bald acceptance of the situation.

"Did they give you a reference, or character?"

The girl shook her head. "What do you think, sir?" she asked derisively. "I tried for a place with other dressmakers, but couldn't get one. Then I tried getting a place in service, but there's not much hope for girls without references. I had a bit of money put by, but it didn't last long, and I told the landlady what state things was in. She weren't a bad old soul, and I guess she meant well, 'cause she told me about a woman that ran an academy, she called it, who was always looking for quick, bright children to train. I thought she meant for service, and went along, and that's when I found out she trained 'em to be thieves."

Walter tried to keep his face impassive, but it must have registered some of the shock he felt. Mary noticed it, and gave a bitter half smile.

"I were shocked too, sir. But Ma weren't there to look after me, and the lady seemed kind enough. It meant a clean place to sleep, and food to eat, and–well, I didn't have to think too long, is all I can say.

"There were more than two dozen of us, boys and girls, and we got trained up in all manner of picking pockets. I started as a looker-out, following along of the others to make sure there were no police about, nor anyone taking too much notice. But the looker-out doesn't get as big a share, 'cause of not taking much of the risk, so I tried my hand at the picking, and found I was good at it, on account of being quick with my hands. I worked at this with two lads, but they took to spending more and more on gin, and once they started in on their drinking they didn't want to work anymore of an evening. One night when they'd been drinking more'n usual they tried to have their way with me, and I fought back and got away. I didn't dare go back to the academy after that. I'd been thinking of coming here–or someplace like it–for a time. I've been lucky up to now, as I've never been caught, but most everyone does get took, sooner or later. That means prison, or transportation." She shivered.

"So you came here to make a new start?"

"Yes, sir. Mr. Audley said that if I worked hard and stayed out of bad ways I might train up to be a servant and get a place at a respectable house." She looked thoughtfully at Walter. "Is that why you've come here, sir?' she asked shrewdly. "To find a girl to work for the gentleman in the country you talked of?"

Walter gave a small smile. "You are quite right, Mary. What I am offering is the opportunity for you to make a fresh start–an *honest* start–far from here, at a good house, in the country in Gloucestershire. My employer has a daughter, who is inclined to be somewhat–wayward, shall we say. Her mother died two years ago, and no governess has been able to keep control of her. The Colonel is now looking for a companion for her, someone close to her own age, who will not be shocked by her behavior, but who will be able–perhaps–to temper her excesses."

"A fresh start," said Mary thoughtfully. She looked toward Mr. Audley.

"It is a good offer, Mary," he assured her. "You are being given a rare opportunity."

Mary eyed him for a moment, then turned again to Walter, who felt that he had seldom undergone such searching scrutiny. She obviously trusted what she saw, however, for she gave a sharp nod of her head.

"It's done then," she affirmed, holding out her hand with a sudden movement that took Walter by surprise. He found himself returning the handshake, reflecting as he did so that he had never, in all his days, struck a stranger bargain.

• • •

Walter felt–not without some justification–that he was a good judge of character, but it was with some trepidation that he introduced Mary Daniels to the Kingsley household. It was true that the Colonel had given his secretary carte blanche to act as he best saw fit, but on the journey to Gloucestershire he could not help but wonder how the old soldier would react when he was told of Mary's history. And Constance–what of her? How would she take to this unusual girl?

When they arrived at the house, Mary was put in the charge of the housekeeper, whose first task was to find the girl some decent clothes. "I can alter them if needs be," Mary announced, as if pleased to be able to demonstrate her worth straight away. While this was being sorted out, Walter met with the Colonel, and explained the situation.

"My brother-in-law is an excellent man, and I believe him when he says that the girl wants to put her past behind her," he concluded. "Nothing I have seen of her in the last four-and-twenty hours leads me to think he is wrong."

"At this stage I have very little choice. I have already given Miss Martin her notice, and I have neither the wish nor the inclination to search for yet *another* governess. The one thing I am not sure about is how much of the girl's history I should tell Constance at this stage. What do you think, Somers?"

"I would advise you to wait, Colonel," said Walter. "Miss Constance will decide matters for herself. If she takes to Mary, then her history will not matter one jot, whereas if she takes against her–well, the girl could be the Duchess of Devonshire, and it would make not a bit of difference."

• • •

Their meeting took place the following morning, for Mary, exhausted after the events of the last few days, had fallen asleep over a meal of bread and butter and warm milk in the kitchen, and the housekeeper had put her to bed. “She’s not in a fit state to meet anyone right now,” she’d told Walter. “But she’s a dab hand with needle and thread, I’ll say that for her.”

Constance was summoned to the library at ten o’clock. Impressed by the solemnity, and novelty, of the occasion, she arrived promptly, and was waiting when Mary was brought in. Walter had expected the girl to look nervous, but she seemed quite calm. He was also impressed by the change in her appearance. Freshly scrubbed, wearing new clothes, and with something approaching a tinge of color already brightening her cheeks, she looked a far cry from the girl he had met in London.

The Colonel wasted no time. “Constance, this is Mary Daniels, who’s been brought from London to be a companion to you. Mary, this is my daughter Constance. She can be somewhat headstrong, but I hope the two of you shall get along.”

For a moment neither girl spoke, and Walter sensed that they were trying to get the measure of each other. Constance was the first to break the silence.

“So, Mary Daniels, you’re from London, are you? I don’t expect you’ll know any of the same people I do.”

“I don’t suppose I will, miss,” replied Mary in a steady voice. “I daresay a few of them might have passed me in the street, but they wouldn’t have taken any notice of me.”

“No, they wouldn’t.” Constance darted a sideways look at the Colonel. “My father says I’m headstrong. Does he expect you to tame me, then?”

"No, miss. A body can't be tamed unless she wants to be. I expect I can keep up with you, though, better'n a governess could, and keep you out of some trouble."

"We shall see. I don't expect you know much about horses, being from the city."

"I wasn't always from the city, miss. Me da was a groom, and I used to help him sometimes, when I was younger."

"Where is he now?"

Walter drew in his breath, ready to intervene. Before he could say anything, however, Mary shrugged and said calmly, "Don't know, miss. He got kicked by a horse and took to drink and run off on Ma and me. And my ma died two years ago, when I was fourteen, and I've been living by my wits for the last year, doing things as a proper young lady like yourself shouldn't hear about." Mary tossed her head, in a manner that would have befitted Constance herself. "Anything else you'd like to know about me, miss?"

Constance stared hard at her for a moment. "My mother died two years ago. Did they tell you that? And you know something about horses. So we have two things in common, Mary Daniels."

With a sudden movement she stepped forward and tucked Mary's arm under hers. "I think we shall get along splendidly. You're certainly an improvement on Miss Martin, and all the other Misses who came before her." She glanced toward her father, then said in a conspiratorial whisper, "And I do want you to tell me about those things I shouldn't know of." Then, more loudly, she added, "But first I want you to come with me to the stables. We have a new horse, Regulus, and I want you to see him." A beaming smile lit up her face. "Oh, we're going to have *such* fun–I just know it!"

• • •

The late-September sun cast a mellow glow through the library windows, revealing a scene which would have been almost unthinkable only a few months earlier, but which was now increasingly commonplace. Constance was curled in a capacious armchair, a book on her lap, while Mary sat at the desk, diligently practicing her handwriting. Peace hung over the house, which made the sound of Constance snapping her book shut all the more startling. Mary looked up.

"Oh, it's all right, Mary, it's simply that I've no patience for reading just now, when hunting season is so close to hand. The first meet is only a fortnight away. Oh, it's so exciting! And such a house party that's planned. It will be the best thing that has happened since you came to live with us. Aren't you excited too?"

Mary put her pen down. "Not so much as you, Miss Constance, for I shan't see much of it. But I'll come and watch you ride out with everyone. I said I would."

Constance frowned. "It would be *so* much better if I could go astride. That way I could ride Regulus. Perkins had to concede the other day that I'm *still* the only person who can manage him properly. Father said that I could ride him astride if I contrived to keep my legs decent, but there is simply no way I can manage that in my habit, as Father knows."

"I have had a thought about that, miss."

"Really? Oh Mary, tell me!"

"Well . . ." Mary paused. "I thought that if you could find me out an old pair of riding breeches from one of your brothers, I could alter them to fit you. Then you'd be decent."

Constance laughed in delight. "You *are* clever!" Then her face fell. "But Father would never allow me to wear trousers in public."

"Now, the Miss Constance I met in April would never have let that stop her," said Mary, with mock severity. "But I thought of that too. If I take one of your habits, I can sew the two together, with the breeches inside, and then make a slit up one side of your habit. That way the breeches are hid, in a manner of speaking, but you can still ride astride and be decent."

Constance clapped her hands together. "You think of everything, Mary. Now if only there were going to be some young men here, to see me! Apart from my brother Charles and whatever friends he brings, who will all be stuffy bankers like him, the youngest man is likely to be Arthur Pemberton, and he is nearly *thirty*." She made it sound as if he might as well be nearly a hundred. "And he's to be married anyway, it was in *The Times* not long ago. She is the daughter of Sir William Warren, the Cabinet Minister. I met her once, at one of the schools I attended. Her father was a Director, and she came down with him on Prize Day."

"What was she like?"

"Oh, rather pretty, I suppose, in a frail sort of way. She seemed one of those dreadfully prim and proper girls, who probably think that a morning spent looking at prints and doing needlework, followed by a round of visits and good works in the afternoon, and then playing piano in the evening, is an exciting day. Father says that she is ideally suited to being a politician's wife, as she will never cause Mr. Pemberton any scandal whatever."

"Is Mr. Pemberton a politician, then?"

"Oh, no, but his father is one of the richest men in England, and Mr. Pemberton is marrying a politician's daughter, so Father says that the whole matter is as good as arranged."

Mary shook her head. "It seems a very odd way of deciding things, Miss Constance. If it's all settled in that way, what's the good in women asking for the right to vote? Seems as if we'd have no say in the matter anyway."

"I don't pretend to understand these things, Mary, any more than you do. But if Mr. Pemberton is content to marry that ninny, then I've no use for him, whatever his age." She leaped up from the chair. "Let's go find those breeches, and see what can be done."

• • •

By the time of the hunt weekend, Constance could barely contain her excitement, and her high spirits could be felt everywhere in the house. Mr. Somers, passing Mary in the hallway, commented on it.

"It's rather like the old days, Mary, before you came. It does make me realize what a difference you've made. And it's made a difference in you, too."

Mary blushed. "I have you to thank for that, Mr. Somers. You've been very good, taking time to help me with my reading and writing and sums."

"It's been my pleasure, Mary. To be honest, it makes something of a change for me. There is only so much I care to hear about the Siege of Sebastopol in the course of a day, and at the rate the Colonel is going I shall be hearing about it for a long while yet."

He was interrupted by the sound of running feet, and then Constance appeared, somewhat out of breath. "There you are, Mary! My aunt wants you to see about repairing her gown—she's torn it somehow, and is in such a flutter about it. Will you come?"

They hurried along the hall in the direction of Mrs. Millington's room, Mary laughing in Constance's wake.

"There's no need to rush so, miss, the gown isn't going anywhere!"

"I know, but I don't want to miss anyone's arrival." They were at the top of the main staircase, and both girls stopped, drawn by the sound of activity in the entranceway. The Colonel was greeting a tall, dark-haired man, quietly but fashionably dressed, with an air of authority tempered by a quick smile, which was directed at his host.

"Ah, Mr. Pemberton. So pleased you could come. My sister–your hostess–is not here to greet you, I am afraid, and I've no idea where my daughter has–Ah, there you are, Constance!" He had turned at the sound of his daughter descending the stairs, while Mary hung back, watching. "Mr. Pemberton, may I introduce my daughter, Constance."

"Miss Kingsley. It is indeed a pleasure to meet you."

"I've read about you in the papers," said Constance, her head slightly to one side, as if measuring him up.

"Only good things, I trust, Miss Kingsley."

"Well, they say that you're very rich, and that must be counted a good thing." Colonel Kingsley spluttered, but Constance continued speaking. "And that you're to marry Sir William Warren's daughter, and go into politics. I met her once, at my school. *One* of my schools, that is," she corrected herself. "On Prize Day. *I* didn't get a prize," she added hastily, as if wishing to distance herself from that possibility.

Mr. Pemberton laughed. "That does not seem entirely surprising, Miss Kingsley, unless they award prizes for being forthright, in which case I suspect you would have walked away with all of them."

"Perhaps I would, had I stayed long enough. But I never stayed very long at any school."

Colonel Kingsley intervened. "Constance, that will be *quite* enough for now. I am sure that Mr. Pemberton wishes to be shown to his room after his long journey. And I am sure that you have something to do. I hear your aunt calling," he added, in something like relief. "Please go and see what she wants."

"Yes, Father." Constance turned back to Mr. Pemberton. "I shall see you at dinner, sir. I hope that I am able to sit by you."

"You will sit in the place assigned to you, Constance," said her father, making a mental note to consult his sister about the seating arrangements before they went in to dinner. "You shall have more than enough opportunity to speak with *everyone* during the course of the weekend. You're not to monopolize Mr. Pemberton, d'you hear me?"

• • •

At dinner Constance was, to her chagrin, placed at some distance from Mr. Pemberton, but she could not help noticing that he looked her way more than once, each time with a smile that made her feel a little weak on the inside. It was not a feeling she had had before, and it frightened her a little, but she could not stop herself wanting him to look her way again, and again.

When the meal had been cleared the company rose, and Constance's aunt led the ladies to the drawing room, where tea and coffee were served. Constance tried to take an interest in the conversations going on around her, and answered a few questions which were directed at her, meanwhile hoping that her father would not keep the men too long over their port. There was still no sign of them when her aunt signaled that it was time for her to retire, and although she protested, Mrs. Millington could not be persuaded. Constance took her reluctant leave of the company, and as she left the drawing room heard the sound of voices in the hall. Turning, she saw her father and the other men walking toward her, the scent of cigar smoke heavy in the air.

"Ah, Constance, off to bed? Yes, I'm sure you would like to stay a few more minutes, but your aunt has obviously decreed otherwise, and I am not going to contradict her. Goodnight, my dear." And with that he disappeared into the drawing room.

Mr. Pemberton was among the last of the men, and when he saw Constance he stopped. "I am sorry to have missed the pleasure of your company this evening, Miss Kingsley," he said, with a courteous half bow. "Do you hunt with us tomorrow?"

"Yes, I do, Mr. Pemberton. I wouldn't miss it for the world!"

"Nor would I, Miss Kingsley. Now I must bid you goodnight." And before she could protest, he took one of her hands in his, raised it to his lips, and bestowed the faintest of kisses on it. "Until morning, when I very much look forward to seeing you again."

• • •

"And he kissed your hand, miss? The cheek of him!"

"I believe it's very much the vogue on the Continent." The girls were in Constance's room, and Mary was carefully putting away Constance's things while the other girl regaled her with the evening's events.

"Well, we're not on the Continent, miss, we're in Gloucestershire. And I don't know as it's right for him to be doing that, hardly knowing you, and him about to be married."

"Oh, Mary, he didn't mean anything, I'm sure. We've exchanged a few dozen words, that's all! And yet . . ."

"What, Miss Constance?"

"At dinner this evening, I felt–well, odd, every time he looked at me."

"Could be you're sickening for something, Miss Constance. If I were you I'd be abed, so as to be ready for tomorrow. You want to be fit to go hunting, don't you?"

"I most certainly do, Mary. Oh, I can't wait to see Mr. Pemberton's face when I arrive on Regulus!"

Mary glanced at her sharply. "You mean your father's face, don't you, miss?"

Constance waved a hand. "Of course." Under her breath, however, she whispered "But I do want to see Mr. Pemberton as well!"

• • •

The morning dawned clear and bright, and Constance–never a late sleeper–was awake even earlier than usual. A tray of breakfast was brought up and left mostly untouched, and she fussed so much about her appearance, and that of the riding outfit, that Mary was thankful when it was time for her to depart. After tidying the bits and pieces which, as was customary, Constance had contrived to spread across the room, she went downstairs, where she encountered Mr. Somers.

"Good morning, Miss Mary! Off to see the riders depart? The Colonel says we may go into the front drawing room to watch the spectacle. It's quite a sight."

"I've seen the hunt before, Mr. Somers, but never from this close."

"Yes, I forgot you come from the country originally." They were at the drawing-room window, looking out at the bustle of scarlet and black in the courtyard. "Now that I see you in the light, it's easier to remember. You look like a country girl again."

Mary blushed. "It's kind of you to say that, Mr. Somers. I just wish that some of the other poor girls–and lads, too–that I knew there could have the chance I've had."

"And what will you do with this chance, Mary?" Noting her puzzled look, he added, "You won't be Miss Constance's companion forever. Have you given any thought as to what you will do in the future?"

"No, Mr. Somers, that is, not really. I thought I'd like to go on to be a lady's maid, perhaps, but . . . you'll think it very foolish of me . . ."

"I assure you I will not think you foolish, Mary. What is it you would like to be?"

"A schoolteacher," she said in a rush. "It's what my grandfather did, and two of my uncles, Ma said, and–women can be teachers now, can't they, Mr. Somers? At some schools?"

"Indeed they can, Mary, and I don't think you're foolish at all. I think you would be a very fine teacher one day, if you–Good heavens, is that Miss Constance? What on earth is she wearing?"

It was indeed Constance, who had ridden into the forecourt on Regulus. She was sat astride, and Walter turned to Mary.

"Did you know about this?"

"Yes, Mr. Somers. It was my idea, with the breeches and all. The Colonel said as long as she didn't show her legs and cause a scandal she could ride astride."

"I don't know about not causing a scandal," muttered Walter. "Judging by the reaction, she's on her way to one. Who's that man beside her?"

"That's Mr. Pemberton. I saw him yesterday, when he arrived."

They were deep in conversation, seemingly oblivious to the looks and remarks of everyone else. Mary had no idea what they were saying, but she was struck by how well matched they seemed. High atop Regulus, Constance's head was at the same level as Pemberton's, and she looked happier than Mary could remember seeing her. It was a happiness that seemed destined to be short-lived, as the Colonel was making his way toward the pair, a dark look on his face. But at that moment the horn sounded, and the riders were off, Constance and Mr. Pemberton near the head of the field. Within moments they had disappeared from view.

• • •

It was late before the riders returned, and there was barely time for Constance to wash and change for dinner. Mary had expected her to be full of news of the day's events, but Constance was subdued, and disinclined to talk. At dinner she was once more seated at a distance from Mr. Pemberton, and once more she was conscious of his glances toward her. The odd sensation of the night before was still there, but different, somehow, in a way which made her feel as if everyone and everything else was somehow muted. The only clear and stable thing was Mr. Pemberton, and Constance found herself counting the minutes until the meal would be over.

At last she could escape to the drawing room, where she tried to pay attention to the chatter of two middle-aged women whose names she could not recall, and whose conversation struck her as reaching new heights of tedium. She hoped that her father would not keep the gentlemen as long as he had the evening before, and was relieved when footsteps in the hallway signaled the arrival of the other guests. She straightened herself in her chair, and tried not to look as the doorway opened. She was afraid that Mr. Pemberton would come straight to her side, and more afraid that he would not. She fixed her eyes on a painting on the far wall, and waited.

"It is a passable landscape, Miss Kingsley, but surely not *that* absorbing a piece of artwork," said a low voice at her side, and she turned to see Mr. Pemberton. His eyes were merry, and a smile tugged at his lips. "Although with my customary lack of tact, I am prepared to hear you say that you are the artist, in which case it is a most assured–nay, amazing–piece, and should be on display in the National Gallery."

Constance laughed. "I am glad to hear that there is someone else as tactless as I. Remind me to inform my father that I am not as singular in that respect as he seems to think. I would ask you to sit down beside me, but my father said that I was not to monopolize you."

"Ah, but he surely cannot object should I decide to monopolize *you*," said Mr. Pemberton, drawing a chair closer and sitting down. "I was afraid the weekend would be full of the same people–or at least the same *type* of people–I am always encountering."

"And what sort of people would those be, Mr. Pemberton?"

"Good, virtuous, dull people who say only what one wants to hear, have not an original thought in their head, and whose conversational stock-in-trade amounts to gossip which would be dull even if it was new, which it invariably is not."

Constance's eyes gleamed with laughter. "Why, Mr. Pemberton, how do you know that I am not one of those people? That I will not say things merely to flatter you, or that my thoughts are original, or that my conversation will amount to anything more than details of the latest scandal, real or imagined?"

"Because if you are one of those people, Miss Kingsley, then I am very much mistaken, and have no business contemplating a career in politics."

"Ah yes, your political career." Once more Constance cocked her head to one side, in a gesture which he was coming to realize was habitual with her—a way of sizing up the world, and those in it. Seeing the look that crossed his face, she asked bluntly, "Is that what you want?"

He gazed at her in silence for some moments, before saying softly, "Do you know that you are the first person who has asked me that simple question, Miss Kingsley? Everyone—my father, my fiancée, her father—seems to think that the matter is preordained, and that there is no point in even mentioning it, let alone querying it. They all want it, and so the assumption is that I want it too."

"But you must want it, or at the least you must have wanted it, at some point, else why would you be marrying Miss Warren?"

Pemberton laughed. "Dear me, Miss Kingsley, what an extraordinary person you are, to ask that question! Has it occurred to you that I might love her? I thought all young ladies believe that true love is the only acceptable and acknowledged basis for a marriage. It says so in all the popular novels, or so I am told."

"I have only recently started reading the popular novels, Mr. Pemberton, so you must excuse my ignorance on that score. What I see and hear around me leads me to believe that people marry for all manner of reasons, and if love is one of them, then they are exceptionally fortunate. You parried my question very well, but did not answer it, which makes me think that you might make a very fine politician. So I will ask again. Is that what *you* want?"

"To go into politics? Or to marry Miss Warren?"

"Either. Or both."

Again there was silence between them, and Constance felt as if the entire room had hushed itself out of sympathy. She knew that all around her was the hum of conversation, the clattering of china, the murmur of the footman as he refilled cups, but she could not hear it. The world had shrunk down to her and the man who sat beside her, so close now that she could have reached out and taken his hand, and the realization that she wanted to do that–or wanted him to reach out for her–shocked her. It took a moment for her to realize that he was speaking.

"If you had asked me either of those questions as recently as this morning, Miss Kingsley, I would have said yes to both. A qualified yes, perhaps, but there seemed no choice on either matter. Miss Warren is universally hailed as a paragon of all that a man should want in a wife, and it is equally understood by the world that the man who marries her will go into politics, his way there eased by her father's influence and reputation. Having made the decision to marry Miss Warren, I accepted the other as a matter of course. But now–well, let me say that I am questioning both decisions."

"And what has led you to question them, Mr. Pemberton?"

Constance asked the question with a lightness she did not feel. She was conscious, suddenly and sharply, that the future course of her life might well hang in the balance, and she braced herself for his answer. It was not long in coming.

"I saw a girl, on horseback," he replied simply, his eyes never drawing away from hers. "A laughing girl, confident, assured, prepared to risk the censure of others in order to be happy. A girl such as I had not thought existed. Now that I know she does exist, I am prepared to move heaven and earth to be with her."

Constance found that she could not speak. Her face, however, seemed to tell Pemberton all he wished to know, for he sat back in his chair and gave a short nod.

"Here comes your aunt," he said quietly, then, more quietly still, "It will be difficult, and you must prepare yourself for that. But I will find a way." More loudly he said, "I must not monopolize you any further, Miss Kingsley, and I see that your aunt wishes to speak with you. I hope that we may continue our very interesting conversation on another occasion."

• • •

Despite Constance's best efforts, there was no opportunity the next day to speak privately with Mr. Pemberton. Her aunt was persistent in her efforts to ensure that Constance assisted her in her hostess duties, and her father once again kept the gentlemen late after dinner. It was not until Mr. Pemberton was leaving that she had a few words with him, and they were merely lighthearted pleasantries on both sides, conscious as they were that others were listening. When he took her hand, however, Constance had to conceal her start of surprise, for he pressed a folded piece of paper into her palm. Then, with a nod and a smile, he was gone.

The note, which she did not open until she was in her bedroom, was brief.

> My dearest Constance, if I may so address you, I hope that you are constant by nature as well as name, for I am determined that we shall be together, no matter the difficulties that lie ahead. I will be in touch as soon as I am able, and you will then tell me if my hopes for a future with you are founded upon rock or sand.

She had committed the letter to heart by the time Mary came into the room, and the face she turned to the girl made Mary stop in her tracks. Constance seemed to be glowing, and Mary felt that if she moved too close she would be burned. "What is it, Miss Constance?" she cried, alarmed. "Are you ill?"

"Oh, Mary, I am far from ill. I am the happiest person on earth! That is what I am."

"Why, whatever can have happened?" Mary's face clouded. "This is something to do with Mr. Pemberton, isn't it, miss? What have you done?"

"Nothing–not yet. But we have talked, and he has given me this note, in which he says that he is determined we shall be together."

"But how, miss? He's to marry Miss Warren, isn't he? How can he be with you, and still be a–well, a gentleman?"

"He won't marry Miss Warren," said Constance, her voice ringing with confidence. "He will marry me, as soon as it can be arranged."

Mary stood in shocked silence. "But Miss Constance," she said finally, "I don't see *how* it can be arranged. There's Miss Warren, and her father, and his own family, to say nothing of the Colonel. He will never approve."

Constance gave an imperious toss of her head. "If my father will not give his approval, then I shall marry without it."

"But–" Mary tried to put her thoughts into words. "How can you know he loves you? Or that you love him? Why, three days ago he was a stranger."

"It sounds like the worst sort of contrivance from a popular novel, I know. But such things do happen in real life, else novelists would not write of them. You do not have to know a person for months or years to realize you love them, and that they love you. Such is the bond between us. We *know* it, Mary." She rose, and took Mary's hands in hers. "You must believe me. Say that you do, and say that you will help us."

Mary looked long and hard at Constance. Then, as if reassured by what she saw, she nodded her head.

"I'll help you, miss," she said with a sigh. "Although where it will all lead is a mystery. I can only hope there's a happy ending."

• • •

The next few weeks were a fraught time for both girls. Mr. Pemberton was as good as his word, and within days a letter arrived from him for Constance. She shared its contents–and that of the others which followed in regular, and rapid, succession–with Mary, but would not let her read them.

"For they are very personal in nature, Mary," she explained. "And if you do not read them, you can tell my father as much if he ever has reason to ask."

"How will you live, Miss Constance?" Mary asked once. "You've no money of your own, and nothing will come from the Colonel, and Mr. Pemberton will almost certainly be cut off by his own father."

"He has thought of that," said Constance. "He thinks of everything. He has some money of his own which his father cannot touch, and an uncle who emigrated to western Canada within the last year has done very well in business there, with the railway going through. He has promised Arthur a position with him should he ever want one. Imagine that, Mary! Traveling all that distance to the far side of another country, through mountains and forests!" She spoke of it as if it were little more than a grand adventure, and Mary chided her.

"It's not a game, Miss Constance. It means a heap of troubles, and estrangement from your family, and hardship. And what will become of me?"

"Why, Mary!" exclaimed Constance. "You will come with me, of course! Mr. Pemberton has been quite positive on that point. And I shall need a friend, more than ever I do now. Say you will come with me."

"I'll think on it, Miss Constance. I can't say fairer than that, now, can I? And there's a long road to walk before we get to that point.'

• • •

In the end, Mary was wrong, for events came to a head only two days later. It was after breakfast, and the Colonel was in his study, where he had been joined by Mr. Somers.

"Good heavens," said the Colonel, looking up from his copy of *The Times*. "Somers, have you seen this? It appears that the engagement between Mr. Pemberton and Miss Warren has been called off, and the lady is to sue him for breach of promise."

Walter gave a whistle of surprise. "Startling news indeed, Colonel, and somewhat unexpected. There was certainly no talk of such a thing when he was here only a few weeks ago, so it is very sudden."

"I wonder if he has said anything to my daughter. I know she has been receiving letters from him; quite a number of them, in fact." His eyes narrowed. "Indeed, I have wondered at the quantity of letters to and from Mr. Pemberton. I hope that–" He left the sentence unfinished, and rose suddenly from his chair. "Come with me, Somers. We will find out if there is anything to those letters which my daughter is not divulging."

Walter, a feeling of misgiving rising within him, followed the Colonel upstairs, and waited while he rapped on Constance's door. It opened, disclosing Constance and Mary within. The Colonel entered, Somers behind him.

"Constance, do you know anything of this?" queried the Colonel, pointing to the relevant article. "You have been receiving letters from Mr. Pemberton, and writing him in return. Has he spoken of the matter to you, or mentioned it in any . . . Is something wrong?"

Constance's face had gone pale, and her entire body had stiffened. She opened her mouth, but before she could say anything her father took a step backward, as if she had struck him. "Dear God, tell me that you are nothing to do with this! Tell me, on the name of your dear mother, that you are not the cause!"

Mary and Walter could do nothing more than watch—the one in sympathy, the other in something like horror—as Constance took a deep breath. She raised her eyes to her father's face, and said quietly, "I cannot tell you that, Father. I am sorry."

Silence held steadily over the room, the only sound that of a clock ticking on the mantel. For several seconds it was as if everyone within the room was frozen. Then the silence was exploded by the sound of the Colonel's hand crashing down upon Mary's dressing table.

"Sorry! *Sorry*! You *will* be sorry, my girl, unless you can tell me that this is all some girlish whim, and that you—*both* of you—have thought better of such madness."

"It is very far from a whim, Father. Mr. Pemberton has asked me to marry him, and I have said yes."

There was another silence, as the Colonel digested this news. He suddenly looked very old. His gaze traveled from one face to another, as if seeking answers, then returned to Constance, who was still standing, ramrod straight, in front of him. "There will be no marriage," he said, his voice heavy. "Mr. Pemberton may do as he pleases with regard to Miss Warren. I would have credited him with far more sense, but he has made his bed and must lie in it."

"What do you propose to do, Father?" asked Constance. She spoke quietly, but there was a steeliness and determination to her voice that Mary recognized immediately. "Lock me in my room?"

"I will, if that is what is needed to prevent you doing something which will bring ruin and scandal about your head, and upon this family. In fact, I shall do just that. Mr. Somers, Mary, leave this room now. We will see how effective being confined to quarters is, and leave Miss Constance to reflect upon her folly." Ignoring the protests of his daughter, the old soldier turned to the door and, before Constance could move, was on the outside locking it, Mary and Walter looking on in silence.

"That will keep her safe for now," said the Colonel, pocketing the key. "Mr. Somers, please be so good as to come with me to my study. We must discuss this matter immediately, and see what can be done." The Colonel walked stiffly away, and Walter, after a quick glance at Mary, followed him.

When they were out of earshot, Mary moved to the door. "Miss Constance," she whispered. "Miss Constance, can you hear me?"

"Yes, Mary," said Constance from the other side of the door. "What am I to do? Father can't keep me locked in here forever, but he can try to stop us getting married."

"How can he do that, miss?"

Mary made an impatient noise. "I'm not twenty-one, so I need his consent. He can arrange to have me sent away, to the Continent, perhaps, where I shall be out of harm's way, or so he thinks. Or he can apply to have me made a ward of the court, so that legally I can't marry until I'm of age. Unless . . ."

"Unless what, Miss Constance?" asked Mary, after a moment's silence.

"Unless we can make our way to Gretna Green, and marry there. Hush"–as Mary tried to speak–"give me a moment to think. Yes," she continued, "that is what we must do. I can be married there, quite legally, without Father's consent. The law is different in Scotland."

"How will we get there? And are you sure Mr. Pemberton will agree to it?"

"Yes, I am sure," said Constance, confidence in her voice. "But we shall have to get word to him." She thought for a minute. "If I write a letter, will you be able to take it to the village and ensure that it gets posted? It may be difficult–my father or Mr. Somers might well suspect that you know something about this business, and watch your movements."

Despite the gravity of the situation, Mary could not suppress a small laugh. "I managed not to get caught while I was picking pockets in the streets of London, miss. I daresay I can get to the village without being spotted."

"And what about getting me out of this room, Mary? Can you manage that too?"

"I daresay I can, Miss Constance. Mr. Somers says I don't forget anything I've learned. We'll see if he's right."

• • •

It did not take Constance long to write a letter to Arthur Pemberton, advising him of the situation, and setting forth her plan.

> If you are serious, my dear Arthur, then you will be waiting for me three days hence, at midnight, near the turning to the village a mile from the house. Do not respond to this letter, as it will not reach me. If you are waiting, that will be all the response I need and want.

The letter was duly dispatched, with no one the wiser. Then commenced three days of waiting, during which time the mood of the house was black and heavy. Mrs. Millington, who had been told of the situation, had taken to her room with what she called a nervous collapse, and Mary was kept busy tending to the invalid. She was not allowed to see Constance, who was still in her room, her meals brought up by a servant under the supervision of the Colonel, who kept the key. There was, of course, no word from Mr. Pemberton, and Mary could not help wondering nervously what the outcome would be.

The appointed day came at last, and it took all Mary's skill at deception to maintain a steady countenance whenever she encountered another member of the household. She was particularly desirous of keeping out of the way of Mr. Somers, who always seemed to be searching her face when they met, as if looking for confirmation of something he suspected. When, after Constance's evening meal had been delivered, Mary knocked on the door of the Colonel's study, she was almost sorry to see the secretary within.

"Yes, girl, what is it?" asked the Colonel, his voice weary and his face seeming to have aged by ten years. His desk, usually neat, was strewn with papers. "We are rather busy, as you can see."

"Yes sir, I realize that. I just wondered if–well, if it were possible for me to see Miss Constance. I'm that worried about her, and it couldn't do any harm, if someone else were there with us."

"Out of the question." The Colonel rose and went to stand in front of the fire, which he gazed at unseeingly. "My daughter must be made to realize her folly. It will not be long now before the entire matter is settled." Mary tried not to look startled, and hoped that Mr. Somers had not noticed. "I am arranging it so that she cannot marry before she is twenty-one without Mr. Pemberton regretting the day he met her," he continued, and Mary allowed herself a small sigh of relief. "A few more days should see it done. Until then, my daughter is to have no visitors."

"Please, sir," cried Mary, moving to where he stood, and clasping him impulsively by the arm. "Please, let me go to her. If you could hear her crying, as I have–it would melt a heart of stone, it would. You can't deny her the small comfort of a friendly face and voice, surely, sir?"

The Colonel was clearly moved by her appeal, and patted her on the shoulder. "There, there, Mary," he said, not unkindly. "You're a good girl, of that I'm sure, and I know that you mean well. But my mind is made up. My daughter is to have no visitors. I am sorry."

Mary nodded. As if realizing the liberty she had taken, she let go of the Colonel's arm and moved back.

"If that's your final word, sir, then I can't change your mind. Forgive me for asking, but I only wanted to do what I thought best."

"I know that, and it does you credit. My daughter does not deserve a friend such as you. However, I must ask you to leave us now. Mr. Somers and I have more work to do, and it is getting late."

Mary bobbed her head. "Yes, sir," she said meekly. "I'm sorry to have disturbed you, but I had to try." She glanced at Walter, trying to read his face, but it was impassive. "Goodnight then, sirs," she said quietly, and took her leave. When the heavy door closed behind her, she took a deep breath. Then she squared her shoulders, said, "Well, that's that, then," under her breath, and made her way to her room.

• • •

The clock had struck twelve, and darkness and silence had fallen over the house, when the door of Mary's room opened. She took one last look behind her, then took a firm grasp of the small valise she was holding and crept through the shadows to the door of Constance's room.

"Is that you, Mary?" asked a voice from the other side, before Mary could tap. "Do you have the key?"

"Yes, miss, I do." Mary fumbled in her pocket, and drew out the brass key which she had abstracted from the Colonel's pocket only a few hours earlier. She fitted it into the lock and turned it, and the door opened to reveal Constance on the other side. She was dressed soberly in warm traveling clothes, and was holding a small case. Mary glanced at it. "Is that all you're taking with you, Miss Constance? It doesn't seem a lot."

"It will be enough, Mary. More than enough, if Mr. Pemberton is not there. But he will be. I know he will." She spotted the valise in Mary's hand. "Have you decided, then?"

"Yes, miss. I can't stay on here, whatever happens. So I'll throw in my lot with you and Mr. Pemberton, if you'll have me."

Constance grasped Mary by one hand. "Of course we will, dear friend. There is nothing I–Good heavens! Mr. Somers!"

Mary turned, and saw the secretary standing beside her. Even in the faint light emanating from Constance's room, she could tell that his face was pale and set. He looked from one girl to the other before fixing his gaze on Mary.

"It was very cleverly done," he said slowly. "No wonder you never got caught, Mary. I was watching closely, and even so I almost missed it."

"You knew?"

"I suspected."

"Have you–have you said anything to the Colonel?"

Walter sighed. "No," he said at last. "I have not."

"And–will you say anything?" It was Constance speaking, but it was Mary the answer was directed to.

"I do not know, yet. Is this what you want?"

Mary met his gaze frankly. "It is what Miss Constance wants. We are going now, to meet Mr. Pemberton."

"And thence to Gretna Green, I suppose, and from there–what are your plans then?"

"Mr. Pemberton has money of his own, and business interests in Canada. We will book passage on a ship from Liverpool and sail as soon as we can. The Colonel will surely set folk in search of us, but he mayn't think to look there, and we'll be gone before they can find us."

Mr. Somers shook his head. "It is a risky step and a bold venture, but then I am sure you both know this. And I know you both well enough to realize that these facts are unlikely to stop you."

Mary seized his arm. "You will not raise the alarm then, Mr. Somers? You will let us go?"

He gazed down at her in something like sadness for a moment, then gave a small smile. "Yes, I will let you go, and the Colonel will be none the wiser–for a few more hours, at least." His smile faded. "I wish you the best, Miss Constance, you and Mr. Pemberton. You are both very brave. I only hope, to misquote Mr. Dryden slightly, that the world is well lost for love. And you, Mary." He took his hand in hers and held it a moment. "I am glad to have known you, Mary Daniels. Miss Constance is a very fortunate girl indeed, to have so true a friend. I hope that, whatever happens, you will let me know of your fate, and where I may write to you. You came very suddenly into my life, and I would hate to lose you in so dramatic a fashion. No, say nothing. You have not much time, and the longer you stay here, the more chance there is of discovery."

"Thank you, Mr. Somers," said Mary, suddenly close to tears. "Thank you for all you've done for me. I won't forget."

"No, we won't forget," said Constance. "Come, Mary, we must go. Mr. Pemberton will be waiting." She picked up her bag, and the two girls stole along the hallway. Mary paused at the turning, to look back; then, with a small wave, she was gone, and silence settled over the house once more.

"Will he be waiting? I wonder," mused Walter to himself. Then, with a shake of his head, he pulled Constance's door shut. "We shall all know soon enough. Either way, it will be an–interesting time ahead, to be certain. *Very* interesting."

• • •

From a letter written by Miss Beatrice Wardour to her friend Miss Evelina Lancaster

Vancouver, British Columbia
August 1887

My dearest Friend,

I alluded, in my last letter, to the difficulties the school was facing. This place, which was scarce more than a village but a few short years ago, is now a bustling city. Alas, the growth in population has put a huge strain on the school, which has not been able to keep up sufficiently to accommodate the large number of students who wish to enroll. As Principal I have been agitating, for some time, for an increase in funding to allow us to expand, yet my pleas were falling on deaf ears, for our elected officials have many pressing affairs to which to attend. Just when all seemed bleakest, however, an angel–or rather, angels–stepped forward in the form of Mr. and Mrs. Pemberton. They are fairly recent arrivals, even by the standards of this place, having been here for less than six months, but he has already amassed a quite sizable fortune, having speculated wisely in property, the value of which is increasing almost daily. He has endowed the school with a fund sufficient to meet its expansion needs, with the promise of more to follow should it be needed. His wife, who is considerably younger than him, came with him to see the school, and commented on their future need for the facilities the school provides–a reference, I take it, to the forthcoming increase in their family number. They have also, most providently, supplied me with a new teacher, a Miss Daniels, a good, quiet, sober woman whom Mrs. Pemberton called a dear friend of long standing. I am sure she will prove an asset to the school when lessons resume, with much of value to teach the students.

From Miss Wardour to Miss Lancaster

Vancouver, British Columbia
April, 1888

Miss Daniels has settled in so well, and is such a favorite with the pupils, that I do not well know how I would replace her, which is why I was pleased when she informed me that her forthcoming marriage will not in any way impede her in the carrying-out of her duties at the school. It was only very recently that she informed me of her engagement–perhaps she was worried that it would mean the curtailment of her employment, as is the custom in some establishments when a woman moves from the single to the married state. Her fiancé came with her to the school the other day, so that we could be introduced. He seems a very decent young man, Mr. Summers (I believe it is) by name, only recently arrived from England. He is to work for Mr. Pemberton, whose mind is much occupied by the new addition to his family, or so Miss Daniels tells me. Who would have thought that someone so placid and quiet should harbor such a secret as a fiancé! There is apparently much truth in the old adage about still waters running deep.

Mercury Retrograde

MARY ROBINETTE KOWAL

With her father's giant orrery turning over her head, Hannah sat in a chair and watched the clockmaker make his adjustments. The great brass and enamel model of the heavens swept through its rotation with little ticks from within its base. Etched in gold and silver, the signs of the zodiac wrapped in a band so that, even in daylight, an astrologer could see where the planets lay. Lit by the sun streaming in through the large glass windows of Sir Phillip's study, the planets rotated like women dancing in scarlet, cerulean, and primrose ballgowns.

Mr. Whitaker peered through the brass door in the side of the mechanism and frowned. His neat starched collar contrasted beautifully against the dark skin of his throat and made his jaw appear even firmer than it was. Rumor had it that his mother had been a Rajah's daughter, but he denied that. Whatever the truth, the result was a man who caused the fashionable young ladies of London to swoon whenever he walked into a room. Hannah was not immune to his charms. Not at all.

Mr. Whitaker picked up a wrench and reached inside the orrery's base. His movement checked almost immediately as his coat snagged on a gear. Yanking his arm free, he glanced at her father before turning to her. "Miss Miller . . . I need to remove my coat in order to reach inside. I apologize, but, it is very snug."

Hannah masked a smile. He hardly needed to apologize for that, except Papa was in the room. "By all means. I shan't be shocked. My father often works in his shirtsleeves, don't you Papa?"

"Eh?" Sir Phillip looked up from the star chart he was working on. He was not normally in his study at this time of day, but Lady Richardson was due for an astrological reading. It was most inconvenient, but she tried not to let it show.

"Do you not work in your shirtsleeves sometimes?"

"Oh, yes. Quite." He had an ink stain on his index finger from dipping his pen with too much haste. Sir Phillip peered over his glasses at Mr. Whitaker. "Will it be ready for the Crystal Exhibition?"

"Certainly. Only . . . I need to make an adjustment to the interior mechanism and my coat is in the way, I am afraid."

"Ah . . . yes. Well, carry on." He went back to the charts, nibbling on the end of his pen.

"You see." She smoothed the folds of her hoop skirt and smiled. In truth, she had hoped Mr. Whitaker would need to remove his coat. He was widely reckoned as a prodigy with clockworks, and at the tender age of eight-and-twenty had been engaged by the Prince Albert himself for his automatons. That he was also tall, slender, and had waves of dark hair did nothing to diminish Hannah's interest in his work. "Do let me know if there is anything I can do."

He hesitated only a moment longer, then pulled off his frock coat and hung it over the chair next to her. Leaning down, he whispered, "How much did you slow it this time?"

"A quarter turn," she whispered back.

Rolling up his shirtsleeve to expose a muscled arm, he again picked up his wrench and reached inside the machine. He stared at the far wall, but appeared to see something deep within the machine instead.

"Papa . . ." Hannah looked around as if just thinking of it. "Is it time for Lady Richardson?"

He pulled out his pocket watch. "Dear me. It is." He bundled up his papers and hurried out of the study, leaving her quite alone with Mr. Whitaker.

Only when the door had shut did Hannah dare think of Mr. Whitaker as Gideon.

She came to the side of the machine and leaned against it, watching her love work. His dark hair curled around his brow. His eyes, narrowed in concentration, stared at nothing as he worked by feel. He glanced up at her, with an imitation scowl imperfectly masking a smile. "You make me regret teaching you how to make the adjustments. Your arms are more slender than mine."

"I could undo it, if you like."

He grinned. "And allow you to get grease on your dainty gloves?"

"Well, I would take the gloves off."

"Even worse. Grease under your delicate fingernails. Where is . . ." He grunted and closed his eyes as he fiddled with something deep in the machine. "There." A slight metallic scraping emitted from within, and the orrery sped.

Hannah looked at the watch hanging from the chain about her neck. "Shall I time it for you?"

"Please."

As Mercury swept past, Hannah noted the time. The second hand ticked as the planets and stars swirled by. When Mercury completed its revolution, she said, "Two minutes, thirty-six seconds."

"A little too fast . . ." He frowned and eased the wrench around. Then he cursed. Something metal clattered inside the machine, as though he had dropped the wrench. Scowling, he stretched his arm deeper.

He jerked back, yelping. The machine stuttered. Gideon did not pull his arm out, though she could see the muscles of his shoulder bunching under his waistcoat. He pushed at the machine with his other hand, straining.

Hannah spun, skirts swirling around her, and threw the switch on the giant mechanism, halting the machine.

Gideon rested his head against the side of the base. "Thank you."

She knelt by him. "Are you hurt?"

"Only my pride." He jerked his arm again and scowled. "My shirtsleeve is caught in a gear."

Hannah peered into the machine, heart still racing though she tried not to show it. She had thought his arm itself had been caught by the machine. The sleeve had been caught in the gears. It looked as though it were in the process of trying to eat his arm. "What can I do?"

He wrinkled his nose. "Try walking it backward. Slowly. Grab . . . grab Mercury as your handle."

"All right." Hannah stood. It was her fault, for adjusting the orrery's timing in order to throw it off. They got to see each other so rarely since he had finished the installation. "I am sorry."

"Do not be." He pulled on his sleeve again. "I know better than to stick my arm in a running machine."

Hannah put her hands on the enameled sphere of Mercury and walked it backward. "Look. Mercury is retrograde. I feel rash . . ." She felt some resistance from the machine.

"Stop!" He ducked his head and peered inside. "The fabric is wound around the gear. Flesh and fire! This is what I get for showing off."

"Shall I cut your shirt free?"

He scowled. "I like this shirt."

"Do you really think it is going to be salvageable after the gear is done with it?"

He sighed and compressed his lips. "You have a point, though I do not have to like it."

Hannah patted him on the back. "There, there." She skipped to the table where her work basket sat. At night, the large windows gave her father a better view of the stars, but during the day, this room had the best light in the house for needlepoint. She pulled out her shears and came back to crouch next to Gideon. Holding the scissors up, she paused and leaned against him. "Since I have you captive, my dear . . . when are you going to speak to my father?"

He winced and looked down, picking a ball of fuzz off his trousers. "After all of the work is finished. I do not want to come to him as a suitor while I am still in his employ."

"He adores you."

Gideon rubbed the back of his neck. "He admires my work—when it isn't being sabotaged by his daughter. It is the other that I worry about . . ." He held up his free hand to display the dark skin there as if it were not obvious that he was talking about his Anglo-Indian heritage. Dropping his hand, he nodded at the scissors. "Are you going to free me?"

"Yes. But I will not be patient forever." The opening in the mechanism's base required Hannah to kneel behind Gideon. She pressed her torso against him, feeling the ribs of her corset give a little against his firm back. She slid her arm along his into the machine. With both of their arms inside, she could not see the fabric she needed to cut. Hannah tried to work the scissors by feel, but Gideon flinched. "Did I cut you?"

"Only a nick."

She tried again with the scissors, but he stiffened. The gear had his shirt pulled so tight around his arm that she could not cut while their arms were blocking the view. Hannah pulled her arm back out. "I have a better idea."

"Do tell, because I do not want your father to catch me stuck like this."

"Oh, but it is so delightful to have you here." Hannah held her breath and leaned forward to kiss his cheek, startled at her own daring. Perhaps even a clockwork Mercury could inspire rash behavior when retrograde.

Gideon blushed, his deep complexion darkening further. A smile rounded his high cheekbones. "I will admit that I now see the benefit of this, albeit temporarily." He glanced toward the door, which was hidden by the base, then stole a kiss from her cheek.

The room seemed to warm as Hannah blushed with pleasure. "Well . . . it seems to me that what you need to do is to remove your arm from the shirt, and then it will be that much easier to remove the shirt from the mechanism." If she had thought that the room seemed warm before, she felt a wave of heat from her toes to the tips of her ears as she suggested this.

Charmingly, Gideon blushed even deeper at the suggestion and ducked his head. He seemed to find it necessary to adjust his tie even though the silk was perfectly tied in a four-in-hand. He cleared his throat. "There must be another way."

"Certainly." Hannah stood up, dusting off her dress. "We can pull the gear all the way out as well. It shouldn't take you long to repair . . ."

Gideon screwed his face up and peered into the base of the machine. "It was just a timing adjustment."

Remembering that his predicament was entirely her fault, Hannah twisted her hands together in front of her. "I am so sorry about that."

"It is not your fault. I only thought . . . I thought that if I repaired it fast enough, we might have some time alone."

"We do now." She sighed, wishing that he felt comfortable coming to the house without an errand. People would talk if he called on her, and there was enough gossip about him already. "Are you sure that you don't want to try removing your shirt? I am certain it will be easier to get the sleeve free."

Gideon chewed his lower lip. "All right. But go on the other side of the machine."

"Gideon . . . are you modest?"

"One of us needs to be." He flashed his disarming grin again. "Besides, if your father returns while I am disrobed, I would prefer not to be assaulting your virtue with a view of my manly chest."

Hannah giggled and shook her finger at him, but she moved to the other side of the orrery nonetheless. She also picked up a mirror that belonged to a partially disassembled telescope. Holding it so she could see over her shoulder, Hannah watched Gideon struggle one-handed with the buttons on his vest. "Do you need help?"

"I am fine." He twisted the button around, coming no closer to slipping it through the buttonhole.

"I do not mind."

"Your father . . ."

Hannah sighed. "We could have you over for dinner and you could talk to him then."

"Is he in the habit of inviting craftsmen to dinner?"

"You are hardly just a craftsman. You are a scientist as well."

"Very kind of you–blast." His fingers had slipped again on the button.

Hannah put her mirror down and shook her head. "This is silly. It will be but a moment." She swept around the orrery and knelt next to him, skirt puddling a little onto his lap.

Gideon slid back as far as he could, but Hannah stopped him with a hand on his vest. If anything, that made him blush deeper. Utterly charming.

"I promise not to hurt you." Hannah ducked her head and undid the buttons on his vest with ease. As she moved to the buttons on his shirt, her hands shook a little. The room really was too warm for this time of year. "I . . . um . . . I need to take off your tie."

He nodded and looked out the window, swallowing. His breathing seemed faster as she pulled the silk out of its knot and laid the fabric across her lap. Free from the confines of the collar, his neck was breathtaking. Hannah had to remind herself to inhale, and then it almost hurt to breathe. She undid the last button, revealing his undershirt and the hollow of his collar bones. Hannah slid the shirt off his shoulder. His skin seemed as though it could burn her hand. So smooth. So warm.

The only sound in the room was his breath and the rustle of silk as she leaned forward.

A vein pulsed in his neck, keeping time with her own heart. Gideon pulled his free arm out of the shirt. He twisted to slide the other arm free, and the muscles in his upper arm bunched and gathered. Fascinated, Hannah put her hand on his biceps.

The door opened. Crockery shattered on the floor.

Hannah jumped to her feet, tripping over her skirt. She stumbled back from Gideon–Mr. Whitaker–and turned to face the door. Her father stood in a puddle with the pieces of a tea set at his feet. His lower legs were soaked. She forced her gaze up to his face.

Normally genial, he was a vivid red. A vein pulsed out at his temple. "What is the meaning of this?"

Mr. Whitaker scrambled to his feet, tearing his shirt free from the machine. "I–My shirt was stuck. In the mechanism. Your daughter–"

"My daughter will go to her room and wait for me there." Her father stood back from the door and pointed to the stairs.

"Papa–I was only trying to help."

He pointed again.

With a glance back at Mr. Whitaker, Hannah hurried from the room. Her father said, "Thank you for your time, Mr. Whitaker, but your services will no longer be required."

• • •

In her bedroom, Hannah paced from the window to her dressing table and back again. She had heard Mr. Whitaker clatter down the stairs in a hurry. When she had looked out the window, he was striding down the street, buttoning his greatcoat with his hat perched at a precarious angle on his head. She pressed her hand against the glass, and the handprint was still there. She stared at it each time her circuit brought her back to the window. She was half tempted to leave her room and go speak to Papa, but she was too frightened of the rage she had seen on his face. Never had she seen her father more than mildly perturbed.

A knock at her door. Hannah halted by the window. "Come in."

Her father opened the door and stepped in, face stern. He carried a tray with hot cocoa and a slice of Robertson's cake. "I thought you might be hungry."

Hannah wrung her hands. "Papa, about Mr. Whitaker."

He set the tray on her dressing table. "I am so sorry that you were exposed to that. I had been warned that his Indian blood would tell, but his work was so good." He turned a cup on the tray, staring at the dark liquid inside. "My ambition has harmed you, and I can only offer my apologies for that."

For a moment, Hannah could only stare at him. She swallowed and found her voice. "Papa, you have misunderstood completely. Mr. Whitaker was stuck in the mechanism, and the only way to free him was to remove his shirt–"

"And it needed to be you to do that? It needed to be done while you were alone?" He shook his head. "I can see how it would seem reasonable to such a pure heart as yours, but any civilized man would understand how very wrong such an action would be."

"But–but it was my idea."

He lifted his head at that and turned to stare at her, dismay mixed with revulsion.

Coming closer, Hannah tried again to make her father see that it was not Mr. Whitaker's fault. "He thought it was not right but I . . ."

"Have I failed you so completely? Your virtue is your most prized possession, and you would toy with it so? With a mongrel clockmaker? With any man, really, but with someone who has only the veneer of civilization allowing him to mix with his betters."

"His father was a British admiral."

"Who should have shown better sense than to be taken in by a harlot. You have not seen the state of undress their women habitually parade in, but I assure you that no virtuous man would be tempted by such a display." He shook his head. "His father's morals were clearly weak, and any benefit the British blood might have conferred on the son is lost."

"Mr. Whitaker is not like that. He is good and modest and blushes at the slightest impropriety and–"

"And how do you know that?" Her father jerked his head up.

Heart racing, Hannah took a step back. "I . . . we . . . that is–he was going to speak with you, but wanted to wait until the work was completed."

Her father turned away from her, but she could still see him in the mirror. His jaw was clenched tight and his mouth puckered with distaste. "Am I to understand . . . do you have an attachment to Mr. Whitaker?"

This was not how she wanted to tell him. In all of her imaginings, this was not how she would approach her father, nor what his reaction should be. She had pictured coming to him in his study and speaking of Mr. Whitaker's gentleness and intelligence. Her father would be surprised, of course, but only because they had been so careful not to let their mutual regard show. He would recover from the surprise, and be delighted to have such a son. Mr. Whitaker's clockworks could only help with his astrology.

The reality was so far different. "I thought you liked him."

"He does good work. I admire that. I regret that you confused the two." Facing her, he seemed to have mastered some of his emotion. "I trust, understanding my feelings now, you will no longer have any regard for him."

Hannah shook her head and backed farther away. She had to make him understand. Turning, she hurried to her wardrobe and pulled it open, digging inside until she found the star charts she had draw up. "Look–he is. We are destined for each other. See how perfectly we fit?"

Her father strode across the room and snatched the charts out of her hands. "You will disregard these fancies. That you 'fit' well does not mean that he is an appropriate object for your affections." He rolled them into a tight tube. "You will stay in your room until you have had the opportunity to consider your actions."

"Papa . . ." Hannah reached for him, begging him to relent. "I love him."

"I am very disappointed in you." Turning on his heel, he walked briskly to the door and left her alone in her room.

• • •

Hannah pulled her cloak tighter about her and leaned over the telescope, trying to spot Mercury in the sky. She had gone over her father's star charts, but the results did not please her in the least, and she was determined that the location of the actual stars must be different than what the charts showed. Every chart she had drawn up showed that there was no way in which she could marry Gideon.

Mercury sat firmly in Cancer, just as it had in the star chart.

She sighed, breath steaming into the air, and straightened. From the roof, she could see over most of London toward the Thames. The innumerable gas lamps that lined Pall Mall cast a glow that obscured much of the night sky. It had become harder and harder to see the stars as more of the gas lamps went in. She suspected that before not much longer, her father would need to spend most of his time out at their country estate to do his work. After Gideon, she had no hope of him letting her remain in the City. She had not even been outside the house for the last two weeks.

Carefully, Hannah put the cap back on the telescope and lifted the heavy brass instrument. She headed back inside, the flannel of her dressing gown catching against the wood as she pushed open the door. If her father knew that she was on the roof, he would have much to say.

Hannah set the telescope on its tripod back by her father's desk and picked up the taper that she had left in his study. She made her way down stairs, candle flame dancing against the walls. She would just have to study the charts longer. If the conditions were not favorable, she would need to change the variables and hope she could find a pattern that would fit.

The stair creaked as she crept back down the stairs. A moment later, her father's door opened. "Hannah? You should be in bed."

"I–I could not sleep." That was true enough. "I was just trying to clear my head."

He frowned, brow creasing with worry. "I will have Robertson send up some warm milk."

Hannah wanted to laugh–as if warm milk would do anything to ease her heart, but she had to be calm and rational or her father would never let her leave the house again. "Thank you. That would be very kind."

He stepped into the hall, then hesitated. "My presentation at the Crystal Exhibition is tomorrow. Would you like to accompany me?"

"I would be delighted. I hope it is well received." Hannah dropped a small curtsey of thanks before she retreated to her bedroom, leaving her father smiling. It relieved her that he was letting her out of the house, even supervised. But more importantly, Gideon would be at the Exhibition with his automatons.

She lit the candle by her bed with the taper and pulled the charts out from under the bed. Crouching on the floor, she studied them again. If the current variables did not work, she would plot the outcome backward. If she started with them happily married, what conditions would get them there?

Hannah worked the figures until Robertson arrived with the warm milk.

• • •

The Crystal Exhibition Hall, now filled with people, nearly took Hannah's breath away. She had understood from newspaper accounts that the glass structure was the largest of its kind and a feat of engineering. The newspaper engravings, however, told nothing of its scale, and made it seem only a very large orangery with perhaps a more interesting shape.

On the carriage ride up, she had repeatedly thought that the building was large and then, upon realizing that it was farther away than it appeared, that it was even larger than she thought. It gleamed in the sunlight as the various planes of the arced roof caught the light. Within, full-size living elms graced the wide halls making them seem more like avenues than an indoor space.

Her father kept her close as they walked through the press of people to his exhibit stall. The abundance of silks seemed as though the crowd had taken the entire rainbow and woven it into cloth for dresses. The gentlemen walked at the side of their ladies in deep black frock coats, providing a setting for these jewels of England. Hannah scanned the throng for some sign of Gideon. If he were here, surely she would be able to spot his warm skin among the pallid masses.

With his automatons, he would be sure to attract a crowd, particularly if His Royal Highness visited the booth. More than one overheard conversation mentioned Prince Albert and that he was supposed to be in attendance today. Perhaps if she told her father that she wanted to see the Queen's husband, then she could follow his entourage until he arrived at Gideon's booth. Hannah bit the inside of her cheek. That would never work. Her father knew Gideon would be here, and would never let her out of his sight. She sighed.

Her father patted her arm. "Are you all right, my dear?"

"The press–I have been so much at home lately that I have grown unused to crowds." This had enough truth that it did not feel as though it were a true lie.

"Would you like to go home? I can spare Robertson to send with you." He tipped his hat to a passerby.

"No, no. I want to see your triumph." This, too, was true. He had worked hard for a space in this exhibit. Gideon's orrery was to be part of his demonstration about how the stars influenced the lives of every person.

"That is good of you, my dear."

Whatever else her father said was lost–across the great hall, she heard Gideon's laughter. They were passing a booth with automatons arranged artfully. Inside, Gideon spoke to a gentleman and a lady, demonstrating his piano player. The manikin, with its porcelain skin, looked almost real as it played a minuet upon a dainty pianoforte.

Gideon's teeth flashed as he smiled. He bowed and gestured to the next machine, a clown who juggled. As Gideon lifted his other hand to wind it, his gaze lifted as well. The moment when he saw her was unmistakable. There was first a smile of recognition, quickly cut off and replaced as his face drooped into sadness. Lowering his head, he wet his lips and looked away before mastering his expression and facing the couple again. He wound the clown, but his gaze followed Hannah as she walked.

She turned her head almost over her shoulder, watching him.

"What is it, my dear?"

Hannah snapped her attention forward again. "That woman had a remarkable dress." She swallowed. "I swear she had four tiers of flounces. It was quite the thing."

"I thought perhaps it was Mr. Whitaker." He glanced at her, and Hannah was forced to look down.

She could not even think of a creditable lie.

• • •

With a sigh, Hannah straightened from the star charts and rolled her neck to try to ease some of the tension. Her heavy braid hung over her shoulder and she toyed with the ribbon tying the end of it. The candle flickered as she sighed again. She had worked the charts over and again till she was certain about the answer.

She did not like it, but it was an answer.

According to the charts, she could marry Gideon and keep her father's good opinion of her only through one path. They had to elope. She could not see how that could possibly make her father agree to the marriage, but when she had changed variables around in the equations, looking for a clear path, only one had fit.

Not just any elopement. Oh, no. They had one chance and one chance only. According to the star charts, she must elope with Gideon at 11:43 on the night of Thursday, the fifth of July. Even varying a minute caused the outcome to change. What was maddening about this equation was that it told her when to elope, but it did not tell her what would happen to change her father's mind, only that it would change.

Hannah sighed again, and shadows bobbed around the room. She put her head on her hands and massaged her scalp to make it stop aching. How she wished she could consult with Father about the calculations. It was not an option.

So, she drew out a fresh sheet of paper and began drafting the equation again, checking her math for the fourth time.

• • •

Hannah walked down the street with her father, on their way home from visiting one of his clients. She stopped in front of a window to admire the bonnet inside. "Have we a moment?"

"Hm?" Papa turned and frowned at the window. "Do you not already have one like that?"

"Do not be silly. I have a steel-blue one which goes with my blue dress with the cut steel beads. This one is dove gray, and would be perfect with my spotted silk." She pouted, hoping that she was not overdoing the girlishness. "I will need new gloves to go with it, but it would be just the thing to wear to Lady Richardson's tea."

"I quite like your green dress. And the bonnet with the little white flowers."

"That one? It must be redone before I can wear it again. It still has a pelerine, and those have been out of favor for four seasons at least. Really, Papa . . . if you want to present me at court this year, I must have the right clothes to be truly 'Out.'" She tilted her head to the side with a look that she had practiced in the mirror. "Please may I go in? Look–Hatchard's Books is just across the street. You can browse and wait for me there."

He hesitated and looked around them. "Well . . ."

Hannah put on a look of hurt. "You can see the door from there. If you are afraid I will run away . . ."

"No, no." Though it was clear that was exactly what he had been thinking. He had not let Hannah leave the house without him for the past several weeks. "Of course I am not worried about that. I was just wondering if I should not come in to pay for your bonnet."

Hannah laughed at that, and it was a genuine laugh. "Papa, I have had a line of credit with Cunningham's haberdashery for the past three seasons. Do you not pay attention to the bills when they come in?"

"Oh! This store. Yes. Well. Yes . . . I shall be just across the way, then. If you are sure you do not need me." He waited, though, until she actually went into the store.

The shop bell tinkled to announce her, and Mrs. Cunningham looked up from behind the counter. "Good afternoon, miss. What might I do for you today?"

"I wonder if might see the dove-gray bonnet in the window." Hannah glanced across the street as the milliner fetched the bonnet. Her father stood inside the bookstore, staring across at her. She pulled her attention back to the room and tried not to fret about his distrust.

Certainly, what she was about to do was not trustworthy.

Mrs. Cunningham brought her the bonnet and Hannah pulled her own off, setting it on the counter. She tried the new one on. It was charming, and exactly what she could wish for. "Perfection, as always. Have you gloves to match?" She took the hat off and turned it over, admiring the construction. It really was exquisitely made.

"I do. Just in from Milan. Quite lovely." She set a hatbox on the counter. "And what length and size for the gloves?" The shopkeeper opened a drawer in one of the cabinets ranging below the display shelves.

"Elbow-length. Six and a half." Hannah pulled out an envelope addressed to Gideon from her handbag while the shopkeeper rummaged through the drawers. She tucked it inside the hatbox, setting the hat atop it. "Could I trouble you to deliver this and the gloves for me?"

"Of course." The shopkeeper straightened with a pair of gloves that exactly matched the hat. "Just write out your direction and I will have them sent along promptly."

Hannah took the slip of paper the shopkeeper gave her and carefully wrote out Gideon's address.

• • •

Hannah sat in the parlor downstairs, sewing on yet another cushion cover for what would eventually be a full set for the dining room. She had completed five of them so far, as the sort of thing young ladies of quality were supposed to do. Well, no. Other young ladies did needle-painting for the walls, but she could not stand to make things of little use and no beauty. This way, at least, no one would spend any great time looking at her handiwork. She was creating a full set of the zodiac for the cushions. She had Pisces underway now.

Gideon was a Pisces. Hannah sewed the star sign's thigh with as much outward calm as she could muster. Had he gotten her message?

Her father sat at a table across the room with Lady Richardson, who had come for a consultation and stayed for tea. The woman's pug nosed around the room, snorting as it smelled every corner. If it chewed on her father's slippers again, Hannah would have to . . . do nothing except smile and laugh along with her father's client.

Robertson entered the room with a package held in front of him. "Miss Miller? This has just arrived for you."

Hannah forced herself to set her needlework down calmly. "Thank you, Robertson. I will just take it upstairs."

Her father looked over, frowning. "What is it, my dear?"

"My new hat, Papa." She wrinkled her nose and smiled as she took the box from their butler. "You know how girls are when they get new clothes. I must go try it with my dress immediately."

Lady Richardson raised her quizzing glass and turned, chin quivering. "A new bonnet? Oh, I must see. Stay and model it for us."

Her father spoke before Hannah could demur. "Yes, yes. I want to see it on." He turned to Lady Richardson "This stopped her in the street this morning. Absolutely stopped her. She is growing up, my little girl." His mouth compressed for a moment, as if remembering how much she was growing up.

"Oh . . . Well. My hair is not right for this." She had no idea what would be in the box when she opened it. She hoped that Gideon had sent a letter, but even that might be too easily discerned.

"Nonsense, my dear." Lady Richardson waved a gloved hand. "Let us see this famous bonnet."

"Of course." Hannah set the box on a marble side table and tried to block it with her body without appearing obvious. She undid the strings tying the brown paper around the box and caught her breath. The shopkeeper had written Gideon's address on the lid. Carefully, she tilted it away from her so that it did not show and set it top-down on the table. She peeked into the box, removing the mass of tissue paper surrounding the hat. At any moment, she expected an envelope to drop to the floor and reveal her subterfuge.

In the box was only a hat. Frowning, Hannah pulled it out and turned it over. Nothing had been tucked into the lining. The only thing below it was the pair of gloves. She could not restrain a sigh.

"I hear a sigh of delight, Miss Miller. Let us see, my dear, let us see."

Hannah lifted the hat to her head, and tried to compose herself. She turned around, still tying the bonnet strings under her chin. "Well?"

"Oh! So becoming. Come here, Pug, see what a nice bonnet this is. What a nice bonnet."

Hannah's father beamed at her. "It is very becoming indeed. You are as pretty as a picture."

"Thank you, Papa–"

Claws scrabbled on marble behind her. Lady Richardson shrieked. "Pug! No. Bad dog. Very bad dog."

Hannah spun, the bonnet falling backward off her head. The horrid little dog had gotten onto the table and was worrying the tissue paper. His hind leg kicked the box lid, sending it spinning. Hannah dashed for it. She could not let her father see the address. He would recognize it, even without Gideon's name. The little dog continued to push and worry at the papers. It tipped the box over, barking now as Lady Richardson hurried toward it.

"Oh, Pug. No. No!"

The dog jumped down with Hannah's gloves in its mouth. The room dissolved as Lady Richardson and Hannah's father gave chase to the little beast. Hannah took a moment to toss the box lid into the fire and joined them.

The little dog scampered under the chairs. It ran around tables. It bounded across the sofa. Stopping only occasionally, the pug would shake the gloves viciously. Hannah ran after it but it scurried to take refuge under the cherry coffee table. Her father got down on his hands and knees to chase the beast. Lady Richardson stood in the middle of the room calling her dog, as though it would listen to her.

"Pug. Come here. This instant." She clapped her hands. "He does like his little games."

Hannah circled around the table and crouched, her mass of skirts billowing out on either side to make a barrier the dog could not pass. As it tried to dart away from her father, it ran headlong into the wall of silk. Hannah snatched for it, but the little dog backed away and all she caught were the gloves.

Her eyes widened as she felt paper crinkle inside the gloves. Gideon's letter? Delighted to have a new game, the pug hung on to them ferociously, growling as though it were a much larger dog. Hannah was in no way willing to let the little dog have the gloves or the paper they contained.

"Oh, tug! Pug loves tug." Lady Richardson shook her finger at the dog. "Gloves are not for playing, young man. You let go of them at once."

The dog paid no attention to his mistress. It also paid no attention to Sir Phillip approaching from behind. Grabbing the little dog around the waist, Hannah's father secured it. Startled, the beast yelped, dropping the gloves so suddenly that Hannah fell over backward. Something crunched under her back as she landed.

The little dog began to howl, yelping as though it were being slaughtered. For a moment, she thought she had landed on the dog, but it was safely in her father's arms.

Lady Richardson cried out and hurried across the room, finally moving with anything resembling urgency to lift her dog from Sir Phillip's arms. "Oh, poor Pugsy-wugsy. Has you hurted yourself? Poor thing. Poor, poor thing."

Hannah gritted her teeth as the dog continued to whine. She rolled to her knees, trying to get her hoops and petticoat arranged around her. Sir Phillip appeared by her side to offer his hand. Hannah gratefully placed her hand in his, using the one that held the gloves to manage her skirts as she stood. She caught her heel on a fold of fabric, halting her for a moment while she shifted her weight to free the trapped silk.

"Your hat. I am sorry my dear. It looks as if it has suffered quite a casualty." Her father undid the ribbons that still held it at her neck and pulled the poor crushed bonnet from where it had lain on her back.

"I shall buy you a new one. Naughty Pug." Lady Richardson nuzzled the little dog, who responded by licking her nose. "And gloves too, those look quite the worse for wear. What a naughty boy, yes you are. Are you a naughty boy?"

"My lady is very kind." Biting her lips, Hannah took the crushed bonnet from her father and carried it and the gloves across the room to the hatbox. "I am going upstairs to freshen up a little, Papa."

"Of course, my dear. I will send Robertson up with your tea."

With her thanks, Hannah made her escape and barely restrained herself from running up the stairs to her room. In the safety of that chamber, she dropped the mangled hat and its box on her bed. Hands shaking, she went to the window to pull the letter out of the gloves. The moment it was free, she recognized Gideon's handwriting and a wave of relief and joy washed over her. Until she unfolded it and saw that fully a quarter of it had been obscured by the drool of Pug.

All along the side of the page, the words had blended into a mass of ink, leaving her to puzzle out sentences which missed their beginnings:

> . . . you, is a very alarming notion, which I can only ascribe to . . . have missed you more than I can describe. The plan you propose sounds . . . do not think we should attempt it, and yet, it is hard to see our way clear without . . . patient, my love. I shall think of you and we will not be long

She wanted to scream with vexation. Resting her head against the glass, Hannah stared out at the street and watched the pedestrians and carriages pass below. Vendors went down the street carrying blocks of ice. A man with a cow stopped when a housewife stepped out her door to wave him over. He set down his stool and milked the animal. A matron led a string of schoolchildren all in their dark blue uniforms on the other side, heading to the park. She stared, wishing to see Gideon.

Hannah took a slow breath, pressing her ribs against the confines of her corset. The specifics of his letter did not matter, ultimately. She knew what she must do, and she would leave her home at 11:43 on the 5th. It was the only course.

• • •

Hannah sat in her bedroom with her bag packed. A single candle burned on her nightstand. She held her watch in her right hand, the chain looped about her neck, and stared at it as the minutes ticked past. In four minutes she would go downstairs.

If she shielded her eyes from the candle, she could just see a slice of sky. If she leaned out the window, she could just see Mercury edging retrograde into Leo. Papa would have a clearer view from his rooftop observatory and with such fine, cloudless weather he would stay out all night. Any other night, she would join him as he studied the heavens for the astrological promises they held, but her own quicksilver youth waited for her on the street below. Tonight she was thankful that her father was on the roof performing some observations, and would not hear her when she left. She listened, nonetheless, to the creaks of the house as it settled for the night. The letter to her father lay on the pillow, waiting to tell him where she had gone.

A carriage rolled past, steel wheels rattling against the pavement. The horse stopped in front of the house. Hannah hurried to the window and looked out, clenching the pocket watch. Had Gideon arrived?

A dark carriage stood in front of her door. She looked at the watch again. Two minutes longer. She could go down now–No. No, she knew that Mercury retrograde inspired rash decisions, so she must guard against that. She could wait two minutes.

The seconds ticked past more slowly than she could imagine.

One minute. Hannah picked up her bag with one hand. She had packed only two dresses, and would send for the rest once they were away. If this worked. Please, God, this must work.

Finally, the minute had ticked into 11:43. Hannah let the watch drop on its chain and eased her bedroom door open. She picked up the candle and slipped into the hall. Setting her bag down, Hannah pulled the door shut behind her, wincing when the latch shot home. It seemed as though a gun had gone off in the quiet of the house.

Carefully, she picked up her bag and snuck down the stairs. She had spent the past week learning where the floor creaked and avoided those spots. Her dress hushed along the carpet. Hannah had worn a wool dress, too heavy for the season, but quieter than silk or cotton.

She reached the bottom floor and tiptoed across the marble entry, trying to keep her heels from making any noise on the floor. At the door, she blew out the candle and set it by the front.

Hannah shot back the lock, wincing as the small sound magnified into an echo up the stairwell. She opened the door and stepped out.

The carriage door opened and Gideon climbed out to meet her. "Dearest . . ."

She ran to him. "I was afraid you would not come."

"I have . . ." He wiped a tear from her face, and Hannah was surprised to find that she was weeping. "And now you must go back inside."

"What? No–no, we have to elope, now. Tonight. It will not work any other night." She tried to push past him to the carriage.

Gideon stopped her, his strong hands on her shoulders. "If I cannot approach your father like an honorable man, what makes you think he will ever accept me?"

"The stars–"

"Are bright points in the sky." Her father stepped out from a shadow next to the stairs.

Hannah stumbled back, heart pounding. "Papa. Gideon, we must go."

"No, no, dearest." Gideon captured her hand. "I will not–not like this."

"Come inside, both of you." Sir Phillip turned and opened the door to the house. He held it while Gideon led Hannah, protesting, back inside. Her father lit the candle by the door and gestured to a chair. "May I ask you to wait here while I speak to my daughter?"

"Of course, sir." Gideon offered him a bow and sank into the chair, setting his hat upon his knee.

Stunned, Hannah followed her father into the drawing room, standing in the middle of the room as he lit the candles on the mantel. She still clutched the carpet bag. All she had to do was turn and run back out of the room to Gideon's arms. She held still. Tonight was for rash decisions. She must think. She must act rationally. But how had her father come to be outside? In his silence, she heard accusations of foolishness and dishonor. She sank into the chair. He was right. How could she have thought to run away with a man without her father's blessing? She had placed more faith in the charts than in her father.

Her father settled into a chair by the fire, and mopped his brow with a handkerchief. Hannah saw his hands tremble. She dared a glance at his face. Above his beard, his face was drawn and tight. He flinched at her gaze. "How have I failed you?"

Her heart froze. "Papa?" She had not foreseen this.

"I must have failed you."

"You will not let me marry Gideon."

"Have either of you asked? No. I found you alone, with him disrobed. What was I to think?" He scowled and wadded the handkerchief into a ball. The candles stood behind him, casting his face into shadow.

"You might have listened to me when I tried to explain."

He sighed. "I thought you were being taken advantage of but . . . but then your Mr. Whitaker wrote to me today."

"He–What?"

"He wrote to tell me that you wanted to elope tonight. With Mercury in retrograde–in Leo, of all places!" He rose and turned away from her as if trying to contain himself. "You know that a night such as this invites rash decisions, and yet you followed one. Why else, if I have not failed to teach you?"

"But, Papa, I planned it weeks ago, before the retrograde motion." Her voice dwindled as she realized what she was confessing. Hannah wrapped her arms around herself to hold back the sudden nausea in her gut. "That makes it all right, doesn't it? I–we love each other, and–it was my idea. I promise you."

"So I surmised from Mr. Whitaker's letter, though he was very gracious in not blaming you at any point." Sir Phillip pinched the bridge of his nose. "I hardly know what to think, here. My daughter . . . my daughter has planned an elopement. Why?" Her father turned back to her. "Why didn't you want to wait? Why didn't you want my blessing? What did the stars tell you?"

Hannah dropped her head. "All of the charts said you would say no. All of the charts had said 'no,' save the one I used to plan tonight." She held her breath, waiting for his answer.

"My dear . . ." His voice broke. He crossed the room and knelt in front of her. "And you truly love him?

"I do, Papa." Hannah kept her head down, not able to bear to look at him. She smoothed the folds of her skirt over and over, trying to find order in the wool fabric. "I know it was wrong of me to not tell you, but at first I was not certain and then, because I was, I wanted–I had this dream of how we would tell you and then . . . and then I was foolish and everything went wrong."

"Eloping? You cannot think that would repair it." He sighed, sinking back onto his knees with a groan. "But I will grant that I did not realize how much Mr. Whitaker meant to you or you to him, until he wrote. I thought it was a childish infatuation."

She shook her head, unable to speak.

"Well . . . well." Her father handed her his pocket handkerchief. "Here. Wipe your eyes."

Hannah took it and pressed the cloth to her cheeks. One corner bore the initials she had embroidered for him Christmas last. For some reason, that made her weep in earnest. "The way you talked about him–his heritage . . . I did not–I was not going to run away forever, Papa. The stars–"

"Hush now, let us have no more talk of the stars. Or if we do . . . why not? He has shown himself to be a man of integrity. Tonight is a night for rash decisions." He pushed himself to his feet and strode to the drawing-room door, flinging it open. "Mr. Whitaker, will you join us?"

A rustle of cloth, and then Gideon stood in the door. "Sir?"

"My daughter says that she loves you. And you her, I understand."

Hannah half rose from her chair, gripping the arm for support.

"Yes, sir." He turned his hat in his hands. "Yes sir, I do."

"And you wish to marry her?"

Gideon looked past Sir Phillip, meeting Hannah's gaze. She trembled at his smile. "Very much so."

"Then sir, you have my permission to address my daughter." Sir Phillip stepped to the side, tucking his hands behind his back.

After only a moment of hesitation, Gideon came across the room. Hannah met him, hands outstretched. He took them with his large, capable fingers. With a breathless laugh, he got down on one knee. "Miss Miller, would you do me the honor of being my wife?"

"Oh, yes." Not caring that her father was in the room, Hannah bent to kiss her quicksilver youth, and blessed the stars for allowing her father to make a rash decision.

False Colors

MARIE BRENNAN

The skies were clear and the winds fair for Plymouth, the *Hesperides* flying before them like a swan, her wings unfurled from the yardarms and bellying out full. On deck, the gusts were strong enough to flick sailors' tarred tails of hair forward over their shoulders; higher in the rigging, they were strong enough to knock my shoulders forward and test the set of my feet on the rope beneath. I grinned into the afternoon sky, momentarily letting the wind carry my concerns from me, away into the distance, as if to drown them in the deep.

I loved these moments aloft. The mast swayed in great arcs with the pitch and roll of the ship below, which had alarmed me greatly in my midshipman days. Now I found it exhilarating. And it was one of the few places aboard a frigate where one could feel truly alone.

Nearly three hundred men on the *Hesperides*, packed in cheek by jowl, and a trifle bloodied by our work at Algeciras two weeks before. But good spirits prevailed: our squadron had sunk two Spanish vessels and captured a French seventy-four, with scarcely more than a dozen killed on our side. It was remarkable how rapidly a decent victory could improve morale.

A decent victory, and the prospect of shore leave ahead. Our harbor was approaching, visible on the horizon without need for the spyglass thrust into my breeches. Duty called, as it always did. I called down to the deck in a strong bellow, then gripped the backstay in my calloused hands, piked my body upward to wrap my legs over, and slid down the thick rope with practiced ease.

Perkins was waiting for me below, hat in hand. I accepted my cover from the midshipman with a nod and, settling it upon my head, made my way aft through the routine bustle of sailors and ropes, all the bones and sinews and blood that kept the ship in flight across the waves. The *Hesperides* was more battered than her men; a thirty-two-gun frigate had no business in a battle between ships of the line. But broken yardarms, splintered deck planks, shattered rails—those could all be repaired, and would be. Leave would give us time to rest, and everyone was eager to get to it.

Except the lieutenants of the *Hesperides*, who faced a different fate. I found Harry brooding on what remained of the taffrail, broad shoulders hunched inside his coat, sea-colored eyes slitted against the force of the wind. "Plymouth in sight," I said, as if he might not have noticed, and got only a grunt in response. "It's only a party, Harry."

It gained me a half smile. "I thought you hated parties."

I did. They were invariably attended by mothers with unmarried daughters, who saw a promising young lieutenant as a reasonably likely prospect. Dedicated rakes might enjoy that game, but as Britain's least eligible bachelor, I found it nothing short of torture. Still—"It's good to get off the ship once in a while."

"Never long enough to see your sister, though. Does it bother you?"

"I wish Victoria's health were good enough to allow her to come south," I said. "But the mail packet should bring another letter, which is always good." It meant my arrangements were still holding.

"No Almack's for her," Harry said, his gaze still fixed outward. "No society at all, for an invalid. It must be hard."

I found it odd that he should say so. Neither of us had ever been to Almack's–though one heard the tales, even out at sea. Did he miss the elegance of that life?

For my own part, I did not. This was what I loved best: sails and rigging, rudder and hull, the salt spray peeling at my face. Life on land would be safer, for sure–I never yet heard of a dancer at Almack's losing a hand or leg to someone's misstep–but with less of glory in it, and less *purpose.*

I did not voice these thoughts to Harry. There was no need: he and I were joined in our love for the sea and the service that commanded our loyalty. He was my dearest companion in all the world, and I, if I did not miss my guess, was his. We had been friends since my first day as a midshipman, and had hardly been separated since, excepting my brief and ill-fated assignment to the *Persephone.* We understood each other even without words.

Usually. Yet I had no idea what troubled him today.

From behind us came a familiar, hated voice. "Looking ahead to the whores? There will be none for us. Fine ladies instead, much good may it do."

If I had little need to share my thoughts with Harry, I had even less desire to do so with Byrom. But did not like having him at my back, and so turned to face *Hesperides'* second lieutenant. "You'd prefer Plymouth's pox-ridden women? Myself, I'd sooner lick the sores of a leper–it would be safer for my health."

A faint, supercilious smile often lurked about Byrom's mouth; now it grew nastier. "Indeed. Perhaps your preferences lie elsewhere, Ravenswood."

My back went rigid. For words like that, I could call him out, and any man alive would call it justice. But if I did . . .

Byrom knew his hold over me, and missed no opportunity to exert it.

Rage boiled in my veins, less for the present insult–merely the newest in a long series–and more for the despicable position into which I had fallen. The thought had even entered my head, during the battle, whether it might not be worth the cost to shoot Byrom where he stood. Him, and then myself: I almost believed I had rather endure hell's punishment for a suicide than the ordeal I suffered now. Though if the devil had any sense of irony, my punishment would be exactly what I sought to escape.

I received the bosuns' yells with gratitude, for they broke me from my black and murderous thoughts, summoning me to my work. Without speaking, I pushed past Byrom and went to do my duty.

Harry followed me down to the ship's waist. In a voice I hoped was not clear to the men's ears, he said, "Honestly, Simon–no one could fault you if you called him out."

"Granger doesn't like his officers to duel," I said, pausing to let some of the men swing up onto the ratlines, heading aloft to reef sail.

"But he's given you no command against it."

"That's a lawyer's argument, Harry, and unlike you."

He winced, and I regretted the barb. But the anger in his tone wasn't directed at me. "*I* should like to see you call him out."

If only I could. But Byrom would never accept the challenge.

"The Navy's golden boy? Lowry wouldn't like it if I damaged his future lieutenant." Much less killed him, as he deserved. The rage flared up again.

"They intend him for promotion, obviously," Harry agreed. "Lowry takes prizes aplenty, and gives their command to his officers; the Admiralty rarely revokes the promotions. They say the *Inimitable* may be the finest ship our yards have turned out. Lowry will be in a hurry to test that."

Which meant Byrom might be a commander within a year, and a post-captain soon after. I wondered if God had placed me in this position as punishment for my sin. But why wait so long to inflict it? And why punish innocents along with me?

Determined to turn my thoughts from their course, I bent to the task of bringing the ship into port. "Never mind Byrom. Let's go to meet our doom."

• • •

Our doom consisted of genteel music, finely dressed gentlemen and ladies . . . and one face whose unexpected presence struck me with the force of a musket ball.

Lady Katherine Deverell stood beside her husband in elegant lace, her hair coiffed in the latest fashion, greeting her guests with a smile and the graceful extension of one gloved hand. All that gentility was as good as a disguise, compared with the hoyden she had been, years before; and yet I should have recognized Kate Lyon were she painted like a harlequin.

Her eyes fixed on me even before Captain Granger finished his introductions. There was no way she could fail to remember the name of Simon Ravenswood; it had not been so many years as that. But how much did she guess?

"You seem to know the gentleman," Lord Deverell said, noticing Kate's interest–as any man might who has fifteen years on his pretty young wife and knows it.

I spoke before she could. "The lady and I were acquainted in childhood," I said, my tone cordial but distant, to lay her husband's fears to rest. "Before she went to Italy. She was good friends for a time with my sister Victoria. We have not seen each other in many years."

Kate's eyes narrowed. But she could hardly say anything, not there in front of everyone, and I felt mixed relief and regret as we made polite small talk and then moved away so that she and her husband could greet their other guests. Either, I supposed, would be short-lived; I could hardly avoid her for the entire night. Whether I wanted to or not . . . that question, I could not answer.

Nor did I have time to consider it. Before long, I had another matter to distract me.

I had met Harry's family before, and greeted Mrs. Wycliffe and her daughter with a smile and a well-practiced bow over their hands. The third lady with them, however, was unknown to me. "Lieutenant Ravenswood, may I present Miss Charlotte Fanning?" Mrs. Wycliffe said, ushering the girl forward. She beamed fondly at Miss Fanning. "Harry's fiancée."

Despite my self-control, I stuttered visibly in my bow. Fortunately, the angle concealed my expression from the ladies–I could only hope Harry himself had not been watching. By the time I straightened, my look was one of pleased surprise. "Harry said nothing to me of an engagement!"

It was not the best response. Miss Fanning smiled awkwardly; no young lady would like to hear that her husband-to-be has kept her a secret. But Mrs. Wycliffe gave her son an indulgent pat on the arm. "He is dreadfully superstitious. I cannot deny that the life of a naval lieutenant is a dangerous one, and difficult for his family; I'm sure your own sister feels the absence keenly, Lieutenant Ravenswood. But it's nonsense to think that speaking of good news will bring ill fortune in return."

Superstitious? No more than any sailor. Why had Harry not said anything of this to me? We might leave a great many things unspoken, knowing the other would fill in what had not been said, but this was close-mouthed even for him. I was not some dockside fortuneteller, to ferret out secrets I had not been told.

He would not meet my gaze, either, when I glanced at him. Well, he could hardly offer an explanation here, in front of the others. But I would have to press him for one later.

I realized by the faltering smiles of the ladies that I had let myself fall into too long of a silence. To Miss Fanning, I said, "My felicitations to you both. If Harry is half so attentive to his duties in marriage as he is in the Navy, you will be well situated indeed."

Even as I said the words, I winced inwardly; that was not the most graceful compliment I had ever offered. It seemed I was doomed to spend my evening shifting from one awkwardness to another.

I should have trusted that thought. It would not have saved me, but it would at least have prevented me from feeling such misplaced relief when Granger drew me away. "There is someone you should meet," the captain said, leading me across the room. His next words put a leaden weight in my stomach. "You and Byrom both."

He collected the second lieutenant and guided us to another group of women, four in number. One older, and three younger; they looked familiar, though I had not met them before. As soon as Granger introduced them, I understood why. It took no dissembling at all to show the pain I felt as I said, "Ma'am, my sincere condolences on the loss of your son."

Mrs. Warrington gave my hand the tiniest squeeze as I released hers. "I'm glad to make your acquaintance at last, Lieutenant Ravenswood. Percy wrote often of you in his letters. He considered you his greatest friend aboard the *Persephone*."

He had his eyes from his mother, I saw, a warm and trusting brown. All his sisters shared them, too. To face his family en masse, with Byrom standing rigid at my side . . . I wondered what Percy Warrington had written of *him*.

Byrom was too canny to show that side of himself so publicly, though. With smooth courtesy, he said, "It was an honor to serve with your son, Mrs. Warrington. One of many fine men lost that day."

His platitude made me grit my teeth. These ladies deserved better than such empty words. "I don't know if you were aware, ma'am," I said, "but Captain Monmouth intended that he should stand for lieutenant at the next opportunity. I have no doubt he would have passed."

The possibility of tears glimmered at the corners of her eyes, but she held her sorrow in. "Thank you, Lieutenant Ravenswood; it is very kind of you to say so. We desired nothing more than that he should serve with valor."

Nothing more than that he should serve, and return home safely. I tried to block out the memory of his face, and failed.

The eldest Miss Warrington twisted her fan in her fingers and said hesitantly, "If–if I may–"

You may not, I wanted to say, for I could read in her expression the words that were coming. And would have rather faced a French broadside, armed with nothing but a knife.

"Could we beg you to tell us what happened? To the *Persephone*, I mean."

My gut clenched. "The account of it was published in the *Gazette*."

An account I knew by heart, for it was a digest of my own words to the Admiralty. I kept a copy next to my heart, the paper much battered with folding, and even now it seemed to burn a hole through my ribs. The mother laid one hand on her daughter's arm–not to quell her, but to take up her cause. "The *Gazette* says so little, though, only the barest outline–"

"That is a kindness to the families," I said, my fingers curling tight. "The details are not something ladies should hear."

"Please, Lieutenant," she said with quiet dignity. "He was my only son. No insult intended to Lieutenant Byrom, whose conduct was so gallant–but you were such a friend to Percy; I had rather hear it from you."

I had no need of suicide to place me in hell. I was there already. But worse than this would be to allow the unsuspecting Mrs. Warrington to hear the tale from *him*.

Byrom stood at my side, a grenade ready to go off if I made the slightest error.

Fixing my gaze in the distance, and hoping they would credit the tension in my voice to the unpleasantness of the memory, I opened my mouth and lied.

• • •

I fled as soon as I could afterward, out of that elegant hall where I did not belong in the slightest. How I found my way to the gardens, I could not say, for no one had shown me the path, but the next thing I was aware of was the fresh evening air. It cleared my head, though my stomach still roiled with sick shame and fury.

Oh God, the lies stuck in my throat, clawing it bloody. I had thought myself at my deepest nadir when I stood before an Admiralty board and gave my word of honor that the demise of the *Persephone* had gone as I said, leaving myself and the heroic Lieutenant Byrom as its only survivors. But that was nothing, *nothing* compared to this: lying to the face of a grieving mother.

Cold comfort that Percy had behaved with every bit of valor and honor I imputed. Far more than *I* showed now. And yet, what other choice did I have?

None. Byrom had me trapped, as effectively as if he held a pistol to my head. He could make me crawl, make me relinquish the name of gentleman—everything I had built up for myself, he could and did strip away from me, leaving me a despicable, dishonorable *thing*.

"Victoria!"

The name, hissed just over the rush of the breeze, snapped me back to alertness like a gunshot. Someone else had come into the gardens.

I had not survived so long in the Navy, however, without developing strong nerves. I startled, but no more than anyone might upon being surprised, and turned where I stood on the path, boots crunching in the gravel. As if I did not know who I would see.

Kate hurried to join me, tugging her pelisse up to cover her bare arms. "Don't worry," she said as she drew near. "No one else is out here. I am not such a fool as to say anything where another might hear. Oh, Victoria, it *is* you!"

My heart skipped a beat every time she said the name—a name I had scarcely heard in ages, scarcely even dared *think*, lest thought lead to action, and action betray. If Byrom's gaze threatened my carefully constructed facade, Kate's voice stripped it away, revealing the truth that lay behind: not Simon Ravenswood, but Victoria.

Kate's eyes danced in merriment as she halted before me. "I couldn't believe it when I saw you, that you would have the cheek to show up in such a fashion–oh, you must tell me what is going on! Where is Simon?"

There was no possibility of lying. Kate would never believe me if I pretended she was mistaken, and would be insulted if I tried. My mouth was as dry as bone. I heard my own voice as if it were a stranger's: habitually at the lower edge of my range, low enough to pass for a man's light tenor. "Dead."

The merriment in her eyes staggered, faded, died. "What? But why haven't you–" Understanding dawned, as she remembered why my twin had entered the Navy to begin with. "The inheritance."

I nodded.

"But Victoria, to pretend to be Simon–I know we played at it when we were young, masquerading as boys, but he's a lieutenant; they will catch you out–" Again the flow of words stuttered to a halt. Her lips parted in amazement, or perhaps horror, as she realized her own error. "How–how long have you been doing this?"

The number startled even me, when I spoke it. "Six years. He died during his first leave."

I saw her look at me again, this time seeing not Victoria, but Lieutenant Ravenswood. My weathered skin, my sinewy hands, my hair in its rough tail, the dark strands glinting reddish-brown where the sun and wind had bleached them. The heavy wool of the coat hid the rest: the scars of battle, the whipcord strength where feminine softness should have been. I made a spare man, but so would my twin have done. Taking after our father as we did, I had little that needed concealing.

"Heavens, Victoria," Kate whispered, staring frankly. "How have you *done* it?"

Wryness twisted my mouth into an unfamiliar smile. "With difficulty."

She covered a giggle with her hand, and waved for me to go on.

The wind tugged strands of hair into my face. "It's possible to get privacy on board a ship, though far from easy. And you can even piss standing up, if you know the trick–" I broke off, wincing. "I'm sorry."

"Not at all," Kate managed, despite her ladylike blanch. "Though now I *do* believe you've been six years in the Navy."

I looked away in embarrassment. No need to tell her the other graphic details. I was fortunate that my nature, or perhaps the physical strain of my life, made my blood come rarely. "Officers rarely strip down, not like the men. And I have done my d–my best to avoid any error that might lead to corporal punishment. They would know me quickly enough, if I removed my shirt."

"But to attempt such a masquerade in the first place . . ." She wrapped her pelisse more tightly.

"I panicked," I admitted, barely loud enough to hear. "Without Simon, I had nothing. No future, nor any hope of one. Our uncle's terms were quite clear: we received our stipends only so long as Simon was in the Navy, and the rest of the money would come only when he made post. Absurd, to think I could take his place–and yet it was the only thing I could think of."

Kate sank down onto a bench, still dazed. "Hannah Snell did it; why not you? Though she was a Marine, which I suppose is different. And a woman grown, not a twelve-year-old child." She shuddered, likely at the thought of my youth. "However did you manage?"

"What choice did I have? When I came back I told them I had fallen from my horse and struck my head; it can damage the memory. I had bought those books before Simon went away, to learn what he would be doing–"

"Sailing manuals," Kate said, nodding. "I remember."

Manuals I had studied obsessively–far more obsessively than my twin did. "I knew names from his letters, and put them to faces when I reported back; it was enough–though hard going at first."

"And so you've been trapped all this time," she murmured, touching my wrist in sympathy.

"Trapped?" The word felt odd on my tongue. "I suppose that, in the early days, I saw it that way. I made a rash decision, and had no way out of it; I could not desert, they would not release me from the service, and to admit the truth would be worse than continuing to lie. Had it not been for Harry–Lieutenant Wycliffe–I don't know if I could have endured it."

Her gaze sharpened at the name. "Does he know?"

I shook my head, perhaps a touch too vehemently. "He is my dearest friend, but no. I could never tell him."

Kate raised one eyebrow, as if she heard something in my tone. I was not about to admit, even to her, the incident that occurred–or rather, *nearly* occurred–the night I was made lieutenant. Harry and I had both been drunk, which was both cause and cover; I did not think he remembered how close we came to kissing.

She allowed the issue to rest, but her next question was nearly as awkward. "What will you do when you are made post? Will you stay? I imagine it would be easier for a captain to keep secrets."

It would. But I could not tell Kate the true answer: that I had no hope of success. Even if I escaped disgrace, there were hordes of lieutenants in the Navy, all competing for a far smaller number of commands. I lacked the political connections that could aid me, and without them, I might never get my step.

Movement caught my attention. We were no longer alone in the gardens; several figures had come out onto the terrace. What excuses Kate had made to follow me I did not know, but we could not go on like this, talking so privately. Her husband would begin to wonder, if he did not already. Feeling both relieved and reluctant, I said, "We should go."

Kate caught my sleeve as I stepped away. "Victoria–"

My face hardened. "You must not call me that."

"Simon, then–Lieutenant Ravenswood." Her lips quirked on the name, but only in passing. "Quickly–does *anyone* here know?"

I offered my arm again, and she took it smoothly, as if I were any gentleman. How much should I admit to? "Granger," I said under my breath.

"Your *captain*?"

"I was wounded–a shot to the thigh." All of this sotto voce, as we crossed toward the house. "I didn't witness the scene myself, being unconscious, but at that range the ship's surgeon could hardly miss the truth. He told Granger."

Kate pinked again. She didn't used to be this easily embarrassed; all that schooling in Italy had wrought changes. "What did he do?"

"Told the surgeon to dig the bloody thing out before I took an infection, and he would address the matter when I woke. By the time I did, Granger had decided to let me stay."

An oversimplification, but we were too close to the other guests for me to relate the rest of it. In actuality, Granger had listened to my story, while I quaked in my skin. Then he told me, in deceptively level tones, that I would be testing for lieutenant at the next opportunity. After I failed, he would have me out of the service on terms that would save him the awkwardness of explaining how a young woman had got past him all that time.

But I had not failed. And I wondered sometimes whether Granger had ever expected me to.

• • •

"You tell the tale so prettily," Byrom murmured in my ear a little later, knowing it would stick under my skin like a barb. I turned my back on him and walked away, but it did no good; I could feel the pressure of his satisfaction on me like a weight. With the Warringtons giving me tearful smiles whenever I passed, by the time Harry drew me aside, I was more than ready to play the bear.

"I'm sorry," he said, pacing the side parlor to which we had retired. "I should have told you long since. About Miss Fanning."

My answer came sharp. "No, I quite understand. It is a private matter, not to be shared with outsiders."

"Damn it, Simon!" He rounded on me, hands clenching. "That isn't it, and you know it. I cannot think of anyone less an outsider to me than you. We were sniveling middies together; you've been covered in my blood, and I in yours. We might as well be brothers."

Harry's words put a cramp in my gut. Talking with Kate had been a mistake; it made me Victoria in my own mind, twitching every time Harry called me Simon. And for him to call me *brother* . . .

What I wanted was impossible, and I knew it. Even before the arrival of the unfortunate Miss Fanning. But that did not stop me from wanting it.

The tightness in my throat made my voice come out dangerously high. "Then why not tell me? Our friendship–" I forced myself to say it. "Our *brotherhood* has rarely been a thing of words. We understand one another without them. But an engagement is a devil of a thing to leave unspoken."

Harry's shoulders sagged inside the heavy wool of his coat. "I . . . oh, hell. Mrs. Fanning is a dear friend of my mother's. They both wanted the match, and I thought . . . I don't know what I thought."

I damned the lightness that rose inside my chest. "Don't you wish to marry her?"

"It hardly matters, now," Harry said unhappily. "I've asked for her hand; I can hardly take that back."

No, he could not. No more than I could take back the rash decision that had put me on-board the *Hesperides.* Even though it meant Harry knew Victoria Ravenswood only as a fiction, a sickly sister living in rural penury. But would he have given her a second thought, had she never donned the mask I wore now?

We made our decisions, and then we lived with them. Both of us were too honorable to do otherwise. "I'm sure it will be all right. You're a good man, Harry, and I'm sure she's a good woman. There are worse foundations for a marriage."

"And better ones, too," he said, gazing downward in dejection. But it did not last: he straightened his shoulders, donning once more the martial bearing we had both learned to maintain, and we went back out to the party.

Where I caught Byrom's gaze, narrowed in suspicion that I had withdrawn with Harry. A hint of a leer bent his thin mouth, and had I been in range at that moment, I would have smashed it with my fist.

My fury, thwarted of its target, bent back upon myself. Had I not just been congratulating myself on how honorable Harry and I were? For him, it might be true, but never for myself. My eyes were drawn, as if by a magnet, to the Warrington sisters and their mother. I had lied to their faces. I had no honor left. I had allowed Byrom to strip it from me, out of cowardice and shame.

There is a kind of madness that takes a man–or a woman–when the call comes to leap from the deck of one ship to another, boarding for the chance of a prize. With Marines shooting from the tops and the cutlasses of the enemy waiting, a man must be mad to fling himself across that gap. And yet time and time again he does it, out of optimism or patriotism, for bloodlust or for a cause, but most often of all for one simple reason: he cannot bear the thought of seeming a coward before his friends and comrades. His honor requires him to charge into the teeth of his own destruction.

Sometimes he may hope to emerge unscathed. I had no such expectation. But with Harry promised to Miss Fanning, and Byrom about to be rewarded for his crimes, I found I could no longer bear the weight of my own dishonor. With the madness of battle boiling in my veins, I went in search of Captain Granger.

• • •

We two, at least, could speak in private without occasioning comment. We returned to the garden, not far from where I had walked with Kate; I found it easier to breathe in the free air.

This might be one of my last chances to enjoy it.

"I apologize for troubling you, sir," I said, locking my hands behind my back to keep them from trembling. "A party is neither the time nor place for a matter of this sort, but I fear I cannot, for my own conscience, keep silent any longer."

Granger grew still, as I had seen him do a thousand times before: a flicker sighted in fog, an unidentified mast on the horizon, that might yet prove dangerous. The last time he had directed such alert study toward me, I was a midshipman, unable yet to stand for the wound in my thigh, explaining to him why I had chosen to masquerade as my twin brother.

When a thing must be done, it is better to do it quickly. I had learned *that* lesson from our ship's surgeon. "The account I have given of Byrom's actions aboard the *Persephone* is false."

The rest of the words poured out of me as if I had rehearsed them: crisp and dispassionate, a lieutenant's report on an unsuccessful naval engagement. But this time, instead of the positioning of the ships and the set of the wind with respect to the nearby shore, I spoke of the incompetence and cowardice of the *Persephone*'s first lieutenant, the despicable Edmund Byrom. I could not lay the loss of the ship and her men entirely at his feet; we'd had a damnable run of bad luck, before and during the battle with the *Aigrette*. But from his actions as officer of the watch to his final, despicable flight, Byrom had disgraced himself and the service. And I would rather cut my own throat than allow him to hold command over men once more.

Granger kept silent through my recitation, not even asking for clarification on any point. When I finished, he stood facing the wind, jaw set in a hard line. I knew what he would say, and braced myself for it.

"You lied to the Admiralty. Why?"

My own failings were harder to voice. But I had begun; I must continue. "When we washed up on the Spanish shore . . . I lost consciousness. Byrom went through my clothing, looking for anything of value or use, and discovered my secret. When I woke, he presented his demands: I must help him to safety, and afterward must never speak a word of his errors. I must present him as a hero–say that he fought valiantly to save the *Persephone*, and was responsible for saving me. If I did not, he would expose me as a woman."

"And what makes you tell the truth now?"

I bent my head, unable to stand straight while I admitted it. "The Warrington family. Lying to them . . . I must write a letter, I think. With the true story. Nothing of what I said regarding Percy was false, but they deserve to know who should be blamed for his death."

"You think you will have the opportunity to write a letter." This voice, too, I had known before; Granger used it when his fury must be private, rather than bellowed to the world. The surgeon had cleared the infirmary and its surroundings before the captain came to see me, but I do not think anyone would have heard his words if they were standing on the other side of the curtain. They were intended for one set of ears only, and fell upon them like hammers. "I protected you, Ravenswood. And this is how you repay me."

My eyes closed, of their own accord; I forced them open again. "I am sorry, sir. Which means very little, and I know it. But the only compensation I can make is to ensure that Byrom is disgraced as he deserves, whatever the cost to myself."

He grunted. "Whatever the cost. I told you before that you could be hanged for what you have done; you would be dependent upon the leniency of the court, and their wish not to be seen as laughingstocks, for any lesser punishment. But now you have lied to an Admiralty board. They will execute you for that."

"Sir . . ." How could I put it into words? I could not; some parts of it, Granger should not hear anyway. He would not want to know the role Miss Fanning had played in sending me to this desperate end. But some parts, I could say. "If I did not speak, Byrom would have more chances to get men killed. Should I value my life above theirs?"

Granger exhaled sharply, not quite a snort. "A very noble sentiment. Do you actually mean it?"

My back went rigid. "Sir. Ever since I took my brother's place, I have striven at all times to serve His Majesty's Navy as the best officer I can be. The immutable fact of my sex has always undermined that; I am a woman, and I must lie about that fact, and both those things make me less than a gentleman. But I have done my utmost to behave as a gentleman in every other respect, to counterbalance those flaws by the perfect execution of my duties. Byrom took that from me: he provoked me into weakness and cowardly self-preservation. If making restitution for that failure costs me my life, then I will pay it gladly."

Granger met my gaze for a long, wordless time; then he let his breath out in a sigh and shook his head. "Damn it, Ravenswood. You're a better gentleman than most whose sex and birth gives them that name. When I sent you to test for lieutenant, I knew you were *capable* of passing; you knew your work better than some men whose political connections have made them captains. The question was whether you would try.

"It would have been easier had you failed. Whether the cause was deliberate choice or simple panic, I could have had you broken, and then you could have escaped with very little consequence. But you insisted on trying. Your brother was made midshipman, but *you* and no other made yourself a damned fine lieutenant." He sighed again, looking away from me. "Now it may have earned you a hanging."

His speech had produced such a muddle in me that I stood with my jaw loose. Granger had said to me at the time that I deserved the rank of lieutenant, but never had he spoken with such glowing praise. I had been prepared for his rage, even if he condemned me to execution. To receive an accolade instead left me staggering.

I could think of nothing to say. I expected hanging; I had no plans for avoiding it. Granger considered for several long minutes, then shook his head. "I don't see a solution, but that doesn't mean one can't be found. I received orders when we came into port: we leave again just as soon as we return to Plymouth. A short cruise only, perhaps two or three months. But to lose two of my three lieutenants now would be disastrous; it therefore follows that I must keep you both. By the time that is done, if no better answer has presented itself . . ." He sighed. "Then you will have to desert. And upon our return, I will make certain Byrom is condemned for what he has done."

From the standpoint of the greater good, it was success. Byrom would be kept away from any position that might allow him to lead others to their deaths, and I would escape with my life. But I would lose everything else I valued.

The service.

Harry.

Simon could hope to keep something of his friend, even after marriage. But with Simon gone, what could Victoria hope for? Charity might move Harry to correspond occasionally with his friend's invalid sister, but we could never meet. He would know me in an instant. And I could not bear to receive distant, cordial letters, when Harry had been closer to me than any save my own twin.

But my personal feelings did not signify. I had done what I must, and with that, I must be satisfied.

• • •

In the aftermath of my revelation to Granger, I wished at first that I might speak privately with Kate, without arousing her husband's suspicions. We had once been great friends, before her family shifted to Italy; together we had gotten ourselves into no end of trouble by dressing as boys–that being part of the reason it was thought better to school her in a foreign country–and surely, if I were to share my woes with anyone, it should be her.

But Kate was out of my reach. And besides, it was not to her that I wished to unburden myself.

I found Harry avoiding the dancing–and, I rather suspected, his fiancée. What a fine pair we made: both of us miserable, for no cause we could publicly admit. He took gratefully to my suggestion that we walk outside. I could not tell him what troubled me, but at least I might take comfort in his company.

"I owe you an apology," I said as we left the lights and laughter of the house behind. "For what I said before, regarding Miss Fanning."

Harry shook his head, hands locked behind his back as if we paced the quarterdeck. "No, you were right to chide me. Such dishonesty was not fair to you, or to her."

"Dishonesty!" The word burst from me, carried on something that was almost a laugh. "You didn't lie, Harry. You simply . . . *postponed* a truth." The brief ripple of merriment faded quickly. "No, I can hardly condemn you for that. Not when I have done so much worse."

The admission was not one I had intended to make. Harry paused on the graveled walk, turning curious surprise on me. "Whatever do you mean, Simon?"

I should never have begun on this topic; having started, I could not stop. No, it went back further than that. It became too late the moment I opened my mouth to Granger, and let the weight of Byrom's secret slip loose from where I had kept it stowed.

"I have lied to you, Harry. To everyone. I have no right to lecture anyone on matters of honesty."

The startled silence that followed would not last, I knew. I had said too much. Harry could not possibly let the matter rest, not after that.

His reply, however, took my breath away. "I'm sure you had good reason."

Another impulse to laugh, though I was not amused in the slightest. "Oh, no. I wish I could say it was so. But my reason is nothing more than a despicable urge to preserve my own skin." Bitterness laced the admission, even more than I had shown in front of Granger.

We walked on another few steps. Then Harry's shoulders went back, and he raised his chin. "I know you, Simon, and I know you to be an honorable man. That is enough. You needn't say anything more. Whatever matter drove you to lie, you'll find no condemnation from me."

Warmth and pain alike burned me within. I had not looked for forgiveness, and did not deserve it in the slightest; yet the fact that Harry gave it, unquestioning, made me feel—if only for the briefest of moments—that I had not, after all, lost everything I valued in the world.

If only he had not given that forgiveness to *Simon.* To an honorable *man.*

It should have been enough to shut my mouth. But my long stalemate with Byrom might as well have been a mist that was at long last clearing from my vision, and with it gone I could see clearly once more. My own well-being did not matter in the slightest, when weighed against the damage that man could do, if given more authority and scope for his flaws. My impending desertion might discredit me, and therefore allow Byrom to escape censure for what happened to the *Persephone*, but sooner or later he would err again. And if others were on guard for it, he might yet be stopped.

Yes. I'd had enough of lying. Whatever the cost to me, the time had come to tell the truth.

"Harry, I'm a woman."

That . . . was not what I had intended to say.

I stopped, a pace after Harry did. How was it that my knees continued to hold me? The habits of battle, I supposed, that kept my body strong even when my mind was boneless with fear. I could not bring myself to turn and see Harry's face. He said nothing, and the rest of the truth limped out of me, quieter and less passionate. "I'm not Simon. I'm Victoria."

A soft crunch of gravel from behind me, as if his weight had settled from the step he did not take. An exhalation of air, cut off, as if he began to say *How?* or something else to that effect, but could not finish the word.

I bowed my head. "Do you recall when you were all given leave, not long after Simon joined as a midshipman? He suffered a blow to his head when he fell while riding." My throat tightened, such that I had trouble going on. "The truth is that he died. The one who returned to the ship was not Simon, but me."

Six years. It would not take long for Harry to calculate the span for himself. He had known Simon, the *real* Simon, for a scant few months. The man he called friend was no man at all, but me.

Yet that friendship was real, and I owed it to him at least to meet his gaze. When I turned to face him, he shook his head, not blinking. "Why?"

"The inheritance," I said. Harry knew the situation well enough; he did not need it explained. Which was fortunate, as I could not have said more if I wanted to. Now, far too late, the enormity of what I had just done struck me. The captain had granted me one final cruise in which to plan my exit, but that was now impossible. I had managed, barely, to live with Byrom when he knew my secret; I could not do the same with Harry.

Which meant I would never return to the *Hesperides.*

Harry shook his head again. I'd seen men with similar expressions, after they suffered a blow to the head in battle. Dazed and uncomprehending. "Why tell me now?"

The unbinding of my true self let the anger loose, that I had tried to keep in check before Granger. With undisguised venom–both for Byrom and for myself–I related the truth of the *Persephone*'s demise, and the second lieutenant's subsequent blackmail. To this I added the admission that I had confessed to the captain, earlier that evening.

"And damn it all, it isn't *fair,*" I burst out, when I thought I was finished. "I may hope to block his promotion at the very least, and surely his own flaws will damn him in time. With my word against his, though, I have little hope of his removal from the Navy. Not if I am revealed, or forced to flee. And why should *he* stay, when I must go? I am a hundred times the lieutenant he is!"

Harry's expression had closed down during my explanation, hiding his reactions behind an impassive wall. He looked up as I finished my tirade, though, and he nodded. "It's true. You have done very well. For a woman."

My heart twisted almost into a knot.

Then he added, very quietly, "Or even for a man."

His praise might be less fervent than Granger's, yet it meant so much more to me. Even that light, however, could barely touch the darkness that had settled over my spirit. "Much good may it do me," I said, as low as I had ever been. "If I don't wish to be court-martialed and hanged, I shall have to find some exit from the service, and likely it will be as a deserter. My only satisfaction will be that I have put a hole in Byrom's hull, to sink him in time."

"That, at least, I will be sure to see happen," Harry said, in a tone scarcely less intense than mine.

It strengthened me, to know I did not stand alone. "Thank you." I hesitated, wondering if Harry was now regretting the forgiveness he had offered, before I'd even told him the truth. I *had* to know. "I hope we may at least part as friends, on that count if no other."

Harry's reply was long enough in coming that I almost gave in to despair. But at last he nodded, not looking at me, and said, "Yes. S–Victoria–we are still friends."

It was not friendship I wanted from him. With the barrier of my deception stripped away, I could admit that to myself; I had loved him for years, as more than a mere companion. But I must release that now, as I had released all other hopes, and be grateful for what I might keep. His friendship, and the sound of his voice, addressing me at last by my true name.

I wished it felt less like a knife in my heart.

"What will you do?" he asked. "After you leave."

I aimed for an air of carelessness, and came at least within shot of it. "I will figure something out. My skills are many, if not those of a lady. Come, we should return to the party; your family and fiancée will be wondering where you have gone." I had not intended to mention Miss Fanning. Where had my restraint gone?

But Harry, it seemed, was as eager to escape this dreadful embarrassment as I was. Distracted, he said, "Yes. Let us go back. I have matters I must attend to."

• • •

The evening was nearly at an end, and I had drunk more than was wise. What else should I do, though? The waters in which I sailed had shallowed without warning; I was surrounded by shoals on every side. (And my imagination was determined to wallow in nautical metaphors, as if to rub salt in the wound of that loss.) Byrom and Granger and Mrs. Warrington and Kate and most of all . . .

Where had Harry gone?

I could not find him, nor Kate. In my search, however, I ran afoul of Byrom, who trapped me against one wall of the ballroom, malicious pleasure on his thin face. "You did well with those women, Ravenswood. Such a touching tale; I nearly wept to hear it. Perhaps I'll have you set it to music, next."

Staring into his calculating eyes, I found I could no longer recall why I was protecting his secret. What loss could I suffer, that I would not suffer regardless? My life? There seemed no reason why I should preserve it. The battle madness that had made me speak the truth to Granger was back, but colder this time.

"I thought I might sell my story to a newspaper, instead," I told him, through a smile that could more rightly be called a baring of teeth. "Tales of blackmail always attract such prurient interest."

It took a moment for him to absorb my words. Then his own expression hardened into a snarl. "You know I can destroy you."

"And I, you," I answered. "A pretty impasse, is it not?"

Byrom scoffed. "No one will take your word for it. Not when I expose you for what you are."

He did not know I had already told Granger and Harry. He did not know I had already embraced my fate, robbing his threat of its force. "Plenty of people will be willing to believe it when I expose you for what *you* are: a coward and an incompetent, unworthy of your rank, or even the name of gentleman."

His face purpled with rage. Through his teeth, he said, "If you weren't a worthless bitch, I'd call you out for that insult."

Now, far too late, Harry appeared. He had reentered the ballroom with Kate, and was making his way past the dancers toward me. What had the two of *them* been doing together? It hardly mattered. "You don't dare face me, and you know it," I said.

Harry only heard my reply, but even a blind man could have seen the threat in the air. His hand closed around my arm. "Come with me, Simon. I need to speak with you, in private."

Was it habit that made him still call me Simon, or a friendly concern for my dying masquerade? It didn't matter. The name,

I think, lit the final fuse, for Byrom knew it to be a lie. As Harry tried to drag my resisting body away, the second lieutenant laughed, making no attempt to quiet it. "Always together, Wycliffe, eh? Hoping to make him your catamite? You'll find a nasty surprise if you do."

All around us, conversation died.

Harry dropped my arm. Body taut as a line under tension, he turned to face Byrom fully. And I remembered, with fierce joy and sudden fear commingled, Harry's words on board the ship, before we came here. *I should like to see you call him out.*

I could not. But *Harry* . . .

His voice could carry over the roar of guns in battle; he only used a tenth of that volume now. It was enough. Everyone within a dozen paces heard him. "For that insult, *sir*, you will beg my pardon on your knees–or you will meet me on the field of honor."

Byrom licked his lips, a quick, nervous flick of the tongue. He had gone too far, and he knew it. He could provoke me all he liked, and I could not call him out for it; no man need accept a challenge from a woman. But he had always confined himself to that safe target, minding his tongue around those who might rightly demand satisfaction. My secret was no defense for him now: the public implication that Harry was a sodomite would stand regardless. And that challenge must be answered.

Lord Deverell had heard it. So had Kate. And Granger, too, who spoke into the silence. "Mr. Byrom. Your words are an insult no gentleman could accept. Will you apologize?"

The second lieutenant's gaze slid to me. I held my breath, wondering if he would do it regardless: expose me, simply for the vindictive pleasure of my destruction. But then his attention returned to Harry, and a thin smile spread across his lips. He had, I realized with leaden horror, found a better way to hurt me.

"I will not, sir."

The captain's tone was grim. "I dislike my officers to duel, but in this case, it seems unavoidable. Lord Deverell, I beg your pardon for this disruption. Although the law may often look the other way when gentlemen agree to settle their differences in combat, the practice *is* illegal. We will not trouble you–"

"Nonsense," our host boomed. Kate was by his side; had she whispered in his ear? I had not been watching her closely enough. "If the gentlemen are in accord–regarding the duel, that is; not in the matter of the insult–then I see no reason why they should not be allowed to resolve the matter as they see fit. And one really needs dry land for this sort of thing, not a ship's deck. I volunteer my terrace."

It was not the proper form; a duel should be delayed until the following day, to give heads time to cool. But with the *Hesperides* preparing to set sail again, there was justification for concluding the matter tonight, and Harry did not hesitate to take it up. "I thank you for your generosity, my lord. If Byrom concurs, I would be glad to face him now."

All eyes turned to the second lieutenant. The purple of anger had drained from his face, leaving him white, but he nodded stiffly. "I agree. Let it be done."

We swept toward the garden doors in a chattering crowd, Lord Deverell calling for a footman to bring his dueling pistols. Some of the ladies hung back, but others, Kate among them, came along. I could not spare any attention for her. To Harry I growled, "What are you *doing*? I did not ask you–"

"You didn't have to," Harry said, before I could finish. "I won't kill him–at least, I don't intend to. They'd put me on trial for that, and I'd be left ashore while I waited for the acquittal. But he deserves this, and we both know it."

Servants hung lamps to brighten the terrace, until it was as good as day out there. Fawcett, the Marine captain who had accompanied us to the party, stood as Byrom's second; he made no attempt to pretend he supported Byrom's cause, but honor demanded that *someone* observe the proper forms on his behalf. I, still reckless with my impending doom, declared myself Harry's second. Granger opened his mouth to object, then subsided, granting me this measure of vicarious satisfaction. Byrom's eyes promised murder for me, once he was done with Harry, but I no longer cared.

Fawcett and I agreed to the terms without difficulty. One pistol each, which we loaded under each other's supervision. The men would fire simultaneously at a distance of ten paces, and if one or both be disabled, the duel would end there.

I had seen Harry go into battle before, and feared for him, but never like this. However just his cause might be, this time, I could not fight at his side. If he should be wounded–God forbid, wounded badly . . .

I was not often given to praying, reasoning that God had little cause to favor a woman as impertinent as I. But I prayed now, that Harry be safe, and Byrom suffer the fate he deserved.

We gave the pistols to the duelists, and Lord Deverell himself counted off the paces. "You will turn on the count of three, and fire when I give the word, gentlemen."

Harry's eyes met mine, where I stood to one side. I should have spoken before this began–should have told him how I felt–we left too many things unsaid–

"One," Lord Deverell said. "Two."

As the word "three" left his mouth, Byrom spun and fired.

And something knocked me to the ground.

• • •

At first, my mind was an utter blank.

When at last I managed to form a thought, it was: *What a damnably stupid way out of my troubles.*

A babble of voices deafened me, words leaping clear in brief, half-comprehensible fragments. *Early–misfire–bad aim–cheating bastard* . . . And Byrom, claiming over and over again that it was an accident, that his gun had discharged as he turned, what shocking bad chance that I had been struck.

I pressed one hand to the spreading wetness on my coat. Lord Deverell was bellowing for Byrom to stand his ground and receive the return fire, and through a gap in the men now crowding around me, I saw Harry with his pistol outstretched.

"Harry," I said. It was soft, and could not possibly have carried over the noise of the crowd. But his head turned nonetheless. I met his gaze, and I shook my head. However much I despised Byrom–the murder I saw in his eyes before had been for me, not for his opponent; he had planned this from the start–I did not want Harry to kill him. He would be put on trial for murder, and even with an acquittal, the stain of that would follow him forever.

Harry's eyes returned to Byrom, and his lips peeled back in a snarl. Then he fired.

Byrom screamed. Through the legs around me, I saw him drop to the ground, clutching the shattered ruin of his knee. I had no doubt that Harry had struck what he aimed at.

Then I was being lifted and carried inside, while someone went for a doctor. It was all over, if not in the way I had expected; my secret would be lost entirely now. I rather wished Byrom had struck me somewhere more immediately lethal, so I would be spared the indignity that was about to come.

But no. I was laid on a sofa, and heard Kate's clear voice giving orders; when the door shut, I was very nearly alone. The only ones who remained knew the truth, and were friends besides: Kate, and Granger, and Harry.

"My husband has a *lot* of money," Kate said, when I focused my eyes on her. "Enough to buy one doctor's cooperation, certainly. And we three shall keep your secret."

Granger unbuttoned my coat with impersonal hands, then dragged up my shirt. The white corselet that flattened my meager bosom showed clearly where Byrom's round had struck: my right side, just below my ribs. "I'm no doctor," he said, probing the wound, "but I think it missed your intestines. You have good odds of surviving this, Ravenswood."

"She had better," Kate said sharply. "I can't tell if you have spoiled our plan, Victoria, or played into it beautifully."

Plan? I remembered then what had preceded the insult and the duel: Kate and Harry, returning to the ballroom together. Like a pair of conspirators, ready to carry out their scheme.

Kate smiled at me. She could not entirely hide her worry, but it was mixed with a mad gleam I remembered from our childhood misadventures. "It goes like this. Miss Fanning has no more enthusiasm for her impending marriage than Lieutenant Wycliffe does. Familial pressure, however, prevents either one from admitting that openly. Now, the good lieutenant and I were not in agreement on the notion of faking your death, but as circumstances have presented us with this, ah, *opportunity*–"

She faltered, eyes going to my bloodstained body. Harry cleared his throat, and stepped into the breach. "If my good friend Simon were to beg me to look after his sister . . . I'm sure Miss Fanning would understand."

For one grinding, dreadful moment, I had a vision of myself as an invalid in truth, incapacitated by this wound, living as a spinster on the charity of Harry and his wife. But no, Kate had said something about lack of enthusiasm for the marriage. *Miss Fanning would understand . . .*

Oh.

The sudden acceleration of my heart could not be good for my wound. Byrom disgraced, publicly, by his own hand, and now Harry was offering me–

No. It was *not* everything I had dreamed of. I closed my eyes, because I could not bear to let anyone see the shame there, the temptation to accept this crumb, because without it I had nothing. With so much else gone, I had only my dignity, and clung to it with all the strength I still retained. "I don't want your pity, Harry."

Above me, silence. And then he spoke. "It isn't pity. It's . . ." A pause, in which I thought my heart had stopped beating entirely. "It's affection."

I opened my eyes then, and met his, and saw in them what he had concealed under the shock of our earlier conversation: a mirror to my own feelings.

Feelings he could not admit then; it would not have been right, with him sworn to wed another. He should not admit them now. But that single word was more than enough. We were not simply friends, as he had said in the garden; we had not been *simply* friends for years, even if my masculine facade had forced us to call our bond by that name, or to divert it sideways into brotherhood. I knew, suddenly, that he remembered the near kiss the night I was made lieutenant.

Harry blinked, and I realized from the burning in my own eyes that I had been staring into his for some untold moment. My tongue, working once more, gave voice to a laugh. "It's fitting, I suppose, given my strange life, that I should be proposed to while bleeding on Kate's sofa."

"It is not *quite* a proposal," Kate corrected me, after Harry and I had gazed at each other for another eternity. "We must put it about first that you have died, or rather that Simon has, and then Miss Fanning can release Lieutenant Wycliffe. But there must be no *actual* dying on your part, do you understand?"

"Yes," I agreed, not looking away from Harry. It was hard to speak; my lips wanted to stay stretched in a smile forever. "No dying."

How could I die? I suddenly had all the reason in the world to live.

• • •

I played the part of the invalid passably well, I think, courtesy of Byrom's cowardly shot, and my subsequent long recovery. The wedding was small, out of consideration for my supposed weakness–much greater in story than in truth. It was just as well: fewer guests meant fewer people to wonder at the bride's oddly weathered face, or less-than-graceful bearing in her gown.

Afterward, Harry and I walked in the garden of his family's house. A breeze was blowing, and out of habit I raised my head and inhaled deeply. But the air carried no hint of salt.

Harry did not miss the sudden melancholy in my expression. "You miss it, don't you."

I sighed. "I miss a great many things. For all its bad parts–the danger, and the brutality, and the restrictions of shipboard life–I felt honored to be in the service. More than anything, though, I miss the sea."

My new husband took my hand in his own. "There are benefits to this peace with France, you know. Unlike a great many lieutenants, I face no hardship in being put off and placed on half-pay. And there are a great many opportunities for a trained officer, outside the service." He looked to the south, toward the distant sea. "Some of those opportunities are much more . . . *flexible.*"

As with his proposal–as with so many of the things he said–Harry left his precise meaning unspoken. I heard it well enough. My breath drew in, calling only the faintest of twinges from my side. "You mean–"

He nodded. My hand tightened on his: still a strong grip, despite my convalescence, and the callouses remained, under my glove. Would the crew of a merchant vessel put up with their captain's wife interfering in shipboard affairs? Surely we could assemble one that would.

I had not lost the sea.

Smiling fit to crack my face in half, I walked on with my husband through the garden, the wind gusting in my ears with a sound like waves.

Mrs. Beeton's Book of Magickal Management

KAREN HEALEY

"Irene, if I am forced to marry the Marquess of Chumley, I will simply die."

Irene Crawford nodded and cast a curling charm on a lush lock of the speaker's black hair, sublimely unconcerned with this horrifying pronouncement. Lady Flora Wittingham was in constant peril of immediate expiration. This day alone, she had been forced to eat cold kedgeree when she arrived late at the breakfast table, wear a pale green day dress that muddied her complexion, and accompany her father and his guest on a gentle walk about Rabton Park's icy grounds while Cyril, Marquess of Chumley, treated them to an extended account of his own grounds in the North.

Flora had, in private, declared all these misadventures likely to herald her immediate removal to paradise, and yet, she had survived to this moment, where she was dressing for dinner in her pretty chambers. Indeed, despite frequent threats of imminent demise, she had survived to the age of seventeen.

An age just right, the Earl of Rabton considered, for a pretty, well-bred gel to be properly affianced to a gentleman of noble title and considerable property. All the better that Lord Chumley not only shared Lord Rabton's politics, but his fondness for lingering over port and pipe. He was also nearing the end of his third decade–a good age, Lord Rabton thought, for a man to take a wife and ensure his succession. Chumley seemed partial to Flora, and needed only to be brought up to the mark.

The Earl had not condescended to ask his daughter's opinion on the match, and would have been astonished to know that she could hold one. Irene Crawford was the sole receptacle of such confidences, but her official title was lady's maid, not confessor. Irene could thus grant Flora neither grace nor absolution–not that such papist institutions would ever be given entrée to the ancient grounds of Rabton Hall–and usually concerned herself with the care of her mistress's clothes, the arrangement of her hair, the mixing of various potions for her complexion, and the casting of such small spells as could assist in these ventures. She tried not to give her opinion on such potentially perilous topics as Flora's inner turmoil, and Flora did her part by graciously declining to request Irene's thoughts on the same.

Consequently, Irene was considerably startled when Flora's hands ceased in their fretting against each other and flew up to grab Irene's own. Irene stilled, staring at her mistress in the glass. Flora's complexion was unusually pale except for two red spots and her large, dark blue eyes positively threatened to spill over with tears.

"My lady?" Irene ventured.

"Oh, Irene," Flora whispered. "I do mean it, you know. I think I will die if Papa makes the Marquess propose to me. And I think–" she drew a deep breath, "I think I would rather I did. I have not even come out yet! I was so looking forward to my season."

Irene was not unsympathetic to Flora's plight. It would be a terrible thing, she considered, to be forced into marriage with a man so much older than oneself, and moreover, one with whiskers so very blond and bristly. Lady Flora had wealth, beauty, and reason, and Irene thought it outrageous that with these advantages, in this year of 1894, Flora was still not free to choose what path in life she might follow. Irene feared that her own path stretched out narrowly, with no allowance for shortcuts, byways, or highways.

And thus, this was a dangerous situation. Flora, however kindly a mistress, was still a mistress, and Irene a servant. And Flora's papa paid her wages.

But instead of giving advice directly, and possibly being held to account for it, Irene could hint at a course of action, and had done so on several occasions when she feared Flora's happiness was really at stake. This was clearly one of those occasions, and she cast around for a way to influence Flora's thoughts without seeming to do so.

"Do you recall that period last year when you were ill and I read to you, my lady?" she began.

"Oh yes. Such lovely books, with happy endings. I did think that Catherine's papa might have relented earlier. Henry was such a nice young man, really. So well read."

"It was *Pride and Prejudice* which has come to mind," Irene said delicately. "Particularly the chapter regarding the proposal Mr. Collins made Miss Elizabeth Bennet. Literature has much to teach us."

"Oh!" Flora said, her eyes widening. Irene took advantage of the shock to gently free herself from Flora's grip. "Why, she refused him! And Mr. Darcy too, though that was only because he was proud, and she knew better later and a good thing too. Do you think I could say no to the Marquess?"

Irene would rather give a direct opinion on whether the

garnets went well with the pink ballgown than answer this question. She ostensibly returned her attention to Flora's ringlets, attempting to indicate with a quirk of an eyebrow that if Lady Flora thought Miss Elizabeth Bennet's actions might be applicable to her own, that was entirely Lady Flora's privilege.

"Elizabeth Bennet had a supportive papa," Flora mused. "He said he would not like her to marry Mr. Collins, and her mama's threats came to nothing." Her face was clouding over, and the tears threatened again. "My mama is dead, and would never be so unfeeling as Mrs. Bennet, but I fear my papa may not be so obliging."

Irene took a gamble. "The Bennet family were in some distress," she said, as if idly. "Five daughters, and an entail. Of course, with no brothers, you can see how Mrs. Bennet thought it best Elizabeth marry to keep the property in the family."

"No brothers," Flora said thoughtfully, and then her stormy brow cleared. "But I am fortunate in mine! I can depend on Jamie to support me, and he comes down from Cambridge tomorrow!"

"Does he, my lady?" This question, hinting as it did of disinterest and ignorance, was, strictly speaking, a falsehood, and Irene resolved to say an extra prayer before bed to atone for it. The homecoming of the Viscount Northcliff, a household favorite, had been all the conversation downstairs for a fortnight.

"Oh, yes, Irene. He is bringing some friend he says could not travel home for Christmas, can you imagine? How horrible! We must be very kind to him."

"Certainly, my lady," Irene murmured, forbearing to mention what would happen should the housekeeper have the least suspicion that she was being very kind to any male guest.

"And I will speak to Jamie the instant he arrives. He shan't allow Papa to make the Marquess propose," Flora concluded, and looked radiantly beautiful in her relief.

Irene allowed a moment for self-congratulation, and reset the curling charm that had faded with lack of attention. Concentrating her will, she murmured a few phrases. Dark red light streamed from her hands and lifted Flora's heavy locks—only to fall apart when Flora suddenly twisted, breaking Irene's concentration. Irene flinched in the wake of the failed spell, her fingers burning as if she had plunged them into boiling water.

"Irene! I have just thought—oh, have I hurt you?"

Irene gestured toward her mouth. Flora, reminded of the silence that followed a badly broken spell, went quiet with remorse. But even genuine guilt could not restrain her very real urgency. "I had just thought," she whispered, "that if he were to propose tonight, before Jamie arrived, I would not in the least know what to do or say. Irene, is there anything about refusing a proposal in The Book?"

Irene shook her head. There were, to be sure, dozens of etiquette books that would advise Flora on how to gently and genteely decline an unwelcome proposal, but few accounted for a disobliging papa. The Book of which she spoke, Irene was quite sure, contained no such advice.

"We must make sure," Flora insisted, and Irene let out a breath that would have been a sigh, had her vocal cords been of any use at that moment.

Nevertheless, she left Flora trying to repair her hair with more mundane efforts and hurried up the back stairs to her own room. Her position entitled her to this privacy, and even some degree of luxury, with a mattress not too thin and covers thick enough to banish the chill of Rabton Hall. Irene knew very well that the housemaids envied her the privilege, but she could not despise the treat–not when it allowed her to bend over her scalded hands, and whimper in silence until the wake of the interrupted spell subsided, the pain passed and her voice returned.

Then she reached into her small and crowded bookshelf, a discard from the nursery Flora had long ago left vacant, and retrieved *Mrs. Beeton's Book of Magickal Management.* Yes, this venerable publication was The Book in which Flora placed such trusting faith, and why not? With its aid, Irene had achieved what the godless might term miracles.

Full of good sense, admirably organized, and clearly written, The Book rarely failed its devotees in the practice of household magick. In this, it was unlike lesser publications, which often resulted in the death of the ill-advised practitioner by the consumption of poisonous concoctions, the dissolution of bodily unity in the event of a particularly strong wake, or, as in the unfortunate case of one poor housekeeper from N–, the transmutation of the human form into that of a vase of lilies.

No, servants who sought the assistance of Mrs. Beeton rarely damaged themselves in permanent fashion. A restless lady of the house who moved before the completion of a curling spell could cause pain, but never dismemberment.

When Mr. and Mrs. Crawford had regrettably departed earthly soil two years earlier, The Book and considerable magickal talent had been among the few possessions they could bequeath their only child. Fortunately, before her own untimely demise, the Countess of Rabton had been of a kindly disposition, and lady's maids with magickal ability were both all the fashion and exceedingly rare. She had thought Irene a neat, good sort of girl with nice manners, and no looks to speak of–a perfect addition to the household.

Irene might have once cherished other ambitions, but she was too practical to ignore the workings of necessity. Indeed, as she moved down the stairs, The Book under one arm, she focused with the ease of long practice only on her current task, allowing no whimsical fancies to escape, however entrancing they might be.

The sound of another voice in Flora's chambers, however, aroused both her curiosity and her concern. The voice was certainly male. Had the Viscount Northcliff returned early, and gone to greet his sister in her suite? Even as Irene thought it, however, she recognized the voice.

It was that of the Marquess of Chumley.

Irene froze. For his lordship to enter Flora's chamber–while she was unchaperoned, no less–was quite beyond the bounds of propriety, and if any hint of such an event got loose, Flora's reputation would be irreparably blemished. But a man who might enter a lady's chamber might have even less scrupulous activities in mind.

Irene crept closer, ready to raise the alarm at the first hint of danger, and brave what scandal resulted. In so doing, she inevitably overheard the substance of the conversation.

"–do think you should leave," Flora was saying, her usually pleasant voice pitched high.

"Come now, Lady Wittingham–may I call you Flora? And you must call me Cyril."

"You may not, sir."

"But when we are man and wife, such a confusion of syllables as 'Marchioness Chumley' would be a bother, do you not think so?" His voice was a warm, wheedling thing, like a garter snake winding itself into a summer nest.

Flora's voice was beginning to sound desperate. "Please leave, sir. This is most improper."

"I will not, until I have an answer to my question. Come,

Flora, will you not make me the happiest man in the Empire?" It was a question, but the Marquess did not appear to be asking. He delivered each phrase with measured certainty.

Irene's fingers adjusted their grip on *Mrs. Beeton's Book of Magickal Management*, which, in addition to its other admirable qualities, was amply proportioned and weighed a good five pounds. If the Marquess became any more importunate, she vowed, she would burst into the room and beat him as she might a rug. For a moment, a wistful thought escaped Irene's otherwise firm control. If only she had access to more potent magicks, if only the bailiffs had left the inheritance of her father's books after the sad, shabby little funeral. But they had been valuable, and the debts substantial, and Irene would have to make do with what she had.

"I . . . don't know how to answer you, sir," Flora was saying.

Irene frowned, and edged closer. There was something odd about Flora's voice, as if she spoke half asleep. Irene, who had woken Flora every morning for nearly two years, was very familiar with that drowsing tone.

"Say yes," his lordship said in that same slow cadence. "It is a good match, and your father wishes it. You do not wish to disappoint the Earl, do you?"

"No," Flora said.

"You want to be a good girl, don't you?"

"Yes," Flora said.

"Then you will marry me, won't you, Flora?"

"Yes," Flora said, so quietly that Irene had to strain to hear through the thick wooden door. "Yes, Cyril, I will marry you."

"Excellent," his lordship said. "And you will be happy. I cannot abide women who mope. I will go to your father now, and we will marry in the spring."

Even with this warning, Irene had scarcely time to scramble

away, but by the time the Marquess opened Flora's door, Irene was proceeding towards her mistress's chambers at a decorous and unsuspicious pace. Lord Chumley paid Irene no attention at all, striding past with a self-satisfied smile so wide his whiskers could do little to conceal it. Irene, on the other hand, stood still and stared after him in the rudest manner. Then she shook herself all over and went in to her mistress.

Flora was sitting on the edge of the bed, perched precariously on her bustle. Her hands were clasped under her chin, her eyes wide, her pupils very large. "He has gone to my father," she said. "We are to marry in the spring. Oh, Irene! How happy I am!"

She looked happy indeed, but Irene knew Flora's joy had no natural cause. For as the Marquess of Chumley had walked out of the room, she had seen it–an insubstantial tracery of white lines that limned his form and formed a glowing tangle of shapes above his head. It was the white aura–the very sign and signal of magick most foul.

• • •

Irene suffered through the rest of the evening in silence, a silence which went largely unregarded by the rest of the household. Flora was too full of raptures about her darling Cyril to pay any attention to anything else as Irene finished her preparations for dinner. Mrs. Framble, the housekeeper, did note at the dinner of the upper staff that Irene seemed even quieter than usual. She resolved to keep an eye on the girl, lest she be sickening for something.

The news of the engagement, in the traditional course of such joyous tidings, had flowed swiftly downward through the household staff, and all agreed that His Lordship the Marquess of Chumley was a decent choice for Lady Flora. Of course she deserved a duke, but there was none available, so a marquess would have to do. Irene chewed the inside of her lip more than the good Bakewell pudding served to her by little Elsie, the scullery maid.

The white aura! Could she have been mistaken? Irene had never seen it before. She had thought the white aura the province of desperate criminals in city stews, and penny-dreadful novels. She had never expected to encounter it in the honorable surrounds of Rabton Hall.

But she had always been especially skilled in making out signs of magick invisible to nonpractitioners, and it had been clear as a summer sky as the Marquess made his smirking way down the hallway without even a glance in her direction. And Lady Flora's affections had changed suddenly–and inexplicably, were anything but foul magick the cause.

So, then, the diagnosis was made. Irene nodded, passed the salt mechanically, and set herself to determining a cure.

Irene could not accuse a marquess of employing evil magick, certainly not to his face. Neither could she approach the staff more senior to her with this conundrum, as she would have done with anything less serious. Irene considered going directly to Lord Rabton, and had Mrs. Framble not spoken at an opportune moment, she might well have, and this story might have had a much sadder end. For the Earl of Rabton, though not an evil man, was disinclined to listen to such nonentities as lady's maids at the best of times, and if Irene had the effrontery to bring him a tale certain to disrupt both his household and a most fortuitous engagement, the results might have been most determinedly against her favor.

But Mrs. Framble did speak. "I hope this friend of his young lordship is a good sort of gentleman," she said.

"All I know is that no valet attends him," the butler said in stentorian tones, and at this sign of poverty the senior staff shook their heads, all save the first footman, who was most eager to gain experience acting as valet for Mr. Simon Young, and Irene, who brightened considerably at this reminder of the Viscount's homecoming.

"Is the Viscount Northcliff delayed?" she asked.

"Why, no, Irene," Mrs. Framble said. "Not that I've heard. We are to expect him tomorrow morning."

"How nice," Irene said, and sank back into her thoughts. Mrs. Framble eyed her sharply. The females in the Earl's employ (and, though Mrs. Framble was not aware of it, at least two of the males) were forever falling in love with the Viscount Northcliff, who was thankfully too well mannered to take advantage of these infatuations. Nevertheless, whenever lovesickness afflicted Mrs. Framble's girls, they spent too much time sighing and not enough scrubbing. An engagement, with all its attendant bustle, was not an opportune time for a lady's maid to lose her head over a gentleman, and Mrs. Framble resolved to take steps, should any further signs appear.

Irene, pleased with her new plan of action and unaware of Mrs. Framble's suspicions, completed her duties for the day and returned to her solitary room. She finished the taking-in of one of Flora's old gowns for herself, released her plain brown hair and braided it neatly, and composed herself to prayer. "Please, God, help me make it right," is not the most eloquent petition ever uttered silently in the dark of a person's soul, but what Irene's prayer lacked in eloquence–and in originality–was more than surpassed in its sincerity.

• • •

"My God," said Simon Young. "It's enormous."

"It is an ancient pile of rock," said James, Viscount Northcliff, as he swung down from the Rabton family carriage. "But it's home. Take the brown trunk up to Mr. Young's room, would you, Bains? There's a good chap. Be careful, it's four-fifths books."

"You said I would find time to study," Simon protested mildly, still staring up at the impressive bulk of Rabton Hall.

James slung an arm over his shoulder and hustled him through the oak doors. "A ruse, old boy. A damnable lie, be it known. We're here to wench and carouse our way to the hell they reserve for bad scholars."

"You're teasing me," Simon said, blinking his large gray eyes behind his spectacles. "You are, aren't you?"

James laughed and let his friend go. "Couldn't let you molder in the stacks all hols, Simon. It's Christmas! But there'll be time for your books, never fear. Ah, Caldwell, very good, where might I find Pater?"

"In his study, my lord, with his lordship of Chumley," the butler supplied.

"Oh, what a bore. And Flora?"

"In the yellow room, my lord."

"Excellent. We'll go pay our respects, Simon, and I will show you a few things around the place, and then you may spend as long as you like with your books before dinner. Do remember to dress for it, won't you?"

James was a good-humored man of twenty, and if selfish considerations of wanting male company his own age for Christmas had prompted him to extend an invitation to Simon, he had been at least equally moved by concern for the well-being of his studious friend, who had grown pale and thin during a trying term. The bounty of his father's table, James thought, was just the thing to improve Simon's health, and being removed from the allure of the Cambridge libraries was certain to cheer his spirits.

Accordingly, as he entered the yellow room, he kept a close eye on his friend, and was startled to note a sudden flush in the sallow cheek as Simon beheld Flora for the first time, wearing her prettiest pink frock and sitting in a chair near the fire.

"Flora, may I introduce Mr. Simon Young? Simon, this is Lady Flora Wittingham, my sister."

Simon murmured something inaudible about the pleasure.

"Mr. Young, how do you do?" Flora asked, distractedly offering her hand. James, who thought his sister pretty enough, but inclined to fretting and an excess of sensibility, really saw her radiant beauty in this moment, and felt pity for his friend. But Flora did not notice Simon's condition, releasing his hand at once and turning to her brother. "Have you heard, Jamie? I am to be married."

James observed the color draining out of Simon's face and moved at once to cover his friend's embarrassment. "Really?" he said, almost at random. "Jolly good show! To whom?"

"To the Marquess of Chumley. He is with Papa now, discussing the terms of the marriage settlement."

"To Chumley!" James ejaculated. "Well, that is certainly–I mean to say that–"

"Is it not wonderful?" Flora breathed. "I vow, I am the happiest woman alive. Oh! Here he comes now! My darling lord, have you met my brother Jamie?"

"Chumley," James said, nodding.

"Northcliff," the Marquess returned, equally coolly.

"And this is–" Flora paused.

"Mr. Young," James said, startled again. Flora was a scatterwit, but not an unmannerly one, and once introduced to someone, she had never before neglected to commit their name to memory. He was embarrassed for his friend, and worried for his sister, who instead of apologizing for her slip was gazing at her intended with something very like worship in her eyes.

Simon's own eyes were filled with something closer to despair, and though James had intended to take his friend on a tour of the portrait gallery, and point out the rare books in the library, he did not prevent Simon from making his excuses and slipping away.

The mystery only deepened over dinner, where Flora's conversation was all of her wedding plans and the happiness the engagement had given her, while Chumley smirked into his soup and smiled at James with what he thought was an almost insolent air.

James begged off shortly after Simon did, and took himself to his room, sending away his valet before that gentleman could do more than remove his boots, and preparing himself to think through the problem.

The instant Bains departed, however, he was replaced, by a small young woman of about seventeen. He vaguely recognized her as one of the upper servants. Elda, was that her name? No, Irene. He was almost sure she was lady's maid to Flora.

James hoped he would not have to gently ward off a clumsy attempt at seduction. Irene's eyes were pretty, but her skin was marred by freckles. Her mouth, too, was wide and mobile, not the tiny pout James thought he favored.

Then the girl opened her mouth, and if her appearance had surprised James, what she had to say stunned him entirely. "I am Irene Crawford, my lord, your sister's maid. I beg you forgive me this intrusion, but I must tell you that the Marquess of Chumley cast a spell to break your sister's will and force her to accept his proposal, which he made in her chambers last night before dinner. I saw the white aura, my lord. The Marquess is an evil magician and no true gentleman, and he has ensnared your sister's heart by unnatural means."

The pretty eyes were passionate, the freckled skin flushed with anger, and the wide mouth bit off each word with little white teeth.

James, as if in a daze, thought that Irene Crawford might have some looks after all. Then the true import of her speech struck him, and he stiffened. "You accuse a gentleman of base and illegal magick, and with no proof other than your word," he said.

Irene held herself very still. "I do, my lord."

"Knowing that if I take umbrage at this insult to my father's guest, you risk being turned out of this house without reference, without hope of future employment, and with no funds to ease your passage."

Irene bit her lip. "Yes, my lord."

James let out a short laugh and collapsed into a chair. "Thank God for you, Irene Crawford," he said.

"My lord?"

"I would that one in a hundred had your insight and honesty. I would that one in a thousand did! Flora's letters said nothing of favoring this guest–rather the opposite–yet now she fawns upon him. The Marquess of Chumley is the subject of more than a few whispers among the clubs. I suspected something underhanded, but my own magickal talents are meager, and I could not discern the cause."

"No, my lord," Irene said unthinking, still dizzy with the relief that she was not to be turned out into the night.

James's black brows lifted. He was unaccustomed to contradiction, especially from servants. "No?"

Well, Irene thought, she had come this far, and he had named her honest and insightful. She could do no less than honestly tell him the results of that insight. "No, my lord. I have a . . . knack for adjudging magickal talent, and I sense that you have great potential in the art, yet to be applied."

"Ah," James said. "So I am not untalented, merely lazy. Well, you may be right–Simon certainly thinks so, though he helps me with my cantrips all the same, the good fellow. But Flora, Irene. What are we to do? She has consented, she appears happy and well content with the match, and Pater will certainly never dissolve it upon a suspicion."

Irene refrained from pointing out that his "we" presumed a great deal, and said only, "No mere suspicion, my lord. I know what I saw."

"Pater is unlikely to accept the knowledge supplied to him by–forgive me–a lady's maid."

Irene smiled ironically. "That is what I am, my lord. What is there to forgive?"

James felt unaccountably discomfited by this calm reply, but reapplied himself to the problem at hand. "I suppose I could claim that I witnessed the white aura myself," said he.

"If it came to court, my lord, you would be discredited by the barrister's truth incantation," Irene said.

"If it came to court, Pater would be furious and Flora humiliated," said James. "But I'd rather that than see her married to a seducer who employs foul magicks, by Jove. You are right, however. Any barrister would discredit my statement directly. Would you testify, then, Irene?"

"I would," Irene said, though her heart quivered at the thought. A lady's maid who testified against the will of her employer would be unlikely to find another position in service. It would be the factories or the fields for her then, or the workhouse.

James saw her shudder and divined its cause. "That must remain a last resort," he said. "I would rather not haul you in front of the magistrate, if it can be at all avoided. What if there were a counterspell that could break this enchantment?"

Irene frowned, and James had the half-conscious desire to smooth the wrinkle in her brow with his finger. "I do not know of any, my lord."

"Nor I, but Simon may. He cannot apply them, but there's not a fellow in our college that can match him for magickal theory. If he could turn up such a spell, would you help me cast it?"

Irene's face flooded with color and James, realizing his error, sprang to his feet. "I do apologize. It was very improper of me to ask, I beg your pardon." Asking a woman to join him in magickal undertakings! He castigated himself most bitterly for the lapse.

But Irene recovered her composure and lifted her stubborn chin. "No, my lord, you need not apologize. You are moved by concern for your sister. I should be glad to help you and Mr. Young in any way I can."

"You are sure?" James asked anxiously. He could not see any other course of action that might free Flora from the clutches of Chumley.

"Quite sure," said Irene. "Although I beg your discretion."

"Of course," James said. "Let's see. Shall we all three meet tomorrow evening in the library? No one goes there."

Irene considered it. The housemaids most certainly entered the library to dust the rows of unopened books, and Mrs. Framble to make certain they did, but that was during the daylight hours, when there was more light to see to their duties. The great fire would be banked after dinner, and the room should remain empty until the dawn, when little Elsie would arrive to set it burning again. "Late evening, my lord?" she suggested.

"Yes, shall we say midnight?"

"A proper hour for countering foul magick," Irene said, with approval.

James, who had not known that, smiled rather foolishly and bid her a gracious goodnight.

Irene, as she hurried up the back stairs to her narrow bed, reflected that his young lordship was really very handsome when he smiled. It made his eyes look particularly bright.

• • •

Mr. Simon Young, Irene discovered, was more than willing to assist the Viscount and herself–he was positively eager.

"Cad," he was muttering to himself as he rummaged through musty tomes, energetically marking pages with scraps torn from a piece of parchment resting in his lap. "Bounder. Rake. Despoiler of innocence."

"Simon," James said sharply, standing as Irene came hesitatingly into the room. "This is Miss Crawford, of whom I spoke."

"What? Oh, yes, charmed," Simon said, rising and nodding at Irene. "So you've a strong talent, James says?"

"I suppose so, sir."

Simon smiled at her. "Suppose you recite Faulkner's Apprehension of Skill for me?"

Irene obeyed, and Simon whistled as the golden bar solidified in the air, until it seemed nearly tangible. "A talent indeed, Miss Crawford! Well, I've found several things that might help. Take a look at this."

Irene looked over his shoulder, very aware that she was in a room late at night with two gentlemen, but his lordship was leaning against the mantel, some distance away, and this scholarly Mr. Young surely had no harm in him.

To her dismay, however, the cantrip to which Simon pointed was all in Greek letters. "I cannot read this, sir," she said.

"Oh, of course. Well, let's see, in the Roman alphabet, it would be something like this." He began to sketch out the transliteration on another parchment scrap, and Irene watched with interest. "Now, as to the meaning . . . this piece is unclear, but I think the author meant the fourth quadrant, and this must mean 'by moonshine,' although the quarter of the moon is not defined."

"Mrs. Beeton says that for cleaning a room befouled with magick of ill intent, the full moon is best," Irene said timidly. "Would that apply in this case?"

"It agrees with Solomon's Scroll," Simon said, checking a reference and scribbling something else on the translation. "Hah! There, much better balanced among the humors. Who is this Mrs. Beeton? I have not read her work, but she seems like a sensible scholar."

James laughed, but even when Irene, blushing furiously, revealed that the Beeton in question was but a writing woman who had made a collection of household magicks, Simon would brook no delay until The Book was fetched down from Irene's room for him.

"This is a most wonderful work!" he exclaimed. "See here, James, where the ingredients are listed aforehand? And the language is most clear and accurate. By Nimue, I wish that all magickal works were organized upon such principles."

"Perhaps we can apply them to the spell to *save my sister*," James suggested, and was, despite the circumstances, highly amused when both of his companions turned identical startled faces toward him.

"An excellent thought, my lord," Irene murmured, and she and Simon fell into a discussion of what herbs could best be substituted for those not available in her collection. James, seeing that she sat down at last, allowed himself to fall into a chair by the fire and watch the dying embers fade, one by one.

"I think we have it," Simon said, and raked his hair back from his weary brow. "James? James?"

"Mmph? Yes." James roused himself and looked at his triumphant colleagues. "Wonderful! How shall we go about it?"

"Miss Crawford pointed out that tomorrow night is the full moon," Simon said. "She has her part down admirably. I will coach you in yours tomorrow during the day, and we will meet at midnight to disrupt his lordship's spell. Agreed?"

"Certainly," James said. "Miss Crawford, you look exhausted. Will you not rest?" And he solicitously escorted her to the library door.

Simon, engaged in gathering up his books, did not notice this courtesy, and would not have thought anything of it if he had, but Irene was most flustered. In her haste to return to her room and the two hours of slumber she could yet snatch, she did not see little Elsie with her scuttle and hearth brush. But

Elsie saw her, and saw who had taken her to the library door, and vowed she would not speak a word, no, not to anybody. Elsie greatly admired Miss Irene, who was so clever, and knew so many things.

• • •

The confederates met at midnight on the next day, and Simon lost no time in stressing to the two spellcasters the difficulty of the spell. "Once you begin, you must continue," he said. "It is possible–even advisable–to pause and gather your strength along the way, but this is a very powerful spell. If it is broken, the rebounding forces of the wake may do you real harm."

"Harm?" James said sharply, noting Irene's flinch.

"You may be crippled," Simon said. "If you have gone too far in the spell, and then lose your will, it may destroy you both."

James turned to Irene. "We can find another way," he said. "I ask too much."

Irene shook her head. "There is no other way, my lord. It must be done, and it must be done tonight, for who knows when another such opportunity will present itself?"

"I agree," Simon said, sounding unusually severe. "If it were done when 'tis done, then 'twere well it were done quickly."

"We aren't assassinating the King of Scotland, Simon," James protested.

"It will take near as much strength of will as that wicked deed did, James, and you must, even before the spell itself, combine your wills. I can tell you how it's done, but you know I am magick-blank myself. I cannot prepare you for the sensation, having never felt it."

"Will it be strange?" Irene asked.

"They say it is a peculiar feeling," Simon said carefully. "And it may take some time, so you should begin the attempt at once. If you are ready, Miss Crawford?"

James was beginning to be truly alarmed, and wished that he had listened to his tutors in the arts magickal. But there were so many other occupations in a university town for a young man with plenty of money!

"If you please, sir," Irene said, "I brought down The Book. It mentions the combination of wills only in theory, but I thought his lordship might like to read that section."

James fairly snatched The Book out of her hands and applied himself to the indicated pages, which treated the subject as being between two of the same sex as a matter of course. The scandalous practice of combining will between man and woman would never be treated by the renowned Mrs. Beeton. "It recommends we begin facing each other, and thinking of images that are suggested by a third party," he said after a moment. "And . . . I must hold your hand. I do apologize for the affront."

"No apology is needed, my lord," Irene said, and though she would not admit it, even to herself, her hand trembled with something other than fear as she placed it in his.

The combination took longer than even Simon had feared. Irene found it very difficult to fall into the requisite ease of mind and trust in her partner, whereas James discovered that his mind would wander inconveniently about, without fixing on the images Simon patiently built in their minds. It was hard to picture a tree swaying in the breeze, or a babbling brook, or the motion of waves upon the shore (which Irene had never seen) when Irene's brow was crinkled, and her mouth so pursed up with intent.

But at last, after many hours, Irene was sufficiently weary, and James sufficiently desperate that the connection was made.

It happened in the space between seconds. All of a moment, Irene was atrociously aware of his lordship's body. He had broad shoulders, and she could feel them straining against his coat. His dark hair touched the back of her neck in a soft caress. Most shocking of all, the long legs she had observed now gave her a view of the top of her own head. It must be simple to be so lordly, when one was so tall!

James could also feel every inch of Irene's skin as if it were his own, and it moved him no less. Her left boot was too loose for her little foot, and stuffed with cloth to make it fit. The pins in her hair pricked his scalp. Her corset pressed uncomfortably against her–

"Ahem!" James said. "It *is* most peculiar, isn't it?"

Irene nodded, her eyes very wide.

"It is late," Simon said urgently. "Or early, I should say, and the moon will soon set."

James lifted his chin. "Very well. At your leisure, madam. On a count of three?"

Irene crumpled the dried dandelion roots in her left hand as James scattered the salt with his right. And so they were committed.

There is a school of thought, much favored by the gloomy-minded, that posits that if anything can go wrong, it will, at the worst possible time. Irene was inclined to follow it, while James was diametrically opposed to any approach to life so lacking in hope, yet they both gasped in unison as the door opened and the Marquess of Chumley made his entrance.

Flora was on his arm, clad only in her nightgown, and her face was beautiful, but as blank as that of a statue, with no animating spark to give it vivacity. The Marquess paused, and laughed harshly as he assessed the spell in progress.

"What's this? I had thought to find sport, and instead I find meddlers! Stop," he told James and Irene.

James gritted his teeth against the words that rose within him, for anything he said would interrupt the spell and unleash the devastating wake against he and Irene both. Though he would take harm and face death to save his sister, he would not condemn Irene to that fate. Irene, who felt much the same, began her part of the chant, pronouncing every word with a tranquility she was very far from possessing. There was no way out for them but through.

"You must stop," Simon said, over her sweet, low voice. "Come, man, they have begun, and will not cease–you are already undone. Let Lady Flora go and you may yet have time to flee."

"If they stop now, they may yet live," Lord Chumley said. "But if they do not, the same cannot be said for Lady Flora." And with no further warning, he placed his strong white hands about Flora's throat and began to squeeze.

Irene and James watched in horror as Flora, still as empty-eyed and smiling as a doll, began to turn red, then blue. It seemed that after all these years of dramatic threat, Flora Wittingham really might simply die.

"You devil!" Simon shouted, and threw himself at the Marquess. He was tossed back by a crackling wave of blue sparks, rolling to land with a thud against the unforgiving stones of the mantel. Lord Chumley, the white aura nearly solid around him, laughed as he returned his attentions to Flora's slender throat.

Irene's grip strengthened on James's hand, and he did not

leap to his friend's aid as he longed to do. Instead, he turned his attention to her–her hand, warm in his–her breath, fast but even–her heart, pumping steadily in her breast. He felt her will as if it were his own, hard and strong, while his own warm easiness flowed between them. They united, simply and fully, and as James chanted the Greek words, he felt as if he spoke them with Irene's soft lips. A dark glory rose in both of them, and with the last of their strength, they turned it outward, to the evil fog that clouded Flora's mind.

The spell left them, as gently as dandelion seeds wafting on the breeze, and they fell into each other as they sank to the floor, replete.

And defenseless.

Lord Chumley's eyes glittered as he unceremoniously thrust Flora from him and began to gather his power for a thrust at the pair, nearly senseless in the aftermath of their spell. The white aura glowed, his hands moved confidently through the motions of the death spell–and he staggered, falling forward against the mantel.

Flora, once released of her bondage, had assessed the situation at once, and, strengthened by her indignation and the righteous horror she felt at the scene enacted before her appalled eyes, had caught up the nearest likely weapon. *Mrs. Beeton's Book of Magickal Management* cracked sharply across the back of Lord Chumley's head.

At the distraction, his will failed him. The spell broke. And the wake washed over him in a rushing wave, all light and fury. It was so cacophonous a noise that the Earl of Rabton, turning over in his massive bed, dreamed of the Russian guns at Balaclava, and Mrs. Framble, drowsing, hoped that washing day would not bring thunder, and little Elsie, carrying her scuttle along the hallway, squeaked and ran swiftly to the library door.

But what a tableau revealed itself to her wondering gaze. There were Miss Irene and his young lordship, leaning upon each other as they strove to rise and regain their wits. There was her ladyship, hurrying to Mr. Young's side as he sat up and put a hand to his poor head. There was The Book, which she had often seen Miss Irene consult, pages ruffled and spine cracked, ignobly discarded on the floor.

And there were the remains of Cyril, Marquess of Chumley. His spiritual part had been consigned to the Great Judge, and though earthly residents may anticipate the outcome of that courtroom, naught but the Lord of Heaven can proclaim the final sentence. But the fate of the corporeal body may be more easily ascertained, and that of Lord Chumley was nothing but a flurry of white ash, even now drifting down to settle on the library hearth rug.

Elsie saw Lady Flora in her nightgown bending anxiously over a young man, saw Miss Irene near swooning against the Viscount Northcliff, and vowed once more that not a single breath of what she had seen would pass her lips. Then, quiet as the church mouse she resembled, she withdrew from the gap in the library door, and nearly from our story.

"Jamie," Flora said. "Jamie, did I dream? I had such horrible nightmares, I thought that he–That I–" Here she had to struggle to hold back her tears, but hold them back she did, while Simon patted the air above her shoulder with awkward tenderness.

James knelt by his sister, and explained what had happened. Her gasps and cries soon modulated to an icy silence, and she stared at the dust of the late Marquess with real hatred. "Well, then, I am glad I did it," she said. "The white aura! What a detestable beast! And Irene, I am so grateful to you. You are a true friend."

Irene, hovering on the edge of the little group, could only duck her head and murmur that the lady was too kind. The ash on the floor was beginning to bother her, lying as it did in the uncannily accurate shape of a man.

"No, no, it was a wonderful spell, how clever of you and Jamie to think of it!"

"It was Simon's spell," James said, seeing that his friend would not. "He turned it up, and he and Irene perfected it. I did hardly a thing."

Flora gave Simon a smile of melting adoration. "Oh, Mr. Young! I am so very grateful that you came to my aid."

"You're welcome, Lady Flora," Simon said. Emboldened by this new ability to complete a sentence in her presence, he courageously offered Flora a deep bow.

"Gracious, it's nearly dawn!" James exclaimed. "You had better go back to your room before the household rises, Flora. Simon, how's your head? Shall I call for a physician?"

"I'm quite well, and shall bid you my own farewells. Miss Crawford. Lady Flora."

"Mr. Young," Flora said, and swept into her very best curtsey, so that she quite robbed Simon of the ability to speak again.

James waved them out and blinked at Irene where she was methodically sweeping up the remnants of the late Marquess of Chumley. "Lord, Irene, you don't need to do that."

"Someone must, my lord. Do you want me to leave it for little Elsie, when the ash has been ground into the carpet?"

James had not the least idea who little Elsie might be, but the picture of Irene clearing away the dust of this enemy offended him in a way he could not voice. "I want you to stop and listen to me," he said. "And you, Irene, what do you want?"

Irene stood and stared at the tips of her boots, hurt. After what they had shared–what they had felt–should she be paid off with a few half-crowns and a kind word? Well, of course she should, and she knew it well, but her heart rebelled within her. She would not take his money.

"Nothing, my lord," she said, and slid into her voice a hint of surprise at the mere suggestion.

"Irene," James said, and some catch in his voice made her lift her eyes to his. "I mean it most sincerely. Please tell me your dearest wish, and I give you my oath that I shall make it come true."

And Irene, at his word freely given, at the strange look in his dark eyes, at the thrilling tone of his voice, felt the dams of self-control that she had kept so well tended for two long years break, and the secret dream within rushed out as if borne upon a river in furious flood.

"I wish to learn magick, my lord!" she said. "I know I can do more than curl hair and mix skin-brightening potions. I want to study spell theory as Mr. Young does, and make the incantations as clear to casters as Mrs. Beeton has. I want to test variations of spells for ease and efficiency and I want to . . . I want to make my own spells, too!"

James smiled, and Irene thought she saw mockery in it. But the raging waters could not be so easily penned up again.

"In these enlightened days, ladies can learn medicine, and practice it, including those cures that magick only can accomplish. Miss Edmona Lewis is greatly admired as a sculptor. Mrs. Gaskell's novels are adored. But the universities will not let women take degrees, even could I find the money for the fees, and private tutors are far beyond my grasp. I will never–I wish that I–" Irene snapped her mouth shut and stood, hands clenched at her side, shoulders heaving with her fervor.

James gazed upon her, and thought that the ways of the Almighty were wondrous indeed. So Irene wanted to learn the ways of deep magick?

"Then by my name," he said softly, "you shall, my lady."

Irene sighed. "I am not a lady, my lord."

"Would you like to be?"

"My lord?"

"Irene, you have known me for nearly two years, during which time you have been constant companion to my sister. Do you think you could address me by my Christian name?"

"No, my lord."

"Then, Miss Crawford, I shall not address you by yours. It is unseemly, you know, for a gentleman to do so without permission."

"To a lady, my lord."

"Yes, Miss Crawford."

Irene bit her lip. "I really think it is too bad, my lord, for you to be making such sport of me."

"I am not, Miss Crawford, I assure you, and I beg your forgiveness for having led you to believe that I was. The truth is that I am afraid. Can you guess why?"

Irene would not guess, though a wild hope had sprang up within her, like the fancies she could not now dismiss with all her strength of mind. Still, she could not believe their fulfillment, even when James sank to one knee on the library hearth rug.

"Miss Irene Crawford," said the Viscount Northcliff, "will you marry me?"

• • •

The Earl of Rabton was horrified by the tale his children had to tell the next day, in which all the credit of the counterspell's research went to Simon, and all the glory of its casting to James. Irene appeared nowhere in the story, at her own request. He pumped Simon's hand twelve or thirteen times, and called him a good fellow, a very good fellow indeed, and offered him the best port in the cellar.

It was almost a pity Mr. Young was a mere scholar with no title nor property to speak of, for Lord Rabton intended still to look far higher for his daughter's future happiness, but as a houseguest, he thought, Mr. Young was very handy indeed.

Not a week later, Irene Crawford dutifully reported that she had discovered Lady Flora's bedroom empty, and the resulting fuss enveloped the great house. If anybody thought that Irene had gone in much later than the lady's usual rising hour, none mentioned it in the uproar.

The turmoil was only increased when a stable boy confessed to having readied a carriage in the very early hours of the morning at the instructions of Mr. Simon Young, who had said he must make haste to catch the first train to London. No mention had been made of a passenger, yet Mr. Young had loaded a quantity of luggage, much more than the single trunk he had brought with him.

The butler, quailing in every part, ordered the Earl awoken. When that furious gentleman discovered the letter his daughter had left upon his desk, all doubt was gone, and all hope lost. Flora and Simon were eloped to France.

It was with the greatest of difficulty that the Viscount Northcliff made it clear to his father that any plans to chase the couple were doomed to failure, and, moreover, would only spread the scandal throughout the country.

"We will put it about that they were married here, very quietly, and that they journey on their honeymoon," he said.

"Simon will have the sense to make sure they travel as husband and wife in name, until it can be in fact. By the time the season begins they will be home, and the tabbies may chatter as they will."

At first Lord Rabton raged with many threats of action both legal and violent, and then elected for more domestic punishment. With great ceremony he declared he would never receive his daughter again, casting her out utterly. "And you shan't see her either, you pup!" he roared.

Here James grew autocratic, and informed his father that he would not obey any such injunction. "And truly, sir," he added, becoming now beseeching, "you would not wish to never see Flora again. You know you would not."

It was a masterly performance, the footmen agreed, but they listened, all agog, as the unheralded second act began.

"Sir," said James. "I must tell you now of my own engagement."

A more feeling son might have refrained from sharing this news at such a trying time, but a perceptive son could not fail to hope that, having exhausted himself already, hearing of the insalubrious connection of his son and heir to a lady's maid could scarcely raise the old man to more anger.

This hope, alas, was too ambitious. The Earl declared that he should most *certainly* never see his son again, nor provide for him neither.

James was confident that his father's anger would fade, and, moreover, had inherited a great deal of property from his mother. Nevertheless, he was saddened by this breach, however temporary it might prove to be. But, "As you wish, sir," he said, and the old man was checked for a moment by his son's dignity.

Still, he could not bring himself to relent so quickly. "And take that gel out of my house on the instant," he added. "For I am master here!"

This order, at least, James was happy to obey.

Irene, with her bags neatly packed, waited in the courtyard, oblivious to the outrage of the cook, the excitement of the kitchen maids, and the confused goodwill of Mrs. Framble. She saw James hurry toward her in his greatcoat, and the corners of her wide mouth lifted in the smile that she wore, ever and always, for him.

• • •

The tabbies did gossip, of course, for in these impudent times, discretion is counted a sin, and tale-telling a virtue, one especially celebrated by the so-called gentlemen of the press. The family reconciled, after Lord Rabton felt enough time had passed that he might be magnanimous in forgiveness–and meet his grandchildren, among whom he was thereafter a great favorite.

But among those who cared not for forgiveness nor family feeling, much was made of the poor Earl of Rabton, who was so unfortunate in his children. Especially since those children, little caring of their father's woe, shamefully persisted in showing every sign of being blissfully happy.

And little Elsie the scullery maid kept her self-imposed silence most loyally, but for the rest of her long and fruitful days, she treasured what she had found left for her on the library hearth rug the day Miss Crawford and the Viscount Northcliff had left Rabton Hall–a battered copy of *Mrs. Beeton's Book of Magickal Management.*

The Language of Flowers

CAROLINE STEVERMER

"A leek? What sort of madman sends a bouquet of flowers containing a leek?" My older sister thrust the offending bouquet at me. "Take it away, Olivia. Do what you wish, but if you must sketch it, oblige me by throwing the leek away first."

I was used to Iris's high flights. "You haven't even glanced at the card. You don't know who sent it. Iris, consider. It might be from someone you admire."

Iris turned up her nose. "I couldn't admire someone who would do such a thing, and I don't care in the least who sent it. Whoever he is, I shall not grant him a single dance."

"If you don't know who sent it, how will you know who not to dance with?" The leek was surrounded by pink and white carnations, signifying pure and deep love. I examined the card that accompanied the bouquet. "You might wish to reconsider. It's from Lord Camborough."

Iris sat before her dressing table and took up her hand mirror. "Lord Camborough has the soul of a turnip. He must, to send me something so grotesque."

My older sister was in the middle of her first season. Her debut had gone well, and scarcely a day went by without an invitation to Lord Someone-or-Other's ball. Iris has dark hair, a radiant complexion, and a neat figure. Add dress sense–Iris has that to a high degree–and a keen awareness of what other people think of her. If anything, Iris's mastery of that mystery surpasses her genius for what suits her–and the result is a perfect recipe for social success.

I loved hearing my sister's tales of high society, but I was well content to be a spectator at the social whirl. I had my watercolors. The studies I painted of the floral tributes Iris had received had already filled two of my sketchbooks. Since Iris's debut in society, I'd become expert in interpreting the language of flowers. It was fascinating to see which gentlemen were quick to express their affections with the cliche of red roses, and which displayed more discretion and imagination. I liked what I'd seen of Lord Camborough very much, but I have to admit I found the leek alarming. My judgment rested solely upon his few afternoon calls upon Iris and Mama, and what I had seen of him among the other guests during the ball held at our house. Appearances could definitely deceive.

At the age of seventeen, I was still in the schoolroom under the care of our governess, Miss Amberly. My much younger brothers, Charles and William, had recently graduated from Miss Amberly's lessons to a tutor of their own, Mr. Louis Hugo. I often sat with Charles and William for their Latin lessons. Mr. Hugo didn't mind teaching me, and Mama and Papa thought it would do me no harm to learn a little Latin to go with my new interest in botany. It was better than letting me kick my heels idly while I waited for my own turn to come out into society.

I did my best to conceal from everyone how much I was dreading my debut. Iris had taken society by storm. I knew I would be a sad disappointment when my turn finally came. I have my sister's coloring, but there the likeness ends. I am proud to resemble my father in my disposition and temperament, but I also inherited his long nose, his wide mouth, and his decided chin. I take comfort in the knowledge that I have also inherited his common sense. Looks aren't everything. Even Iris admits she needs a bit of good advice now and then.

"A leek symbolizes domesticity," I explained. "I think we are to understand that Lord Camborough perceives the domestic genius within you. Optimistic of him, you must admit."

"Domestic genius? Why would anyone want to congratulate me on my domestic genius? That's what servants are for, aren't they?" Iris studied her face in the mirror and frowned. "The man thinks he knows me better than I know myself. I must teach him a lesson. I shall not grant Lord Camborough a single dance, not even a reel."

"Lord Camborough is wealthy enough to satisfy Mama, and kind enough to satisfy Papa. His entire family is sensible and well behaved." I pointed out. "Not many titled gentlemen can make that claim. The leek was a mistake, I admit. But he may have been trying to be original. Everyone tells you you're beautiful. No one else expresses admiration for your domestic side."

"Very well. I'll forgive him the leek." Iris smiled at her reflection. "I put so much store in your opinion of him that I shall relent and dance with him after all. A reel won't hurt me."

I could not help a most unladylike snort of amusement. "If you are pretending to take my advice in the matter of Lord Camborough, I know you have some other motive. Be honest."

Idly Iris tilted the mirror this way and that. "I will be more civil to Lord Camborough than he deserves, but only to make you happy. In truth, my heart is already half spoken for, and not by a gentleman who does his courting with leeks."

I suppressed a sigh. "Who, then? Who is it this time?"

"Oh, you know who it is I mean." Iris put the mirror aside for a moment to gaze at me with her heart in her eyes. "Have I put myself to the trouble of learning new dance steps for anyone else?"

My heart gave a little lurch of dismay as I took her meaning. The madera, a traditional European dance, had taken London by storm early that season. It required lively music in three-four time and dancers with sufficient stamina for its flashy spins and reverses. The craze to dance the madera originated with a mysterious young man named Mr. Michael Smith. New to society, rumored to be a foreigner, he had set a new fashion for the dance, which he performed with great dash and style. As soon as the madera was fixed as the height of fashion, Iris had begged for dancing lessons. She was determined to dance the madera with the fascinating Mr. Smith.

Dancing masters who knew the fine points of the madera were hard to find. By a stroke of luck, a tutor had been found within our very walls, for Mr. Louis Hugo admitted he knew how to dance the madera. He told us he'd learned the dance when he was on a walking tour through Falconberg back in his student days.

Charles and William and I had watched as Mr. Hugo walked Iris through her first lesson, while Miss Amberly presided at the piano.

"You must hold yourself straight and tall at all times." Mr. Hugo positioned himself and Iris as if they were about to waltz, one hand holding hers, the other resting lightly at her waist. "Shoulders back. Stand tall. Head high, heart high. Imagine you wear a crown." Mr. Hugo was not much taller than Iris, but as he held her, he seemed much more commanding than usual. Although he was at least twenty-five, his age and faint scholarly stoop had disappeared entirely as he readied himself for the dance. With his fine posture and his fair hair, he seemed to wear an invisible crown himself. "So."

"To imagine a crown would be presumptuous," said Iris. "I shall imagine I wear a tiara instead."

Mr. Hugo's expression was one I knew well, the same blank courtesy with which he corrected me when I got my declensions wrong. He let Iris's remark pass as if she hadn't spoken. "In your head and shoulders, you must be dignified. But in your lower extremities you must prance. Think of the stag and the doe in the forest."

With patience, Mr. Hugo showed Iris the steps. At first they moved slowly, with many false starts and corrections. Then Miss Amberly struck up the madera at half time. They moved through the steps without error.

"Very good," said Mr. Hugo at last. "You have some aptitude. Miss Amberly, may we have the music in the proper tempo?"

Miss Amberly obliged. The sprightly music combined with the prancing steps to fill the music room with gaiety. Mr. Hugo turned Iris this way and that, they spun forward and back, dazzling even in the close quarters. When the music stopped, Iris curtseyed as Mr. Hugo bowed. As they stepped apart, Iris was panting with laughter. "That is delightful! I feel as if I've been cantering about on horseback."

"Very good," said Mr. Hugo as my brothers and I applauded. "A few more lessons and you will be capable of dancing an acceptable madera."

"Acceptable?" Iris bristled. "I think I already surpass all the other ladies I've seen dance the madera."

"I am sure you do," Mr. Hugo agreed. "But there is more to the madera than this. Tomorrow we will meet here again. I shall teach you to reverse." He studied Iris critically for a moment, then added, "I shall *try* to teach you."

"I can learn the reverse," Iris assured him haughtily. "I shall."

Mr. Hugo returned her haughty look with interest. "Good. I trust you will. But be ready. Practice the steps you've learned today."

"Practice with me," demanded Charles, with William right behind him. "Play again, Miss Amberly, do!"

So it was that we made Miss Amberly play her sheet music over and over. Mr. Hugo made critical remarks, while Iris and I, with Charles and William as our partners, danced and laughed together. My skirts were still up and my hair was still down, but in the glorious gallop of the madera, I had a taste of what lay in store for me when my turn in society came. My heart was as light as my feet.

Our lessons went on for three wonderful days. I had my turn with Mr. Hugo, and found myself determined to surpass Iris. He issued orders and I followed them. I kept my shoulders back and I pointed my toes. I found myself spinning until I was giddy with the joy of the music and the motion.

"You see," Mr. Hugo said triumphantly, as we completed a turn, "that is exactly how it should be done. Head high, heart high. Excellent! Do as your sister does, Miss Malvern, and you will excel at the madera."

I did my best to conceal my pleasure at this praise as Mr. Hugo released me, dizzy and breathless, to sit between my small brothers and watch as Iris practiced. He pushed her this way and that, criticizing her mercilessly, but Iris was as competitive as I, and she soon mastered the finest points of the dance.

At last Mr. Hugo declared himself satisfied with the result. Lessons were at an end. I missed the music and the merriment. I also found myself missing Mr. Hugo's imperiousness on the dance floor. I had grown to like Mr. Hugo a great deal.

It pleased me to hear him order my sister about. He seemed immune to Iris's charm, a rare thing these days.

The night Iris finally claimed her dance with the fascinating Mr. Smith, I hung on her every word. In her bedchamber after the ball, I almost felt I had been there with her.

"I wish you could have seen me. Mr. Smith asked me to dance a waltz with him, but I was bold. The next dance was a madera, and I hinted I would prefer it to the waltz. Those dark eyes of his held such surprise, but he took my meaning. We joined the other dancers on the floor and the music started. Oh, Olivia, words can't describe the beauty of it! It was like floating! Everyone watched us. I could tell. We were made to dance together, Mr. Smith and I. He said so afterward."

"That was bold of him." I was avid for details. "Did you keep your shoulders back, the way Mr. Hugo taught you?"

"Yes, of course, and I pointed my toes ever so." Iris fairly glowed with remembered pleasure. "Such an air of majesty he has when he dances, yet he is all modesty away from the ballroom. Mr. Smith said he was surprised to see such finished detail in a dancer here in London. Only the girls of his homeland dance with such polish and such fire. That's what he told me."

"Will he dance with you again?" I asked.

Iris was almost too pleased with herself to speak. "He made me swear I would grant him a dance at the Bascombes' ball tomorrow night. I have promised always to save the madera for him."

Iris's dancing had created a sensation. Every night I joined her in her bedchamber afterward to hear the details of her triumphs. Soon Mr. Smith would dance the madera with no one else. Iris admitted rumors flew. The attention shown her was very nearly more than a well-bred young lady should attract, but Iris did not let it turn her head. She behaved with such discretion and modesty, not even the strictest chaperone could honestly fault her.

Mr. Smith was only one of several gentlemen to show an interest in Iris, but so far he was the only man for whom Iris returned much interest. With every turn on the dance floor with him, her preference for him had grown more marked.

Now I braced myself for Iris's confession that she loved Mr. Smith, a man she'd hardly spoken to except when dancing. "Mr. Smith the foreigner, you mean. Papa won't like that."

Iris put her mirror down on the dressing table and addressed me sternly. "Mr. Smith isn't truly a foreigner. He may have rather European looks, but he has lived in England since infancy. I defy you to name a single foreign element in his character."

"The way he dances," I said. "Everyone remarks upon it."

"He does dance the madera with a particular flair," Iris conceded dreamily, "but that is only because it is the traditional dance of his subjects."

Sharply, I said, "His subjects? What subjects?"

Iris gave me a searching look. "You mustn't tell."

I put my hand over my heart. "Never a word. I promise."

Iris held up her hand. "You swear on your honor?"

"Swear on my honor," I assured her. "Tell me."

Iris came to sit beside me, sliding very close on the window seat. In a whisper she confided, "Mr. Smith is not his real name. In truth, his name is Prince Michael Von Falconberg, true ruler of the principality of Falconberg."

"Falconberg?" I echoed. "Where might that be, pray? Miss Amberly never mentioned any such place in my geography lessons."

"Miss Amberly doesn't know everything in the world." Iris sprang up indignantly and returned to her dressing table. "It isn't on maps anymore. It was most unjustly granted to the German crown to appease Von Bismarck. If you don't believe it, ask Mr. Hugo."

"Mr. Hugo?" I was puzzled. "What does he know of such things?"

"Oh, everything." Iris smiled. "I didn't wish to ask Mr. Smith these questions directly, so I applied to Mr. Hugo. He had it all at the tips of his fingers. Mr. Hugo knows a great deal about Falconberg and any number of other kingdoms gobbled up by Von Bismarck and his ilk. Powermongers."

"Why then does Michael Von Falconberg, true ruler of Falconberg, call himself plain Mr. Smith?" I asked.

"Really, dearest." Lord Camborough had once told Iris her laugh was fascinatingly like a ripple of fresh water. Now she rippled freely at me. "You are so naive. He must hide his identity. He has powerful enemies. He has come to London to seek help from friendly interests, but he has powerful enemies who would do him harm if they knew his true identity. Therefore he keeps it a secret."

"Yet he told you." I didn't try to keep the doubt out of my voice.

Iris gazed at me with fond superiority. "He did not wish to, but I persuaded him, at last. I have earned his trust."

I didn't like the sound of that. "How on earth did you earn his trust?"

"How should I know?" Iris gave another little ripple of happiness. "He admires me, as I do him. I have won his complete confidence. He knows I deserve it."

Her sincerity made my stomach twist a little with dismay. "You're fond of him? You favor him over the other gentlemen pursuing you? Then I am sorry for you."

"Sorry?" Iris's eyes went wide. "Whatever for?"

I had to be honest. "If he is who he claims to be, he can never marry where his heart lies. A prince must choose his mate by policy, not by preference."

Iris lifted her chin. "Every rule has its exception."

"Does it? Is that what Mr. Smith tells you?"

Before Iris could answer me, Anna the maid brought the news that Lord Camborough wished to know if Miss Malvern was at home to him.

"I am," said Iris. "Tell him I shall join him directly."

She turned to me, triumphant. "There. Does that content you, my dearest sister? Only to make you happy, I am willing to receive a man who sends me leeks. I shall listen to his amiable rubbish for a full twenty minutes, and even dance with him at Lady Worbury's ball, all to please you."

"I am not the one whose contentment matters," I countered. "Think of Papa and Mama."

Iris gave me a glittering smile. "I do, dearest. Believe me. I do."

• • •

After the dance, Iris once again let me keep her company while Anna helped her to change out of her silken ballgown. The petticoats, the pantalettes, the crinoline, and the chemise all took time and patience to set aside in their proper order.

"I was as good as my word. I gave Lord Camborough a waltz in addition to his reel, and neither of us mentioned the leek at all." Iris, now in a nightgown and a silken wrapper, played with her hairbrush as Anna took the pearl-tipped pins from her hair. "He's too good for me, Olivia. You'll have to take him in hand yourself."

I couldn't help laughing. "I don't believe Lord Camborough would give me a second glance, even if he is still unattached by the time I make my debut."

Iris smiled fondly at me. "You don't see yourself as we do, dearest. Those big eyes of yours will have the gentlemen at your feet when the time comes."

"Piffle." I didn't believe Iris for a moment, but I appreciated her effort. "Who else did you dance with?"

"Who do you suppose?" Iris brushed her hair with languid grace. Dreamily, she added, "He told me how beautiful Falconberg is in the spring."

I asked crossly, "If Falconberg is so beautiful, why doesn't he go back there?"

Iris smiled at me pityingly. "There is more to a throne than the right to claim it. That's what he told me tonight. He has come to London to win friends for his cause. Given his qualities, it is no surprise that his efforts have been rewarded. Soon now, very soon, he will return to Falconberg and claim his throne. I only wish I could be there to see it."

If there is anything I detest more than being patronized, it is being patronized by Iris. "No, you don't. Men don't give up power willingly. There will be bloodshed, maybe even outright war. Your Mr. Smith endangers these friends of his if he seeks to press his claim."

Iris gave me another maddeningly indulgent smile. "You sound just like Papa."

"Good," I snapped. "That means I'm making sense."

Iris rippled out her charming laugh. "I've let you stay up far too late. You're so cross with me. Mama and Papa won't like it if you're grumpy in the morning. You'd best be off to bed now."

It is a measure of how annoyed I was with Iris that I went to bed without even a token protest. She might think herself in love with a prince, but I knew there was something amiss. She might not listen to my advice, but she couldn't stop me looking after her. If Iris was mooning over Falconberg in spring, someone had to be sensible.

• • •

Lady Worbury's ball came a few nights later. As usual before a social event of any importance, Iris was besieged with floral tributes from every gentleman who hoped to attract her favorable attention at the ball. By teatime, my sister's bedchamber was fragrant with the assembled bouquets. I came in with my sketchbook to inspect them while Anna was putting the finishing touches on the gown Iris would wear that evening, white silk ornamented with embroidered forget-me-nots and love knots of blue ribbon. It was Anna's task to make sure the love knots were all firmly affixed and properly tied.

Lord Camborough had sent the bouquet most suitable for the dress, simple blue violets for faithfulness, but I knew Mr. Smith's offering would be preferred despite its unbalanced design. It sat in a place of honor on Iris's dressing table, the asymmetry of an arrangement designed to express a particular sentiment rather than to enhance the recipient's beauty.

I examined the bouquet with interest. There were irises, of course, which meant a message. Given my sister's name that was the obvious thing to send. When it came to the language of flowers, Mr. Smith was nothing if not obvious. There was a single red tulip, far out of season, as an expression of love. Red roses surrounded the tulip, symbolizing undying and passionate love. A bit of ivy wrapped the roses, hinting at marriage. So far, nothing out of the ordinary. I looked more closely, and my heart lurched.

Nestled beneath the roses and all but concealed by them, a bunch of pennyroyal leaned against the tulip's stem. Pennyroyal meant "flee away." Within the pennyroyal was tucked a single egret plume, white as snow. What could a feather mean but "fly with me?"

I inspected the bouquet in silence. If I showed the flowers and feather to Mama and Papa, I would destroy any chance that Iris would find happiness with Mr. Smith. If I was right to suspect Mr. Smith was no prince at all, it was surely my duty to raise the alarm. Even if Mr. Smith was by some chance a true prince, he would never stoop to marry a commoner like my sister.

Anna had noticed my interest in the bouquet. "Mr. Hugo brought it upstairs himself."

My voice sounded strange even to me. "Has Iris seen it?"

"No, not yet. Mrs. Malvern has the headache, so she is having a lie down, and your sister is reading to her. Shall I go tell her it's come?"

"Yes, do." When Anna had gone, I seized my chance. I plucked out the pennyroyal and the egret feather. The bouquet looked oddly sparse without them, so I took some carnations from another offering and tucked them into the empty spot. I started to hide the pennyroyal and feather in my bodice, but paused when I noticed a bit of green paper was wrapped around the shaft of the feather. My hands shook as I unwrapped it.

Meet me in Eden at two o'clock, it read. *Be ready.*

I could see it all, how it would be at two in the morning. The quiet house, the empty street, the lover's carriage drawn up, waiting. That carriage would leave without its intended passenger, for Iris must never know the rendezvous had been set.

I crumpled the note and turned to toss it in the fire. Caution halted me. Proof of Mr. Smith's scheme might be important. I put the pennyroyal, the feather, and the note into my bodice. It was scratchy, and I probably smelled distinctly of pennyroyal, but it was safe for the moment.

That night seemed to last a hundred years.

As I had guessed, Iris turned up her shapely nose at the blue violets sent by Lord Camborough. She added the tulip to the bouquet of forget-me-nots that went with her ballgown, a hideous dollop of scarlet against the gentle blue, and tucked a bit of the ivy in besides. The ball lasted for hours, but Iris was home again, complaining of the headache, by one o'clock. I sat with her while Anna gave her a cup of cambric tea and put her to bed. Then I pretended to go to bed myself.

The house was dark and silent by two o'clock. Like all expert hostesses, Lady Worbury had chosen a night with a full moon to make travel by night easier and safer. From my perch on the nursery window seat, I could see moonlight filled the street below. I had dared to hope the message had been a ruse or a mistake, but just after the clocks struck two, a carriage had turned down our street and pulled up at the gate.

Even as I watched, the door of the carriage swung open. A man in a cloak descended, unmistakably young and energetic. He did not approach the front door. Instead, he walked out of my view, in the direction of the kitchen garden behind our house. Could that humble garden be Iris's Eden?

I could bear waiting no more. I started downstairs, soundless in my kidskin slippers. If I told Mr. Smith point blank that Iris wouldn't come with him, surely he and his coachman would take themselves off. If not, I would be obliged to raise the alarm, but only if it was absolutely necessary. If the household knew of this, Iris's reputation would be in shreds. Even Lord Camborough's devotion could not stand such a blow.

I had descended two flights of stairs before I was stopped on the first-floor landing by a hand grasping my wrist. I gasped and twisted, but found myself held fast.

A grim whisper in my ear. "Go back to bed, Miss Malvern. This caller is not for you. I shall see your intended off the premises for you."

I gasped again for I recognized the voice as Mr. Hugo's. "I'm not Iris. Let me go!"

The iron grip left my wrist. "Miss Olivia! I beg your pardon."

In unison we whispered, "What are you doing here?" then I added breathlessly, "Iris didn't see the message. I stole it. You must have seen it when you brought the bouquet up."

"Do as I tell you and go back to bed," Mr. Hugo whispered through gritted teeth. "I will take care of everything."

It was a tempting proposition. I could go back to my room and lie down in my bed and pretend I knew nothing whatever about anything. In the morning, it would all be over. For a moment, I wavered. Then I thought of Iris. What did a tutor know about dealing with a man like Mr. Smith? What did any gentleman understand about the perils to a lady's reputation? I put temptation aside. "Iris doesn't need to know this ever happened. But I must come with you, or I'll raise the house."

Mr. Hugo said nothing, but the way he exhaled through his nose spoke volumes about his patience–and lack thereof. When he spoke at last, I had to strain to catch the words. "Very well. Stay out of the way, whatever happens. This man's a villain. You must let me deal with him." He picked up a bundle and started downstairs. I hastened after him.

I had all I could do to keep up with Mr. Hugo. He must have known the house as well as I did, for he moved through the darkness in perfect silence. Mr. Hugo had keys, I was interested to discover. I'd thought only Papa, Mama, and Jamison the butler had all the keys to the house. Apparently I was wrong.

With only the faintest click of the latch, Mr. Hugo opened the door to the garden. We stepped through, careful not to let the pea gravel underfoot crunch unnecessarily. The night was cool and fragrant. The moonlight was bright enough to cast shadows. I could smell the nearby river on the breeze that stirred my hair.

Mr. Smith's voice, pitched low, came at once. "Is that you, my love? I thought we might have been betrayed."

I yielded to a base impulse and did my best to imitate Iris's voice. "What are you doing here?"

"Love laughs at locksmiths." Even by moonlight, the flash of Mr. Smith's smile was charming. "I've come to claim my own."

"That's a remarkable coincidence," said Mr. Hugo as his bundle hit the ground with a metallic clink. "So have I."

"Iris?" For the first time, Mr. Smith sounded uncertain. "What have you done?"

I stepped out of the shadows. "Iris isn't coming. Go away."

"Get behind me." Mr. Hugo stooped and to my surprise drew two swords from his bundle. "I've taken the liberty of choosing the weapon. Sabers."

Mr. Smith stepped forward. "I don't know who you think you are, but you're not wanted here. Where is Iris?"

"Iris isn't coming. Now go away," I said firmly, "or I will raise the house."

"Do so, by all means," Mr. Smith countered, "and your sister's reputation is ruined."

Mr. Hugo held out the sabers. "Choose your weapon, you fraud. You're going to rue the day you decided to pass yourself off as Michael Von Falconberg."

"Oh, am I?" Mr. Smith inspected the weapons Mr. Hugo held out to him. "Quite sure of that, are you?"

"Quite sure." Mr. Hugo's voice was cold. "I've been longing to try occasions with you. Whoever you are."

Mr. Smith's laugh held a sneer. "I don't know what you mean by that, but I only fight with gentlemen."

Mr. Hugo sneered back. "I too prefer to fight with gentlemen, but in your case I shall make an exception."

Mr. Smith took one of the sabers. "Before I make you eat that insult, tell me your name. I like to know who I'm killing." Moonlight glinted on the bare blade as he took a practice swing.

Mr. Hugo came to solemn attention, holding his saber as if it weighed no more than a teaspoon. "Prince Michael Christian Ludwig Hugo von Falconberg. I won't add 'at your service' because I dislike unnecessary lies."

My stomach twisted as I realized what a blind fool I'd been. Of course Mr. Hugo was the true prince. He knew all about Falconberg. He knew every subtle step of the madera. He also showed every sign of knowing how to fight with a saber.

"Do you really?" Mr. Smith came on guard. "I enjoy them immensely."

Mr. Hugo's voice was as cold as moonlight. "You have stolen my name, you have tricked those who are friendly to my cause, and you have deceived the daughter of the man who has given me sanctuary in exile. Prepare to make amends."

Astonished and appalled, I retreated until my back was to the garden wall. Duels were not just illegal, they were most unfashionable. I'd never wished to see one. Now I was about to. I feared I was going to see bloody murder.

For a moment, the duelists stood perfectly still, each mirroring the other's pose. Then the fight commenced. Sabers clashed and slid, glinting in the moonlight as the fighters sliced and swung.

I rejoiced at the dismay on Mr. Smith's face. His expression soon told me Mr. Hugo's skill was the greater. This man had tricked my sister into believing him a prince. He had tried to elope with her. What would Iris's fate have been, had he succeeded in his plan? In the drama of the moment, I judged death was too good for Mr. Smith.

The fight lasted only two minutes, and ended when Mr. Smith's saber flew out of his hand and struck the garden wall with a clang like a dropped saucepan. Mr. Hugo–Prince Michael–put the edge of his saber to Mr. Smith's throat.

Mr. Smith fell to his knees. "I yield."

Eyes narrow, nostrils flaring, Prince Michael regarded Mr. Smith with loathing. I found it impossible to see mild Mr. Hugo in him anymore. He held the impostor helpless, but he did not speak.

"I said, I surrender." Mr. Smith tried to move away from the blade at his throat, but Prince Michael was relentless. Smith subsided completely, gazing at him in real fear. "I'm at your mercy."

I regarded Smith with disgust. How could anyone, even Iris, ever have believed this smooth deceiver to be the prince of anything?

"Just so." When Prince Michael spoke, it was strange to hear the mild tones of the Latin tutor again. "Like any young lady foolish enough to believe a word you say. Perhaps we should go to Miss Malvern's father, so you can explain yourself and make amends."

"Let me up and I shall," Smith promised. "I shall do anything you say."

I protested, "No, you mustn't tell Papa."

The men gazed at me with identical startled expressions. They had forgotten I was there, I'm sure of it. Enraged, I left my spot in the shadows. "Typical. You haven't spared a thought for Iris in all this, have you?"

"Miss Malvern is safe," said Prince Michael. "He will deceive her no more."

"There's safe and then there's safe," I said. "She won't elope with him now, and that's a good thing." I had to resist the urge to nudge Smith with my toe. He was utterly despicable and deserved a good kicking, but it would be most unladylike to administer it myself. "Her heart will be broken, but that can't be helped. The real danger is to her reputation. She has let her name be linked to that of a base pretender. If he's exposed as a fraud, it makes my sister a laughingstock, and worse still, an accomplice. No one must know of this."

"No one will hear of it from me," Smith assured me.

"You've taken money from the people you fooled into thinking you were a prince," I continued. "You must give it back."

"I can't," said Smith. "I've spent it."

"You astonish me," said Prince Michael drily.

"You must confess your deception and make what amends you can." I pressed on, thinking aloud. "You must tell Iris how you have taken advantage of her trust. Once she knows how false you are, her love for you will die."

Smith smiled. "Sure of that, are you?"

I yielded to unbearable temptation and kicked his leg. My slippers were so light, it hurt me as much or more as it did the impostor.

"Ow!" Smith's eyes crossed as the tip of Prince Michael's saber moved to brush the bridge of his nose. "Oh, very well. Yes, miss. I'll do anything you say, miss."

"Begin by standing up," said Prince Michael gently. "Slowly."

As Smith obeyed, I said, "We'll go inside and find something to write with. You must make a written confession."

At that moment, the door opened and Papa emerged from the house. He was wearing his brocade dressing gown and carried a lamp in one hand and a pistol in the other. "What is the meaning of this?" he demanded. "Olivia, go to your mother at once!"

"Papa, what are you doing up at this hour?" I knew it was feeble, but it was all I could think to say.

"What does it look like I am doing?" Papa growled. "The servants woke me when they heard the racket you and your friends have been making. Hugo, I am surprised at you."

"How do you do, Mr. Malvern." Smith spoke with friendliness surprising in a man held at saber-point. "I'm very pleased to make your acquaintance, sir."

Papa studied Smith with dislike. "I know you. You've been hanging about my daughter Iris. I don't want you to see her again, understand?"

Smith bowed elegantly. "As you wish, sir."

"Papa!" Iris joined us in the garden, her maid close behind her. "What are you doing?" She gasped as she saw Smith held at the point of Prince Michael's saber. "Put that down, Mr. Hugo. You might hurt someone." She flew to Smith's side. "Michael, are you hurt?"

"What the devil are you doing here, Iris?" growled Papa.

"Only a little." Smith smiled bravely at Iris.

"I kicked him," I told Iris. "I confess it. I don't know who he is, but I can tell you who he isn't. He's not Prince Michael of Falconberg. He's probably not even really called Michael Smith."

Smith made another elegant bow. "Allow me to introduce myself. Walter Robinson, at your service."

Iris regarded him with horror. "What did you say?"

I pointed to the man we'd known as Mr. Hugo. "He is Prince Michael of Falconberg."

Iris recoiled. "You!"

"Do you think it wise to reveal your identity so soon, Hugo?" Papa asked Prince Michael.

"I cannot permit this mountebank to go on exploiting the friends of Falconberg," Prince Michael replied. "Nor could I let him elope with your daughter."

Iris had been regarding her Mr. Smith with horror. At Prince Michael's words, she turned upon him angrily. "Elope! Who said anything about eloping?"

I produced the note, now much crumpled, from my bodice. "He did. Here's the message he sent you."

Iris took the bit of paper from me and read it by the light of the lamp Papa held. As she read, her expression changed from disbelief to incandescent rage. She turned first to me. "How dare you steal my private correspondence?"

"I had to." I extracted the feather and the wilted pennyroyal from my bodice and held them out to her, a full confession of my guilt. "I do apologize."

Iris's voice had gone alarmingly soft. "What are these weeds?"

I explained the symbolism of the pennyroyal and the feather. "You see the danger you were in," I finished.

"I see the danger you are in," Iris countered, "for keeping this from me. If a man sends me a leek, it does not make me a marvel of domesticity. If a man invites me to elope with him, it does not make me do so. If you couldn't leave the bouquet alone, you should have told me. The message was for me. You should have let me decide what to do about it."

"You were fascinated by him," I reminded her. "I've never understood why. I didn't know what you'd do."

"You were quite fascinated with me, you know," Walter Robinson murmured. "No one could blame you for it."

"You." Iris came to stand directly in front of the man she'd called Mr. Smith. "Did I enjoy flirting with a man we all believed to be a prince? Of course I did. Your attention made me more interesting to others. Who wouldn't enjoy that? But would I have run away with you? Don't flatter yourself. Break Mama's heart, dishonor Papa, and ruin my family name? For you?"

Iris laughed scornfully, but I knew my sister too well to be fooled. I could hear the sadness underneath the scorn. No matter how she denied her feelings for the false prince, I could guess where her heart lay.

"Iris, come away." I took my sister's hand and drew her toward me. "Leave this to Papa. Let's go in."

To my surprise, Iris listened to me. She let me lead her away from the false prince and the true one. We left the gentlemen in the kitchen garden, explaining themselves to Papa.

When her maid and I had her tucked safely into her bed, I patted Iris's hand. "I'm sorry. I should have told you."

"Yes, you should have." Iris wouldn't look at me. She smoothed the coverlet this way and that. "But there's something I should have told you."

I gazed at my sister blankly. "There is?"

"I lied." At last Iris looked at me. Her eyes were clear and her voice was back to normal. "Until I learned to dance the madera, I wasn't as popular as I let you think. I made up all sorts of stories about the balls I went to, but in truth, the invitations I received had more to do with Papa's position than with my looks."

At first I thought she was joking, but her expression was quite serious. "Why on earth did you do that?"

Iris looked back at the coverlet. "It was easier that way. I didn't want to tell you how frightened I was, or how snobbish Lady Worbury can be, or how alone I felt. At first I didn't want you to be scared, because soon enough it will be your turn to come out into society. But you were so interested, so impressed. I loved that. I didn't want you to know what a hard time I was having. I wanted you to look at me as if I were the belle of the ball."

"But you *were* the belle of the ball," I protested.

"I was when I danced the madera." Iris put her hand over her eyes. "Now everyone will laugh at me, for I thought I was dancing with a prince, and all the time he was a fraud."

"You have danced with a prince," I reminded her. "A prince taught you the steps in the first place."

To my great relief, Iris gave a little ripple of laughter. "I can't believe it. Meek little Mr. Hugo. A prince."

"He wasn't meek when he was teaching you to dance. And you should see him with a saber." I remembered the duel. "Papa has given him sanctuary in exile. That's what he said."

Iris leaned back against her pillows. "Papa knew all along?"

"He must have." It was my turn to shake my head. "I should have guessed. Charles and William are too young to need a Latin tutor yet."

"I should have guessed too," said Iris. "No Latin tutor ought to dance like that."

"Is it truly as bad as you say," I asked Iris timidly, "being snubbed and having gentlemen tread on one's toes?"

"Sometimes it is." Iris took my hand. "But sometimes it is splendid. There is music and dancing, and lovely things to eat. There are men like Lord Camborough, who couldn't snub anyone if he tried. You'll have time to ready yourself for it."

I gazed at Iris in wonder. Her love and care for me made my throat tighten.

Iris held my hand tight in hers. "I'll be there to look after you. Don't worry, Olivia. You'll have a season to remember. I promise."

Mama and Miss Amberly descended upon us then, and I was sent to bed in short order, my ears fairly ringing with the scolding I received.

From that night on, Iris told me the truth about her experiences in society. She was right. People did laugh at her for believing Mr. Smith's lies, but she wasn't the only one they laughed at. In a few weeks, it was all forgotten.

Prince Michael Christian Ludwig Hugo von Falconberg went home to claim his rightful throne. Papa arranged it beautifully. He writes to us regularly, letters in his own handwriting, not his secretary's.

Lord Camborough asked Papa for Iris's hand in marriage. Iris had told Papa to say yes, and he did. Lord Camborough and Iris are betrothed. When they are married, I am to be maid of honor. Next season, it will be my turn to make my debut in society. I'm not dreading that anymore. I won't need to pretend to be someone I'm not. My sister will be there, and she'll look after me.

The Dancing Master

GENEVIEVE VALENTINE

Compliance with, and deference to, the wishes of others is the finest breeding.

–Routledge's Manual of Etiquette, 1875

No person who has not a good ear for time and tune need hope to dance well.

–Routledge

• • •

The dancing master was summoned to Evering Park before the last of the winter frost had burned off the lawn, so that Leah could polish herself before the London Season began in the summer.

"Are you sure that's enough time to keep Leah from making a spectacle of herself?" asked Reg at supper.

Leah lowered her fork out of sight of the table and debated her chances of landing a successful blow on his leg, if she tried.

Their mother, however, was the sort who kept a firm eye on which piece of cutlery was in use, and what for, and she cleared her throat and glanced at Leah over the bridge of her nose.

"I hope both my children might keep from making spectacles," she said, with warning looks at each of them in turn.

Leah set down her fork. Reg smoothed his dark hair and shot her a triumphant look.

Her father added vaguely between bites, "I'm sure all will be well. And Reg, naturally, as Leah's brother, you will use your superior knowledge of all our upcoming Society to assist her."

(He said it with a sigh; he wasn't fond of London. Leah was already seventeen, and her mother had yet to prevail upon him to take them.)

Reg, who had already spent three summers in London doing whatever it was young men did when they went to London in the summer all alone, looked Leah up and down for a moment with a look of mild horror at the realization that she would be linked to him in public.

"You needn't act as if I'm Medusa just because I can't waltz," Leah snapped.

"Leah," said Mother, "don't be peevish. Everything is settled; do let's all try to be settled, too."

Leah stared at her fork without blinking until the next course came.

• • •

Miss Hammond had been another of her mother's clever ideas, and had replaced Leah's governess two years ago as a genteel companion, in preparation for that inevitable Season.

("She had a good family," Mama had told her with a sigh, two years ago, as they sat in the morning parlor and waited for Miss Hammond to appear and throw her vocation on their mercy. "And some prospects, once."

That was when Leah began to worry about London.)

Of all her mother's schemes, however, Miss Hammond had been by far the best. She was only nine years older than Leah, and had a way of looking at Reg as if she wished she could light him on fire, which kept Leah from being peevish more often than anything else could.

As Leah knocked on Miss Hammond's door, she could feel a weight already falling off her shoulders. Miss Hammond would know what to do.

(The thing that frightened her most about going to London was that she was still so often foolish, about little childish things.)

Miss Hammond was dressed for the evening (occasionally she was summoned to provide music in the evenings, if Reg was out, and they could enjoy music without him groaning about it), and Leah was comforted just to see the familiar deep gray bombazine in the candlelight.

Miss Hammond had been reading; the book still sat open on her little table, next to her lamp. (She read essays and histories and love stories, one after another, and made a little chain of pockmarks around Father's library.)

"I can't bear to go to London," Leah said without preamble. "I'm going to throw myself from the attic window. Shall you come?"

Miss Hammond smiled and stepped aside.

"Why don't you come in, first," she said, "and tell me what's happened."

• • •

To attempt to dance without a knowledge of dancing is not only to make one's self ridiculous, but one's partner also. No lady has a right to place a partner in this absurd position. Never forget a ballroom engagement. To do so is to commit an unpardonable offence against good breeding.

–Routledge

• • •

Mr. Martin came highly recommended by the Ladislaws ("Their oldest girl married a Duke," said Mama, with a significant look at Leah), and if one was to welcome a dancing master for as long as Leah required one, then he was the only sensible choice in the matter.

And he was going to come, and Leah was going to learn everything she could from him.

("Your mother is only trying to make sure you don't have any worries when you're there," Miss Hammond had said, tucking some stray hair behind her ear, looking as young as Leah. "Suffer a little now, so that when you have your Season you are secure in yourself, and then you're free to enjoy the evening when you're in the ballroom. I'll be there, if you have any worries, but it's much better to study before one recites, no?"

Leah thought about that. A moment too late, she said, "All right."

Back in her own room, she had looked at her round, ordinary face in the mirror for a long time, her mousey hair and strong nose, two small dark eyes that flickered and shook until she blew the candle out.)

• • •

Reg had gone into town for the morning on some pretense, and Father had declared he wasn't in to visitors, so it was only Leah and Miss Hammond and Mama to greet him when he came.

"Reg should have to study with Mr. Martin, too," Leah said. "He promised not to make a spectacle of himself in London."

"He learned his manners at school," said Mama, as if that was an endorsement.

Leah would have been more than happy to learn dancing if it could have been part of an education in London. It would be worth suffering a mazurka every so often if you were also learning mathematics and history and articles of law.

"Mr. Charles Martin," announced Stevens, and Leah pushed the thought aside and stood to greet the guest.

Mr. Martin was tall and handsome, and had blond hair carefully curled; he wore yellow gloves, and his blue coat was almost too sharp for the fashion, and he entered with a smile that felt larger than it was, so Leah had an impression of white teeth, though she had seen none.

"Lady Clement," he greeted, with a bow one degree more formal than necessary.

Mother stepped forward with her arm held out just so. "Mr. Martin, a pleasure to meet you. This, of course, is my daughter Leah."

Mr. Martin bowed and lifted one hand slightly, palm up, to take her hand.

But Leah had laced her fingers together, and though she thought she might extend a hand and have him take it, somehow her fingers wouldn't move, and so she just stared at him.

He blinked, adjusted his expression back to a polite smile, and slid his eyes past her.

"And this is Miss Hammond," Mother said. "My daughter's companion."

"Charmed," said Mr. Martin, turning his face to catch up with his eyes.

Miss Hammond curtseyed, and Leah watched her, for a moment, turn into a lady–the smooth dip of the motion, the lowered eyes, the glance back up to him, smoothing the skirt in a discreet sweep of the palm as she stood.

It was exactly the way a lady should look when meeting a gentleman, and Leah's heart sank just looking at it.

"If I might suggest, Miss Clement might change into a low bodice for our lesson." Mr. Martin turned to Mama and explained, "It's a common request, among the dance instructors most familiar with the Season. One might learn the correct form straight away, and it is an extra source of ease, I find, to practice on the instrument on which one intends to perform."

The idea of wearing her low bodice in front of Mr. Martin the stranger, who hadn't even looked at her when he suggested it, made Leah's hands go cold.

But Mama nodded at her, which meant the decision had been made, and there was nothing left for Leah to do but obey.

Miss Hammond moved to follow, but Leah snapped, "Don't trouble yourself," and kept walking.

As she turned for the stairs, Leah could hear Mama saying, "She can be clever, Mr. Martin, but she's always been a bit peevish. My apologies. Too long in the country, I suspect."

• • •

The lesson took place in the ballroom.

Evering Park was an estate landed enough to have a true ballroom, even though they hadn't hosted anything grander than a dinner party since Leah could remember.

("Your father isn't fond of a fuss," Mama had said once or twice, when Leah asked. Then she had closed the doors of the ballroom with a sigh and moved for the little drawing rooms where they spent their evenings.)

As Leah walked in, Mr. Martin was examining the room with the air of a tenant. Miss Hammond was hanging back near the doorway, watching him.

"Excellent room," he said, and tossed a grin over his shoulder at Miss Hammond–then at Leah, as he caught sight of her. "It's a bit of a trick trying to teach the new dances with nothing but a morning parlor at one's disposal. One should see how a dance moves over a room in order to be able to dance it with grace."

"This might not be big enough," said Leah.

Miss Hammond squeezed her hand for a moment. "Leah, don't underestimate yourself. Many girls with less to recommend them have managed to muddle through a Season or two and come out all right on the other side."

"All right" meant "married," but it couldn't be true–Miss Hammond had had her Seasons, and now here she was. If Miss Hammond couldn't manage, Leah couldn't imagine how she would.

But that was an unkind thing to think. (For one of them, or both of them. It was hard to say.)

"Right," said Mr. Martin, who was hanging his greatcoat carefully across one of the chairs. "Now, Miss Clement, your mother didn't mention to me how much you already knew about dancing."

Leah remembered vaguely that her cousins the Fosters had thrown a family party at the Hall, when she was thirteen or fourteen. She had practiced beforehand with Lily Foster, and then shuffled her way through some dance where you met and parted with strangers all the way down the line, and sometimes met up in quarters so that your right arms joined in a star, and throughout the whole affair Lily had been trying valiantly to give her silent reminders as to what was coming next.

"I think it's safest to assume nothing," Leah said.

Mr. Martin checked a laugh. "Right. I see. And Miss Hammond, you strike me as a young woman of the world–do I have the pleasure of an assistant in this endeavor?"

Miss Hammond inclined her head. "I'm a little out of fashion," she said, "but happy to help if I can."

Mr. Martin was quiet a moment, looking at her, and then turned to Leah.

"Why don't we begin with making an entrance," he said, and turned to indicate the open doors. "I'll be your escort, and Miss Hammond will provide the sage advice that only a lady can communicate to another of her kind."

Leah looked at Miss Hammond, who was smiling at her, and nodding for her to go on.

"A young lady," began Mr. Martin, "always enters a ballroom quietly, so as not to draw attention to herself by causing any disturbance to others at the party. She should, rather, be noticed because of the refinement of her carriage, her manner, and her grace. Her first dance happens before she ever takes the floor."

He held out his hand, palm down. "So, Miss Clement?"

Leah took a breath (her ribs strained against her corset), rested her palm on his hand. His kid gloves were fitted tight, thin as skin, and he was watching her with sharp blue eyes.

He smiled; she had the impression of teeth.

"Let us begin," he said.

They walked nearly the length of the ballroom, as he said, "No weight on the joined hand," and, "Hold the chin slightly lower, so people don't think you're displeased," and once, "There's no hurry, Miss Clement."

"Yes," said Miss Hammond with a grin, "perhaps let's not gallop," and Leah flushed to her temples and forced herself to walk so that the toe of one shoe touched the heel of the other.

"Well done," he said, and for a moment his thumb brushed the edges of her fingers.

It startled her; it was like skin, just like.

She looked up at him, at his bright blue eyes and his quarter of a smile and his shoulders held with more ease than any gentleman she'd ever met.

As they turned to walk back up the room, Leah glimpsed her mother in the doorway, passing out of sight.

• • •

> A lady cannot refuse the invitation of a gentleman to dance, unless she has already accepted that of another, for she would be guilty of an incivility which might occasion trouble.
>
> –*Manners, Culture, and Dress of the Best American Society*, Richard Wells (1891)

• • •

"I'm thinking of inviting your cousin William, Reg, to come and stay," said their mother at supper, three days later. "You know there's hardly any sport worth having on his grounds, this time of year."

Cousin William Foster was the heir to the Foster estate in Surrey, and only a few years older than Leah, and she set down her spoon in the soup so suddenly it splashed.

From the look on Reg's face, he wasn't any keener to have Cousin William come and stay, which made Leah wonder why Mother would think to invite him.

But Mama was pointedly not looking at Leah, and Leah began to worry.

"I'm sure that's not necessary," Leah said.

(She wished Miss Hammond took supper with them–she would know what to say that was roundabout and polite that could put the invitation out of the question, but Leah was here alone, and her face hurt from practicing a smile that showed no teeth, and now she knew her mother had been watching her with Mr. Martin, and looking at his smile, and making plans.)

Her mother glanced at their father. "It might not be strictly necessary, but won't it be nice for Reg and Leah to spend a little time with their cousin before the crush of the Season, Father?"

Leah stared at him, willing him to look at her and take her side–he had to know what was happening when an eligible cousin was invited to stay, it was what had happened with him and Mother.

But Father only glanced up from his soup and said, "Quite right," with a smile.

Nothing was quite right, Leah thought, though there was no saying why.

There was no saying anything at all.

("A lady can never go wrong by being economical in conversation, and avoiding strong opinions," said Mr. Martin. "In the dance, it's a distraction from your fine form, and in company, it can be seen as an attempt to distinguish oneself."

"But I'm supposed to distinguish myself," Leah pointed out. "There are Dukes in London, and my mother has expectations."

Mr. Martin tilted his head like a bird. Then he looked at Miss Hammond and said, "I see we might want to have some lessons in conversation."

Miss Hammond said, "If you like," with that coquette smile, and when Mr. Martin turned his back she gave a smaller, real smile to Leah.)

She sat in silence through the rest of supper, and waved aside the beef and the pudding with custard; her appetite had gone.

"Very good, Leah," said her mother, as if she really was

proud. "I'll make some enquiries about a modiste of repute, and we'll see what's to be done with your figure, how's that?"

Leah didn't answer; under her fingers, her knife turned over and over.

• • •

"You know why, don't you?" Reg asked.

They were on their way upstairs to retire, after two hours in the drawing room where Leah had flipped nervously through a manual of etiquette Mr. Martin had recommended, not paying any mind to what she saw, and not even wondering that there was so much.

Usually Reg smoked with Father in the dining room, and stayed up later than Leah was allowed. It was rare that he left with her; now Leah knew why.

"I suspect it's because Mr. Martin is handsome."

"I knew it," said Reg, curling his lip. "You're in a fancy."

"Hardly." Leah flinched at the speed of her answer, and amended, "On the contrary, there's something about him I truly do not like. He's a fine instructor, but really, don't imagine I need Cousin William to come and shame me out of something."

Reg raised an eyebrow. "That's not what Mother thinks, clearly."

"Well, then she should spare our cousin and just send you to watch over me," Leah said.

Reg barked a laugh. "God, no! Bad enough to suffer through ten balls a Season looking into a sea of gormless faces from which you have to pluck a wife trained never to think anything of matter. I'm not about to be lectured through the mazurka with my own sister by our Mr. Martin on top of it all."

He took the stairs two at a time, vanished into his room.

Reg had never talked to her before about how he spent his time in London. Given what their mother hinted about his finances, she had imagined him at gaming tables and horse races.

She wasn't sure if this was better, or worse.

• • •

At their next lesson, Leah walked with Mr. Martin until both he and Miss Hammond were content with her carriage, the incline of her head, the lightness of her expression, and the length of her step.

("Please, let's not gallop," said Miss Hammond once, with just enough of a smile that Leah obeyed.)

Mr. Martin stopped; she kept her hand hovering a hair's breadth above his.

He smiled. "Well done, Miss Clement. Now, might I interest you in taking refreshment?"

Leah glanced down and up through her lashes, slid her fan half open to indicate mild fatigue but not disinterest, and smiled without showing any teeth. "Yes, thank you, Mr. Martin."

"No, Leah," said Miss Hammond softly from her chair, with a quick shake of her head. "You can't accept. He is not a close enough friend of the family."

Leah wondered why it sounded like such general custom to bring young ladies into Society, loose them into a sea of strange men, and then starve them.

"I've accepted refreshments from men at parties," she protested.

Mr. Martin gave her a long-suffering look. "At family parties, or among your neighbors, of course you may. But London is a different creature."

For one wistful moment, Leah pictured the streets threaded through with dragons.

"And how close is close enough?" she asked. "Would Cousin William be able to fetch me some refreshment at an assembly, or would I have to hope Reginald is within shouting distance before I expire?"

"Your cousin would be an excellent choice," Miss Hammond said, as if refreshments at a ball were the only thing being discussed. Maybe it was; Miss Hammond didn't employ the same style of hints that Mama did.

(Still, it felt like being thrown away, somehow, and Leah scowled.)

Mr. Martin added, all kindness, "These rules, Miss Clement, are in the interests of your comfort, that you needn't worry about your reputation in the slightest respect by making some unwitting error."

Leah wondered who would be so anxious to ruin her reputation that she had to constantly be on guard for offers of punch, but looking at Miss Hammond, she saw this was something to be taken very seriously.

It might be serious enough to explain why she had seen so little outside this county, and why she had never before been taken to London.

Her busk cut into the top of her right thigh, right through her skirts. She'd have a bruise, tonight, when it came off.

"All right," she said. "Then when he comes, I'll ask him."

• • •

Engagements for one dance should not be made while the present dance is yet in progress.

Never attempt to take a place in a dance which has been previously engaged.

–Routledge

• • •

Cousin William arrived four evenings later, punctual to the minute, and Leah nearly slipped on the stairs in her hurry to get into her place in the parlor before he could get out of the carriage and be announced.

(She had visited Miss Hammond's room to let her give the final word over her dress. The pearl earrings, with no cameo necklace, were deemed most suitable–a young lady of taste, apparently, needed no other adornment.

"Won't you come with me?" she'd asked Miss Hammond. "You're my companion, I should have you with me."

Miss Hammond had tried a smile, and pinned closed the wire of Leah's left earring before she handed it back.

"That's not the sort of thing for which I'm required," she said.

The pearls were heavy, somehow; they ached in Leah's ears.)

She skittered for her place in as ladylike a manner as she could, under her mother's glare.

"Sir William Foster," Stevens announced, as soon as Leah was settled.

Leah smoothed her skirt for an excuse to wipe the dampness off her palms.

Reg shifted his weight back onto his heels, with one creak of the floorboards, and sighed.

William came in with his hat still tucked under his arm, his shoulders pushed so far back that he seemed about to tip over.

She remembered him from the Christmas her family had been invited to celebrate in Surrey. He was taller now, and seemed slightly underfed, and had sharp features in a face that would probably grow to be respectable.

(They had the same nose, she thought.)

He bowed stiffly, then stood up and looked at Mama as if unsure how formal to be.

"It's a pleasure to see you . . . Aunt?" he ventured finally.

He flinched as he spoke. Maybe he'd been suffering under a dancing master, too.

"William," said Mama, coming forward and taking his hands. "It's such a pleasure to see you. I trust you had a pleasant journey?"

"Of course, thank you."

"Reg has been so looking forward to seeing you," she said, without looking at Reg, "and of course Leah has been hoping all day for a glimpse of her cousin. You know how fond of you she's always been."

So, they weren't even waiting a full day before the hints began.

Leah held her breath, worked on her smallest, blankest smile. It fell apart; her lips were dry, and sticking to her teeth.

It seemed to take a moment to sink in (Mama was still going on about refreshment and Stevens taking his things and wouldn't he care for a seat), but then William looked over at Leah, his expression too polite to be disgusted, but trying its hardest.

Leah's stomach sank.

• • •

In the drawing room, Cousin William had to be refreshed and given a brandy, and had to relate to Father and Reg the quality of hunting back at home, and to Mama the quality of company, which meant that for nearly an hour Leah could get away with sitting silently on the sofa beside Mama, twisting her hands in her lap and trying to determine the best moment for escape.

(She had picked up her manual of etiquette on her way inside, and it sat on her lap, if she dared to ignore the guest.)

"And what entertainments are to be had at the Hall this time of year?" Mama was asking.

"Not many," said William, looking into his brandy.

He didn't elaborate, and Leah nearly laughed at Mama's face as she struggled for a response.

"That must be unfortunate for your mother and sister. I know how fond they are of good company."

"Mother and Lily are, yes," he said finally.

"And we look forward to seeing all of you," said Mama. "How do you find the Season?"

"I don't," he said. "Indifferent health has kept me at home the last two springs."

If nothing else came of this, Leah could at least take some comfort that peevishness ran in the family.

"I see," said Mama.

It was cool enough that William glanced up and seemed to cast about for a way to save the sentiment.

"They pass their best wishes to Leah," he said, "and look forward to seeing her during the Season."

"Oh, so do we," said Reg. "She's getting all the training of a diplomat headed for another continent. It's great fun to watch her trying."

William's mouth thinned, and he glanced at Leah and then at Reg. "Charming."

Leah's cheeks blazed.

She opened the book, just for something else to look at besides his disapproving face. It had been nearly an hour;

family honor had to be satisfied by now. Even being lectured by the manual had to be better than this.

Three pages later, she closed the book again.

"Please excuse me," she said, standing up. "I have a headache."

Mama followed her, and caught her at the doorway.

"Leah," she said, "this is extremely rude. I expected better of you."

"Oh, don't worry, Mama," said Leah, "you've made it very clear exactly what you expect. Goodnight."

On her way upstairs, she told Annabelle to send for Miss Hammond, on an urgent matter.

• • •

As soon as Miss Hammond arrived, Leah dropped the open book on her bed and pointed at it.

"It says here I can't decline an invitation to dance," Leah said, voice shaking.

Miss Hammond picked up the book. (She always examined facts; she never got carried away.)

"You mean at a private ball," she said, closing the book. "That's correct."

Leah planted her hands on her hips. "But if he's a stranger, can't I make some excuse? Strangers can't feed me; surely, then, they're not allowed to put their hand on my waist or just–or just impose that way."

She was shaking with anger.

"Unfortunately, that's not the case." Miss Hammond sighed. "At a private ball, the hostess has chosen all present; it goes without saying that everyone is of impeccable character and equal to your time in a dance."

She made a face that mirrored Leah's feelings on the matter.

Leah wondered how many men Miss Hammond didn't care for had put their hands on her waist.

It was a terrible thought.

Leah shook her head, made fists at her sides. "I don't understand it. First Cousin William is lured in, and then I'm told I have to be pleasant and accommodating to strangers all Season long! It should be one way or the other–either I should be allowed to make my own choices, or William and Mama should just settle arrangements, and then at least I won't have to pay attention to Mr. Martin anymore."

She sank onto the bed, tried to catch her breath.

Miss Hammond sat beside Leah. "What's wrong with Mr. Martin?"

His smile worries me, Leah wanted to say, but it sounded foolish, and she didn't want Miss Hammond to think she was inventing in her anger.

"Nothing," said Leah. "Except that he keeps asking me to do what I cannot do."

Miss Hammond smiled, the candlelight flickering across her face. "You'll learn, Leah, I'm sure–you have the potential to be a very passionate dancer, if you apply yourself, quite good enough for your cousin or anyone else."

"My pins are too tight," said Leah.

For a moment, Miss Hammond lifted her fingers as if to reach out and touch Leah's hair herself.

Leah sat perfectly still, held her breath.

Then Miss Hammond got up and rang for Annabelle.

"The good news," said Miss Hammond, "is that, at private balls, if any man is worth having, you have filled twenty minutes, and if not, you can at least beg off afterward and never have to acknowledge him again. That's a lady's right."

It seemed an awfully small one, but Leah supposed she would have to make use of what she had.

"And at public assemblies, you can refer any unseemly gentleman to me," said Miss Hammond, then smiled so that her nose wrinkled slightly. "I am not afraid to play the dragon for you."

Leah closed her eyes as the door shut, to hold on to the smile a little longer, before night sank in.

• • •

> Never lower the intellectual standard of your conversation in addressing ladies. Pay them the compliment of seeming to consider them capable of an equal understanding with gentlemen.
>
> –Wells

• • •

When Leah arrived in the ballroom for her next lesson, William was waiting.

He stood at one of the windows, with his hands clasped behind his back like a parson, and a furrow between his eyes where he was squinting against the sun.

Why did it make Leah so low, just to look at him this way?

"Good afternoon," he said without moving.

She said, "Apologies if my mother sent you."

From behind her, Stevens announced, "Mr. Martin for Miss Clement," (Leah jumped), and a moment later Mr. Martin was swanning into the room with a grin for them both.

"Excellent," he said. "Furnishing your own partners, even!"

"William Foster," William said, frowning, and Mr. Martin grinned and bowed and finished the introduction, and then without a pause he said, "With both of you here we can practice some of the round dances after we attempt the waltz. Miss

Clement applies herself," he told William, "but round dances can get the best of any lady unless she has a mind for figures."

Leah flinched.

"I see," said William.

Leah said, "I'm sure Cousin William doesn't intend to stay."

William turned to look at her. The furrow was still there. "I'm more than happy to be of service."

"Wouldn't Reg come looking for you?"

His lips thinned. "I expect so."

(It was said the same way he had said, "Charming," when Reg had crowed about her tutelage.

Interesting, thought Leah.)

But just as William glanced at her and moved to leave, Miss Hammond appeared at the doorway.

She smiled and nodded to Mr. Martin, glanced at Leah, and turned at last to William.

"Miss Hammond, I presume," said William. "It's a pleasure to meet you."

She curtseyed.

"I wish you a pleasant lesson," he said.

Miss Hammond's eyes went wide, and she said in that tone she reserved for company, "Oh, can't you stay?"

"My cousin would rather not, I think."

"It's no trouble," William said.

Leah scowled.

Mr. Martin cleared his throat. "Well, if someone must break this stalemate, I would treasure a fourth. If we may begin?"

Miss Hammond gave Leah a reproving look.

Leah folded her hands, gave the smile Mama had taught her was neither rude nor enthusiastic.

"Of course, Mr. Martin."

Reg passed by the doorway; he was dressed for riding, and as he crossed the open space he made a face at Mr. Martin's back, and fled.

"Truly, you may go with him, if you'd rather," said Leah, under her breath. "It will be no offense."

"It is no offense to stay," William said. "I'm not particularly fond of hunting."

It was an unusual thing for a gentleman to admit. (Father was very clear that a gentleman who didn't care for hunting was a gentleman deficient, though perhaps cousin William was rich enough that he could afford whatever pastime he chose.)

Mr. Martin had taken his place in the center of the room, and he turned to face them, grinning.

"Right. Let us begin the waltz!"

(The waltz; the dance that put a young lady full in the arms of some young man she could not refuse.

Leah pressed her hands closer together.)

Mr. Martin held out his arm with a bow, and Miss Hammond, blushing, and with a glance over her shoulder to Leah, took it.

She was embarrassed, Leah thought; her cheeks were pink, just at the place they disappeared under the plaits of her hair.

"Though it may seem stylish," he said, and on *stylish* his voice was a warning against drawing attention, "it is still better to hold up one's skirt than to try to mend a rip in between the waltz and the quadrille. So, Miss Clement, if fashion dictates a train, please care for it. A gentleman will understand."

Miss Hammond obligingly removed her right hand from Mr. Martin's, and caught up her skirt in the pressed-together flat of her hand, held with the thumb. An inch of gray flannel petticoat appeared above her right boot.

William blinked. "And what would the man do with his hand, then?"

(Leah remembered that this Season would be his first, too.)

"Behind his back, of course," said Mr. Martin, and demonstrated. "A gentleman never questions the desires of a lady."

It looked quite dashing when he did it, maybe even more than it did when their hands were joined.

Not that Leah would ever say so; she guessed that the last thing Mama would want was for her to distinguish herself by being stylish, or any other thing.

"The man steps backward," Mr. Martin said, "so that the lady may step forward and preserve her hem." He demonstrated, and after a tiny hesitation, Miss Hammond followed him, her hand tightening a little on the edge of Mr. Martin's shoulder as she tried for balance.

"From there, it's a simple pair of steps, and then into the next turn," Mr. Martin said. As he spoke, he was already moving faster, too fast for Leah to understand what was required of her, though Miss Hammond followed with no trouble.

(Of course she would have no trouble with dancing, Leah remembered; Miss Hammond had had prospects, once.)

Mr. Martin was humming now, and his golden hair caught the light every time he came in line with one of the windows, where the afternoon was going.

"It's really no trouble," Mr. Martin said as they passed, his smile flashing, his hand on Miss Hammond's back.

(Leah curled her fingers around the edge of the chair.)

William shifted beside Leah, glancing from them to her and back again. She suspected he was wishing he had accepted Reg's invitation before an even speedier exercise was introduced.

Leah hardly cared; she was fixed, watching Mr. Martin and Miss Hammond.

They turned circles within circles in the little empty ballroom, Mr. Martin's smile growing as he hummed a song for them to keep time to, that one inch of Miss Hammond's gray petticoat flashing in and out of sight like a dove's wings.

• • •

That afternoon was the waltz.

Tuesday was the polka.

Wednesday was the quadrille.

"It's a simple enough dance as regards steps," said Mr. Martin. "But an ease of carriage is what makes it a pleasure to watch, and to dance. Let us practice, then, and think of effortless grace."

"Oh Lord," Leah said under her breath, "we'll be here until Sunday, then."

William covered a laugh in a cough. Leah wasn't sure if it was compliment or mockery.

Two hours of practice later, she still was sure of nothing, except that grace should never be counted among the things in life on which she could rely.

"You look perfectly all right," William said, with a narrowed glance at Mr. Martin. "He's just trying to be worth his fee, I suspect. You didn't tread on me once."

"Comforting," said Leah, and he almost smiled.

(It must have been a comfort, though; the next round her hands weren't even shaking.)

• • •

Thursday was the mazurka.

"The trick to the mazurka," Mr. Martin advised, "is the

sharp, clear action of the feet, and the easy movement from figure to figure."

He was demonstrating, counting off the steps, as he and Miss Hammond skipped this way and that; when he sank onto one knee, she held his upstretched hand in the tips of her fingers, and moved around him like a bright ribbon around a maypole.

Leah and William stood side by side, watching the dance unfold. Leah felt almost calm about it; the dance made so little sense that it seemed any mistakes could be covered up by swiftly changing direction, flinging out an arm, and hopping in a circle.

"Leah," said William, "I hope your shoes are sturdy."

Miss Hammond looked over, smiling. "I'm sure it will be second nature, Mr. Foster."

He inclined his head. "Then I might ask for your guidance, Miss Hammond."

Miss Hammond glanced at Mr. Martin; he frowned, barely, and then a moment later he was smiling at Leah, holding out a hand, saying, "Let us begin!"

As it happened, Leah could acquit herself quite well in the mazurka.

The same could not be said of her cousin.

Finally even Miss Hammond was required to sit out to recover herself. William bowed her into a seat, and seemed on the verge of retreating, until Mr. Martin said, "Now, let us see how well the students learn from one another!"

(He spoke to William, but watched her all the while.)

With the look of a martyr, William took hold; his hands were cold, and Leah felt a flash of sympathy.

"Don't worry," she said. "I'll make a fool of myself before you do."

"We'll see about that, I suppose," he said, but there was a ghost of a smile on his face, and his fingers were a little steadier as Mr. Martin counted off the beat, and with Leah holding him back from a wrong move twice, they muddled through.

(He stepped on her toe, once, but when he moved to apologize she made a little warning face, and the corners of his eyes folded up when he smiled.)

When they finished, Miss Hammond applauded.

"Well done, Leah," she said. "Lovely!"

Leah flushed, and pulled her hands from William's.

"We'll see how long it holds," she said. "Miss Hammond, you must promise to practice with me in London, so it's fresh when I venture out."

Some little shadow crossed Miss Hammond's face, but she only said, "Of course, my dear."

William was looking at her–too solemnly, she thought, there was no hope for him with a dance like this–and she had already started to ask him what he saw to make him so grave when the dressing bell rang, and it was time to change one low bodice for another.

Friday, William did not come.

Leah promenaded and quadrilled with Mr. Martin until her whole vision was filled with golden curls, and bright smiles, and two blue eyes that Leah did not like.

• • •

"So," said Mama at dinner on Saturday, all smiles, "Reg tells me that you've been spending some of your afternoons with Leah during her dance lessons, William? That's very kind."

"It's certainly something," said Reg, and took a punctuating sip of soup.

"Leah and Mr. Martin are very kind to let me join," William said. "I have much to learn before the Season, I think."

"I'm sure Leah enjoys your company," she said.

"You might ask her," William said.

It was just calm enough to sound polite, and just pointed enough that Leah looked up from her plate.

Mama blinked, and turned to Leah.

"Leah? How was today's lesson?"

They had practiced round dances again until Leah was relatively certain she wouldn't cause a knot in the figure; then they had turned to waltzing, for quite a while after the steps had been learned, and for a purpose Leah couldn't guess.

("I suppose it's just as well," Leah said. "I should get used to it now. There's no good in going to London just to get seasick from it in someone's ballroom."

"That would make a banner night," William said, and she'd been so startled she laughed.)

"Thorough," she said. Then, struck by something a little perverse, she added, "William is a very steady partner."

That got his attention.

He looked up at her with a strange expression, seeming on the verge of speaking, until Mama turned her praises on him; then he was trapped in polite nothings for a while longer, and by then it was Father's turn to rouse himself and talk about all the sport William had missed, and so they didn't say another word.

(She placed it more quickly than she wanted to admit; it was the same expression he'd had when she'd laughed at his joke, and she had stopped worrying about her feet, and for a moment they had been comfortable together.

But then she had glanced at Miss Hammond–she didn't know why–and when she looked back, he looked as solemn as before, and Leah was back to feeling as though all the manuals in the world were useless.

Miss Hammond had been waltzing with Mr. Martin, smiling as if she had stumbled on another Season, and Leah had wondered what sort of prospects could have ever passed her by.)

• • •

> The lady who gives a ball should endeavor to secure an equal number of dancers of both sexes. Many private parties are spoiled by the preponderance of young ladies, some of whom never get partners at all, unless they dance with each other.
>
> –*Routledge*

• • •

After dinner, Father must have been in high spirits, because when he led Reg and William into the drawing room, he was already looking for Leah, and even though she only caught ". . . little demonstration," meant over his shoulder for William, she could guess what was coming.

"Oh, yes," said Mama, turning to her. "A splendid idea. And Miss Hammond can accompany. Stevens, please ask Miss Hammond and Mr. Martin to come down."

"Good heavens," said Reg, "this is like watching someone being sent to the gallows."

"That's enough of that," said Father, and Reg finished his brandy with a sour face, and said nothing more.

William finished his, as well, and then stood holding the glass as if looking for a way out.

Leah's sleeves cut into her shoulders, and she felt as though the waist of her skirt had gone suddenly too loose, and would fall as soon as she stood.

She concentrated on the tips of her fingers. It was no worse here than in the afternoon; this was much better than some great ballroom in London with everyone watching her to criticize. Why was she so anxious?

"Lady Clement," Miss Hammond said from the doorway. "Thank you so much for the invitation to join you."

Leah glanced up sidelong at Miss Hammond in her deep gray dress, who didn't seem at all disconcerted that she was being summoned to be of use.

(She had prospects, Leah thought fiercely, that's what made it all so terrible–she deserved better than Leah ever would.)

Mr. Martin came in a moment later, still fixing the last of the knot in his cravat.

He glanced at Miss Hammond, who had already seated herself at the piano.

"I see there's to be dancing," he said a moment later, giving the room a bow.

Mother smiled. "If you would oblige us," she said, "we would dearly love some entertainment this evening."

"With greatest pleasure!" He held out a hand. "Would you care to quadrille with me, Lady Clement?"

And so it began. Leah partnered with William for the quadrille, and then through a mazurka for which Mama herself played the music, so that Miss Hammond could make a fourth.

For the waltz, Miss Hammond was invited back to her seat, and as Mama and Father partnered up, Mr. Martin held out his hand to Leah.

"Miss Clement," he said, and when he smiled she had the impression of teeth where there were none.

(A lady couldn't refuse an invitation at a private party; all men there were of impeccable character.)

"Of course," she said, and picked up her skirt in her right hand.

They made circles around the evening parlor, William frowning at them from a corner, and Miss Hammond at the piano in glimpses no longer than a blink, watching Mr. Martin and Leah as if there were tears in her eyes.

Something about that look–something about it all–was overwhelming, so that long after Leah was safe back in her seat, her heart was pounding.

• • •

Leah couldn't settle in, the whole time she was preparing for bed.

Miss Hammond's face at the piano was haunting, was a sign of something dreadful.

(It's as if she was jealous, Leah thought–she didn't know why–and for a moment her heart turned over.)

Alone in her room, she clutched her dressing gown closed, and looked at herself in the mirror.

She looked older.

Courage, she thought over and over, courage, courage, until she could walk up the stairs and knock gently on Miss Hammond's door.

Miss Hammond was still dressed, and when she opened the door she seemed startled to see Leah.

"I'm so sorry," said Leah, "but I had to see you. Is it all right?"

Miss Hammond blinked, and something sad and fleeting moved over her face.

"Of course," she said, and stepped aside.

Her desk was cluttered with books in neat stacks, and some abandoned writing, and Leah smiled at it as she sat on the bed.

Miss Hammond took a seat beside her. "What's the matter, Leah? You look as if you've seen a ghost."

Leah's neck was burning; her ears were on fire.

"I don't want you to worry," Leah said. "About William, I mean." She looked up, fixed her eyes on Miss Hammond's green eyes, willed her purpose to be clear. "I don't care for him."

There was a moment of quiet; Miss Hammond blinked, looked down at a spot on her skirt and brushed it away.

"You'd do well to marry him, I think," said Miss Hammond. "He's a clever young man, and I waited five Seasons for a man half as kind as he is."

Courage, Leah thought; courage.

"What if I don't wish to marry?"

Miss Hammond half smiled. "Then you have doomed yourself to disappointment one way or the other, and I am sorry for you."

"But surely you can understand," Leah pressed.

Miss Hammond's mouth thinned. "Leah, I could not be more fond of you, but rare is the woman who dreams of growing old in the servants' quarters of someone else's house. If a good man offers, I advise you to take him."

Leah shook her head so hard that her pins stung her scalp. "But that's not–" she couldn't breathe, had to struggle to speak. "That isn't where my heart lies."

Miss Hammond looked at her, for a long time. The candlelight carved her face into a pool of dark, two wide green eyes, a slice of light along her jaw.

Leah's hands were fists in the bedspread.

Finally, Miss Hammond cleared her throat.

"Leah," she said, as if her own voice pained her. "Leah, there's no happiness in it, if you follow your heart and ignore the world."

No, Leah thought wildly, that can't be true, that can't be true.

(Not always, she amended, her heart beating against her stays. Miss Hammond read romances; sometimes, if you loved someone enough and weren't afraid, maybe the world could be ignored.)

Miss Hammond reached out for Leah's hand, pulled it back, folded it under the one in her lap like a dove's wings.

Leah's eyes stung; her fingers stung; her tongue was going dry.

"Leah," she said. "I'm sorry."

Oh God, Leah thought; oh God, pity!

Her heartbeat nearly knocked her over, and when Miss Hammond opened her mouth to speak again, Leah croaked out, "Please, don't," scrambled down from the bed, stumbled out (her stockings snagged on the floorboards).

If Miss Hammond called after her, she didn't hear; her breathing drowned out any other sound.

• • •

Leah was too embarrassed even for tears, when she got back to her own room.

She could only close the door and turn the key with shaking hands, and pull the blankets nearly over her head, as if she could keep out her own folly.

Her heart was pounding; she felt ill, she was going to faint at any moment.

Her fingertips stung as if singed, where she had touched Miss Hammond's blanket.

She was the very greatest fool! What had she done, to be so forward?

(Miss Hammond's little look of pity–oh, God, she was ill, she was ill.)

The grandfather clock in the front hall struck one, then two, and still Leah lay half awake, half dreaming of some way to draw back from the door before she knocked, and walk back into her own room, and never to see such a terrible look from Miss Hammond again.

• • •

Leah woke from a fitful sleep while it was still dark, with enough purpose to know she had to try to make amends.

She took the stairs in stocking feet to wake Miss Hammond with apologies, and beg her to stay on for the Season, and to promise never to speak of it again.

That was how she became the first in the house to discover that Miss Hammond was gone.

• • •

> Withdraw from a private ballroom as quietly as possible, so your departure may not be observed by others, and cause the party to break up. If you meet the lady of the house on your way out, take your leave of her in such a manner that her other guests may not suppose you are doing so.
>
> –*Routledge*

• • •

Her parents met her in the breakfast room to look over the note Miss Hammond had left and discuss what was to be done.

"It seems to be in hand," Father pointed out. "They have dismissed themselves with all possible speed, and can hardly expect references. I'm not sure what's left to be done."

Leah's mother had more feeling on the subject; she reread

the note several times as if it was of great import, instead of just a polite rescinding of a post and a wish for general goodwill, and even when she spoke she couldn't look away from it.

"We must do something," she said. "We have been taken greatest advantage of! We must put an announcement in the paper condemning them. This is despicable licentiousness, and under our roof! If word gets out, imagine what they'll say about us!"

"They'll say you dismissed two troublesome servants as soon as you suspected anything amiss," said Father.

"They'll say we allowed unspeakable liberties under our roof," Mother snapped. "We must expose them."

"No," said Leah, "you won't."

"But they might well be married by now! They might this minute be on their way to some other county to try to present themselves as a respectable couple!"

"Then let them," snapped Leah. "They're no concern of ours, now."

"Leah, what on earth has come over you, that you speak to me this way?"

Leah grit her teeth. "It is only that I was the person principally injured by this deception," she said, as calmly as she could. "I feel that no goodwill can come to me from bringing this matter to other eyes."

"Well, I see what good they have done your manners." She turned to Father. "What do you think of all this?"

Father sighed and rubbed his jaw and considered. Finally he said, "The Ladislaws had nothing but praise for him, which is how he came to our notice. If we say no good of him, then he will not come to the knowledge of our acquaintance, and that will handle the matter."

He didn't mention Miss Hammond at all; she had, of course, already vanished from consideration. Either she was now Mrs. Martin, or she would fall even farther than she had already.

Mama looked from Father to Leah; her hand holding the letter still trembled.

"Very well," she said at last. "I may mention to the Ladislaws, when we see them in London, what has happened, so they do not recommend him to any other families. Then, perhaps, that will be an end of it. For the moment, I must try to compose myself and decide what should be done about preparations for the Season."

After she had gone, Father nodded, said, "I'll be in my library, I think," and vanished likewise.

Leah doubted that Mother would keep the matter wholly quiet, but a small victory was still a victory, and at least, for once, her thoughts had been heard by her mother.

She would have to take her comforts where she could find them, for a while, or she would go to pieces.

(There was another note that Mama hadn't seen. It was even shorter, and by now was blurred with tears, and Leah had memorized it after reading it only once.

Dear Leah,

I have taken a chance at happiness. I know you will understand me; I pray you will give me your blessing. I wish nothing but the best for you.

With great fondness,

Marie

If you loved someone enough and weren't afraid, the world could be ignored.)

Someone rapped gleefully on the doorjamb.

"Well," said Reg, "it's a wonder how fast word travels when there's any real news."

Leah pinched the bridge of her nose. "Reg, go back upstairs."

"And miss this? Hardly." Reg grinned. "This is the first good bit of gossip we've had in ages. And you should be proud of trying to keep Mr. Martin from coming–for once, you had the right idea about someone."

"Leave it alone, Reg."

He shrugged. "I'm only saying, it's just as well you never thought much of him. Mother thought you very vexing about it, but things have borne you out, I'd say, and now we're well rid of two troublemakers."

"Reg," she said, and the word snapped against her teeth.

"Take a compliment when it's offered," said Reg, all astonishment that she might take offense. "You had more sense than that Hammond woman, at least, not that it's saying much."

Leah's throat burned. Her fingernails cut into her palms. "You're just being hateful because you're too idle to know anything. You don't know anything. Leave it alone!"

"I know that Miss Hammond had you wrapped around her little finger, sure enough. I was beginning to worry you'd pick up some terrible habits–"

"That's enough."

It was William.

Leah turned; he was indistinct (her vision was blurred, she was going to cry any moment), but there he was, framed in the doorway, his posture betraying his anger.

(How did she know what his posture meant? Everything was strange, impossible and strange.)

William took another step into the morning parlor, his arms crossed over his chest. "I suspect Mr. Martin wasn't the only one under this roof who has no care for his reputation, Reg," he said, with a pointed inflection on her brother's name. "And Leah has made it clear that the last thing anyone needs is your half-formed opinions on the matter, so I suggest you leave off."

Reg pulled a face. "Christ, Foster, you're not married to her yet."

"I haven't yet read where you need to be married to someone to note them when they speak," said William.

Reg groaned theatrically, but a moment later he left, his footsteps exaggerated all the way back upstairs.

William moved no closer. Quietly, he asked, "Are you all right?"

"Oh, quite," Leah tried, but her throat had closed (her collar was too tight), and she could only manage to shake her head and pinch her mouth closed.

"I see," said William. Then he bowed and said, "You'll excuse me, I've recollected some business."

When she was alone, it was easier to breathe; she could breathe enough to go out into the garden, and to turn some corners, and make sure she was alone before she sat down and wept.

• • •

William was sitting alone in the morning room when she came back.

Though he looked up as she passed, he didn't call out for her, and she debated going upstairs to wash her face before she met him.

But she was slowing down; she was stepping inside.

(His face had dropped all its politeness; he looked a little ill. Somehow it helped.)

He half rose, then sat back down, placed his hands at his sides and on his knees and back again.

She took a seat in the chair beside him.

"That was kind of you," she said.

He shook his head. "Your brother is no better than some. I think he knows it."

"I think he is beyond caring," Leah admitted. "My parents are not so intractable, but some things are just lost causes."

He looked at her (the furrow in his brow, his nose that was just like hers).

"I'm sorry she left," he said finally.

There was nothing in the words that sounded like triumph–it sounded like sympathy, and for a moment she struggled to breathe.

"Thank you," she managed.

There was a little quiet.

It struck her, suddenly and too late, that her parents might have schemed for William to be alone with her like this.

Her mother would be scrambling for any good news that might overshadow the terrible inconvenience of the dancing master running off with the governess; an engagement would be just the thing to crow over, in London.

He cleared his throat. "Leah, I have something I'd like to say to you."

Leah closed her eyes, steeled herself, looked at him with her polite smile at the ready.

(*I waited five Seasons for a man half as kind*, Miss Hammond had said, before she ran away.)

His gaze was fixed on the floor at the other side of the room.

"I know that–I know your heart is not inclined to me," he said. "But I have nothing to look forward to in London. I know hardly anyone, and I am not at ease among strangers. I feel you understand me in this."

She thought of their afternoon lessons, where he had walked through his round dances with the look of a man being led to the gallows, casting long-suffering looks at her when Mr. Martin couldn't see.

"There was a reason they hired me a dancing master," she said.

A shadow of a smile crossed his face. "Quite so."

But the thought of Mr. Martin only made her think of Miss Hammond, sneaking out the back way in the dead of night, just under Leah's own window, and vanishing into the dark.

She took two or three careful breaths, her busk pressing back against her ribs.

"My heart is broken, you know," she said.

Her voice was quiet and sounded somehow far away, and for a moment she was afraid of how it must seem, to sound so sad about some governess (she was still so often foolish, about little childish things).

But he didn't laugh at her. He laced his hands together, looked at the ridge of his folded knuckles. He was flushed, just at the tips of his temples.

"But a broken heart can mend," he said. "I am sure that someday, you will find someone for whom you care."

She tried to imagine that day. She tried to imagine walking into a ballroom in London and seeing William, and her heart turning over; she tried to imagine seeing some sparkling Countess laughing and glittering with diamonds, like in one of Miss Hammond's novels.

But it was only Miss Hammond she thought about, Miss Hammond waltzing across the empty room, one inch of her petticoat showing, where she had picked up her skirt to pretend the glory days had come again.

"William," she said, stopped. She was trying to put words to something that still ached too much to name.

She tried again. "You are very kind, but my heart is a contrary creature–I dare not give you any expectation."

He nodded, as if there had been worse things, and took a breath or two, and then he looked over at her.

"With no expectation," he said, "I would be honored to be your friend, if you need one, in London or anywhere else."

The tips of her fingers went a little warm, as she looked at him, as if they had been singed and were coming to life.

"You're just saying that because you don't know how to dance the mazurka unless I keep the time for you," she said.

"Quite so," he said, solemn.

After a moment, he smiled.

After a moment more, so did she.

The Garden of England

SANDRA MCDONALD

My name is Ashna, and until this morning I was one of the many servants employed by the memsahib and her husband. The husband died three days ago. Now the memsahib lies bloated and motionless in her bed, black flies sticky on the sheet someone pulled over her corpse. Her yellow hair spills out from under the sheet and down to the floor. I'd like to cut off a handful and wave it in victory. Never again will she berate us, belittle us, or treat us like mangy dogs in our own village. But it's impossible to feel triumphant about anything. This is a house of death, and any survivors have fled to the hills.

All that's left are rooms filled with the memsahib's treasures–her silver combs and gold jewelry and the money chest my older sister Saidie said she keeps under the floorboards of her closet.

On my knees in the stifling heat, I push aside a dozen fine dresses and pointy shoes. Foreigners are so fussy and strange with their fashions. The loose board is in the far corner, held in place by one lonely nail. The wooden chest beneath is stuffed with English paper money. I tuck as many notes as I can into my waistband, replace the chest, push the board back into place, and hurry out to the dining room–

The girl is there. The missie sahib. The ugly, disagreeable child that I've helped feed and wash and dress for two years now, ever since I came here as but a girl myself.

"Where is everyone?" she demands from the doorway. "Where is my breakfast?"

She's in her sleeping gown, and her hair is messy, and if she knows her parents are dead she doesn't seem to care. On the dining-room wall beside her hang small paintings of the land neither she nor I have ever been–England, where the Queen lives in a dozen different palaces and chops off your head if you break the law. To get there, you must cross an ocean filled with magnificent whales. Once you arrive, they fill you with pastries and roasted nuts and haggis. In England girls can go to a fine school, just as the memsahib did, or ride enormous trains through wild forests, or live in cities that are alive with music all night long.

Mary stomps her foot. "Answer me, Ashna! Don't just stand there and look stupid."

If I flee, she might raise enough noise to alert a patrol. It would be easier to put a pillow over her face. She's too small and weak to put up much of a fight. No one has ever loved Mary Lennox, and no one would miss her. But Saidie would say, "She's just a child." Saidie, whose heart was bigger than a mountain.

"Is miss very hungry?" I ask.

"Of course I am! No one brought me dinner and no one brought me breakfast, and if my old ayah is gone then where is my new one?"

Her ayah was Saidie. Saidie, who died yesterday morning after days of vomiting and moaning and shriveling up, no matter how many offerings I made to the goddess of cholera.

She was nineteen years old. After our mother died she became a second mother to me, but I never thanked her.

In Hindi I say to Mary, "You are as selfish as the memsahib and deserve to be all alone."

"Speak English!" she orders, her face turning red.

As patiently as possible, as humble as I can, I say, "I am your new ayah. I'll bring you breakfast, and then we'll wash and then we'll play a game. Please wait in your room."

Before she can answer, I hurry to the kitchen. The cupboards are open and in disarray. Dirty dishes are stacked in the sink and a pitcher of milk has gone sour on the table. Through the windows I can see hungry dogs roaming in the compound between the house and the empty servants' huts. There's nothing here to feed the girl. She'll fuss and complain, and meanwhile I should be on my way to the hills, away from this rot and sickness–

The front door opens and a man calls out, "Hullo! Mrs. Lennox!"

I peek around the corner. Three Englishmen have entered, their army uniforms dusty and faces grim. One of them, Barney, is tall and red-haired and not much older than I am. Twice he's kissed me under the shade trees where no one could see us. I like his kisses, all firm and sweet. I also like how he smells, leather and gunpowder and strong English soap. When he looks at me he doesn't see a poor country girl, good only for labor. He sees someone pretty and smart, he says, ready for great adventures.

"Who are you?" demands Mary's voice, shrill.

"My goodness!" says the oldest of the soldiers. "There's a child!"

The best thing would be for me to slip out the back door

now, while I can. But this might be my last chance to see Barney for a long time.

I step into the hall and bow and say, "The sahib and the memsahib both fell very ill. There was nothing we could do."

The oldest soldier says, "Who are you, then?"

"My ayah," Mary announces crossly. "She's supposed to be bringing me breakfast. I'm famished and I'm thirsty."

I dart a quick glance to Barney. He isn't looking at me at all. He's watching Mary with a soft-hearted look on his face. The memsahib rarely allowed Mary in her company, and few people outside the house have ever seen her. He probably considers her to be a small, helpless thing in need of sympathy. He doesn't know yet that she has the heart of a snake.

The third soldier has drifted away and found the memsahib's bedroom. He returns with a green cast to his complexion and shakes his head. "No good news there, Colonel."

"What are we to do with you, I wonder?" the colonel muses.

They decide to take her to the clergyman, who lives in a bungalow nearby. As the only servant left, it falls to me to make her presentable and pack her things in a suitcase. "I want my white dress," Mary says. "I want my blue mirror." She doesn't say anything about her dolls or other toys. Finally the bag is packed and the soldiers lock the house behind us, though I don't think that will deter the thieves soon to come calling.

Barney doesn't say anything to me until we are all walking down the road with his companions and Mary at the forefront. I get to carry the suitcase.

"Ashna, what will you do now?" he asks, his voice low.

"What should I do?" I murmur. "My people are gone."

He thinks about it for a moment. "Stay with the child. Keep

her happy. The family back in England might reward you handsomely."

I don't need any more reward than the money I've stolen, but I can't tell him that.

"I'll come see you," he promises. "Tomorrow or the day after. You'll wait for me, won't you?"

I quickly squeeze his hand. He looks pleased, but not bold enough to kiss a native girl out here where other soldiers might witness us.

The Reverend isn't happy to see Mary. He and his wife have five quarrelsome children of their own that shout all day and run around in dirty feet. The colonel appeals to first his sense of decency and then his sense of greed with a promised donation to the church. I'm part of the deal as well. Before the day is over I've been put to work scrubbing the floors, and seeing to the smallest children's needs, and ironing the clergyman's shirts. Over tea, Mrs. Reverend worries and frets. She tells her husband that people are said to be dying in the hills and villages everywhere.

"The Lord will keep us safe," he tells her.

Their god won't keep me safe, though. He has rules about robbing people. Lord Vishnu would not approve either, nor would the prophet Mohammed, nor any of the lamas who travel the road to Lahore. Perhaps I should donate it to the Buddhist monks who come begging with their bowls. But that would only arouse suspicion. I decide to confide in Barney, but he doesn't visit on the second day, or the day after that, or even the day after that.

Meanwhile the Reverend's children take an instant dislike to Mary, and she to them, so all she does is sit in her room and command me to entertain her even when Mrs. Reverend wants me to wash the dirty clothes.

"You're my ayah, mine!" she rages when I try to excuse myself. "No one else can have you."

The Reverend loans me a missionary's Bible to read to Mary each night. I don't like it. It's in English, not Hindi, with many unfamiliar words to stumble over. Mary is no better at reading, having constantly driven away the governesses who came to the house. Barney promised to teach me more, but that was long ago, before the hot season. He hasn't come to see me at all since we came here. I pray that he hasn't fallen ill. When I see a flash of uniform in the lane a few days later my heart jumps, but it's the British colonel.

"Her uncle in Yorkshire sent a telegram asking that we return Mary to England with her ayah," he says.

"The girl?" Mrs. Reverend asks, startled. I think she wants to keep me. "How odd."

"Miss Lennox needs a servant, of course," the colonel says. "Someone loyal enough to have stayed behind when all the others fled."

He doesn't ask me if I want to go. The English are always making decisions and then presuming we agree with them. Staring at the stars that night, I test the idea in my head. Saidie's last words to me were, "Live a good life, Ashna." I don't think she meant leaving our entire country, sailing away on an ocean full of whales, and living in a land full of white people with funny rules and stiff clothes.

Or maybe she did.

But what of Barney? He hasn't come or sent word. Surely he has plans for our future. The next morning, at dawn, I walk to the garrison and ask for him. They keep me waiting at the gate. The sun is hot on my head and I haven't had any breakfast. After a long time, a young corporal tells me Barney has been transferred to the Punjab.

"Perhaps he left a letter," I say.

The corporal averts his eyes. "Sorry. He left nothing."

When I return to the bungalow, Mary screams at me for running away, and Mrs. Reverend puts me to work scrubbing every pot in the kitchen.

I could slip away in the night to some place far from here. Find a husband, bear him a dozen children, live my life in the endless cycle of dust and monsoons.

Instead I go to England. To find a good life, just as Saidie wished.

• • •

The trip by steamship will take two weeks. We are sent in the company of an army officer's wife. She cares only for her own son and daughter, a set of twins she is taking home to enroll in a boarding school. The English frequently show their love for their children by sending them far away. The twins don't like Mary and Mary doesn't like them, and to all of them I'm invisible unless they need me to fetch, clean, or fix something. Each night I get to sleep in a blanket on the floor.

But the ship! It's enormous and bewildering, full of noise and motion that's much more splendid than anything at home. Day and night, the smokestacks churn out embers and smoke. Many passengers fall seasick, but to me the movement is like a splendid dance between wood and steel and water. We pass through the Suez Canal into the Mediterranean Sea and to the Atlantic Ocean. I know all of this because of Khazin, one of the Lascars who serve as sailors and servants. Whenever possible I meet up with him on the little corner of deck reserved for nonwhites. He teaches me about currents, which are like rivers in the ocean, and how the captain navigates by using a sextant and charts.

"Have you seen many whales?" I ask him.

"As many whales as there are beautiful specks in your eyes," he says.

I let him kiss me on the mouth. He tastes different than Barney–more like coffee and tobacco, like someone who has experience of the world. I rise up on my toes to reach more of him, but a lookout from above calls out a stern rebuke. He reports me to the officer's wife.

"Dirty girl." She hits my hands with her knitting needles. "Don't you have any decency?"

Mary doesn't understand why any girl would let a boy put his mouth on her. "It's disgusting and dirty."

I'm brushing her hair, which is thin and limp and nothing to be proud of. "Didn't your father kiss your mother?"

"He would never," she says emphatically.

Each night the officer's wife reads to the children about an orphan boy named Oliver who falls in with a group of pickpockets. Apparently there are many child thieves in London. Their leader is named Fagin and he's no worse than any British officer, but there's also a nasty man named Bill who is cruel to everyone. There are half-brothers and lost lovers and Bill kills Nancy, but if there are any parts about kissing, the officer's wife omits them. I don't think the memsahib would approve of Mary listening to stories about murderers, but she seems enthralled, and it's a disappointment to us both when we reach England without hearing the ending.

"The wicked get punished, of course," the officer's wife says. "That's always the end of the story."

She doesn't know about the memsahib's money, which I've taken to hiding in my shoe. She's probably always lived in a good house with fine clothing and every need met. This money is my back wages, and Saidie's, too, and is restitution for everything the memsahib and Mrs. Reverend and the other British did–spreading disease, and not giving us their doctors and medicine, and letting their men make girls pregnant. It's money I deserve for serving Mary and her ill temper, and for all the tantrums to come now that England is a flat, brown lump of land on the horizon.

"Come away from that porthole, Ashna!" Mary snaps. "Tie my shoelaces."

Before we left, the Reverend's congregants donated clothes for me. I have two plain blue dresses, one pair of stockings, a pale chemise, a pair of sturdy shoes, and a dark gray coat that hangs heavy on the shoulders. They also gave me two black gloves and a black hat. All these things seemed silly at home, but when we step off the gangplank in London I'm extraordinarily glad. The stiff wind pushes us along the dock. I have to hold tight to Mary's hand lest she be carried aloft and dumped into the waves.

"I hope it's not always this cold," she mutters, the first sign from her that maybe she's worried about the future as much as I am.

In a large terminal we have to stand in lines, pass an inspection and answer questions. Finally we're allowed through to a street jammed full of horses, carriages, and men shouting in odd accents. The ruckus is overwhelming. Even back in the bazaars, you'd never see so many people and so much chaos. The air smells like rotting fish and animal droppings. The officer's wife takes us in a cab to a hotel. A woman is there, dressed in a purple dress and a black hat with silly purple flowers on it.

Her name is Mrs. Medlock and her mouth drops open when she sees me. "No one told me they were sending a black girl!"

"Yes, well, good afternoon and good travels to you," the officer's wife says, immediately bustling off with her children.

Mrs. Medlock's disapproval of my skin color is matched by her disapproval of Mary's plain looks, but it's not as if she has a choice about either. She's been instructed by Mary's uncle to bring us to his manor, and that she will do. In the morning she leads us to a train station called King's Cross to travel to Yorkshire. Everyone has to sit properly in a carriage, with no one allowed to ride on the top or hang from the back. Mary sits by the window, as cold and disinterested as ever. Mrs. Medlock has no choice but to either sit silently or talk to me.

"I suppose you've never seen a train before," she says.

I try to stay polite. "We have trains in India, madam."

"You've never ridden on one like this," she sniffs.

"Neither Miss Mary nor I have ever been on a train, but I rode an elephant once."

Her eyes narrow. "That's preposterous. Young women do not ride elephants."

"A man brought one to the village and the children rode three at a time," I tell her. "They're quite friendly, unless you get them mad. Then they make horrible noises and trample people underfoot."

Mrs. Medlock harrumphs and turns her gaze out the window.

• • •

They say India is big, but England seems endless. The weather is miserable, and a nasty draft seeps through the gaps around the windows. Everything smells like engine smoke. Mary stares at the countryside for hours without a single comment. I don't know if she misses her mother the way I miss Saidie, or if she has any emotions at all except for periodic rage. If I carried that much anger around in me I'd have a headache and stomach-ache and yell at my servants, too.

When Mrs. Medlock speaks again, it's to tell us about Misselthwaite Manor. It's six hundred years old, and has a hundred rooms of fine furniture, but most of them are locked up. Mr. Archibald Craven, the master of the house, was born with a crooked back but nevertheless married a quite lovely woman who died some years ago.

"He's never recovered from his grief," Mrs. Medlock says. "Keeps himself away most of the time, or locks himself in his study when he's home. Don't expect to see him or hear from him. He won't concern himself with little girls or black servants."

At the next stop, Mrs. Medlock purchases a lunch basket full of chicken, bread, and tea. She and Mary share most of the meat and leave only a little for me. Mrs. Medlock is slightly more generous with the tea. I don't understand why the English like tea so much. It always tastes bitter, even full of milk and sugar. Mary and Mrs. Medlock both nap after lunch and then, finally, after dark has come, the train pulls into a station and a conductor calls out, "Thwaite! Thwaite Station!"

They leave it to me to carry Mary's suitcase, my own small bag, and the parcels Mrs. Medlock bought while in London. Out on the wooden platform, the rain and wind lash at us again. The stationmaster ushers us inside a small brick building and speaks to Mrs. Medlock with a strange accent.

"Tha's brought tha' young 'un, but who's tha'?" he asks.

Mrs. Medlock adjusts her bonnet. "Nothing but a native girl."

The stationmaster eyes me frankly. "From Africa, is tha' it?"

"From India, sir," I tell him, my teeth chattering.

"Such a strange world," he says. "Tha' carriage is outside for thee, Mrs. Medlock."

It's a fine carriage, attended to by a footman in a long dark coat. A lantern hangs from a hook and sheds watery yellow light around us. The footman helps Mrs. Medlock and Mary inside, then turns to take the packages and bags from me.

"I'll take care o' those for tha', miss," he says, cheerful enough, before he gets a close look at me. "Oh! Tha's a . . . I'm sorry. Tha's quite a surprise."

"Not where I come from, I'm not," I say, rather sharply, and climb inside without his help.

After a short trip through the darkened village, we start across a bleak expanse called Missel Moor. It's hard to tell by the small light, but I don't see why anyone would want to live near such a thing–it's bleak and empty and makes an eerie noise with the wind rushing over it.

"It sounds like ghosts," Mary says.

"That's just the wutherin'," Mrs. Medlock replies. "You'll grow accustomed to it."

Mary doesn't look convinced. "Who lives out there?"

"Nothing but wild ponies and sheep," Mrs. Medlock says. "And heather and gorse."

"What is gorse?" I ask.

"Everyone knows what gorse is," Mrs. Medlock replies, and I'd like to pinch her.

Every turn of the wheels pulls me farther and farther from home. Maybe I'll be pulled so far that I'll snap, like string stretched too far. Eventually the road turns uphill and we reach a lodge where we get more bitter tea. The final drive is along a paved road that runs through miles of park that surround the manor. Imagine that, I tell Saidie in my head. A man so rich he owns a forest and a road and a house with one hundred rooms. But it seems very lonely out here, too, and maybe that's the price the English pay for wealth.

The manor appears, as large and foreboding as Mrs. Medlock made it sound. There's a butler and another servant, and they stare at me while the footman brings our bags inside.

"Make sure to wipe them dry, John," says Mrs. Medlock.

John nods and does his work briskly. Now that we're inside, I can see he has blue eyes. Blue like the ocean we crossed, with all its secrets deep below the waves. His face is long and clean, no trace of stubble even though it's late in the day. Barney's face was like that, too. Mrs. Medlock settles things with the other servants and leads us through room after room of furniture. There are no people. I hope there's a fire where we're going, because the cold has settled into my clothes and skin and muscles. Mary is so sleepy that she keeps bumping up against me, and I'm so tired that I can still hear the wind howling over the moor, a constant rush.

When we reach a flight of dark, steep stairs, Mrs. Medlock marches up them without hesitation. Mary rouses enough to grip the rail with fierce determination. I follow, but the steps sway out from beneath my feet. The ceiling spins. Suddenly, without even knowing that I'm falling, I thump my head on the floor. An extraordinary pain shoots up my left leg, red like a hot fire poker.

"Miss! Miss!" says John the footman. He's leaning over me with worry in his blue eyes. But the pain keeps me from saying anything at all, and when he lifts me I slide right away into darkness.

• • •

When I wake, it's in a room finer than any I've ever seen. The furniture is carved oak, very heavy, and the tall window has heavy green curtains on it to mask the light. A fire is burning in the hearth and I'm toasty-warm under clean sheets and blankets. It's like a dream, except for the throbbing pain in my knee and my immediate fear about the memsahib's money.

I lurch upward too fast. The room spins and sends me back to the pillow.

"Easy there!" says a cheerful voice. It's an English girl, my own age, with ruddy cheeks and a plump figure. "You don' wan' to be risin' till you're well enow."

"What?" I ask.

She puts down the tray she's carrying. "Mrs. Medlock said you might not understand Yorkshire. I'll have to speak better. I'm Martha."

I sit up slowly. "I'm Ashna. Is there–do you know–my shoes?"

"You don't need your shoes while you're in bed. Or is that the custom in India? Mrs. Medlock said they do strange things there. Aren't you hungry? I brought breakfast."

The food on the tray smells delicious. There's hot porridge and biscuits with butter, and I'll never say no to butter.

As I eat, Martha chatters on. "I've never seen a black girl before. They say there's black as in Africa black, and black as in India black. Ben Weatherstaff was a sailor once and he claims he's seen them all, even Chinamen, who are yellow. Is that true?"

"There's many different kinds of colors, yes," I tell her.

She feeds wood into the fire. "The Queen herself has a goddaughter blacker than midnight. She was a stolen princess and the king of Africa gave her to England as a gift. I don't think people ought to be given away, do you? That's why they abolished slavery."

There's a knock on the door and Mrs. Medlock enters, as grim as ever.

"Mr. Craven wants to see her," she announces. "Get her dressed and presentable."

"Yes, ma'am," Martha says.

Mrs. Medlock eyes me coldly. "It's unfortunate that you fell. Of course, we all hope for a speedy recuperation. Miss Mary needs you."

Once she's gone, Martha helps me into one of my blue dresses and sits me on an overstuffed chair by the fire. The stocking won't fit over my swollen knee, so she tucks a blanket around my waist.

"I need my shoes," I tell her.

"Such a fuss about those," she remarks, but brings them anyway and then busies herself tidying the bed.

I feel inside the right toe. The memsahib's money is not there. The left shoe is empty as well. Dry-mouthed, I ask, "Martha, did anything fall out of my shoes while I slept?"

"Anything like what?" she asks.

"A small piece of jewelry. From my sister."

"Strange place to keep jewelry," she says. "Is that another custom in India?"

"It was for safekeeping."

"Oh. Well, I wasn't here when they tended to you. It was only Mrs. Medlock and John."

Immediately I suspect Mrs. Medlock. It would be just like her to steal away what's now mine. But before I can figure out how to get the money back, Mr. Craven arrives. His back isn't crooked at all. He has black hair with gray streaks in it and a pinched expression, like he's eaten something bad and his stomach doesn't know what to do with it.

"Well," he says. "You're Ashna. Mary speaks well of you."

Immediately I know him as a liar. Mary has never spoken well of anyone.

"Thank you for your generosity, sahib," I say. "In bringing me here and letting me sleep in this fine room."

His tense shoulders relax a bit. "It's the least I can do after your nasty spill on the stairs. You scared Mrs. Medlock quite badly. Is your knee very painful?"

"No, sir," I say, "although I can't walk on it yet."

"There's no hurry," he assures me. "Martha and the other girls can see to Mary. You must heal and recuperate. Meanwhile, you can tell me all about your homeland. I'm quite keen to learn more about it. I would dare say Misselthwaite owes its prosperity in no small part to the success of the East India Company. Such a shame about the revolution."

After lunch, Mrs. Medlock returns with John and a wheelchair that looks more suited to a small child. John smiles when he sees me and says, "You're lookin' much improved, miss!"

The kindness in his voice makes my face feel warm. "I'm sorry that I was curt to you last night."

"No one's worried about tha,'" he assures me.

"Speak proper English, John," Mrs. Medlock chides him. "Enough chitchat. Mr. Craven is waiting."

Thief, I think. Or maybe the culprit is John. In the book the officer's wife read to us, the children that Oliver met all looked earnest and sincere, but meanwhile they were stealing handkerchiefs and purses. Thieves come in all sizes and shapes, some with purple-flowered hats, some with deep blue eyes.

John wheels me down a long hallway filled with oil paintings of stern-looking men and women. By day, Misselthwaite is no more welcoming than it was by night. Most doors are closed. Some rooms that we pass through have enormous, dim chandeliers. One has a grand piano larger than any I've ever seen before.

"Have you worked here long?" I ask John.

"Two years this past Christmas," he says. It sounds like he's working hard not to speak Yorkshire. "Do they have Christmas in India?"

"Christmas and Easter, and many other holidays."

He makes a thoughtful sound. "Is Christmas the same there? I suppose it can't be, can it, with no snow?"

It amazes me sometimes how much the English don't know about their own Empire. "It snows in the mountains all year round. Some are so tall you can't ever reach their tops, and you'd freeze to death if you tried."

"I wouldn't like year-round snow," he says. "Winter doesn't seem very interesting without summer. But I'd like to see the Taj Mahal once. Have you seen that?"

I admit I haven't.

"And America, too," he says. "That looks interesting. Or Australia! I'd like to see a kangaroo."

"I don't know where Australia is."

"It's very far away. The other side of the world. Bigger than all of Asia, they reckon. I had a great-uncle who was sent there as a convict. They did that before, but now it's a civilized place. It takes months to get there on a ship, and it's full of all kinds of strange creatures, like kangaroos and koalas and bunyips."

Before he can tell me more, we arrive at Mr. Craven's library. It's a large room filled with books from floor to ceiling.

Never, ever, have I seen so many books. I don't think all of the memsahib's money could buy so many books. Marble busts of famous white men sit atop the very highest shelves. The carpet is an enormous weave of red and gold, and Mr. Craven's desk is like a ship anchored at the far end of it. There's a blazing fire in the hearth, and at Mr. Craven's instruction, John parks me right next to it.

"Have Mrs. Medlock send tea," Mr. Craven says from his desk.

"Yes, sir," John says, and gives me a respectful nod on the way out.

Mr. Craven has an ink pen and leather journal. His gaze is sharp. I feel like I've been called before a judge. For the next few hours he quizzes me about every aspect of life back home, from weather to tradition to food. He's surprised to hear that the memsahib and her husband sometimes enjoyed sherbet made from ice carted down from the Himalayas. He's equally startled that I've never seen a widow from my village throw herself on her husband's funeral pyre. He's pleased that I know Queen Victoria is the Empress of India, but not so pleased that I didn't know her husband was named Albert and that he died of typhoid fever. Apparently this happened several years ago, and she hasn't stopped wearing black ever since.

When he asks about religion I know he only wants to hear me say that I am faithful to the English God. I tell him I promised the Reverend's congregants I would attend service each Sunday.

"An excellent vow," he says, but doesn't seem interested in holding me to it.

As the afternoon light wanes he moves from his desk to a settee, and from the settee to a chair next to mine. He spends more time studying me than writing on the cream-colored page. I don't know if he finds me pretty or ugly, or simply something exotic, like a strange fruit brought from abroad.

"It's very interesting, the plight of the colored man," Mr. Craven says thoughtfully. "Once, when I was much younger, I saw a black American man perform in a theater in London. He played King Lear. Such an invigorating performance! Thrilling, simply thrilling. Have you heard of King Lear?"

"No, sahib," I say truthfully.

Mr. Craven puts his pen and journal aside. "It's a tragedy about a man with three daughters. He promises his fortune to the one who loves him best, and makes the mistake of thinking that love is best expressed by flattery and lies."

The fire has warmed the room considerably, and too much tea has made my bladder full. I don't care for stories about fathers and daughters, not since my own father ran away so many years ago.

Mr. Craven sighs. "I have no daughters, Ashna. No wife, not since the day mine died so tragically."

He leans forward and puts his hand on my arm. His gaze is much more intent than Barney's ever was.

"It is a tragedy unto itself to be alone in this house, surrounded by lies and flattery but no real love," he continues. "Do you understand what I mean?"

"Yes, sahib." I dip my head. "A terrible thing."

He smiles softly. "Regardless of skin color, every man and every woman longs for love."

Mr. Craven lifts himself from his chair and bends so close to me that I can see each strand along his hairline. He's put some kind of oil in it that smells like cooking grease. His teeth are yellow from all that British tea and tobacco and his tongue trembles behind them. Before his lips can reach me I yelp and reach down to my twisted knee.

"Oh, the pain!" I cry out. "My knee!"

He jerks back with a start. "Your knee? What of it?"

I put on my most pitiful face. "I think I've sat too long in this chair."

Mr. Craven backs away immediately. He pulls a cord on the wall and a footman appears.

"Take our guest to her room." Mr. Craven returns to his desk. "We'll resume this conversation tomorrow."

I don't know this footman, and he doesn't say a word as he wheels me back to my room. Dusk is coming fast, which means Martha will bring dinner, and after that–well, I'll have to wait until the house is asleep, and wrap my knee stiffly, and then it shouldn't be any problem to slip away.

But this is not India. I don't know the way back to the train station and there is no one to ask. Without the memsahib's money I can't even buy a ticket. I could follow the tracks one way or the other, but which way to London? I'll need a map and a lantern, and food for the journey, and I don't trust anyone who works for Mr. Craven to help me.

"Tha's very quiet tonight, aren't you?" Martha asks when she collects my dinner tray. "It's good to see tha' eat every bit, though."

"Martha, do you live here in the house?"

"Yes, of course."

"Do all the servants? The cook and footmen and Mrs. Medlock, too?"

"Yes, all of us, up on the third floor. Mrs. Medlock's got a fine room. She and Mr. Pilcher, they've been here the longest. Why do you ask?"

I fiddle with the blanket over my bad knee. "I can't stay in this room forever."

"No, that's true. Miss Mary has been asking for you. Demanding you, really."

"She has?"

"No one can brush her hair just right, or fix her laces the way she wants them." Martha carries the tray toward the door. "It'll be a relief for all of us when you're recovered."

An enormous clock counts each hour for me until midnight. The house is very quiet. I tidy the bed because I don't want Martha to have to do it, and rummage in the closet for my coat and shoes. If I hobble very carefully, my knee holds my weight. It aches with pain, but I've braced it by wrapping a pillow sheet around it, and that will have to do. I get ten steps down the hall, each one more precarious than the other, before I nearly fall over a big lump on the carpet.

"Oh!" I say, just as John cries, "Ow!" and sits up.

I throw my hand against the wall for support. "What are you doing there?"

John blinks and rubs the side of his head. "I must have fallen asleep cleaning the carpet. See? There was a spot right there. Where are you going?"

"Nowhere," I say. "I was hungry."

"You were hungry in your coat and hat?"

"You were cleaning the carpet in the middle of the night?"

He grimaces as he stands up. His voice is pitched low, as if worried someone might overhear. "All right. Truth be told, I was worried you might have a visitor in the night. Someone who might . . . take advantage of a young lady far from home."

I nod slowly. It's a relief to have someone who understands

my problem, but that doesn't mean either of us dares to say Mr. Craven's name aloud. "I was worried about the same thing."

"But you can't just go off traipsing along the moor," he insists. "Not in the middle of the night and not with that knee of yours."

"I have no better plan. Do you?"

His gaze goes upward, toward the floors above us. "Misselthwaite has lots of secrets, miss. I think it can stand one more."

Carefully, slowly, he escorts me to a back staircase. My knee really can't stand to hold much, so I lean on him more than is proper. Before we reach the second floor I'm sweating and dizzy. John is patient, however. He lights a candle in a small silver holder to light the long, gloomy hallway.

"No one comes up here," he says. "If tha's quiet, no one will ever notice."

We pass several doors before he extracts a brass key from his pocket. The room he picks is pitch black, but the weak candle-light reveals furniture covered by sheets. John pulls a chair free from its wrapping, helps me sit, and puts the candle on a table.

Hiding up here seems preferable to trying to cross the moor, but I'm worried. Maybe this is a ruse to get me alone, a way to claim first what Mr. Craven wants for himself.

"Why are you helping me?" I ask.

"Doesn't matter," he says. "Mr. Craven was meant to go to London today, but he changed his mind after you arrived. If he thinks you've run off, he'll lose interest here. He always does. Once he's gone, I can help you to the train station. Do you have people you can go to?"

"Yes," I tell him, because it's too embarrassing to admit otherwise.

John studies me for a long moment. "All right, then. I'll find a way to bring you food in the morning. You must promise to be very quiet. If he finds you . . . well, never mind that. In the meantime I'll need one of your gloves. I can drop it on the grounds and make it look like you lost it."

As I give him a glove, our fingers touch. His are softer than they look, and far nicer than Mr. Craven's were. I want to tell him how much I appreciate this, how much it means to me to have one friend, but the words get stuck in my mouth.

"Remember, be very quiet," he says, and then leaves me all alone with the candle and darkness.

• • •

Mr. Craven does not leave Misselthwaite the next day. I know, because I sit by the window from dawn to dusk, peering at the main road from behind the heavy folds of the curtain. As promised, John brought me some bacon and biscuits at midmorning, the food still warm from the kitchen. He said that Mr. Craven had sent the gamekeeper and some of the grooms out to find me, with no luck so far.

"And they won't find you," he promised.

The room is cold, and of course I can't light a fire. I've explored it from corner to corner and back again, as slowly as my knee would allow. Velvet tapestries hang on the walls, embroidered with flowers and vines. There's a big oak cabinet filled with small ivory elephants. A hundred elephants, easily, some bearing mahouts or tiny passengers riding in palanquins. The bed is big enough that Saidie and I could have both slept in it comfortably, and if the blankets smell old, at least they're warm.

There's nothing to read and nothing to do except look out the window. Once or twice I think I hear a distant cry, like a child in pain. I don't think Mr. Craven would hurt Mary, or Mrs. Medlock either, but who else could be crying? Mr. Craven said he had no daughters of his own. At dusk, I curl up in the bed. The candle that John left me is almost burned to the nub, so I lie in the darkness and wait. My stomach is so empty it hurts. He comes sometime later, with another candle and a pail of food that smells delicious.

"Sorry that I had to wait so long," he says. "Cook guards her domain like a rabid little dog."

He's brought chicken and biscuits and turnips, as well as a wedge of cheese and beer to wash everything down with. I try to eat slowly, like a proper Englishwoman would, but it's hard when I just want to shove everything into my mouth at once.

"Don't hold to manners because of me. I'd be starving, too," he says.

While I eat he updates me on the search, and how Mr. Craven has grown even more sour than usual since my disappearance, and how Mrs. Medlock has neither asked nor said anything about me at all.

Which reminds me to ask about the cries I heard earlier.

"You're not supposed to know," John says. "Miss Mary, neither. Mr. Craven has a son, and he's a sickly thing. Not supposed to live long, but he keeps on living and making life miserable for everyone around him."

I thought that was Miss Mary's job, I almost say, but Saidie would tell me to hold my tongue and be charitable. When I leave Mary will be alone here, alone with all these strangers.

"This is an unhappy house," I tell John.

He warms his hands over the candle. "It wasn't always, they say. Mrs. Craven was a beautiful bride. Broke his heart when she died in the garden. He walled it up afterward so that no one can ever go in there again. But that doesn't give him an excuse to be forward with young ladies."

The last few words come out angrily. I think he must have had a sister or cousin who fell under Mr. Craven's attention, but he's protecting her by not saying so. We each have our secrets.

"Do you think he'll go to London tomorrow?" I ask.

"Or the day after. Don't worry, I'll bring you food and maybe a book if I can get one from the library. Can you read?"

"A little."

"Me too. I didn't like school much, and didn't think I'd need it. My father always said I wouldn't need it. He never did. Lived and died in the fields, he did."

"In my village the boys went to school and the girls worked. My sister had to teach me, and she only knew it because of a missionary woman. It's not a girl's place to get a good education."

He stares into the candle flame. "You and me both, held back by other people's expectations. But we're putting an end to that, aren't we?"

During the night, I dream of John wandering through the endless halls of Misselthwaite, a candle in hand, looking for his father. He hasn't spoken of a mother but maybe she's still alive, she and some siblings, too. Or maybe like me he's alone in the world, dependent on fortune and his own resources and divine favors. In the morning I wait and wait, but it takes him a long time to come. He looks tired but crisp in his uniform, and to his credit he's brought not only food but also two books from Mr. Craven's library.

"They say this one's about the moor." He hands over the books. "And this one here is popular, too."

"I appreciate it, John."

He blushes and smiles. "It's not a worry. Mr. Craven hardly reads anything from the high shelves. He's very angry this morning at everyone, so I can't stay long. Is there anything you need?"

Only for him to stay with me today, and to help fill the silence with words, and to keep smiling at me.

"I'll be back when I can," he promises.

For the rest of the day I practice walking on my bad knee, look out the window, and read the books as best I can. The first is a gloomy story about an orphan named Jane who is bullied by a boy named John, and punished cruelly, and later she has to cross the moor and live in a big house with many secrets in it. I think the author must have visited Misselthwaite. The second book is about a boy named David. His father died before he was born, and then his mother marries another man, but the man is no good in his heart, and the man's sister is even more cruel, and then the mother has a new baby and they both die, and David has to go and work in a factory.

John comes back late that night and notices the second book clutched in my lap. "Did you enjoy it?"

"It's terrible! Do they really make children work in factories to pay off their debt?"

"Not so much these days. I'm sorry it upset you. I'll take it away–"

I hold it tightly. "No, I have to finish."

He laughs good-naturedly. "Mrs. Sowerby, that's Martha's mum, she says a good book can make you cry your eyes dry and be glad of it. Come on, eat."

Tonight's dinner is stew with carrots and a thick chunk of bread and some apples from the cellar. He tells me how a groomsman found my glove right where John had left it, and that Mr. Craven is convinced I'm lost on the moor. I tell John more about David Copperfield, and we look at the fine illustrations in the book. His hand brushes against mine again, and my dark hair falls against his sleeve, but he doesn't try to kiss me the way Barney would. After he leaves, I lie in bed thinking about all the orphans in the world, some of us encountering misfortune, and others great success. But who decides our fates? The gods I know, or the God of the English, or Mohammed the prophet? If I knew, I could make the right offerings and prayers, and pray for John, myself, Oliver Twist, David Copperfield, Jane Eyre and even rotten Miss Mary Lennox.

The next morning my knee is much better. John says Mr. Craven is almost convinced now that I've met my demise, but he sent his men out looking for one more day. In the book, David runs away from London and finds a new home with his kind Aunt Betsy. I want to run away too, but first I need the memsahib's money, and thanks to Martha I know that Mrs. Medlock has a room on the floor above this one.

Even in the middle of the day, the hallway is gloomy with oil paintings and unlit lamps. Carefully I follow the brown carpet to the servants' stairs, which spiral upward. The first floorboard creaks under my foot, and I hesitate. If anyone finds me, these days of hiding will be in vain. But I climb one more step, and then another, until I reach a set of garret rooms where the servants live. The floor here is bare and the plain doors are all closed. There are a dozen or more possibilities for Mrs. Medlock's room, but if I start with this first one and work my way carefully–

One of the doors swings open. A cheerful man's voice says, "I'd better be getting back before he misses me–" and I flee right back down the stairs to my hideaway.

When John comes that night, he has good news.

"Tomorrow Mr. Craven's leaving for London. You'll be able to go, too."

We're sitting closer than before, in chairs pulled close to the little table. I've finished the dinner he brought and the house is silent. But the wind is wutherin' again, and it doesn't take a lot of candlelight to see the sadness in John's eyes.

"You won't be able to finish your book," John adds. "I won't know what happens to David Copperfield."

"You can read it for yourself," I say. "It gets easier the more you practice."

He takes my hand. "I'd rather hear it from you."

I think that now he's going to kiss me. It will be better than anyone else's because he is kind. He was strong enough to help me up the stairs and brave enough to try and protect me, and I like the look of his face, the way he sees good in things, that endless blue in his eyes–

John says, slowly, "In England, when a girl looks at a boy like that, it's very hard for the boy to control himself."

"It's just the same in India," I tell him.

I think he's going to do it. Instead he rises from his chair. "I have to go. Tomorrow you'll be free of Misselthwaite. Ben Weatherstaff says that there's a thousand Indian sailors who live in East London with their English wives. You might go there and find people you know. Don't you think?"

"I suppose I might," I say.

He nods. "Good. Goodnight, miss."

I spend my last night at the manor alone in a big cold bed, wondering why John wouldn't kiss me.

The next morning Mr. Craven departs at dawn in a carriage driven by a white-haired coachman. It's raining again, just as the day I arrived, with thick fog rolling through the park around the manor. John brings me breakfast and says we can leave soon. Ben is taking a wagon to Thwaite for gardening supplies, or so he's told the house butler. I can hide in the back of it.

"It won't do well to get there too early," he says. "There's only two trains to London today, and Mr. Craven will be on the first one."

I bid goodbye to my little room and to Mr. Craven's books. John smuggles me down the back stairs toward the servants' entrance. We have to move quickly and avoid everyone. But at the last minute a figure blocks the way, someone large and imposing with a stern look on her face.

"There you are," Mrs. Medlock says. "Our little Indian princess, running away."

"Mrs. Medlock!" John gasps.

"Go outside, John," she orders. "I'll speak to you later."

He squares his shoulders. "I'm not leaving her."

Mrs. Medlock grimaces. "Don't take that tone with me, John Allen. Go outside."

I squeeze his hand and say, "I'll be right with you."

Reluctantly he leaves. Mrs. Medlock considers me from head to toe. I try not to cower. Wind pushes at us past the ajar door, making our breath frost in white clouds. She asks, "What did you promise John for him to help you?"

"Nothing," I tell her.

Her voice is scornful. "Nothing at all? Not your favor, or love, or maybe this?"

From her pocket she pulls out a wad of banknotes. The memsahib's money.

"That's mine," I say. "You took it from me."

"It's not likely yours," Mrs. Medlock replies. "Not unless

they pay servants an exorbitant rate in India. You probably stole it on that ship you came on, or before you left. The rightful owner might offer a substantial reward if I return it. And you can be sure Mr. Craven would explain it away to the police in return for your affection."

Out of the corner of my eye, I see John waiting outside. He's huddled against the wind, looking worried for me.

"I will trade nothing to Mr. Craven," I say firmly. "I'd rather go to jail."

"Easy to say, harder to do," she replies. "Did you really ride an elephant?"

I blink in surprise. "Yes. More than once."

Mrs. Medlock turns her gaze past the door and past John to the moor. "I've never left England. Never had the inclination. Foreign languages make my ears hurt, and I can't imagine going to a place where all the customs are different. Why leave home when you don't have to?"

Despite her confidence, I hear regret under the words. I think she has a story to tell. Not of orphans or adventures but maybe a romance gone wrong, or a lover who died in war, or something else that keeps a person safely chained to the places and things they know.

"Sometimes you have to make a new home," I tell her.

Mrs. Medlock looks back at me as if she'd forgotten I was there. Her gaze is speculative but no longer quite as harsh.

To my surprise, she thrusts the money into my hand. "You'd better leave now if you're going to make the train."

"Why are you helping me?" I ask her.

She looks down her nose at me. "I'm not helping you. I'm removing an unfavorable influence from Miss Mary's life. She doesn't need the likes of you around, does she?"

I don't believe her, but I don't contradict her, either.

"Thank you," I tell her. It's the first time I've said those words to a white woman and meant them. But she's already turned away, and it's time for me to go.

• • •

Ben Weatherstaff is a wrinkled man with a crooked nose and a thick tobacco pipe jutting from his mouth. He's filled the back of his wagon with sacks and a blanket.

"Aren't you the pretty one?" he asks. "Takes me back to my sailing days."

"Let's go," John says.

Mrs. Medlock aside, it would do no good for the other servants to see me leave. I huddle under the gray blanket, which smells like horses and doesn't do much to keep out the rain. John rides up front with Ben. When I peek out for a last glimpse at Misselthwaite Manor, I think I see Mary at a window, her pale face pressed to the glass.

"Will she be all right?" I ask John.

He glances backward. "Who?"

"Miss Mary."

"Mr. Craven won't bother her," he says. "Soon he'll forget all about her, like he forgets about his son."

The road is more rocky than I remember, sending me up and down forcefully. My knee is healed up, but now my backside grows sore. When we reach the broad expanse of the moor, Ben calls back, "No one for miles, you can come out now!" The rain has eased to a fine drizzle and the landscape is as bleak as before, but it's nice to breathe fresh air. John climbs over the seat to share some biscuits. He's not very talkative today, and I think I know why.

"You'll find her one day," I say to him, not kindly.

He looks bewildered. "Who?"

"A nice English girl. Someone who looks like Martha or Miss Mary."

"Is that what I want?" His cheeks turn red. "A nice English girl?"

"The soldiers at the garrison would promise many things for a kiss, but then they'd go home and forget me." The wagon jostles, nearly throwing me against him. "My sister warned me and warned me, but I didn't listen."

John's face hardens as the wagon bounces again. "You think that's what I am? As good as some soldier in a fort who'd say anything? I didn't kiss you because I can't. If I did, I wouldn't want to stop. You deserve better than a footman from Yorkshire."

We've reached the edge of the moor, where the high road twists downhill into the town. There's a distant whistle in the air.

"That's the second train," Ben says, and urges the horse to speed up.

John still looks mad. I did him a disservice, thinking he didn't want to kiss me because I was the wrong color. But he's a fool to think that there's better out there for me than a common footman, or even that I'd want someone else.

"I skipped to the end of the book," I tell him. "They go to Australia. Mr. Micawber and Aunt Betsy and Little Em'ly. They find the courage to leave and go to someplace entirely new."

Steam rises over the trees as the train draws near the town. Ben has to stop the wagon because a cart has overturned in the lane outside the church. "Better run," he advises, puffing on his pipe. "You won't make it otherwise."

John grabs my bag, swings down to the dirt, and helps me climb down. We dash through the mud. The train blasts its whistle and the brakes squeal as it slows down. When we come to the station I reach for my pocket, but John is already pushing coins under the ticket window. He presses a green cloth purse into my hand.

"It's all I have," he says. "Two years of saving my pay. It'll take one person farther than two."

The train shudders to a halt outside. The rain slants down harder, trying to drench the passengers stepping up to the cars.

"I don't need your–" I start, but can't finish. I can't finish because John is kissing me. Here, in the train station, with the ticket clerk gaping at us, John is kissing me with both his hands on my shoulders, his breath hot and sweet like jam. It's the kind of kiss a lover gives his beloved when he thinks they'll never be reunited again. I push against him just as hard, this silly and handsome boy who has done so much for me.

"All aboard!" calls the conductor.

John breaks away, takes my hand and drags me toward the exit.

"I have my own money," I try to tell him. "Use yours for yourself and come with me."

"It's a gift! Don't argue with me."

He practically lifts me up the steps and pushes me into the arms of the conductor. I try to jump right back down, but the conductor says, "There now, missy," and blocks the way. Perhaps he's had unfortunate experiences with young women leaping off. The train is moving already, carrying us further down the tracks with clatter and smoke. I dash into the nearest carriage and push my way past a startled elderly couple.

"Excuse me!" I drop the window open and throw some banknotes down to John. "I don't need your money! Come with me!"

Befuddled, he watches the money twist in the rain and wind. He grabs at a sodden note. "Where did you get this?"

The train speeds up with a burst of noise and strength.

I toss more money. "It's mine! Come with me! Come to Australia!"

John picks up another note. Behind him, the stationmaster is gaping in astonishment. I think John is going to remain behind, to stay with the world he knows, but then he grins and he scoops up another note, runs and plucks up another. His cap flies off and the air drenches his face.

Maybe nothing good can come of this–a white boy and a brown girl, fistfuls of stolen money, the world waiting to disapprove. Maybe Australia will always be just a word, and we'll never get further than East London.

But he's running, running for me, running for our future, and I go back outside to the stairwell and help him hop aboard.

Resurrection

Tiffany Trent

I have never told anyone this before, and I never will again. Just this once, for posterity's sake, I shall be frank regarding my origins, and I shall tell you how it is that an illiterate woman of low birth became one of the most prominent surgeons in all of London. And how that selfsame woman took another woman to wife.

My mother was an opium-den owner's daughter, whom he sold at various intervals to well-heeled customers seeking other diversions in addition to the pleasures of the poppy. She died when I was twelve, and I could see my fate written in my grandfather's eyes. He would sell me, too, to the highest bidder.

That was the day I became, for all intents and purposes, a boy.

I left my grandfather's den, dressed in boy's clothes, my hair shorn as fashionably for a boy of my age as I could manage with shears and a tarnished mirror. Though I could bind my budding breasts and sew pads into my clothes to give myself more of a boy's shape, there was little I could do about my fine and slender hands. For the next few years, I took what rough work I could, glad for the blisters and scars if they would prove me more a man than my fellows.

There was enough Englishman in me, thankfully, to pass, though more than one sneakthief or pickpocket commented on the yellow tint of my skin in certain lights. Still, few dared to challenge me, especially after I beat Billy Jenx fair and square in a boxing match down by the docks when I was sixteen. For a time after that, I ruled the roost, and the name of Jonathan Wells (as I called myself) was known far and wide in the Whitechapel rookery as one to fear.

I soon got the eye of a deliveryman who was looking to offload some of his clientele onto someone reliable and hard, someone known and feared but who wouldn't necessarily cause trouble himself. At first blush, it was honest work–but the deliveries became increasingly odd. Butcher-paper-wrapped jars I was forbidden to open, parcels sodden with what could only be blood. My pickup points were odd, as well. I hoofed it all over London, most often meeting shady characters around cemeteries or sanatoriums. I never once questioned my buyer, a surgeon of high repute in Kensington. The work was easier than any I had done before and paid a bit better, too, and if the parcels seemed questionable, what difference did it make to me? I was merely the messenger boy.

Usually, I went to the surgeon's office for my deliveries. His man would meet me at the back door and take the parcels with the barest of nods, and my purse. But one day, the seller, a new chap who insisted I meet him out near Nova Scotia Gardens, told me I was to take the parcel directly to the surgeon's house and I was to wait for his reply.

I went to the new address with definite interest. I often peered through the iron fences at fancy houses, glimpsing a life through the windows that I could scarcely imagine. Girls in beribboned dresses, their long curls sliding over their shoulders.

Gentlemen with their frock coats and impeccable white gloves. Velvet-covered furniture and clean-burning whale-oil lamps. Curios and whatnots my light fingers could make short work of, had I but a few moments inside. Plenty of the boys out on the street spat at this new money, pretending that they didn't want any of it for themselves. They especially made fun of those who managed to claw their way up out of the rookeries and establish themselves as merchants or clerks or whatever other (mostly) honest trade they might find.

I took a piss at these men myself in the gin palaces and at the baiting pits, but secretly, I couldn't help looking into their windows, gazing at a magic future I wished I knew how to enter.

So it was with great curiosity that I went to the front gate of the surgeon's house and rang the bell, as I'd been told. Normally, these things were done at back gates and in side alleys. That I should go to the front gate was even more curious.

The footman who came looked a little askance at me until I showed him the parcel with its address and note.

He nodded and brought me in by the front door. I removed my cap and dusted my coat and trousers as covertly as I was able.

The man led me into a sort of parlor or study–I wasn't sure which. Books lined the walls. I settled into a leather chair which gave off the pleasant smell of cigars and brandy. "Please wait here," the man said. He looked down his nose as if daring me to steal anything.

He needn't have worried. Everything looked much too heavy to lift, much less stow away in my jacket. Except perhaps for a few heavenly smelling cigars in the humidor on the desk. I eyed the door and the humidor. Just as I was reaching, I heard the door open. I slipped back into my chair.

I expected the surgeon's dour face–though I'd no idea why I assumed him dour, I'd never seen him–and so was surprised when a young lady bustled into view. She didn't see me–I suppose my stillness and the drabness of my clothes helped me blend in a little too well. She wore a gorgeous sapphire-blue silk gown, the sort of color I remembered seeing in the opium den of my childhood. I had honestly missed such color; it reminded me of my mother in one of her lovely gowns–how she lit every room she ever entered. The gown was offset by a diaphanous lace chemisette that both covered and revealed tantalizing hints of her bosom. But it was her slender white neck that held my gaze, the way her braided chestnut chignon rested so regally upon it.

Any man would have been fascinated. I certainly was.

The girl still hadn't seen me. She reached for the humidor and lifted a couple of cigars from it, looking toward the door as she hastily stuffed them into her chemisette.

Then she saw me and started. She drew herself up, masking her surprise with an unapologetic glare that would have turned me to stone had she the power to do so. Her eyes were as blue as her gown.

"It's rather rude to spy on a young lady without introducing oneself," she said.

I raised a brow, but couldn't help smiling. "Some might say it's rather rude to steal one's father's cigars."

The stony facade cracked then. "You won't tell Papa, will you?"

But before I could say anything further, her papa was admonishing her from the doorway. "Wilhemina Constance Grace!"

I stood from my seat at the sound of his voice, lodging my cap firmly between side and elbow.

She blushed and fingered the chemisette where the cigars were hidden.

"I won't tell," I whispered, "if you save one of those for me." I winked at her.

She allowed me a small smile, as her father moved into the room and came to face us across his desk.

"How many times have I told you, this is no place for a young lady. Off with you, Willie!" he said.

"Yes, Papa." She cast a thankful gaze on me as she hurried with silken steps from the study.

Dr. Grace didn't bother to sit down. "Yes, yes. You've come with some papers for me to sign, eh?"

I wasn't sure what I'd expected him to do. I supposed I'd had some idea that he might be polite, that he might actually see me. It's perhaps more shocking that I even held such notions, considering the fact that he was neither polite nor particularly interested in me.

I handed them over. He snatched them and signed them perfunctorily with a too-wet pen. His signature ran in great blotches across the page. He grunted and blew on the ink. I noticed he had a cut on his lip above his mustache on the right–his body servant must have cut him shaving. I'd hate to be the one who'd done that.

"No one must see or hear of this," he said as he handed the dry pages back to me. "I'm paying good money to keep this quiet."

For the first time, he assessed me. "You can keep this quiet, can't you?"

I didn't like the directness of his gaze, but I didn't lower mine. I'd learned not to flinch too much with these gents–in the end, it only led to misery for me. "As well as them who sent this paper will let me," I said.

His hand shot across the desk and gripped my collar. He pulled me toward him. His face was inches from mine. It felt as if I could see every pore of his skin. A twitch started under his left eye that I couldn't look away from.

"Now, see here, you . . ." he spluttered. Sweat beaded his forehead, and his pupils were oddly dilated. His nostrils flared red, rather like a deer or a rabbit run too hard in the chase.

He seemed more like fragments of a person than someone real. That made it easier for me to glare at him and say with no small amount of frost, "Unhand me, sir."

I think he saw me then for the first time. He loosened his hold and I stepped back, adjusting my collar.

"I will swear my own secrecy and delivery of the items on schedule," I said. "I can do no more than that."

"That will be good enough for now. See you do it."

"Yes, sir," I said. I smoothed the documents and shoved them back in their packaging. Sometimes I wished I could read. At others, I was grateful I couldn't. This time, I wasn't sure which I'd prefer, but something told me I didn't want to know what this surgeon was up to.

"And never come in by the front door again, do you hear?" he said. "Use the servants' entrance. You've only to ring the bell by the door and the servants will let you in. Surely I needn't remind you to be discreet when you make a delivery."

"No, sir." I said.

He nodded, then turned his attention to the papers on his desk. I took that as my signal to leave.

A silent butler met me at the door. He showed me through the house, and I marveled at its magnificence. I tried to imagine what it must have been like for Willie to grow up here in this beautiful house with that dreadful man. I hoped, at least, that if her mother still lived, she was kind.

We went out a door and the butler motioned me down the steps. He shut and locked it behind me without a word. I drew on my cap and adjusted it, pulled my coat collar up against the cold. Around a corner, a bleak alley led to a hansom-clogged thoroughfare.

And Miss Willie Grace, desperately trying to stamp out her cigar, fanning smoke away from herself and spluttering in the process. I grinned.

"Oh, damn," she said. "It's only you."

I looked at the crushed and tattered cigar beneath her prim boot heel.

"Too bad," I said. "Now I'll have to smoke alone."

"What?"

"That was the bargain. My silence for one of your father's cigars." I held out my hand.

She pouted at me. "And what if I refuse?"

I leaned forward, every inch the boy. If I was to be taken for one, I definitely had to play the part. "Then I'll need a little something more to assure my silence." I touched the brim of my cap and hoped I gave her a knowing enough glance.

I was quite taken aback when she played along, a wicked tilt to the corner of her mouth. "And just what might that be?"

I edged closer. "Oh, I think you know very well."

"Do I?" she said.

Up until that moment, I truly had been playing a role. I had played it with many girls, even swaggered to a few baitings and other such sport with a dollymop or two on my arm. But always I'd left them as I found them, to the point where a few of them grumbled I must have a preference for men. Yet they'd never been able to prove that, either, more's the pity. I had, up until this point, stayed out of affairs of the heart. My mother had suffered far more than I thought anyone should in the name of Venus.

But the way Willie moistened her lips with the tip of her tongue, the heart-fluttering expectancy of her face, dissolved all my pretenses. Though I had never done it, I knew the way of it, having witnessed it often enough from one end of the rookery to the other.

I touched my lips to hers. And when she yielded, I opened my mouth just a little, in the way the French girls did for paying customers up at the palace. The jolt of my tongue against hers surprised her, for she made a sweet little whimper. She must have liked it, however, because she let me continue.

I was just beginning to realize how much *I* liked it when we heard the door slam and feet come pounding down the stairs.

"Oh, dear Lord," she whispered against my lips. I pulled away and knelt, pretending to pick up the crushed cigar, just before a scullery maid rounded the corner. She frowned when she saw us, saying "Miss Grace" as she hurried by as if she was spitting rather than saying her mistress's name.

We both only allowed ourselves to laugh when we saw her disappear into the busy street beyond.

High color appeared on her cheek. "You must think me awful," she said, looking into my eyes and daring me to think she was anything but impudent and beautiful because of it. "All you wanted was a cigar!"

I took her hand, covered in lace wristlets and soft wherever mine was rough. I lowered my mouth to it as I held her gaze. "You, milady, are far better than any cigar," I murmured.

She blushed fully at that, but didn't withdraw her hand.

How much I yearned to kiss her again in that moment! I had long wondered what the allure of such romantic rituals might be for those I'd seen engaged in them, but now I understood.

And yet, I also didn't. There was so much that escaped me. She was looking at me as any girl looks at her beau, full of hope and longing, ripe as an apple for the plucking, and yet I knew in my heart that she could never be mine. She was further above me than the moon. Not only because of her status and position, but also because of her very sex. If she ever found out what I was . . .

I dropped her hand. "Time for me to be off," I said.

"That's it?" she said. "I won't see you again?"

"Not likely," I said. It was all I could do not to flinch at the coldness in my voice.

To her credit, there was only a little widening of those sapphire eyes to give me any hint of her feelings. She lifted her chin and turned back toward the door of her house. "Good day, then, Mr . . . ?"

"Wells," I said. "Jonathan Wells."

"Mr. Wells," she said. Then, she sailed by me, her silken skirts brushing my leg.

"And to you, Miss Grace," I said, wishing my heart didn't feel like lead in my chest. Wishing most of all that I'd never kissed her and discovered just how wonderful it was.

• • •

I delivered the documents from Willie's father to my customer in Nova Scotia Gardens, hard by a debtor's cemetery and laystall pit. My man was a wily, louring fellow called Jack Stirabout. What his real name was I never knew, nor did I ask. There were rumors he'd once been a butcher, and I didn't doubt that from the size of his great arms and barrel of a torso. He couldn't read but only a little, but he understood at least what the surgeon's signature meant. And when he looked at me, he seemed to see clean through me, like he knew all at once what I was and what I only pretended to be.

"Well enough, then," he said, upon seeing the doctor's hand on the documents. "We'll have the first shipment for the good doctor by the end of the week. See you're here late Friday, eh?"

"Yessir." I thought I said it smartly enough, but the next thing I knew Jack's fingers were twisted up in my collar.

"You walk around here like some sort of bloody peacock, you do, but let me just lesson you, my lad. If you so much as breathe a word of any of this to anyone"–he turned my face to look at the gravestones and pits of offal–"you'll be eating shit at the bottom of a hole with the rest of 'em! And if you don't show, I promise you'll be doing the same!"

He shook me once. "You understand?"

He let me go, and I straightened my jacket and collar. "Yessir," I said, keeping my voice as even as I could. I cursed Tom under my breath for recommending me for this job.

"Right," Jack said. He tossed a few coins at me, which landed all around my feet. "Sod off!"

I picked up the coins as fast as I could and made for my room above the gin palace. Having a room all to oneself was a luxury most could ill afford, but I managed it through the kindness of Mrs. Pennyforth, a good-hearted woman who was grateful to me for keeping the worst of the drunkards away from her girls. Plenty of bluster and one well-placed punch was usually enough to scare the idiots off, but this Jack Stirabout fellow was something else entirely.

I hoped he never went to the doctor's house and found Willie Grace. The thought of his giant, dirty hands on her . . . I shuddered. But there was no reason to think he ever would meet her–why should he? I was the one who would bring the deliveries to the surgeon, and no one else.

Tom had said this was a good, respectable job, but I was beginning to think he had set me up. I suppose it wouldn't surprise me if he had, truthfully. People here would sooner stab you in the back as look at you, especially if you'd toppled one of the rulers of the roost like I had. Billy Jenx had been easy to overthrow. Jack Stirabout, though?

There were bruises around my throat where he'd grabbed me around the collar. I considered not showing up on Friday. I could always find other work, I knew. But Jack had promised me pain if I didn't show, and I knew he'd not hesitate to deliver.

And then there was also the hope that I'd see Miss Wilhemina Constance Grace. I sat on the creaking rope bed, suddenly too tired even to go down for supper. My lips burned with the memory of kissing her, and I couldn't tell if I felt shame or fear or whatever else that brief feeling had been when she'd melted toward me, sweeter than sugar.

All I knew was that it couldn't ever happen again.

• • •

I fought with myself all day about going back to Jack Stirabout on Friday, but in the end, I did it. I went back to Shoreditch around the stroke of midnight. I waited there, chafing my hands and stomping my feet against the cold, nervous as a cat on hot irons.

They came through the darkness, shadows made of even deeper shadow until they showed themselves to be men. Jack and two others I didn't know.

He was kinder this time, clapping me on the shoulder and calling me "lad" as though we'd known one another all our lives. One of his helpers threw a burlap sack over my shoulder. I thought I saw stains as he transferred it, but then it was resting heavy and warm against my back. I didn't want to know.

"Go on, then," Jack said. "Next week, we'll see how you handle an even heavier load." This time his hand on my shoulder was so hard it nearly toppled me.

He laughed and then he and his lackeys disappeared back the way they'd come.

I carried it, trying to stick to the shadows as much as I was able, avoiding all the most well-known constable beats. I entered through the back alley, went up the steps, and rang the bell as I'd been told.

The butler, silent as always, opened the door. He took the burlap sack, which was indeed marked with an ever-expanding dark stain, gave me much less coin than I was expecting, and shut the door.

I stood there for long moments in the flickering light of the gas lantern, staring at the door, before I turned and went back to my little room, feeling more burdened than I had earlier.

When the next Friday came, I found myself more reluctant than ever. I hadn't been able to stop thinking about the stained burlap sack and its potential contents. Nor had I been able to cease thinking about Willie and our impertinent kiss. My thoughts swayed between them, much like the sack I'd carried–heavy and coarse and stained with all that I didn't understand.

Nonetheless, rent was due soon. And Mrs. Pennyforth, despite the "family discount," as she put it, was unyielding on timeliness.

When I arrived at Nova Scotia Gardens, Jack Stirabout was waiting for me with a long sack slung over his back. There could be no mistaking what this was, what they were. An iron spike of fear drove down my spine.

Resurrection men. I'd heard it whispered about that there were men who, for a price, would steal corpses from churchyards for anatomists and surgeons. That some men up in Edinburgh had even been caught murdering people to fit the descriptions the anatomists gave.

I swallowed hard. Before I could back away, Jack came and threw the corpse over my shoulder. I nearly collapsed–it must have weighed as much as I did, if not more. While I was used to toting heavy loads in the brickyards where I'd once worked, so many stones of dead weight, so to speak, wasn't easy to take on all at once.

"Steady on, lad," Jack said, his voice thick with drink, "you've got a long way to go with that one! Best get moving!"

He gave me a shove that nearly sent me to my knees again.

"You don't really expect me to carry this all the way to Kensington?" I said.

His eyes narrowed. "I expect you to do what you're told. Or there'll be worse than bruises around that pretty throat of yours!"

He stalked toward me, and it wasn't just the weight of the corpse that made my knees tremble. It was as if he'd known what I was all along and was taunting me, promising me pain if for one moment I dared to give up this charade.

I turned and started back the way I'd come.

There were lots of stops and starts along the way, times when I very nearly abandoned the terrible weight on my shoulder and ran. And then I would think of that doctor and what he might do to anything or anyone in his path if he didn't get his precious delivery. I would think about how it might just be possible that Willie would be out in the alley smoking again (though heaven knew that was a terribly slim possibility).

"Oy!" someone shouted.

I'd been keeping to the shadows with my burden as best I could, always with an eye toward perhaps stealing a handcart if the opportunity presented itself. But thus far, luck hadn't been in my favor.

I looked round and dread turned my feet to stone. A constable was headed toward me, holding his lantern up and shaking his wooden rattle at me to tell me he meant business.

There was only one thing I could do.

I dropped the body and ran.

He shouted and rattled even more imperiously, but, relieved of my burden, I streaked through the darkness like a shot. I cursed under my breath at the inanity of it–Jack Stirabout and his rabble had clearly meant me to fail. And even as I ran, I worried that perhaps it would have been better to stand firm and take my punishment. Yet I guessed that Jack had people even on the inside. There would be no way I could escape him, unless somehow I had the ear of a wealthy patron like Wilhemina Constance Grace.

I went to my little room. Though of course I had boltholes around the city, my room was closest, and I desired the heat and light of the gin palace to chase away the terror of the dark.

I got hideously drunk that night, and nearly allowed two girls to drag me off together before I remembered myself enough to beg off, and hauled myself up the opposite set of stairs to my own room.

I woke with a start the next day, jolting out of bed to the resounding throb of a headache that seemed almost bigger than my own head. I was surprised that they hadn't come for me in the night as soon as they'd discovered my duplicity.

I gathered up all the coin I'd saved and stowed in various places throughout the room. It wasn't much, but it might buy me a train passage to somewhere. Anywhere was better than London now. I even tossed about the notion of passage to America, but there wasn't quite enough for that. Though I could have stowed away, the idea of hiding in a swaying, rat-infested hold for months didn't sit well with me at all. Perhaps I was getting lazy.

Or perhaps I was just too confident in my ability to get away.

I didn't tell Mrs. Pennyforth or the girls I meant to leave, of course. Just gave my usual wave and nod and struck off toward Paddington Station with my cap pulled low and my coat tight around me, and all my money, little as it was, singing in my frayed pocket.

I was within sight of the station when the two toughs flanked me, taking my elbows firmly and escorting me off toward Shoreditch with nary a word. I didn't say anything, either. There was no point.

Throughout our long silent walk, my thoughts skipped here and there, like my grandfather's little birds dashing themselves against their bamboo cages. I thought about how these men smelled of onions and death. How even if I could escape they would most likely take my money. How Billy Jenx and his gang would slink back into Whitechapel and have quite the celebratory swill at my expense.

And of course I thought of Willie. Sweet, sapphire-eyed Willie whose father was the butcher of all butchers.

Jack's boys didn't take me where I thought they would. We went into a pub that I reckoned was close to Shoreditch. Its windows were so greasy you could barely see in at them. They sat me down hard on the bench. And that's when Jack Stirabout came and plunked a thick pint down in front of me.

To say I was confused was a bit of an understatement.

"Drink up, Jonathan. You've earned it."

I sat straighter. "I don't know what you mean. I didn't make the delivery last night."

Jack waved his hand as if he didn't care. "We'll discuss that later. But for right now . . . *drink.*" He leaned forward and his eyes bored into mine.

And in that moment, I realized something. I'd been running scared ever since I'd started this job. *I* was the cock of this roost, not anyone else. I'd beaten down thugs aplenty to get where I was. I'd eluded the wiliest of them. (Except for Tom, who I still blamed for getting me into this.) I'd met dozens of big, mean boys, and I'd bested all of them. Even if it didn't look like I would best this one, I wasn't going to let him take me down easy.

"No," I said.

"No?"

"No."

Jack didn't bluster. He signaled to his men. The next I knew they both had my arms and legs secured and Jack was coming around the table with the mug of beer. He pinched my nose closed with his giant hand until I was forced to open my mouth to breathe. Then he grabbed my jaw and held it open while he poured the beer down my throat.

Nobody else in the pub said a word. I screamed and thrashed as best as I could, which caused at least some of the beer to go into my lungs and get coughed out.

"Right then, my boyos," Jack said. They dragged me out of the pub. My head throbbed and my feet didn't seem to want to work properly. I stumbled along between them, and they laughed and pretended that even this early in the day, I was already so into my cups that I couldn't walk anymore.

Not that anyone cared, or would have stopped them in this part of London.

After that, there isn't much to recall before I woke hanging upside down. I thrashed in terror, scraping the tips of my nails against the stone. It was pitch dark, and it smelled of dank, rotten earth. I quelled the urge to scream. For a strange moment I thought I'd been buried headfirst, but I realized as I put my arms out that I was, in fact, dangling by my ankle down what must be a dry well.

I craned my neck as well as I was able. The moon glowed like a call to heaven over the lip of the well, occasionally darkened by scudding clouds. My head and limbs felt stuffed with cotton.

I twisted and turned like a worm, until finally, with great effort, I lifted myself up enough to be able to get my hands on the rough rope around my ankle. I wished like hell for a knife then. I worked at the knot until even my calloused hands broke open and bled. But, at long last, I was able to get myself free. I very nearly let go the rope before I realized it was taut and that, more likely than not, if I did let go, I'd never be able to leap up and reach it again.

Furthermore, if someone was waiting above and felt the rope suddenly slacken, they might think to look in and see what I was about.

And then they'd find . . . what were they expecting to find? The dankness of the well seeped into my bones. They expected me to be dead. Perhaps they would even use me as a replacement for the corpse I lost last night. Whatever they'd put in that beer had not been enough, though. Not enough by far. I was a child of the opium dens. I could drink many a man twice my size and age under the table. They'd have had to give me enough to kill a horse, if that's really what they were after.

Climbing up the rope not knowing what I'd find was worrisome enough, but the sheer agony of forcing limbs to work that had been drugged and so long in stasis was brutal. There were times when I thought my nerveless fingers would betray me and open, leaving me to fall to my ironic death on the stones. Others when it seemed that my body was far too heavy for me to carry it back to the world I knew.

I didn't dare to think of what I would do when I *did* reach the top–who I'd meet, if I'd be able to run on an ankle that felt like it was made of sand. But I kept climbing anyway, hastening my own resurrection, because I would not be another corpse carried on another shoulder to be dissected in Dr. Grace's theater tomorrow morning.

At last I could push myself up, albeit weakly, with my legs and haul myself over the lip of the well. I half fell, half jumped off, my ankle giving way beneath me. One of Jack's men snored near me, a flask gleaming on his paunch.

In the brief moon, one eye unshuttered, then the other, as he sat bolt upright and reached for me. The flask clattered away on the stones.

"Oy!" he cried. "Where do you think you're off to?"

He lunged. I scrambled to get my feet under me. Perhaps it was terror or the sheer will to live that made them finally obey. I plunged away through the dark churchyard, stumbling against headstones and the iron grates of mortsafes meant to protect the dead.

The man's cries roused his fellows, who were apparently busy at knucklebones in some abandoned sepulcher. They gave chase, shouting their curses at my back.

I looked back once, to spy their distance, tripped over the corner of an ill-hewn tomb and fell so hard I was sure I'd broken something.

Then the first of them was upon me. He seemed reluctant to manhandle me, watching me as I rolled over to engage him, until someone shouted, "Beat 'im to a pulp. Nuffink else is workin'!"

All bets were off. My mother had taught me a few tricks for dealing with men if my life ever became threatened. I don't think she ever used any of them herself–it probably would have gone hard with her if she had. Most of them involved sharpened hairpins, but there were a few that required nothing but a good show of force and stealth.

I waited until the man was close enough to seize me, even though I knew I was losing time as his drunken comrades wove toward us through the stones. He stooped over me, raining down a few blows on my face and my injured side before I kicked up and out as hard as I could, smashing into his shins with such force that he nearly toppled.

Instead, he bent down to grab the offended body part and I drove my boot into the bridge of his nose. Face burning and swelling, I hauled myself up and ran again before the others could get me.

I ran until I was limping and then until I was hopping on one foot. If I'd seen a lame beggar with a crutch, I swear I would have stolen it from him. As it was, I hobbled until I found myself crawling up the steps to the surgeon's back door.

What I'd do here I didn't know. I lay with my face pressed to the dirty stoop, letting the coolness take the heat from my cheek. I was too afraid to ring the bell, but I put my hands on the door as if somehow I could force it open, and therein find sanctuary.

Imagine when my fingers suddenly met air and then silk. When a stifled scream fell on my ears and then hands tentatively reached down for my shoulders. I tried to roll, and groaned. Something was definitely broken.

Willie called for someone, and then she and the silent butler were hauling me up by the shoulders. I could barely stand on my own–my feet sort of dragged and every breath was pure, knifing agony. I must have made it here just on will alone.

They got me upstairs and into a narrow room that had belonged to a maid, or perhaps the butler himself once upon a time. Willie sent the butler to fetch water and bandages, a bit more oil for the lamp, food if he could find any.

She turned up the wick so that the lamp she'd brought shone brighter, and set it on the table by the bed.

"Now," she said, "what's happened? Who did this to you?"

I shook my head. How could I tell her that her own father was behind it all?

• • •

She cupped my temple and forced me to look at her. She searched my face, taking in all my injuries with an appraising look that was completely unafraid. Her other fingers touched my lips, and I hissed with pain at the realization that they were split. And then I hissed at hissing, because making any noise at all hurt like the devil.

"Where else are you injured?" she said. She reached for my collar and began unbuttoning my shirt, as swift and businesslike as I imagined her father might be in the operating theater. I lunged backward, nearly hitting the table and knocking the lantern to the floor.

"Stop," she said. She put her hands over mine. "I am a surgeon's daughter. I've watched him for countless hours when he didn't know I was there. I've studied his books and notes. I think I can help you, if you'll trust me."

"I know what's wrong," I gasped. "I don't need . . ."

But she pushed my hands away and worked my shirt off, frowning when she saw the binding already in place around my ribs.

I tried to keep her from unwrapping it, but her persistence was the stuff of legend.

At last, when she'd unwrapped me enough to see the truth, she sat back with a soft little "Oh."

I looked down. I could see the bruise spreading along the curve of my left breast, the ugly swelling where I'd fallen over the rough tomb and then been punched before I'd gotten away. I sighed and winced.

"I'll bind you back up again," she said, "before Jameson gets back. Later, we'll need to put a poultice on it to ease the swelling. Can you bear the pain for now?"

I nodded. She bound me back up deftly, her fingertips sending shivers across my skin.

I pushed her hands away when she would have buttoned up my shirt again. "So, now you know," I said. I sat up and away from her, careful of the lantern and the table.

"Yes," she said. "And–"

"And?" I wouldn't look at her. I couldn't. A pain had started in my chest that was worse than the blow to my ribs. It was under my ribs. In my heart.

Her hands were on my face again, turning me toward her and forcing me to look at her. Her gaze was as deep as I imagined the ocean could be, and as fathomless.

"And it does not matter."

I couldn't speak.

"Whoever you are, *what*ever you are, it does not matter to me. I am infatuated with you, Mr. Wells. I hope you feel the same about me."

For all its bravery, her voice trembled on that last note, as if she suddenly realized what she was saying, her brashness.

"Pearl," I said.

"What?"

"My real name is Pearl."

She smiled and then she kissed me with the lightest of kisses just over the split in my lip. "Pearl," she whispered.

"And, yes," I said, as she moved back to look at me. "I am indeed very infatuated with you, Miss Willie."

I wanted to melt into her arms, but I couldn't quite melt into anything except the bed. I couldn't help but think that even if she accepted me, which was miraculous enough in itself, her father never would. I started up, thinking of Dr. Grace and what he would do if he knew I was here, if, even now, Jack was in the surgeon's study telling him what a thief and a liar I was.

But the pain of that movement nearly made me faint.

"You mustn't exert yourself," she said, pushing me back down onto the bed. "And don't worry. It's my secret as much as yours, now. All will be well. You'll see."

Jameson came then, with the things she'd requested. He raised a brow at the two of us on the bed, and Willie stood up quickly, nodded to me, and then left.

Jameson offered me warm cloths for my face. I pretended as best I could that nothing else was wrong, and as he seemed eager to leave, he didn't question me on it.

"A sleeping draught for you, at the lady's request," he said, placing a cup by my bed. That was the first time I'd ever heard him speak.

I left it where it was, convinced it was the very stuff that had gotten me into this mess, afraid if I drank it I'd end up in the one place I could think of that was worse than the bottom of a dry well–my grave.

• • •

Willie came to me again in what must have been the morning. My room had no windows, so I had no way of knowing the time.

She had a furtive look about her, the reason for which she explained as she said, "I slipped away before breakfast. If I don't hurry, Father will come looking for me–he hates it when I'm not at the table on time. But I had to see you, to make sure you were well!"

I nodded and managed to sit upright, after much travail. She hurried to help me. "Stupid, adorable thing," she whispered over my head as I leaned against her, gasping with pain.

"You didn't take the draught," she said.

I shook my head. "That was how they got me the first time."

"Got you? What–you think I was trying to drug you so I could ship you off somewhere?"

"Not you," I panted. "Your . . . father."

"What do you mean?" She was practically glaring at me now. I owed her an explanation.

"I was delivering corpses to your father. But not just any corpses. Victims of murder."

The shock on her face was painful. I didn't like the way it drained her to the pall of the very corpses I'd just mentioned, the dull glaze of understanding in her eyes.

"I was very nearly one of those. They tried to dose me with enough laudanum to poison me. They hung me down a dry well until they were sure I was dead. But it didn't work. I escaped, barely, and came here."

"To the enemy," she said flatly.

"To you," I said.

It was then we heard her father calling, his voice getting louder and more strident as he approached. She fluttered around the room as if she could make a magic door that she could whisk me into, but I knew there was nothing we could do. We were caught. He would have me transported for crimes I didn't commit. Or worse, give me back to Jack Stirabout and his boys. I knew they'd never let me get away a second time.

He burst into the room, all bristling mustache and slick, dark gentleman's clothes. "Willie, what the devil . . ."

And then he saw me.

"You!" he said. "What in blazes are you doing here?"

I opened my mouth, but he kept going. "You'd both better have a damn good explanation, because . . ."

Willie went over and shut the door, leaning against it with that look of absolute confidence I'd come to love and somewhat dread. I would have laughed, if it hadn't hurt so much.

"No, Father," she said. "*You* have some explaining to do."

Her father frowned. "Whatever do you mean? You were the one late to breakfast. You were–"

She held up her hand and, much to my everlasting awe, he fell silent.

"Perhaps you'd like to explain how it is that this boy was nearly murdered last night by thugs who work for you? Or perhaps you'd care to tell us how it is that you justify hiring said thugs to murder innocents for your surgery? We're both listening, Father. We'd love to know."

And now it was his turn to go absolutely pale and still.

"What?" His voice was as flat and sharp as a knife. I wanted to warn Willie to tread carefully now, lest she do herself harm.

"You heard me."

"I know of no such thing." He gestured toward me. "This boy is a liar–you'd believe him over me, my dear?"

Willie lifted her chin and looked at him sidelong. "Any day of the week." She bit the consonants off hard.

It was utterly amazing to me to watch the transformation in both of them. She was tall and regal as a queen. He looked back and forth between us like a whipped dog. "Well, I didn't, I mean . . . that is to say–"

He couldn't go toward the door, so he backed into the other corner of the room. "It's very difficult to advance medicine when one is constantly forced to use rotting specimens!" he blurted out.

We both stared at him. The silence was so sharp I feared it would cut us.

"Here's what you're going to do," Willie said. Her voice was as deadly calm as her father's had been the day he'd threatened me. Strange, how all his composure was gone in the face of his daughter's rebellion.

"You are going to stop dealing with those men. You are going to take Jonathan in and train him as your apprentice, so that eventually he can take over your practice and, if he so chooses, marry me. You will do things honorably and above board. And we will swear that neither of us will ever tell what we know of your sordid, absolutely unforgivable crimes."

She looked at me then, and, though we were both blushing at the thought of our love so boldly (and yet still so secretly) declared, I nodded.

Her father's face went through several shades of red and purple before at last he hung his head, muttering through his mustaches about agreeing. We all shook hands on it before Willie let him out the door, telling him that she'd follow him presently.

She shut the door and took a deep breath before looking over at me.

Then she smiled and said, "I always did get my way."

And that is how I became Dr. Jonathan Wells, Esq., surgeon to a great many of the wealthy families of Kensington. And how Miss Wilhemina Constance Grace became my wife.

Outside the Absolute

Seth Cadin

Looking down the narrow street, more usually identical to several twisting others like it in Manchester, Sam felt amazed at how completely they had, in less than a fortnight, transformed it from its habitual dreary sulk of a state into this marvel of vibrancy, thrillingly full of colors with its joyfully defiant banners and flags. The soot-caked bricks and half-crumbling walls of its tightly packed buildings were still there. The cobblestones in the street itself were still cracked, and missing entirely in a few treacherous places, tripping around which had left more than one careless drunken wanderer battered and bruised. Yet the grime and decay itself now seemed somehow enlivened, as if it were a wildly blooming industrial garden instead of a place for poor people to sleep badly between hard shifts of work.

Or at least, Sam had to assume most of the cobblestones were still there, because every inch of them was now covered by some boisterous activity, until they were blocked from view by the sheer size of the crowd. Being of a less idealistic set of mind than certain of her comrades, she paused to wonder whether the count of cobblestones might indeed have changed from the night before, with a few of the looser ones pried up and piled neatly somewhere not too far from reach.

Her thoughts were interrupted by the passing of one of the very ones to whom she might ascribe the possibility of such . . . *forward-thinking* activity–Tristan, jubilant that his treasured but previously hidden contraptions would soon make their debut, who half yelled above the growing din of the throng, "Can't imagine the Institution's ever had a queue quite like this, eh?"

"Nor would they care to," Sam said absently, still watching the narrow street and thinking about the different ways in which a cobblestone could do damage to the human form. "They'd sooner face the shame of having to whistle for Peeler's lads than have their Royal associated with this lot."

Merchants of the right mannerisms and acquisitions were welcome, yes, Sam thought–a suitable fortune could now sway the otherwise disdainful heads of the aristocracy, who lately had begun to find themselves rather longer on titles than they were deep in purse–but the men and women working to make those merchants rich were not as welcome in the city's small answer to London's assumption that the North was without culture, or indeed perhaps even without civilization itself.

These mere laborers as now surrounded her, though there were so many more of them–and more every day as Manchester boomed both around them and by the work of their rugged, sooty hands–were not yet expected or understood by the ruling class to have even any interest in, or ability to understand, the world of art, let alone to harbor suspiciously political thoughts about making some of their own. Most especially not in ways which defied the entrenched hierarchies of London's Royal Academy, or its highly specific views on what constituted art worthy of critique, let alone display.

"Oh, but it's open to the public, don't you know that, Sam?" Tristan called over his shoulder, with a laugh they shared, knowing that to the patrons of the Institution, the public was a very different entity than the people.

"No, but also not like this!" Sam yelled at Tristan's retreating back. "We've hours yet to open, and already I'm not trusting the place won't burst at the seams!"

The fact that the merchants and workers had already begun to collect, in woodcuts and engravings, whatever pieces of art they could manage to afford, almost to the very moment these were available, was hardly considered worth noting to the members of the Royal Manchester Institution–after all, the minions of merchants were already known to always have their unpleasant little ways of passing their time, not to mention their money, along.

The tiny street already contained more people than Sam–or any of them, except perhaps Antoine–had imagined would rise to the occasion. Yet the Frenchman *had* not only imagined it, but believed in it with such fervor that his passion opened up a way even for those who could not envision it at all to *hope* for it.

Hope for it enough to work for it, separately and together, in each of their unique ways shaping both the fact and the way it had been brought about. As Sam surveyed what had once been a familiar landscape, and was now somehow both more and less itself than it had ever been before, she realized that nothing fundamental about it had been altered, and yet it was a new place nevertheless.

Sam looked down at the carefully hand-sewn frock she had worn that morning, and touched her stolen wig, and understood–though still without knowing exactly what it was she was understanding–that she had some deep and essential connection to the almost occult process which they had all worked so hard to bring about here.

Even as Antoine ascended his old crate and attempted to catch the attention of a crowd who he had not yet realized had no further need of him, Sam felt this had become a place not just refreshed and reformed, but somehow transmuted into a fragment of a different world entirely.

She found herself tracing all the paths that led from the old world to this new one. All the while, she wondered at whether each step taken had been essential to the destination, or whether instead they would have been propelled to this strange and wonderful place regardless of the choices they had made, pulled there by forces beyond their understanding or control.

She felt as though she had been fated to come to this moment, standing and watching as the crowd somehow swelled with even more bodies attracted to all the commotion and spectacle–not to mention the rumors that had been running wild as they'd quickly taken all the complicated steps necessary to prepare for this display, especially when the details of what people (or which creatures, to some minds) were behind its production became known.

Later–with the long chestnut-colored hair (donated by a kind friend who'd decided she preferred her own short-cropped to go with her suspenders) unpinned and returned to its tattered hatbox, and the plain but precious dress hanging once again neatly beside the ragged trousers and workman's rough shirt, which were together all to be found hanging in the room's excuse for a wardrobe–Sam thought it must have been Uncle Andrew and his Shop of Wonders, rather than fate, who set it all in motion, for purposes which would remain forever unknown.

• • •

When he saw it for the first time, all Sam could think was that it would have to do. The carefully hand-lettered sign in its window declared that within were "wonders to behold"–though apparently not, he thought wryly, to be dusted now and again. Wonder might be less dear than its reputation suggested, his cynical mind continued, as he stood there in the trousers, *beholding* it as instructed by the sign, as it was assembled there, in a jumble of creaking shelves and upturned crates, with only the occasional panel of glass to betray the late shopkeeper's thoughts about worth in terms of finance rather than fascination.

Yet it would do–there was nothing for it but to be done. This dusty shed of junked-down marvels consisted of all the valuable worldly goods Sam had ever owned, as of the previous morning, which had been far more surprising than most of those which had come before.

First, news of an uncle–thus also once a brother–previously unmentioned by a sister, also a mother–though admittedly not much of one, Sam thought with more forgiveness than the woman, who'd briskly brought and then left him without a word at the age of seven on the steps of the City Hall, as if to declare he was now Manchester's problem to resolve, was due.

Most everyone's ship is anchored eventually, and few of them find the best ports. Just the closest, he'd thought upon occasion, whenever he happened to think of her. *Just the ones in reach before we crash.*

Now he was in possession of a small new shard of knowledge about her–the youngest brother of Sam's absent mother had been called Andrew, and Uncle Andrew would never exist in the present tense for Sam.

• • •

The first surprising morning of the week was delivered by a man unexpected in himself–in his carefully tailored suit, with his impeccable hat, the smell of London overpowering even the lasting tang that hung around him from the natural effect of sitting backwind of horses on the move. The appearance of his carriage had been the disappearance of several clutches of vagabonds and rag-children, scattered like mice when a cat stalks down the cellar stairs.

He was a barrister, this vision of a hundred hungry nights woven tightly into just one vest, appearing in Sam's row like the demon of money itself.

Surely, Sam had thought before, there would be demons for the evils of the world, just as there were saints and angels for the better aspects, though he'd found himself dubious of a few of those. He'd not previously, however, thought of it the other way around. He had not considered that what was demonic might, at least, play the part of an angel now and then.

The papers were surely official, and Sam found himself thinking of bread and soup again as he looked over the gilt-covered seals. Yet he said nothing, and the barrister said much, though none of it was anything, because the papers said it all, and Sam could, at the cost of his own great effort over many years, read rather well, and knew better than to let himself listen instead, on a morning such as this was becoming.

The verbose papers could have easily been reduced to one simple word–*property*. A piece of land, formerly occupied by a building, for lack of a better word, and all that was contained therein. An unknown Uncle Andrew, for reasons of his now eternally mysterious own, had in a flourish of papers like this transformed Sam from a peasant to an owner of property–not property such as the rough bed he slept fitfully in, or the table he'd made himself out of discarded pine scraps, carefully hingeing together each piece like a puzzle–but property with *value*, enough to call for the signing of papers worth more than the shack in which Sam silently regarded them.

Finally the rich man stopped speaking in the language of his kind and Sam said, "Yes. I understand. Only show me where to affix my signature, and give me the keys to this–" He peered at one of the papers again, hardly able to believe what was plainly stated, "–'collection of antiquities and wonders' which have made a merchant out of me."

• • •

Sam spent the rest of that first day in the trousers, because he knew even the strange and forgiving company he kept would take him more seriously when he approached them as the boy.

He thought of it that way, himself–not so much that he *was* the boy, or that, when so attired, she *was* the girl, but rather that Sam was always Sam, and which side emerged to be worn on the outside of Sam when the day began was an enigmatic matter with its own capricious agenda. Although not so much that Sam could not, when necessary, decide upon which it was best to wear rather than waiting until it felt clear.

Having been called forth and given directions, the companions he'd gathered met him at the address that he could now rightfully call his own the next afternoon–few of them were gainfully, or at least legally, employed, and therefore were lucky if they rose before teatime, let alone ventured forth into the harsh light of day. It was unlikely they'd have arrived before dusk if not for the fact that a pub quite dear to most of them happened to be just across the way, though none of them, Sam included, had ever taken notice of the shop before, so quietly did it keep to itself.

Each had their own reasons for avoiding the daylight–drink, or sloth, for some–but neither of these vices had ever much appealed to Sam, whose own difficulty with mornings came mostly in the form of lying awake for hours before deciding what to wear that day, which door of the wardrobe to open. In this twilight of self Sam would sit, feeling not so much indecisive as impossibly decided–the problem was not which sex to emulate, but that occasionally, in the center of Sam there was a feeling as if, impossible as it seemed, *both at once* would be most appropriate.

Of the thirteen quick visits he had made the day before–delivering a speech that ended with a dramatic and pleasingly bell-like jangle of keys–somehow seventeen hopeful young faces appeared. This was likely due to the part of the speech which had included the promise that anyone who arrived to help Sam empty this place in order to sell its contents as quickly as possible would have some part of the profits thereof distributed back to them.

Sam had been vague on this point, not yet knowing how big the pie he was promising to divide might turn out to be. Yet as he surveyed them gathered and eager for paying work that involved dust instead of soot, he became keenly aware that any size slice at all would do for this ragged assemblage.

• • •

Packed neatly away, the wonders of the shop were somehow even more desolate than they had been in their jumbled time on display. It was how one thing fitted against another, though neither had a regular shape to it–a broken cuckoo clock, hand-carved, tucked sideways against an old shaving mirror, its tarnished brass frame warped, its yet intact glass nestled carefully by a stack of worn rag dolls.

And so on, until all the wonder had been taken away and what remained was just a room, smaller than before, as if its evicted inanimate residents had created over time a way of folding space, until a single shelf came to feel as though whole infinite rows of shelves would pull out from behind it if it were removed. Only dust and cobwebs were there instead, and so the room was smaller now, but Sam wondered–then let it be, with an easy flick of his mind, where he knew all too well there were no maps or compasses when the forest of thoughts there turned wild.

There was a fascinating presence to the walls themselves. Once exposed, they made Sam a little ashamed of his own prior cynicism toward the place. There *was* treasure here, and not the flimsy tin kind men in linen suits sold along the docks in any city with a port.

The tired but satisfied haulers of wonder had, on finishing, found themselves surrounded by panels, five to each wall, and two more in the drop ceiling Sam hadn't even glanced at until now. Each panel fitted into the other like a puzzle, with metallic protrusions and eclipses intertwining so delicately and yet so precisely that it became difficult to determine where one panel ended and the next began.

The skirting boards revealed the answer to this visual conundrum–brass bolts, somehow kept to a perfect shine while the faux wonders were left to decay, held each panel in place along strips of varnished wood–some tree which was dark and surely exotic, from how it seemed to hint at a bigger, deeper world. Sam's collection of workers stood at the center of them, their chatter slowly falling into silence as they contemplated what they had uncovered, and then immediately began a lively debate over what should be done with it.

Sam surveyed them again and found he only knew a few of them well, though the stowaways attached to the core were also familiar for their habit of following wherever their center wandered.

There were Antoine and Tristan, at the moment inseparable despite their frequent fallings-out, the racket of which would echo down the whole row as they cursed and tussled in their rooms on the ground floor of the building at the corner of the street. With them as always was an ever-shifting collection of lads, always just a shade younger than themselves, who seemed to regard them as beyond reproach and correct in all their oft-expressed opinions, which of late had been unsettlingly Chartist for Sam's nervous disposition.

If ever there were men who had no sense to keep their heads down and their names out of the mouths of the rich, it was those two and their pretty young denizens–still, they were also the most talented, devoted and unusual artists he knew, and more passionate on the subject of defying the traditional techniques and accepted subjects of the Royal Academy than Sam could find it in himself to be.

Certainly he felt art should be and indeed necessarily was, by its nature, an exploration in progress at all times–but had never in his own painting paid much attention to why he was going about it entirely wrong, whereas Antoine had come from France and therefore had much stronger feelings on the subject, and Tristan was by his nature a contrarian for whom defiance was less a political or artistic philosophy and more a way of life.

They and their hangers-on made strange company with the rest, who were mostly young women, since Sam had found that those who wore skirts and bonnets as a matter of habit were more inclined to be of an open mind toward keeping company with someone who did so seemingly at random. They were, like Sam, all artists–some painters, some sculptors, a few like

Tristan who did a bit of both and also found fascination in the possibilities of mechanized display–but all united in their determination to keep on scrabbling at the edges of a world which had thus far found them insignificant, regardless of its judgment of their work.

Jyoti was the most colorful, in the long skirts she stitched together herself from what appeared to be pieces of old curtains, in different textures and patterns, creating a strange patchwork in which, for example, a scrap of lush purple velvet was sewn neatly aside a thinly green-striped strip of cotton. Sam imagined she scrounged them up when the aristocracy felt time for a bit of a freshening-up around what they surely called a "cottage," despite its dozens of rooms and staff of willingly cooperative workers when it came to passing on the odd bits and pieces.

She would have been colorful even in white, though, like a diamond–she seemed to fracture light around and through herself as she moved, so that from one angle she looked shadowed by some perilous mystery, and from another bright with inspiration.

She spoke quietly, but there were times when she spoke firmly as well–not insistent, but with certainty, as if the discussion were a chess match she'd already calculated herself winning.

She had that tone now: "There is another way, a balancing."

Antoine, who had been holding forth on the subject of how the panels might be removed and reassembled for display, halted at once, as part of the charm he had which induced forgiveness of his arrogance in others was his ability to know when it was wise to let them speak instead.

Jyoti went on. "What we must do foremost is honor these walls. They are a gift from our greatest patron, the Holy Spirit, who has given us through an unknown artist a way to become ourselves as God wills us to be. Yes, it is true that any gift, once given, is then the domain of the grateful recipient, who may display or alter or even discard it at will and according to his wisdom. So let us use our wisdom, as guided by the Spirit within us."

"We make it part of the show," Sam said. "We use it somehow, not just tear it down and mix it up. She's saying, We found it, it's something we found incomplete, so we have to complete it."

Silence in the room, for once–not even fabric shifting, as each by each they were struck with a vision, and lived in it for a moment . . . before beginning to argue again, but this time in much more specific and useful ways.

Sam slipped away and aside, to stand with one hand resting on one of the exquisite panels, tracing the lines with his fingertips and wondering if Uncle Andrew himself had created this marvel, or merely discovered it and found it an appropriate encasement for his wares. He was so lost in its complexity that he only knew he had company at the last moment, when the delicate scent of powder reached his senses.

Ingrid, unlike Jyoti, rarely wore colors at all, though her paintings were full of them, so explosively vivid and unusual that more than one viewer had felt they must surely be somehow offensive despite any obvious display of crudity. Her dresses were somber, and even the rows of buttons she'd patiently sewn on, each by each, were small, carefully polished fragments of dark shells she had collected, so that they blended into the dark fabrics almost entirely.

When she spoke, it was with a seriousness matching her attire–but also with a bluntness that seemed to echo her paintings, so that the whole picture of her somehow emerged between the two seemingly opposite poles.

"Are you entirely sure of what you're about with this?" She was speaking low and almost directly in his ear, and for a moment he could hardly breathe for wanting to turn and touch her face, and find in her expression reflected what his heart had, through their years of friendship, never found the courage to convey.

"Not a bit," he answered cheerfully, turning indeed, but only smiling, forcing his hands to return from the panels to his sides rather than her cheek. "All I know is that there's no reason we shouldn't have a permanent exhibition of our own, for our kind of work. They have theirs, so let us have ours as well."

He'd meant to speak quietly, but as he finished he found the crowd had fallen silent and turned its attention to him. He spread his hands at them–what more was there to say? And almost in one slow synchronized motion, their regard turned toward Antoine, who was already clearing his throat in preparation to say it, at some length.

• • •

Eventually, the endless talking descended into general agreement that the debate should be moved to the pub across the way, which they had all nicknamed 'the Absolute' so long ago they could no longer remember what amusing absolute they had decided it was on the night they'd so christened it.

Sam could have reminded them that the property was emphatically and officially his own, which they seemed to be forgetting by the moment, but found himself unable to care–unable to really think of it as not belonging to all of them already, despite his distance from their heated discussion over how they ought to shape its destiny. Half their earnings for the work would go directly to the Absolute tonight, he knew, and the rest would slip through their fingers in hardly any time at all.

And so instead of joining them, and knowing she would refrain as well, Sam followed Ingrid when she slipped away, despite feeling all the while that he should *instead* turn down every path that branched away from her. Any small alley or dung-riddled crossing would do, and he'd be a free man again, making choices that were his and not some miserable form of destiny pressing his body forward like a strong wind on the deck of a ship at sea.

Though he had more than a bit of experience trailing a person without being noticed, he could see the moment, on her face, when Ingrid knew first that someone was following her. Sam imagined that, given the secret she had to protect, her senses had long ago become habitually keen in this way.

And so he also saw when she made herself ready, shifting in a way he knew meant she was gripping the handle of her dagger firmly and letting the flat of its blade rest gently under her sleeve. He watched as her other hand gripped a less graceful sachet of herbs with a handful of small rocks nestled inside them, ready in her jacket, so either hand could answer whatever danger might approach her.

At this point, he felt it might be best to make himself known, and coughed quietly before he approached and reached her side.

"Ah," she said, "only Sam," and let her hands release their hidden weaponry, seemingly ignorant of the expression of dismay which passed quickly over him at this pronouncement. She might at least have been a bit pleased, he thought, though on reflection realized that perhaps relief and trust were the same, for her.

"I knew where you'd be going," he said. "If you'd rather go alone–"

"No," she said, perhaps just a bit quickly, and his heart lifted again. "Come along, you can help me with the boards. They do keep trying to keep us out."

• • •

The abandoned chapel, set far back in the wilder parts of the dismal cemetery, had indeed been boarded over once again, but not with much enthusiasm, as if the laborers felt unsure about their task. It was one matter to miss a sermon now and then, but another one entirely to box up a house of God like an oversized wooden rockinghorse bound for the shelves of a private gallery in some posh mother's attic–besides which, they'd been sent out to do it enough times now that it had become a kind of game, which Sam suspected they had reasons of their own for playing.

And so, some distantly heard call to grace summoned from the workers' hearts, or perhaps just a packet of wages too late too often, made it easy for Sam and Ingrid to pry out a loose or rusted nail or three and make a spot big enough to clamber through. He went through first, because it was a trousers day–otherwise, Ingrid would have done so, though Sam suspected neither of them would ever be able to define the terms of this silent agreement between them.

As he expected, first there was an imminence of bats disturbed from their slumber–Sam could think of them no other way but that, as some fabulous single creature with many parts looming up above them, all around them, and then departing through the rough window they had made. All in a tidy column, Sam thought, each knowing where the other was, like humans in a queue, only with wings.

Together in the moldy chapel, which had been stripped bare of pews and altar until the only signs remaining of its former holy purpose were crumbling saints painted on stone in lurid tones, having all this while been falling slowly down the walls in pebbles and chunks. Sam couldn't tell the Marys from the Margarets, but he recognized an ikon of St. Lucy, because of the eyes, or rather the absence of eyes, or rather the presence of eyes but held out on a tray just as neatly as they had once been set into a face.

"Horrible," Ingrid remarked, following Sam's gaze. "And they say we are the deviant ones."

"Jyoti would see it differently," he said, loyally, or perhaps charitably, or both.

"Yes, but she sees everything differently." Ingrid stepped over fallen boards and rocks until she stood at the chapel's center, and looked at him as if expecting something, though nothing else in her eyes told him what it might be.

So Sam followed, and stood beside her, and then moved a little closer, and found she did not move away. They shared a long moment of silence, enjoying it together after the day's hard work and noisy evening, and then–

A beam of the drifting evening light, as they will do, happened to bounce upon a remaining shard of glass in a high broken window, just at the very moment he was reaching to touch her hand–bare of its glove, which she'd torn on a nail and then stripped and dropped outside into the bracken like trash in the gutter.

Thoughtlessly, horribly wasteful, he told himself, and wanted her regardless–or even more, and let his hand keep moving toward her own. Then the sun intervened, and her attention was brought back to the moment and caught, and her hand drew back as if he'd been pressing a viper or hot coal toward it.

"I–I apologize–" he stammered, but before he could make even more of a fool of himself, she reached out with her own hands and took both of his in them, then pulled him as close as he'd longed to be to her for so many years.

"You should," she whispered in his ear, even as she drew him closer still, even though pressing their bodies together meant that if he hadn't already known her secret, he surely would have guessed it then. "You certainly left me wondering long enough."

He would have laughed, but quickly found his lips were otherwise occupied by an even more pleasurable activity, as he needed no more encouragement than that to lean up and let them brush against hers, at last.

• • •

The unnamed committee of outcasts and undesirables who fancied themselves renegade artists met again the next day, and again the numbers had somehow swelled to what seemed surely like twenty or so people milling through the former shop. In Sam's mind it was theirs, though each one of them called it "ours." Our command post, our hideout, Our Gallery. They said it as often as they could in as many ways, delighting themselves each time, though Sam found it totemic, a kind of witchery. They wanted the truth to emerge by collective insistence.

Arguing happily in little crowds, which shifted and reformed with each passing resolution, none of them seemed aware of their own futility. *Theirs*, thought Sam, who felt she'd had enough of the trousers and could trust the group now to allow her the frock and wig for this evening's increasingly organized session of planning. Theirs, but not hers at all anymore, though certainly *ours*, if she stayed.

She knew that she would stay. She saw Ingrid, as unattached to any of their clumps as herself, drifting through the space not as if it were empty, but full instead of different people, in different kinds of clothes.

As Sam watched her, she could almost see them herself–up close, as she never had, rather than from a distance in the street, or as a portrait on a wall. Glittering, hands and throats heavy with the weight of priceless jewels–the women would be graceful and the men resolute, standing just as stiffly in one place as their wives would flow dynamically through the room, one distant day.

Then Ingrid saw Sam too, saw that she was seeing both near her and through her eyes, and this was almost as extraordinary as the moment itself.

They shared, across a field of ragged backs–huddled in now quieter, more conspiratorial and above all else more sectarian groups than before–a look which Sam knew meant the same to each of them, a thought unspoken, *They will rise. This wretched lot will rise. We will pull them up, and drag the other ones down, until the reckoning.*

• • •

They met their third personal conspirator after the third night's debate–moving together to meet her just at the street's corner, at the edge of the light cast by the tall gas street lamp on its twisting iron column. They met her there as if they had arranged to do so, though no mention of it had passed between any of them.

Ingrid, Sam, and Jyoti. Two women, one boy–again today, through the cheap stage magic of trousers and hairpins, and putting his shoulders back more. Ingrid had remarked once upon how Sam walked differently as a girl than as a boy–how Sam's body seemed to have two separate rhythms, side by side, into which it could–or perhaps simply did, without Sam's willing it–slip on any given morning.

Jyoti, for her part, seemed not indifferent but perhaps entirely unnoticing of how Sam changed sometimes from she to he or back again. She spoke to him now the same as she had yesterday when they met, when Sam's magic trick was a hand-sewn frock instead. In her regard there was not the slightest flicker of confusion or awareness that anything about Sam had changed.

She sees differently, just as you said, Sam thought, looking at Ingrid and knowing he could convey this meaning with his eyes. *All the time.*

Sam watched as Ingrid, forgetting to guard her face, seemed to wonder at her own mind, decoding such messages in a glance as quick as the shadows flickering through curtains in the windows above them. He knew that Ingrid considered herself more rational than to have such strange thoughts, share such moments with–

"You don't mind when I'm a girl," Sam observed mildly.

"Do you have the gift?" Jyoti responded before Ingrid could, rounding upon Sam with an affect almost like anger. "You've done that, speaking to thoughts before. You've done it with Antoine, only he–"

"Didn't notice," said Sam. "Wouldn't."

"But we do," Ingrid said, and Sam felt their unity again where, he now reflected, they had begun building a wall. "So is she right, can you–see people's minds?"

There was a precarious moment, a sense that Sam might turn and flee, or even attack them–that he was on the cusp between these impulses and did not himself know which one would tip him. Yet balance returned when he laughed, instead, girlishly but with a rattle that went with the trousers.

"I can pretend to, all right," he said, twinkling all over with some delightful secret and the growing confidence he could share it. "Have done, it's good for a bit of push. But no, Lady Jyoti, I've just a knack for seeing people's faces, and that can be quite like seeing their minds, if you know the way of it."

Both women spoke at once.

"The way of–" started Jyoti, just a moment before Ingrid said, "*Lady?*"

• • •

The second surprising morning of the week contained rather more pillows than Sam was accustomed to, and indeed than he could recall laying his head down on the night before. Those had been two flat rags on the floor of what had been a shop and was now an impending exhibition, whereas these were plush with down and coated in some impossibly soft fabric which, he decided after a moment's cautious thought, was the same color as a young salmon seen through the water of a muddy river.

The bed too was surely not the one Sam had occupied for all the nights and early mornings of seven years–that one was also flat, and so familiar that every piece of straw stuffed inside seemed like an old friend saying hello when it poked him in his slumber.

Then he remembered–Jyoti laughing, Ingrid scowling, himself wanting to flee again but instead letting himself be led, at Jyoti's insistence, to the grand old house he had only suspected was real when he'd let slip the guess of a title. It was the way she carried herself–she *was* surely one of them, but she hadn't started life that way.

And so, as she assured them her parents were away at one of their other houses, attending to their busy social season, he and Ingrid had found themselves just outside the city after walking for what felt like hours, and probably was, which explained the exhaustion with which Sam fell into what must surely be the most comfortable bed in the world.

From which he was too soon pulled by the clanging of a bell, a summons he followed outside until he found, standing next to a squinting and disheveled Ingrid, a beamingly radiant Jyoti, who told him she'd been sent a wonderful vision in the night by God, and that she'd like very much to introduce them to her horses.

• • •

Ingrid seemed to choose not to see it, and Sam wished he didn't, but it was too starkly clear for his mind to reject. Around Jyoti, the horses were soothed in some uncanny way, and when she left them, they looked after her and shifted restlessly in their stalls. Of course she must visit them often, he thought, but still–the way she glided through the barn, and touched them all, and said their names–it felt like a sacrament, a ritual with more power than its components should have the capacity to produce.

When they had been suitably introduced to what must, Sam slowly realized, be Jyoti's closest friends, she led them behind the barn to show them the seed of her idea.

It was a carriage, with a quality to it much like her family's house itself had–so carefully maintained over so much time that for all its glorious worth it seemed nearly ramshackle, a patchwork of aristocratic frugality and the work of some craftsman who cared for his trade in the same way Jyoti cared for her horses.

"Yes," Ingrid said, instantly, before Sam could even see what was meant by this presentation. "We can adorn it, transform it–for the opening."

Sam felt uneasy, sure that as permissive as Jyoti's family might be about their wayward daughter's wanderings through life, they would draw the line at the use of their property for this particular endeavor. They must know it, too, he thought, looking at his companions, but nevertheless both women looked back at him fiercely, as if defying him to disagree. He wished he'd brought the frock, because he sensed it would have somehow given him better ground to stand on with them in this moment.

As it was, he was outnumbered, and only let himself sigh as he said, "Very well. Then I believe it's time we paid a visit to Tristan and Antoine."

• • •

The rough little room was a pickpocket in its wedged corner, with its ramshackle walls built straight up alongside the brick and mortar of the buildings around it, like ivy made of crate splats and bits of tin. The roof was proper thatch, as even artists needed a trade when lacking in patrons, or more precisely to the point, when lacking the necessary traits of character to acquire patronage, such as the ability to regard property as defined in terms of ownership rather than possession. So *two* trades might be more accurate, Sam thought, as in addition to being notorious degenerates and occasional thatchers, the men who resided here were accomplished thieves, with Tristan's mechanical handiness leading in particular for him to a reputation as a fine cracksman.

Let inside by Antoine, who seemed to be expecting them somehow, Sam fell back behind as he was overwhelmed by the many works of art and strange contraptions in various states of completion surrounding them. In green and golden tones, spanning more than half the long wall at the back of the studio, one huge canvas seemed almost to glow with some inner light, as if the artist had somehow imbued the oils with a living spirit.

"Everyone's off working," Tristan said by way of greeting. "And somehow word has gotten round that we're taking all comers, and it's astonishing but it seems to have inspired rather a lot of–"

"Of course," Ingrid said, cutting off his rush of words. She sat just as primly upon a small chair as Antoine lounged luxuriously on a threadbare loveseat in the corner opposite from her.

"Many are called to the arts, to make beauty and create joy," Jyoti started to add, but Ingrid finished for her.

"They're just not normally allowed."

"Nothing's stopping them," Sam started to point out, but when he saw Antoine's head rise in response he waved a hand as if to dismiss his own words. "Never mind. The art will be there. Probably more than we can fit, so it's a good thing we have a carriage to display the rest on, outside, and the Absolute will probably let us use its walls too."

Sam fell quiet as Jyoti explained her vision, and then as Antoine did more than just lift his head, but indeed rose and began to pace in circles. Tristan seemed to be ignoring them all, working at a canvas with his back to them, but Sam knew he was listening by how his shoulders tightened when he heard Antoine begin to speak.

"Not just space. We need to get the most attention we can, or they'll just ignore us. We need to throw an opening so spectacular they'll want woodcuts done of the day itself . . ."

He went on, listing his ideas, but all the while Sam kept his eyes on the tension in Tristan's spine and the way Ingrid kept sending him sideways glances. He resolved, since he was stuck with the trousers anyway, to take Antoine aside and make clear his reservations.

• • •

This proved, once they had slipped away from what had descended into Jyoti's dreamlike proclamations of the fuller details of the vision she felt sure had been sent by the Holy Spirit, to be an even more irritating task than Sam had anticipated.

No violence, Sam had insisted firmly, with a note that indicated he was aware that very different visions of just how newsworthy their little event would become if a riot ensued were already forming in Antoine's mind.

After that, the conversation had become a tangle of misdirection, until he heard Antoine saying, "Still, it might be, or come to be, that one or another of us, perhaps a few in tandem–"

Sam was amazed to find there were yet more tones of voice in the Frenchman's repertoire to distinguish shades of condescension than he had encountered already. "Tandem means two, Antoine, not a few, which doesn't mean anything," he said after a moment of stillness.

"Yet your diversion means everything, because it's how you tell me to stop, and when what is becomes what is not, everything is one thing and nothing is everything."

"Words aren't sport–"

"And you are not sporting, my dear. In my own defense, I seem to recall someone other than myself bringing us on to the subject of words–"

"And meaning. Yes. Aside from your usual drivel, you seem to have understood me quite well."

"You want no part of it."

"I couldn't begin to imagine what you mean, but I will note, on general principle, that I would agree with any vague suggestion of that undefined significance." It was amazing, the lasting effect just a few hours spent in a small room with a barrister flourishing papers could have on a person, Sam thought as he heard himself speaking.

"Ingrid will be in with it," he said. "She knows we need a spectacle to establish Ours right from the start."

Around them, the market was folding inwards on itself, tarps rolling down and workers retreating behind their sheds. After a moment, Sam pretended he hadn't heard and walked away–but it was a moment, and if he'd noticed, Antoine would have too, and would know that once Sam had spent a bit of time alone with this last, undeniable fact, then Sam would be in with it too.

• • •

The days that followed were a blur. Each morning, Sam woke and rushed to the former shop to put a hand in the work that needed doing to prepare, and every afternoon and evening which followed was mostly comprised of the faces of old friends and new acquaintances appearing hopefully over a canvas or around the edge of a sculpture, none of which would ever be accepted to hang in any city's proudly traditional galleries, and almost all of which were accepted for display at theirs.

Yet the work was done and time passed until, with all the pieces in their place, Sam found herself pausing to gather the other contents of her wardrobe before accepting Jyoti's invitation to spend the final night before the opening with herself and Ingrid at her family's otherwise unoccupied estate. Uncomfortable as Sam felt intruding there, the call of the soft bed–and the thought of Ingrid in another room nearby–made her too weak to resist.

And indeed, once the horses had again been greeted and tended, and each of them settled into a different bedroom for the night, Sam found herself, still in the frock, sneaking down the carpeted hallway and slipping into Ingrid's room, where she found her beloved awake and waiting, sitting up half covered in thc bed.

Within a moment they were entwined, only their clothes between them–only fabric, with no room for air, or even time, which stopped for their embrace. Under it, the sense of untouched skin, hidden away but giving off from it a heat which was unmistakably fierce nevertheless.

That Ingrid would let Sam feel the true shape of her body, the secrets she concealed under her long, stern dresses, made Sam feel more privileged than all the deeds of property in the world could ever do.

She whispered her name, and Ingrid gripped her shoulders as if she might suddenly fly away, drawn through the window into space by the same cosmic magnet that had brought her here.

"Only a little while more," Ingrid whispered back, eventually, when the kiss that had seemed to start nowhere ended abruptly as she rolled away. Mentioning time, she summoned it again, and they both looked toward the dark window.

"We'd best–" Sam started to say, but Ingrid was already rolling back to push her away, out of the bed and onto her feet.

"Yes," she said, firmly. "We need our rest, and this is no way to get any." And so Sam headed back to her room, burning but waiting, which was not an unfamiliar sensation.

• • •

And then, hours indeed after Sam's last exchange with Tristan, Our Gallery was officially open.

In the street outside, there were puppeteers and ribbon-twirlers, and at least thirty kites in the air at one moment, though several quickly dropped as they entangled. Antoine had carried on with his cryptic bookkeeping of favors owed from exotic characters, and produced what Sam had to admit was an impressive display of a man's living trophies, the fellow humans he had met somehow along his various ways.

Jyoti's two fine horses standing patiently outside the gallery, attached to a carriage with its sides entirely covered by some of the more unusual works their call for art had attracted, became the centerpiece of what began to feel more like a carnival than an opening.

There was even a lady Sam spied in the crowd who, upon careful inspection, seemed a bit uncomfortable in her dress, and who Sam caught several times slumping her shoulders inward as if remembering suddenly to conceal their width. Another spy in the house of renegades, Sam thought, but left her to her own business. Having had no problem deciding upon keeping with the wig and the frock herself this morning, she sensed the stranger might prefer her privacy than a moment of flimsy camaraderie.

Jyoti's ragtag collection of boys from the park had appeared as well, materializing around her in a cloud of grime and eagerness. They must each have loved her in some burning, unique way, Sam imagined, but she was entirely unaware, and treated them as if they were her personal coterie of angels, and kept them on their best behavior by doing so. They stayed far away from the kinds of young men who tended to surround Antoine and Tristan instead, though an uneasy truce existed between them by the influence of Jyoti's acceptance of each.

If she looked at you as if you were clean, Sam had noticed, you felt clean, even if you'd last bathed on a day you didn't know the name of, let alone its distance in time away from the one you were currently also at a loss to identify. Sam and time had never got on well, and shc suspected this was one reason she and Jyoti did, when they achieved similar orbits, at any rate.

"Have you imagined it, in yourself?"

Inside the gallery, pressed on all sides by the throng, which had waited all morning for this opening, Ingrid's voice brought Sam out of her reverie and into another one.

They stood there at the painting's edge, looking down into the convex in the floor onto which it had been painted. Sam dimly recalled a selection of irregular globes on crumbling stands, a shadow of Uncle Andrew's wonders overlaid upon the creation before her eyes. There now instead was Jean, the French saint, Antoine's muse–burning alive, eyes contorted toward an opening in the clouds hinted at but not seen.

Ingrid and Sam watched as each viewer did what they had each first done–turned their heads upward to follow the line of the martyr's gaze, and found only colorful chalked stars on the ceiling, itself painted in shades of blue so perfect they had to be real. That was Jyoti's work, of course–her memory of some sky she once prayed under and then brought here with her, to translate from her spirit to their eyes.

Around them, all the works hung from the drop ceiling, rather than against the panels, so that the visitors had to follow a spiraling pathway leading them between the extraordinary metalwork and the many unusual and varied works of art facing them from the other side, into a centralized area around the painting on the floor.

But even before the first circuit of visitors had completed the route, the sound of a commotion outside reversed their direction. While the general crowd went toward the noise, Sam and Ingrid followed a more direct route to what they both immediately knew was its most likely source.

• • •

They pushed past the crowds, now all mindlessly moving toward the sound of boots on the march approaching, which echoed down the lane even over the noise of the mob, and went directly for the crowded room on the corner, where they found, as they knew they would, Antoine poised at his window, bottles and cobblestones stacked upon the table beside him ready to be flung. Despite Sam's earlier suspicions, Tristan was nowhere to be seen, though she knew that didn't mean he wasn't off poised to make trouble somewhere else.

"Someone seems to have alerted the authorities," Antoine said blithely, without turning, eyes focused sharply on the street just outside. "Theft of property, causing a public nuisance and general deviance on display–it is a shame, really, but it seems we will be faced with the inevitable violence of the ruling class and forced to respond in kind."

Sam took a step back as she saw Ingrid step forward, just as Antoine's hand reached past the pile beside him, closed around a thin glass bottle. He stood, turned, and tapped it menacingly against the edge of the table.

"I should make you aware," Antoine said, layers of oily charm falling away by the moment, "that my compunctions about cutting you rather badly are few, and much less compelling than the alternative, you–you *creatures*–"

Use his anger, Sam thought. Yet she already knew that Ingrid herself knew everything which Sam did about a moment like this, and certainly much more than Antoine–who, for all his bravado, was nevertheless of the mistaken belief that a fight was a civil engagement with rules, as if performed on a stage. The idea that Sam might be stealthily approaching from one side with a hefty chunk of cobblestone in her hand would simply never appear in his mind, for despite his arrogance and ambition, and his apparent inability to regard human life as important on an individual level, he was to the bone one of the world's truly naive men.

Ingrid was neither naive nor a man, and so in response to his warning she kicked him directly in the most delicately measured scrap of his tailored trousers, the proceeds of his felonious activities always having gone dually toward artistic supplies and his own preening vanity.

When he staggered back she kicked again, this time low and at the knees, and when he hit the floor she stomped his wrist with her boot until his writhing hand let free the bottle, which Sam snatched up and handed to her with a henchman's loyal reflex, this same quality leading her to keep a grip on the rock with her other hand until the tussle had been decided.

"Jyoti wouldn't care for the mess," Ingrid said after a moment's reflection, during which she regarded the bottle as if it were a brush she was considering applying to a canvas, though she didn't sound entirely sure of what she might do next.

Then the moment instead of the bottle was broken as Tristan finally appeared, rushing in with his toolbox clutched to his chest.

"They're coming," he said. "Antoine, we can't. We mustn't. What we've made happen out there–it's better. It's enough. No," he finished, holding up a hand as Antoine started to protest. "We're just having an exhibition to open our gallery, that's all. Sam said it–why shouldn't we? I know what to do. It's not too late, and we don't need you, but if you don't come with us, then I don't need you either."

For all the times they'd hollered similar threats at one another, perhaps it was the simple, flat way in which Tristan delivered this threat which made Antoine sag in defeat, and leave his little pile of inanimate troublemakers behind to follow where his man led them all.

• • •

Outside, between Our Gallery and the Absolute, the massive crowd was waiting, shuffling down the cobblestones in groups of three and five and ten. The word had gone round quickly, and an angry tone was buzzing through them now, as their delight in the festivities turned sour in the knowledge that the law was approaching with all the weight of the elite behind it.

Sam followed, with Antoine between herself and Ingrid, and realized at some point Jyoti had appeared trailing behind them as well, until they were standing at her carriage just outside the gallery. Tristan ascended, pulling himself up on its step to rise just a bit above the crowd, cupped his hands, and yelled, "Barricade! Barricade now, do you hear me? Anyone with strong arms, follow me, and the rest of you stay back out of our way!"

For a moment, Sam didn't understand. But then she saw Jyoti smiling, and rushed after Tristan, whose kit of tools was again clutched to his chest protectively, feeling Ingrid beside her and at least thirty pairs of strong arms pushing behind them.

• • •

Disassembling and removing the panels took less time than she'd thought it would, and Sam quickly realized this was because Tristan must have been at work on them already, loosening bolts here and there in the night, having seen even further ahead than Sam had earlier given him credit for. It still took all the might of what seemed like half the crowd, but working together, they somehow pulled the panels free and maneuvered them down the street, each borne up by several shoulders, until they were arranged in an arc cutting off the intersection neatly in a glistening crescent of magnificently shining metalwork, brass and silver and gold all entwined and alive under the sunlight, as if it had meant to be brought here all along.

They propped each panel up until it leaned on crates and overturned tables and stacks of broken cobblestones, some freshly freed from the street and others retrieved from Antoine's various stashes, which turned out to be tucked away in at least five different places, along with more bottles and other projectiles for the riot he'd so desperately wanted to produce. They finished just as what looked like the full police force of the City of Manchester reached them, marching in form with truncheons in hand.

And they stopped, finding their progress blocked by the fantastic barricade and all the people standing fiercely behind it, transformed by their united effort from a milling crowd of spectators to a silent force of human bodies as impassable as the barricade itself.

One of the officers seemed to be attempting to read out a list of charges, but every time he spoke the crowd hissed and booed and drowned out his attempt, to his clear frustration and confusion.

At this moment, Jyoti broke free of their huddle, and Sam watched in blinking wonder as she walked calmly to the barricade and stood just a little bit back from it, hands at her sides.

"I'm sure there has been some misunderstanding," she said calmly to the man who appeared to be leading this collection of Peelies. "There's no trouble here, sir, just a little celebration of the gifts which God Himself has bestowed upon us." She smiled in her special way, and though most of the crowd couldn't hear what she was saying, they raised up a great cheer regardless. When it had died down, she called to the men who had clearly been sent to shut all this nonsense down. "Why don't you come and join us?"

A laugh rippled through them, and the crowd became lively again, splitting from its unified state once more into growingly separate conversations, though for once, most followed the same general theme. Somehow they had triumphed without fighting the battle, and somehow, in ways they were beginning to understand, this meant they were more free than they had ever known before.

• • •

It was perhaps the strangest standoff in the history of riots that never happened, Sam thought later, as slowly the festivities got back underway and the gallery began to fill again, slightly bigger now inside. People rotated in and out of it, and all around the carriage, as the police fell back in an attempt to determine exactly what procedure to follow against what appeared to be not an armed resistance or general strike, but simply some strange kind of street fair in progress.

After a few hours of waiting on further orders and seeming to receive none, and knowing that while they could themselves remove the barricade but able to see that what lay behind it would only become a serious criminal situation if they actually did so, they seemed to slowly evaporate. Some time later, Sam was sure she saw Jyoti helping a few sneak over the far sides of the barricade to join the fun, their truncheons and helmets left tucked out of sight on the other side.

Distracted by this, standing beside Ingrid with their hands secretly entwined, she didn't notice Antoine's approach, and only knew he was there when Ingrid's hand dropped from her own.

"You've always turned my stomach, you know, *Samantha*," Antoine hissed and spat. "Whatever it is you think you are, parading around however you please, all you do is make life harder for good, *real* men like Tristan and myself, who have no need of your circus freakery cluttering up people's minds even more than they already are."

Sam looked at Ingrid, whose mouth was set firmly. Her dress felt heavy and useless, and all at once she knew she would still be Sam in this moment without it–or with the trousers, or perhaps, unthinkable as it was, wearing nothing at all.

There was no word for Sam, because Sam couldn't be confined by a dictionary or placed neatly on a map. As Jyoti had seemed to understand, Sam was a dynamic force, all woman when she was woman, all man when he was man.

She *knew* it now, believed it now, and yet still needed this woman she loved, her beautiful friend called Ingrid, who'd chosen the name because the one her parents had chosen instead could never suit her–still needed the only one who could understand at all to hold her up in asserting it–to stand with her, and unmake the secret binding them both with the hands of the truth.

Tell them your secret too, she thought at her beloved, meeting her eyes. *Stand with me.*

For a moment, it seemed as if Ingrid heard Sam's mental pleas, and was about to meet them with mercy. Instead, she turned on one perfect heel and walked away, leaving Sam and Antoine both watching to see if she would look back before she vanished out of sight.

And she did, but only at the last, and then the happy masses closed over her like a curtain, hiding her expression from their view.

Steeped in Debt to the Chimney Pots

STEVE BERMAN

> "A friendly sprite whispered in his ear, and saved him from too utter folly. The sprite had not yet forsaken him; woe to him if ever it should!"
>
> –George Gissing, *Thyrza*

Winter 1884

Atop the cold, bronze shoulder of his favorite statue in Hyde Park, a sprite watched the sun die across the sky. He had spent the day tallying the debts still owed on twelve fingers and toes, and the result saddened him. Freedom was an illusion–what he owed to the other Folk who were insane enough to make sick London their home would keep him bound to the city for years. The Folk had a code–nothing could be freely given or expected, and words had to be measured, worried over. Tupp Smatterpit envied humans, and had grown fond of mortal pubs where he saw drinks bought because one man's fortune inclined him to generosity, a word the Folk had forgotten. Or maybe his kith were unable to share true goodwill and affection.

Thoughts of debts and affections made him envision Lind. Tupp wondered why he found the human lad's foolhardiness so appealing.

Tupp tossed his hat, aiming for the bronze sword. It landed at the base of the statue's stone pedestal. He held his breath, expecting a late carriage to come along and trample the hat beneath iron-shod hooves.

Addressing the statue, "What binds you, friend? Poured and cast aside . . . Where's my luck, why only this folly?" Tupp stroked the handsome metal face. He had come to admire a few man-made works about London, especially this statue in the park, an ancient warrior, bared muscular arms and torso that required the severity and strength of metal as their form. Perhaps this was modeled after another creature of legend. Tupp often daydreamed atop the statue that such men still walked secret lands.

But now his fancy was confined to his partner in crime. Tupp closed his eyes and envisioned Lind's features cast in bronze, that sharp nose and small eyes so quick to hide beneath greasy locks. A bit of hair on his chin. No sculptor ever let a masterpiece wear such a wide grin. No, statues are solemn, a word that Tupp doubted Lind even knew.

And how would Lind react if he ever discovered Tupp's idle longing? If only affection could be freely given, freely returned between Folk and man.

Tupp's ears picked up the sound of footfalls on the icy grass. He looked down to see a small figure wearing so long a scarred leather vest that it threatened to trip him. A cobbler to the Folk. A leprechaun with tufts of white hair growing long from his ears.

"You're the one they says is payin' for that rapparee's deeds."

Tupp sighed and nodded. Just how many of the Folk had Lind robbed? Tupp leaped down from the statue and picked up his hat.

"Then you're a gowl to be handin' out glamour to save a human's hide."

Tupp reached into his waistcoat pocket and removed a snuff-box. Once it had been full of glittering, golden powder–glamour, what kept iron sickness at bay and allowed the Folk to disguise themselves. He opened the lid. Barely more than two pinches remained. He offered one to the leprechaun.

He harrumphed as he took his due. "In my day, any mortal so bold as to steal from our kind, we'd make him dance till his soles bled. I could make him a pair of brogues that would clench his feet like a dog's jaw."

"No," Tupp said. "He's mine. So his debts are mine to pay."

• • •

Though he had no watch, Lind knew he was late in meeting his partner in crime, Tupp. As he lost his last farthing the bell of some nearby church had tolled five o'clock. The winter sun set, and Lind stood among grimy boys–costers and shoeblacks, broomers and runners, poor streetlarks all–huddled beside an old coal barge. Though stuck fast for years in the Thames mud, the barge offered protection from both the brutal wind and the wandering eyes of any constable.

Lind shuddered beneath his greatcoat. He should never have spent the day gambling. First, the worst of luck at cards, then wagering over how many chops a man could eat, then this, the lowest, emptying his pockets at three-up–a child's game tossing pennies high and wagering on whether they came down heads or tails.

Thirteen shillings gone. Thirteen shillings, yesterday's take from selling a hob's loot to Kapel. Lind could suffer the pain of losing his own coin–it happened often enough–but to gamble away Tupp's share? He worried how the sprite would react. Would his customary cheer falter? Would he curse Lind?

A sliver of a boy dashed from the direction of the docks and yelled out, "Traps comin'!", and the crowd scattered fast. Lind climbed the derelict barge. Coal dust from the old wood rubbed off on his palms, reminding him of a childhood spent with soot covering every inch of him. He should be running off, but he dawdled, wondering if time spent in prison would be a safer life. The Folk hated iron. Bars might keep them away.

But no constable came. Lind realized that it had all been a cheat, that one or more of the streetlarks must have pocketed the brass and run while the others fled. He looked out at the shoreline, lit by fading sunlight, and spotted three figures running together. One carried a broom–a sweep who'd collected the wagers.

He could follow them. Demand a share of the take. He jumped down onto the shore. The river's muck tried to steal his shoes. He felt the chill reach his stockings as he pried his feet loose and ran after them. Pale faces turned back. With a cry, the three splintered. Lind followed the one with the broom.

The boy headed for a dark blotch in the distance, one that grew distinctive as Lind ran. Another dock, one so dilapidated, like a carcass picked clean at the dinner table, the askew pilings might have been rib bones of some great beast.

Cold air was quick to constrict Lind's lungs, and he had to catch his breath at the first piling. With the sun set, there was little light to see by. So he blinked in disbelief when a weak flame answered his need. Where the black water lapped the shore, a bedraggled figure held aloft a candle lantern. A mudlark? They searched the Thames muck for rubbish that washed ashore. But where was her hamper? And why would she be out so late?

"Lost boy." The mudlark spoke with a country accent, with hints of lush green grass that bent beside the river. The image of gentle ripples on the water filled his head, and, despite the cold, he began to relax against the piling. "Come, let me take you home," she said.

The harsh wind brought to Lind the smell of something dredged from the dark bottom of the filthy Thames, and he fought the urge to retch. Then he glimpsed the mudlark's face. Wet hair clung to gaunt features and empty eye sockets; the squat green teeth within her long jaws belonged to a drowned mule, not any woman. Fear overtook the bile in his throat. It seeped out through the pores of his skin on rivulets of sweat. He *knew* her. He shivered and slipped around the piling so she could not see him. "Jenny," he whispered.

Months ago, after some mishaps that nearly ended with him being caught, Lind had stopped robbing houses. Why risk the noose? That was when he started stealing from the Folk. The small ones. Goblins, mostly. A cobbler with odd ears. What harm could they do to him? And they would never talk to a human magistrate and risk revealing their presence in the city. It was all so easy.

Until he made a terrible mistake. From the safety of a rooftop, Lind had watched one of the Folk sink a net fashioned from rags down an old well. While she looked hideous, he never thought her truly dangerous. So after she'd left, he climbed down the slimy walls and recovered a silver hand mirror and matching hairbrush. The find made him laugh—why would something so ugly keep mementos belonging to a lady, not a frow? Even dry, the handles kept her stink, so Kapel, his favorite fence, had refused to offer a fair price for either.

But when he started working with the sprite Tupp, selling recovered glamour to the Folk so they could survive the pains that living in London brought–all that smoke, all that worked iron–Lind discovered that goblins talked, that word had spread of a brazen human stealing from them. And that Green Jenny liked to drown her victims. Before she ate them.

Lind glanced around the rotting wooden piling. He saw the sweep stepping out from under the dock toward Jenny. The boy wore a smile, which chilled Lind worse than Jenny's terrible face. Glamour hid her true visage from the boy. Lind could not see the lacquer, whatever beauty and cheer she masked herself with. He was a child when soot dislodged by a brownie had fallen into his eyes and cursed him with the Sight.

No one deserved Jenny's fatal embrace, but Lind didn't dare risk his own life to save the poor bloke. He imagined her sharp fingers clutching at his coat's sleeve as they dragged him toward the water. The Thames would be so icy and dark, blinding him to everything but her face as he choked on the river water.

No, not even the promise of a hundred shillings in the sweep's pockets could move Lind. He pressed his back to the piling and told himself that cowards live longer than heroes. In his head Lind said the only prayer he knew, a Hebrew one for blessing wine that Kapel had taught him.

Perhaps the Thames was so cold that it would stop the boy's heart before Jenny began stroking his hair. Lind caught a weak voice calling out, "Mum?" He hoped he misheard and the sound was just the wind.

• • •

Few tapmen in London pour a charity mug for a stranger, so Lind, desperate to get good and drunk, had to be watchful at Boniface's tavern, where he always met Tupp. When he saw an old man slouch beside his drink, he came close. There was more than enough gin left in the cup to swallow, and it was the proper duty of every Englishman to see that nothing went to waste in the Empire. When the bloke's trembling eyelids shut, Lind lifted the tin cup from the scarred table.

Lind scraped the mud from his shoes on the bulldog-shaped andirons set in the fireplace. A fire had consumed much of the log. He couldn't rid his soul of the cold left from seeing Jenny. Before he could finish off that sip of gin, a pearl-gray top hat, a bit battered, landed over the cup's mouth.

"There's no more welcome sign of winter than a trio of hags roastin' chestnuts." With a grin tight between ruddy and round cheeks, Tupp scampered up and onto the mantelpiece.

The handsome sprite wore a fustian coat the shade of caked mustard, and a loose blue cravat that drooped around his neck. A child clown would envy those clothes, but no one in Boniface's laughed at Tupp. Grains of glamour kept the crowd from noticing the odd outfit, not to mention Tupp's crescent-shaped ears and the six slender fingers on both hands. "Mind you, only buy them from the youngest, the maiden, as the meat's the sweeter." Tupp reached over and lifted his hat up. Somehow, in doing so, he stole the tin cup from Lind's hand. He drained its contents quickly, then tossed it into the fireplace where it made embers rise and dance a while.

"If you're so happy for winter, let's toast to it. Buy us a drink." Lind wished he could laugh then and there at Tupp, who often acted as mad as a spoon. A cherished, heirloom spoon.

"And the nuts in the crone's pan might be a touch . . . morbose." Tupp started pressing out the many dents in the brim of his hat.

Lind rubbed at his throat and coughed. "Some drink to fend off the ague I feel risin'–"

Tupp bit down on the brim a moment, then seemed satisfied. To Lind, the hat still looked to be in the same sorry shape. Tupp placed it atop his auburn curls with a rakish slant. "Why are your pockets empty? Didn't you see your Hebrew?"

"I–I . . . No. I'll go tomorrow."

"Just as well. We will have something else for him. Tonight."

Lind wanted to stay with the drunks–the elbow-crookers, he liked to call them–at Boniface's until he was thoroughly pissed. He did not want another glimpse through the strange keyhole of weird. "Could we not stay here? Or, fine, somewhere else. Just the two of us." He put a hand over Tupp's. "There's mischief we can share rather than work another night." But Lind could not bring himself to ask Tupp to indulge in the real mischief he truly wanted to share with the sprite.

He hoped that Tupp would see in his eyes that Lind wanted no more selling powdered glamour to the scrambling child with sharp claws that clung beneath the eaves of St. Giles's Ragged School. No more silent women laundering mounds of bloody clothes in the dark at the Poplar Hospital for Accidents. Once it had been exciting, as if he had learned the greatest cheat in all the world, but now the wonder turned to horror.

Tupp frowned. "If only we could. But I have debts to pay."

"One night? They won't forgive one night?"

Tupp dropped to his feet. "A brisk walk will do us well."

Lind rubbed the disappointment from his face. He understood how avoiding debts only brought misery . . . that, and he did not trust most of the Folk Tupp dealt with. On his own, they would cheat the sprite out of glamour without a second thought.

No matter how fresh the snow, the cobblestones of London turned it filthy. Nimble Tupp walked atop the ashen broth.

Lind never saw him slip, and envied the sprite's dry feet. By the time they had walked several blocks, Lind was shivering, his feet soaked. He asked Tupp if they could hire a cab.

But Tupp refused to spare even a farthing. "Nonsense demands."

Lind groaned. Why did only mortals suffer from nonsense?

They came to a corner with a coffee stall flickering light and warmth from its lit firepan. The smell rising from the pot tugged at Lind's empty stomach. "A mug would warm the insides," he said. "Please, Tupp."

"That it would," said the stallkeeper. "Best thing for you now."

Then Lind spied a set of scrawny limbs covered in ragged clothing move in the shadows of the doorway just behind the stall. He felt the flush of panic seize him. Had Jenny ventured out of the frigid Thames for him? But then he saw the faces of the women who stepped into the firepan's glow. Weak-eyed and wan, but decidedly human.

"Lind, we don't want to keep this one waiting long," Tupp said. "He's a most sallow fellow."

Lind thought all of the Folk were sallow. 'Cept Tupp, who possessed a grin and a wink.

The taller of the women moved next to Lind. Her sunken cheeks told of too many hungry nights. "Spare a penny for me and my sister to warm ourselves? Terrible cold out."

A soft chime sounded from Tupp's waistcoat. Tupp muttered as he consulted one of his many pocket watches.

Lind didn't put much weight on education. How'd reading ever save a man's life? But he knew that the queer markings on the watch's face didn't match any English numbers or letters. Didn't look Hebrew either.

"A pretty," said the second woman, who leaned down to dislodge Tupp's hat and finger his copper curls. "'Ave time for me, 'an'some?"

Lind wondered how she noticed Tupp. He should have been dusted with glamour and hidden from sight, as he had been at the pub. Had the sprite become careless? Had the pinch worn off?

Tupp ignored the woman. "I smell currant cake." He slipped the watch back into a pocket and retrieved his hat from the ground.

Lind saw the greed in the woman's eyes. He understood the promise of gold, the promise of trouble. But it would not end well for the women. Tupp might curse them to wander all night long till they dropped from the cold. Not that Lind had ever seen the sprite do so, but he had overheard Tupp threaten others he *could*.

"Let's be going," Lind said.

"A bit o' that cake would be nice."

"Like sweets?" The one woman stopped down to rub at Tupp's belly. She whispered in his ear while her fingers slipped toward the waistcoat pocket with the watch.

"I prefer cakes to tarts." Tupp's elbow struck her in the chest. She shrieked and fell into the snowbroth.

"'Ere now," called out the stallkeeper. First his pockmarked cheeks and then his chest puffed in readiness, like rising hackles on an angry mutt.

"No," Lind shouted, and reached for the firepan's handle. Pulled loose of the stall, it fell to the wet cobblestones and rolled, spilling hot coals that steamed and hissed as they died.

The women screamed, the stallkeeper cursed, but Lind grabbed Tupp by his collar and pulled him down the street at a run. When the cold air burned inside Lind's chest, they took refuge in an alley. Lind gasped for breath. "No more," he panted to Tupp, who leaned against the opposite brick wall and regarded him with curiosity.

"But you haven't had a taste yet." Tupp held up a stolen currant cake.

"What next?"

"Hmmm?"

Lind rubbed both palms against his watery eyes, wishing he could wipe away the Sight. He wanted nothing more to do with the Folk. Even Tupp was too dangerous to associate with . . . and yet he did not want to abandon the sprite.

When he looked up, he saw that Tupp had grown a foot taller and stood beside him. Tupp blew hard over the cake before breaking it in half. "You asked me to be partners. Now you have regrets?"

"Every day, every hour, I feel as if I'm risking everything, but I have nothing to show for it."

"Nothing? You're with me," Tupp said.

"And you're the only thing keeping me from going mad."

"Shhhh," Tupp whispered. "I'd not say that. The Folk like their mortals mad."

The cake smelled like spring, like how gold should smell. Spit filled Lind's mouth. He took the offered half, noted how it was warm to the touch as if baked within the half-hour. Grit met his teeth at the first bite, and then such sweetness overcame his tongue. Lighter than treacle. Lighter than honey. He couldn't bring himself to chew fast enough, so he swallowed fast as fever spread through him. He felt a bead of sweat start at his temple–or perhaps it was a tear traveling down his cheek–drifting down, along the path to the scar at his chin, where it was damned to freeze. He didn't know why he'd be crying. He didn't have a worry to his name.

The currants cradled in his five fingers went from wine-red to glittering amber. No, gold, like Tupp's watches. Lind started chuckling like some fresh-faced sot. Treasure had been within those women's reach all the time–all they needed to do was pull apart the cake.

"Laughter's better than melancholy," offered Tupp, staring at him while nibbling his share.

Lind nodded, though he didn't understand what Tupp meant. He stuffed the rest of the cake into his mouth, and then wiped the grease from his fingers onto his coat. Reckless thoughts murmured in the corners of his head. Break into some fancy's tall house and steal a billiards table. Or climb a gaslight pole and wait for the first carriage to pass beneath and jump down into the coachman's bench. Or remain in the alley and brush the crumbs from Tupp's lips.

He took a step closer to the sprite. Kissing one of the Folk would be the most enchanting thing. And so he did. Press his lips against Tupp's. He curled his fingers around Tupp's lapels, opened his mouth to compare the sweetness of cake to that of sprite.

Then sudden pain ripped at his guts. Lind bent over, clutching at his stomach, the kiss forgotten. He was so empty, so hollow, as if he'd never swallowed a morsel of food in his life. When had he last eaten? Days? No, it felt more like weeks ago. Starving, he scraped at the cobblestones for whatever grime he could lift on his finger.

• • •

Tupp regretted charming Lind. He only wanted to see him smile and laugh. Then the kiss . . . how long ago had been the last time he'd kissed another? If he could not remember, then too long. But was the kiss freely given? Was a kiss bought by too much ale the same as one given by magic?

Tupp had not anticipated how fragile Lind had become. He had to forcibly lift the lad up from the ground, restrain him from filling his mouth with dirt and frozen water. Lind's sense of daring had cracked like old lacquer. Might there be anything left even if Tupp did manage to satisfy all the Folk the lad had wronged?

When they reached Gilspir Street, the famine in Lind's gullet had faded to a distant echo. Tupp doffed his hat at the gilded cherub roosting above on the Fortune of War's outer wall. Inside, the taproom reeked of harsh tobacco, burned grease and stale, spilled beer. Tupp led the way through the crowd toward a bench set against the far wall where a bony fellow, face hidden under his wide-brimmed black hat, sat hunched talking in whispers to a swarthy bloke with greasy hair falling into his eyes.

"Eur Du's an ankou, a gloomy lot," Tupp whispered to Lind. "When the sun's up, he works as a mute at funerals, walking in the train, dressed all in black. But moonlight brings out his true nature. Before the earth settles on a grave, he's digging it back open. None sacks a corpse faster than Eur Du."

• • •

The bony man lifted a hand to beckon them closer. The unkempt bloke snatched a sack from the floorboards, glared at Lind, and then left. Tupp sat down in his place.

"So, the sprite brought his foundlin'." Air whistled past the remains of Eur Du's nose and made his thick accent all the harder to understand.

"We're partners." Lind forced himself to meet the ankou's gaze. Eur Du sounded French, and looked pox-riddled as well. Perhaps the Continent was also infested with goblins.

"Of course." A hand scratched the ragged hole below his narrowed dark eyes. "Manee interestin' dealin's happen here. Do you know this place's historee?"

Lind sighed. Why did all the Folk waste so much time dwelling on the past? Yesterday belonged to bad dreams. Greed demanded the mind stay sharp and consider tomorrow's worth.

"No? Bodee-snatchers favored this house. Resurrectionists. They'd prop all the bodees on these benches 'round the walls. Had the owner's name underneeth. Wouldn't bee the leest surprise' if right under your ass there might' been a corpse."

Something grabbed hold of Lind's ankle, freezing skin and bone. He cried out, and the patrons of the Fortune of War looked up from their mugs to mutter and stare.

Eur Du's and Tupp's laughter made his face flush. Pranks annoyed Lind unless they were meant as a distraction before a theft. Tupp's amusement felt like a stab in Lind's back.

"So you have . . . ?" Eur Du asked.

Tupp grinned and took from his waistcoat pocket a scrap of newspaper. His nimble fingers unfolded an advertisement for replacement teeth that held a pinch of golden powder settling into the creases. Glamour. The dust every Folk in London needed. Not only to disguise their presence, but to fend off iron sickness as well.

The ankou leaned forward. His breath stank like spoiled meat, and Lind wondered how much of the tavern's stench began with Eur Du. "Is *mad*, is good."

Lind slid the paper way from Eur Du. "Now, your offer?"

The ankou lifted his hat. Fine white hairs, perhaps cobwebs, covered his speckled pate where he kept safe a jeweled ring, which he lifted loose and set on Tupp's open palm.

"As you say, is good." Tupp turned the ring so the smaller red stones sparkled around their older brother. Then he passed it on to Lind. The silver band was cold to his fingers, as if freshly dug from the mounds of snow outside. Or the hard, frozen earth. He imagined Eur Du at work with his shovel, prying at a coffin much as a hungry man would take a knife to a closed oyster.

"Get us drinks, sprite."

Tupp hesitated a moment, then headed for the taps.

Eur Du scraped free a flake of skin hanging from his cheek with one cracked nail. "Eur Du can smell death as perfume. You wear it. Old. Your mother, yes? Bringin' you into the world took her out, yes? That makes you start life a murderer. Eur Du respect that."

Lind slid a hand into his coat and gripped the handle of his knife. Now he hated this one. Perhaps all the Folk. He imagined plunging the iron blade once, twice, into Eur Du's chest.

"But then," the ankou muttered as a black ribbon around his hat rose like a threatened serpent, "all your kind die so easilee, so fast. If I do not see you tomorrow, I assume you dead."

Lind reached for the glamour, folding the edges of the newspaper shut. "Best enjoy this. You'll not see another pinch more from us."

A chuckle wheezed through Eur Du's tiny, sharp teeth. "Do you reelee think he will keep you well, brammig? We may not be able to utter untruths, but know that we can never be trusted. When you no longer amuse the sprite, he will forsake you." The ankou's arm shot forth and covered Lind's hand with its own, a leathery touch that masked an iron grip. "An' then, we'll be waitin'."

Lind managed to slip his hand free. Small grains of earth clung to the lines of his knuckles. Grave mould, he was sure. "You think I trust Tupp? You're wrong, bogey. I know he'll soon be bored of me." He made a show of turning away from the ankou to hide his lie. He watched Tupp carry mugs in each hand. Tupp wore his usual grin, which, for a moment, softened the growing hardness in Lind's chest. For a moment. Then Lind slid the knife out of his pocket and opened the blade. "I'm expecting your lot as well." He hoped his hand did not shake as he stabbed the blade down hard in the wood, a splinter's length away from Eur Du's fingers.

• • •

Before Tupp set the mugs onto the table, he waited for Lind to pry loose the knife and return it to his coat. He smirked. So not all Lind's bluster was gone. Tupp lifted up his hat to reveal a third mug, which he set in front of Lind.

"So we have a deal, Eur Du?" he asked.

The ankou nodded as he slid the glamour close.

The watered beer tasted sour, as if the stink in the ankou's hair had settled on the drink's surface. Tupp started pouring out his mug on to the floorboards and Lind was swift to catch as much of the stream in his own emptied mug. "Why waste beer on haunts?" Lind said, while staring at Eur Du.

Out on the street, Tupp turned to Lind. "I've some errands. We'll divide the take tomorrow night. At the Bridge of Sighs." He took a few steps, remembered that he had traded away his last pinch of glamour, and then turned back. "And bring the rest of the glamour."

"What? Why?"

The Folk cannot lie. The words cannot leave their mouth. They remain trapped in the imagination. And so he could only say, "Because I have no more of my own."

"But you kept more than me."

"Would you have all of London see me?" Tupp asked.

"How do I know who might see you when I have no idea where you go? Errands. Always errands. I want one night to spend together, but you always run from me."

"I'm not sure you know what you want of me."

Lind opened his mouth, then covered it with one palm, as if stifling his words. Perhaps, Tupp wondered, mortals could not tell the truth. "Nothing. Go. Tomorrow at the bridge."

Not every one of the Folk inside London despised or preyed on mortals. One spent most of his time beneath the ground, within the environs of the massive tunnel running underneath the Thames.

It took him a while to find the bluecap tapping at the walls. His calling out "Firma," startled the fairy. Firma blinked its enormous lanternlike eyes. It dropped a small pick and clutched the soiled cap from its head, revealing a corona of pale blue flames rather than hair.

"Few sprites venture down here, Smatterpit."

"Yes." He had never sold glamour to Firma. Bluecaps were rarely seen by miners or diggers. And if they were, it was welcome because they were seen as warning mortals of unsafe conditions. But they had crossed paths before, years ago, and Tupp knew that Firma was one of the very few Folk in London to have kept a mortal lover for decades.

"I need a favor."

The bluecap coughed. Or maybe giggled. "None of the Folk comes to me for . . . for anything."

"I cannot offer much–"

"What favor?"

"Tell me how you have kept your mortal happy for so long."

"Bessie." Firma smiled. "She has burrowed into my heart. I'd not have it any other way."

"But she will die. You will go, but she will die. How can it be more than just some grand banquet, enjoyed for a brief time, but then–"

"But you always remember the banquet. Each course remains with you no matter how you pick away at the plate. I'd not want to miss the meal for fear of the bill." Firma patted Tupp on the shoulder. "Loving anything is not about possessing it. See," he said and reached down for a clod of earth. "I love this dirt, this earth, this England. But do I own it? No. I am merely passing on my way through it, and it meets my touch and sight and smell–" Firma breathed in the dirt "–for a moment. A moment I can cherish or not, but why not cherish then?"

Tupp nodded at this newfound wisdom. "My debt–"

"You owe me nothing."

"But . . . but . . . that is not how we do things." He did not know how to react to generosity.

"You asked me how I have kept my Bessie happy. It is also because I give freely."

"Then I should do the same," Tupp said, and realized there was another of the Folk he had to see, to talk to, that night.

• • •

Hot brickwork burned Lind's palms and knees. Weak light, distant above, teased his eyes. The air tasted heavy with ash, cousin to the soot that blackened every inch of stone and skin and forced him to breathe through his nose or gag and choke. He inched upward along the tight throat of the chimney, then stopped. As a gangly ten-year-old, Lind could easily scurry up tight passages, but it had been six years since last he swept, and a diet of stout and meat had filled out Lind's frame. He found himself wedged tight.

Angry whispers began where he should be alone. Clearing soot was silent, awful work. After the first bitter mouthful, climbing boys kept lips pressed tight unless they dared to call for help. He clawed at the rough edges to push himself toward the roof.

A rough voice from the drawing room below echoed in the chimney like a dog's barking. Mr. Barling demanding Lind climb higher. The whispers became titters. Something sharp bit at the soles of his bare feet. Mr. Barling must have borrowed a hatpin from the missus, perhaps the one with a gaudy faux pearl at the end. A lit match would be next.

Lind struggled but could not inch higher. His lungs ached for a good breath. He knew that if he started to panic, the walls of the chimney would seem to draw closer. Beneath him, the stream of curses came faster and higher pitched, as if the other sweeps giggled at the fireplace's mouth.

Fresh pain along his shins stirred Lind. He blinked at the sunlight that slipped through drapes encrusted with dust and grime. Morning in the room he rented at the end of New Kent Road. He dreamed too often of the past, as if his sleeping thoughts regretted ever running away from Barling's basement.

He tried to wipe the nightmare from his face but found he could not raise a hand. Another binding pulled taut around his neck.

First he cursed, then he struggled more.

The same titters from his dream sounded around the room, soft as a whisper till they deepened to a final gurgle, the laugh of infants. His vision restrained, Lind glimpsed several small shapes scurrying by the cracked plaster walls, around the ends of the drapes, near the mattress. Rats didn't move on two legs. Rats didn't stink like a heap of soft apples.

"Out! Out," Lind screamed and heaved hard against whatever strings or cords tied him down.

Something landed on his stomach, forcing a groan from his lips. Heavier than a rat as well, with tiny limbs around a sallow, pear-shaped frame. Layers of amber-colored wings fluttered. If not for the brass nail it held over him, Lind might have smirked. "The dust of our kin. We want." Tiny, glittering eyes moved back and forth. "Our dust."

He felt cool air on his lower legs. The others must have ripped apart the sheets at the foot of the bed.

It repeated its demand, shrieking the last words and stomping a foot on a rib.

Pixies. The last he'd seen had been caged by Bluebottle the spriggan, a fence at his rag-and-bone shop. He ground them to powder, to glamour, and forced Tupp to collect from the Folk of London. Lind had once felt a sense of sympathy toward Tupp for being under the spriggan's control. Released when Lind and Tupp robbed him, the pixies had swarmed over the spriggan. A horrible but deserved end. But it would have been wasteful to leave behind the milled glamour, so Lind took bags of the stuff.

Lind never imagined pixies would come looking for the glamour. How'd they find him?

Something sharp dragged across the soles of his feet and he screamed.

"Rings on his fingers, bells on his toes, he shall have trouble wherever he goes," sang the unseen pixies, who stank like split casks of last year's cider.

The bindings bit through the sheets, shirt and skin when he thrashed. Several snapped before the pixie atop him could stab down with the nail.

He struck the pixie, its middle giving way to his fist as if he had crushed a rotten apple. Its scream was shrill and awful.

The others flew to the window, breaking glass, or to the door, sending it slamming against the wall. More plaster fell.

Blood streaked the sheets, mostly his own. He plucked a wing from the dead pixie. With the warmth of his touch, it gleamed like a scrap of gold leaf. He ripped the rest free of the corpse. Tupp wouldn't approve, but why trouble his partner's morals by confessing?

He hobbled to the center of the room. The floorboards had been pried apart, revealing where he had hidden his share of the remaining glamour. The pixies would have stolen away with it if not for the heavy chain he'd wrapped around the small bag. Lind didn't care why none of the Folk could stand the touch of iron. The thick links would have charred a pixie's hands to cinders.

He'd have to abandon the room, the building as well. But if the pixies didn't return, something else would come calling, something nastier.

Lind ripped the sheets apart and wrapped the cleanest strips around his bloody legs. He then took everything of worth. The pixies had so thoroughly knotted the sleeves of his second, better shirt that he'd never be able to wear it again. He kept it for entry to the Exchange. As he dropped the worn file and chisel into the small sack he brought along when calling upon a house, a strange sense of awareness filled him. He was looting his own room, and the haul wasn't worth more than fourpence except for what the Folk had brought–glamour, wings, and ring. Suddenly fearful that the pixies had robbed him after all, he went to his pockets. But no, he found the ring where he'd left it and laughed. The Folk weren't so clever after all.

The makeshift bandages allowed him to make the long walk to Houndsditch. Countless restless voices, each seeking to capture passersby, rose from the Old Clothes Exchange. Lind breathed through his mouth to escape the varied stink of sweat-soaked clothes, moldy clothes, and worthless clothes and, underneath the lot, the most wretched rags. But deeper into the Exchange, there'd be worse. His stomach murmured and churned at the memory of hare skins hanging raw, sold close to fatty cakes, the crusts brilliant with grease.

This hour was the busiest for the Exchange, and Lind stood next to the old-clothes men in their uniforms of tight gabardine coats and smocks, armed with fistfuls of stacked hats and shouldering sacks. Each tugged at their beards as they eyed their fellows, their rivals in line beside them. "Solomon never judged so much," Kapel would often tell Lind.

Yet Lind felt so comfortable among them. Did the Sight allow him to peer past their stern faces and thick gabardine? He saw men who acted as brothers when they shared laughter and sips of plum brandy after a deal, white-bearded grandfathers nodding praise over the shoulders of reading children, their language loose from the confines of church to be welcome in the home.

Mr. Barling had boasted to his clients that he considered his climbing boys "me own brood, such li'l dears." But Lind remembered the sound of Barling's footsteps as he left his dears alone in the cramped basement, so dark, often so cold. The gonophs had promised to be brothers. More like that Cain bloke. The underworld of London was no better or worse than these earlier families–kind when the rounds were brought and cruel when the finger comes down.

He sold to the Jew beside him his knotted shirt for a penny. Lind reached the gates and their tollman, Barney Aaron, round of head and belly, held out a hand for a copper. His young son, already thick in the middle and with dull eyes, held a leather satchel that by the day's end would be so heavy it crept near the ground and would tempt any villain in London who guessed its contents.

Oh, he hated how that satchel taunted him. Lind paced some evenings in the company of a gin bottle and devised seven different schemes, including one that required a slavering mutt as a distraction. But once he stole from the Jews, he'd never be able to return to Kapel, so he would arrive at the Exchange early, when the young Aaron hefted a light satchel high over his shoulder.

As he pushed and slipped his way through the narrow paths of the Exchange, fingers tugged at his sack. He ignored the calls around him.

Atop a small stage in the center of the maze, Kapel stirred a kettle over a small stove and shouted through his smoke-colored beard, "Hot wine. Ha'penny a glass."

Lind winced at how clumsily his wrapped legs took the stage's steps. "Two glasses."

He dropped his sack to the wooden boards.

"It's good wine." Kapel poured from the ladle.

Lind acknowledged the lie with a nod. Kapel's insistence that every deal be made with the blessing of God remained amusing. So the old Jew had taught him a prayer over the acrid wine he sold.

"Baruch atah–"

A short figure roaming the Exchange caught his attention. Stockier than Tupp, and with a wide cap of green moss and long, drooping feathers. Passed right near the stage but didn't raise its gnarled head at him.

Lind began the prayer again, "*Baruch atah adoney–*" but then the Folk started a loud dicker over the torn sleeves of a coachman's coat atop one mound of clothes. The attendant Jew argued and showed the lining.

He heard Kapel clear his throat, so he muttered the middle part before finishing. "*Borey pahree hagoffem.*"

"Is good you are so eager, eh?" Kapel winked as he sipped. The wiry hair around Kapel's mouth was darker than the rest of the beard and made his teeth look large. "Will I have to turn out my pockets today?"

He nodded but kept his eye on the Folk who dropped broken eggshells into the palm of the Jew, who seemed pleased with himself. Poor bloke.

He took the ring from his pocket and swallowed the wine, tepid and the more sour for it. He switched hands returning the glass to Kapel, and his fives dropped the ring into the red dregs left at the bottom.

When Kapel set the glass down with the others, the ring had been palmed, then cleaned with some spilled wine.

"A commendable piece," Kapel said softly. "I can give a good price."

Lind pantomimed searching through his sack as he spoke. "I need a very good price, my friend." He would give all the coins to trusting Tupp. Even if it meant Lind went hungry for a few days.

"Nu, don't I offer the best? You are either visiting better people to bring such finds. Or worse."

Lind nodded. "I fear it's both." His legs pained him. He thought of the walk to meet Tupp at the bridge. And then? Another job, more of the Folk, who hated him. Perhaps he should take the coin and leave London for good, escape the Folk. But the idea left him cold. Lonesome and cold.

"I'm up the flue."

"Oh?"

Lind nodded. The words wanted to rush out, and he bit most down. Even weak wine on an empty stomach could make him foolish. He didn't dare talk of the Folk to Kapel. He might be wise, but Kapel would see him mad. Lind had to talk clever for once.

He whispered. "Worse than the traps, worse than a tuck-up fair and watching your mates do the drop." Lind tugged at his collar to emulate being hanged.

"Tell me."

"I've made some . . . well, goods of a sort. There are folk who pay well for them. That ring there, the sorts of loot I've brought you, all came from them. But they're a queer lot, and some aren't willing to buy. They'd rather take. And I don't think they care how they leave me."

"What are you selling, *boytchik*?"

"That I can't tell–"

"Then how can I help you?"

Lind stood there, not sure what to say. He didn't have an answer. There might not be one. He felt trapped by his heart.

"Stealing is no life. Listen to me. What I do is a little sin. You're a little sin to me as well, but one I enjoy helping." Kapel climbed down from the stage and motioned for Lind to follow. "I would be sorry if you would be found dead in some alley."

Lind thought of Eur Du's threat and shuddered. He followed Kapel through the Exchange and watched as the old Jew took his time greeting merchants, arguing over a price, until they reached the gates.

Kapel then turned to him and pressed some folded pound notes into Lind's palm. Lind, displeased that the advice would benefit a bumpkin squire from the countryside and not a dedicated cracksman who knew the streets, the housetops since he was a child, made a show of counting the pounds.

"More than enough for the ring, I think. And for you to leave."

Lind hugged Kapel before leaving the Exchange. Perhaps for the last time.

• • •

On the way to Waterloo Bridge, Lind stopped at a whelk-seller. Half his cart sold for a penny four of the large, pickled snails on chipped saucers, the other offered them live in a tub of cold, scummy water. A little girl shivered beneath a tattered shawl, the ends trailing into the brine and the weight of lead, as she wiped the whelk shells to a shine. Lind bought four from the man. Though bitter, the flesh was firm and would last in his stomach. He wiped his lips, then held out a penny to the girl, who had cautious eyes but quick fingers. Lind regretted that the penny would end up in the man's pocket by the night's end.

The bridge's tollman barely glanced at Lind when he approached the turnstile. "Ha'penny to cross." The man shifted on his seat, and the sound of a bottle rolling about his feet made the man blush and cough. Lind joined the other furtive folk who dared walk the bridge on a barren night. Half were desperate, the other half not to be trusted, which made Lind smirk and wonder to which he belonged.

Lind often found Tupp sitting, or once lying, atop some ledge with his gaze on the west, following the setting sun.

He saw Tupp standing on the stone ledge now, still as a statue, yet a moment of worry stole through Lind. A simple step forward would topple Tupp. Waterloo earned its second name of Bridge of Sighs after women had taken to leaping off it into the Thames. Lind looked over the edge. No boats in the cold water, so perhaps no one else had seen him. Pub talk had said the boats carried Bible and coin for anyone dragged alive from the waters. Redemption of soul and pocket.

Lind advanced stealthily, partially due to his sore legs, but also because this was one of the few times he could observe a wistful expression on Tupp.

At first, Lind thought the Folk could only feel anger or delight–they seemed to only raise their voices in rage or cheer. As if children, awful children, with magic behind their whims and no thought for anyone but themselves.

But in the past month, Lind had glimpsed moments beyond growl and grin. The way Tupp watched him with such interest. Treating any of the Folk as if they were men of London was dangerous. He worried he'd let his guard down and end up like that poor sod who embraced Jenny last night.

Yet, when Lind had stepped close enough to see the wistful expression on Tupp's face, see how the wind made Tupp's blue eyes water, Lind felt reluctance to think that his partner ever meant him harm.

Tupp glanced down at Lind, then gestured for Lind to join him on the ledge.

Why didn't the gusts carry off his askew top hat? Lind didn't want to test his scratched legs against the wind. And Tupp had never made such a request of him before when they met.

"Only one step up. Perhaps two. You are a master cracksman . . ."

Lind sighed. He cautiously climbed up on the ledge. The wind snatched at his coat. He felt it tug him back and forth, then, as if it had decided the water would be a better fate than the stone of the bridge, the wind howled and pulled him down.

• • •

Tupp grabbed Lind before he fell. "You're limping. You're hurt."

Lind sat down. "Oh, some pests came looking for our haul." He reached into his coat and withdrew first the pouches of glamour, and then a handful of coins. "Your share."

"Sizable. Have you ever been to Wessex?"

"No."

"I come from there. And there are days I miss it so much that not even glamour can keep me from feeling sick." He shook the coins. "This could pay for both of us to travel there."

"And what would we do when the glamour runs out?"

"There are fewer Folk there. Less iron, too. But we won't be taking this," Tupp said as he held the glamour out over the water.

"What? No, that's worth a fortune!" Lind reached out until he risked slipping from the bridge.

"True. Although some fortunes aren't measured in coin, but in years." Tupp opened his hand and the bags splashed into the noisome river below.

He pointed out movement below. Jenny's head broke the water's surface, long and limp hair hiding much of her face.

Lind stiffened next to Tupp.

"Your debt is paid, mortal," she said, her voice melodic despite being full of the Thames. "And my silence bought as well, when kith and kin ask where you have gone." Then she sank, as if eager to walk the cold river bottom.

Tupp realized Lind had clenched his hand tight. "Fewer Folk in Wessex?" he asked.

Tupp nodded and smiled. "If you wish, you need only be bothered by one." Tupp leaned in close. The feel of soft lips overcame the rough stone upon which they sat. The heat of the kiss kept at bay the icy wind.

Lind then whispered in Tupp's ear, "And how would we live?"

"I promise 'with great mischief.'"

About the Authors

Steve Berman's tale of how the sprite Tupp and the mortal Lind first met appeared in *The Faery Reel* (edited by Ellen Datlow and Terri Windling). Steve has sold nearly a hundred articles, essays, and short stories since he began writing at the age of seventeen. He has never swept a chimney, but, like Lind, he does enjoy a good wager. His young-adult novel, *Vintage*, is your typical "boy meets ghost" suburban fantasy, and was a finalist for the Andre Norton Award for Young Adult Science Fiction and Fantasy. He lives in New Jersey, the only state in the US with an official devil, with a very demanding feline overlord codenamed Daulton.

Marie Brennan is the author of the Onyx Court series of London-based historical fantasies: *Midnight Never Come*, *In Ashes Lie*, *A Star Shall Fall*, and *With Fate Conspire*, as well as the doppelgänger duology of *Warrior* and *Witch,* and more than thirty short stories. You can find more information on her website, www.swantower.com.

Stephanie Burgis lives in Wales with her husband, son, and crazy-sweet border collie mix. The first two books in her trilogy of Regency-era fantasy novels are published in the US as *Kat, Incorrigible*, and *Renegade Magic*, and in the UK as *A Most Improper Magick* and *A Tangle of Magicks*. You can find out more, and read excerpts from her novels, at her website, www.stephanieburgis.com.

Seth Cadin is from New York and now lives in California. He has one partner, one daughter, and many pet mice. Some of his other short stories can be found in the Prime Books anthology *Bewere the Night*, in volume five of the annual collection from *Three-lobed Burning Eye* magazine, and in the young-adult anthology *Brave New Love: 13 Dystopian Tales of Desire* from Robinson (UK) and Running Press (US).

Karen Healey is the author of YA urban fantasies *Guardian of the Dead* and *The Shattering*, and the forthcoming YA sci-fi thriller, *When We Wake*. She is the winner of the 2010 Aurealis Award for Best Young Adult Novel, and the Sir Julius Vogel Award for Best New Talent, and a 2011 William C. Morris Award Finalist. She is fond of libraries, but not so keen on dusting. You can find more information in her website, www.karenhealey.com.

Leanna Renee Hieber is an actress, playwright and author of the Strangely Beautiful and Magic Most Foul series of Gothic Victorian fantasy novels. *The Strangely Beautiful Tale of Miss Percy Parker* hit Barnes & Noble's bestseller lists, won two 2010 Prism Awards (Best Fantasy Romance, Best First Book), and has been optioned for musical theater adaptation currently in development. *Darker Still: A Novel of Magic Most Foul* hit the Indie Next List as a recommended title by the American Booksellers Association. A member of RWA and SFWA, her short story "Charged" will be featured in *Queen Victoria's Book of Spells*. A member of performers' unions AEA, SAG, and AFTRA, she has worked extensively with the Cincinnati Shakespeare Company, and other regional classical productions. She lives in New York City with her real-life hero and their beloved rescued lab rabbit, working the occasional film or television gig in New York City when not on book deadline. Find her at www.leannareneehieber.com or on Twitter, @leannarenee.

M. K. Hobson's short fiction has appeared in *Lady Churchill's Rosebud Wristlet*, *Sci Fiction*, *The Magazine of Fantasy & Science Fiction*, and many other fine publications. Her debut novel, *The Native Star*, was nominated for the 2011 Nebula Award. Readers interested in learning more are invited to visit her website at www.demimonde.com.

Mary Robinette Kowal is the author of the novels *Shades of Milk and Honey* and *Glamour in Glass*. In 2008 she received the Campbell Award for Best New Writer, and in 2011, her short story "For Want of a Nail" won the Hugo Award for Best Short Story. Her work has been nominated for the Hugo, Nebula, and Locus awards. Her stories appear in *Asimov's*, *Clarkesworld*, and several *Year's Best* anthologies. She is the Vice-President of Science Fiction and Fantasy Writers of America. Mary, a professional puppeteer, also performs as a voice actor, recording fiction for authors such as Elizabeth Bear, Cory Doctorow, and John Scalzi. She lives in Chicago with her husband Rob and over a dozen manual typewriters. Visit her website at www.maryrobinettekowal.com.

Sandra McDonald is the award-winning author of the collection *Diana Comet and Other Impossible Stories*, a Booklist Editor's Choice for Young Adults. She also writes adventure novels for gay and straight teens and science-fiction romances for adults. Her short fiction has appeared in more than fifty magazines and anthologies. She currently resides in Florida with a backyard full of wildlife. Visit her at www.sandramcdonald.com.

Barbara Roden was born in Vancouver, British Columbia in 1963, and is a World Fantasy Award-winning editor and publisher. Her first collection, *Northwest Passages*, was published by Prime Books in October 2009; the title story was nominated for the Stoker, International Horror Guild, and World Fantasy Awards, and the book received a World Fantasy Award nomination for Best Collection. Her short stories have appeared in numerous publications, including *Year's Best Fantasy and Horror: Nineteenth Annual Collection*, *Horror: Best of the Year 2005*, *The Mammoth Book of Best New Horror 21*, and *The Year's Best Dark Fantasy and Horror: 2010 Edition*. Her Sherlock Holmes pastiches have appeared in *The Mammoth Book of New Sherlock Holmes Adventures*, *Gaslight Grimoire*, and *Gaslight Grotesque*. She has written extensively about Victorian detective fiction, most recently for the Barnes & Noble reprints of the complete Sherlock Holmes stories in their Classics imprint (March 2012). "The Colonel's Daughter" was inspired by the writings of Henry Mayhew, and by the real-life adventures of Beatrice Holme Sumner, whose scandalous behaviour shocked late-Victorian England.

Caroline Stevermer grew up miles from anywhere on a dairy farm in southeastern Minnesota. She now lives in Minneapolis, but she sojourned on the east coast long enough to graduate from Bryn Mawr College and have a few adventures in New York City. She has written *A College of Magics* and *A Scholar of Magics*, among other novels, and in collaboration with Patricia C. Wrede, *Sorcery and Cecelia, The Grand Tour*, and *The Mislaid Magician.* She likes baseball, steamboats, trains, and art museums.

Tiffany Trent is the author of the YA steampunk *The Unnaturalists*, and the *Hallowmere* series. She has also published in *Corsets & Clockwork*, *Subterranean Magazine*, and *Magic in the Mirrorstone.* She lives in the New River Valley of Virginia where she keeps bees and herds chickens when not writing. You can find more information at her website, www.tiffanytrent.com.

Genevieve Valentine's YA fiction has appeared in *Clarkesworld* and *Subterranean Magazine*, as well as the anthologies *Teeth*, *Under the Moons of Mars*, *After*, and more. Her first novel, *Mechanique: A Tale of the Circus Tresaulti*, is out now from Prime. She has yet to emerge from the tangle of Victorian etiquette, the scope of which is baffling. Her appetite for bad movies is insatiable, a tragedy she tracks on her blog, genevievevalentine.com.

About the Editor

Ekaterina Sedia is the editor of several anthologies, including the World Fantasy Award winner *Paper Cities,* as well as *Running with the Pack,* and *Bewere the Night.* Her next anthology is *Bloody Fabulous.* She is also the author of the novels *The Secret History of*

Moscow, *The Alchemy of Stone*, *The House of Discarded Dreams*, and *Heart of Iron*. Her short stories have appeared in a number of venues.

Scott Westerfeld is the author of eighteen novels, thirteen of them for young adults, including the trilogies: Leviathan, Uglies, and Midnighters. Scott was born in Texas, but currently splits his time between New York City and Sydney, Australia.

Acknowledgments

"At Will" © 2012 by Leanna Renee Hieber. First publication, original to this anthology. Printed by permission of the author.

"The Unladylike Education of Agatha Tremain" © 2012 by Stephanie Burgis. First publication, original to this anthology. Printed by permission of the author.

"Nussbaum's Golden Fortune" © 2012 by M. K. Hobson. First publication, original to this anthology. Printed by permission of the author.

"The Colonel's Daughter" © 2012 by Barbara Roden. First publication, original to this anthology. Printed by permission of the author.

"Mercury Retrograde" © 2012 by Mary Robinette Kowal. First publication, original to this anthology. Printed by permission of the author.

"False Colors" © 2012 by Marie Brennan. First publication, original to this anthology. Printed by permission of the author.

"Mrs. Beeton's Book of Magickal Management" © 2012 by Karen Healey. First publication, original to this anthology. Printed by permission of the author.

"The Language of Flowers" © 2012 by Caroline Stevermer. First publication, original to this anthology. Printed by permission of the author.

"The Dancing Master" © 2012 by Genevieve Valentine. First publication, original to this anthology. Printed by permission of the author.

"The Garden of England" © 2012 by Sandra McDonald. First publication, original to this anthology. Printed by permission of the author.

"Resurrection" © 2012 by Tiffany Trent. First publication, original to this anthology. Printed by permission of the author.

"Outside the Absolute" © 2012 by Seth Cadin. First publication, original to this anthology. Printed by permission of the author.

"Steeped in Debt to the Chimney Pots" © 2012 by Steve Berman. First publication, original to this anthology. Printed by permission of the author.